What reviewers are saying about the stories in
Moonlight Madness

Moonlight Madness Book One
"Moonlight Madness kept me in nail-biting suspense and delivered a heart-achingly tender story. Ms. Lee has done an amazing job of bringing her characters to life."
—*Keely Skillman, Coffee Time Romance*

"Ms. Lee has created a fascinating world of vampires and shape shifters that I enjoyed reading about… this book is a must read."
—*Susan White, Just Erotic Romance Review*

Moonlight Mad
"If you have never read a Maril will be the one to hook you. M strong, take charge males; be th She is also, hands down, an e detailed sexual encounters that l
—*Joletta Hill, The Road to Romance*

"In addition to the vibrant tussle between the twins, this story also contained explosive sexual encounters that I am accustomed to from Ms. Lee. Each of her sexual escapades is definitely a panty-wetting event and left me breathless with molten hot desire. This is one series not to be missed!"
—*Nikita Steele, Erotic-Escapades*

Moonlight Healing
"This series… finally comes to a head in Moonlight Healing. The love scenes are still fiery and intense. Marilyn Lee has done an awesome job penning yet another tale of the Gautier family and adding another thrilling adventure to the Moonlight series."
—*Angel, The Romance Studio*

www.ChangelingPress.com

Moonlight Madness

Marilyn Lee

All rights reserved.
Copyright ©2006 Changeling Press LLC

ISBN 978-1-59596-387-1

Publisher:
Changeling Press LLC
PO Box 1046
Martinsburg, WV 25402
www.ChangelingPress.com

Printed in the U.S.A.
Lightning Source, Inc.
1246 Heil Quaker Blvd
La Vergne TN 37086
www.lightningsource.com

Anthology Editor: Margaret Riley
Cover Artist: Angela Knight
Cover Layout: Bryan Keller

The individual stories in this anthology have been previously released in E-Book format.

No part of this publication may be reproduced or shared by any electronic or mechanical means, including but not limited to reprinting, photocopying, or digital reproduction, without prior written permission from Changeling Press LLC.

This book contains sexually explicit scenes and adult language which some may find offensive and which is not appropriate for a young audience. Changeling Press books are for sale to adults, only, as defined by the laws of the country in which you made your purchase.

Moonlight Madness
Marilyn Lee

Prologue

Full-blood vampire Vladimir Madison paced outside the big dark RV parked in an RV court between Philadelphia and New York. An invisible barrier his twin brother Aleksei said was alive blocked his passage.

Vlad frowned. With the help of their younger sister, Katie Dumont, he and Aleksei had finally tracked down one of the twins who had been calling out to them. Aleksei had managed to penetrate the so-called living barrier. He'd been gone for what felt like hours. Left alone, Vlad's anger raged. He raked a hand over his long, dark dreads, staring with glowing eyes at the RV.

Father. We need you. You must help us or I'll be coming to call you to account for deserting us.

He sucked in a breath. Those words had haunted and tortured him since his unnamed son had whispered them into his mind weeks ago. At the time, he had no idea the individual calling out to him was his half-vampire, half-shifter offspring. He and Aleksei had spent what felt like an eternity searching for the twins. Each one had called out to him and Aleksei separately. The knowledge that one of the twins had been poisoned lent an air of added desperation to their search.

Vlad closed his eyes, remembering his response to his son's cry for help. *Whoever you are, I await you.* Now here he stood, restless and angry. Using the special bond he and Aleksei shared, Vlad reached out to his twin. A combination of joy and anguish flooded his mind. Whoever Aleksei had encountered inside presented no threat, but brought a level of pain that made Vlad ache for him.

He shook his head, impatient to be allowed inside, to see the males... the men who were his... sons. His sons. Reaching deeper, he made brief contact with the male inside, touching his mind... and felt no particular connection. That was unexpected, as well as unwelcome. Vlad had resigned himself to being a father. Yet, strangely, he did not feel like a father. Was he a father? If so, why didn't Aleksei and his sons—no, there was only one other male inside with Aleksei—but why didn't he come out?

Vlad reached out again, issuing a soft command.

Come.

He felt an immediate and powerful response… one that did not originate from within the RV. In fact, it seemed to come from… Vlad swung around. He found himself facing a tall male with glowing gray eyes, short dark hair, and bared incisors.

"Bastard! Filthy bastard!" The male's right hand shot out with blinding speed. Vlad tilted his head to the side. A clenched fist brushed his ear. Undeterred, the baby vamp pressed his attack. Vlad blocked a flurry of blows with his forearms before losing his temper. He lashed out with a speed of which only a centuries old vampire was capable.

Just as his fist was about to connect with the other male's face, Vlad felt a strange tightness in his chest. Something inside him told him he did not want to hurt the male in front of him. He halted his fist and danced back from the baby vamp. The two considered each other in silence for several moments.

Vlad glanced at the RV. Whatever was happening inside, Aleksei needed to be undisturbed. Vlad turned and flashed toward the surrounding park with the other vampire racing behind him. It soon became clear the baby vamp could not match his speed. Without giving himself time to wonder at his actions, Vlad slowed down, eventually stopping. He turned to face his pursuer and would-be attacker. "I am Vladimir Madison."

The other male took a deep shuddering breath. "I am Etienne Gautier and I know who you are… I know what you are."

The other vampire's voice dripped with venom. His eyes shot off hate-filled virtual stabs aimed directly at Vlad's heart. He clenched his right hand into a fist and pressed it against his chest to assuage the sudden ache there. "Who are you?"

But even as he asked the question, he knew the other male's identity. He could feel an undeniable connection to this baby vamp. It was that connection that had allowed him to stay his hand when he would have delivered a near fatal blow to the other. It was the same connection that had allowed him and this… boy to call out to each other.

This boy—this angry baby vamp—was his son. Vlad gasped, feeling as if the air was being sucked from his lungs. His son. While he had felt nothing for the male in the RV giving Aleksei such pain, he felt a wealth of emotion in connection with this male… his boy… his son.

Vlad allowed his incisors to ascend. He looked at his son with eyes that no longer glowed. What did one say to an adult son one had never met? How did one express an unexpected but powerful need to protect that son? The emotions assailing him were bewildering. He'd only ever felt real devotion with his siblings, Aleksei, Tat, and Drei… and now with this angry baby vamp.

Showing affection or consideration for anyone other than his siblings was alien to him. Yet the anger and pain he sensed in the other male tore at him, making breathing difficult. He had to do something to help his son.

Having no experience of his own on which to draw, he responded as Aleksei had to him and their younger siblings many times. He opened his arms. "I am Vladimir Madison. Come to me… my son."

The other male stood facing him, breathing deeply, his hands clenched into fists at his side, his incisors bared, his eyes glowing. "You are a useless dog who deserted our mother when she was pregnant and left us to fend for ourselves when we needed you most! Now, when we are both adults, you come and want to play daddy of the goddamned manor? You dare expect to be welcomed with open arms? You insolent motherfucker! All you're fit for is staking and beheading! And that's exactly what you'll get, you bastard!"

The venomous words cut through Vlad with the force of a razor sharp knife. But under the hate, he sensed a pain and anguish in his son with which he was all too familiar. It mirrored the feelings which had overwhelmed him when he'd encountered Palea Dumont, the mother he had spent centuries believing had abandoned him. This great grief was what *she* must have felt when he had flung words of hate at her.

He felt soulless and lost. Even when he had thought Aleksei, the person he cherished and loved most in the world, had abandoned him, he had not experienced this depth of agony and despair. No child should drive a parent to these depths of hell. And yet he had spewed hate and rage at she who had borne and cherished him for the first ten years of his life.

How his words and hate must have hurt her… torn into her… shattered her. He had done that to the woman who loved him enough to offer her life to bring him peace. He closed his eyes and called out. *Mother… Mother, it's Vladimir.*

A distant response brought tears to his eyes and hope to his heart.

Vladimir… malchik moy – my little boy… solnyshko moy – my sun. Is it really you or is this but yet another sweet dream?

It's me, Mother. Vladimir. I'm sorry… so sorry.

For what, solnyshko moy?

For bringing you grief and pain when you gave only love and devotion. Forgive me, Mother. Forgive me.

Were forgiveness necessary, I would freely grant it, solnyshko moy. You have nothing for which to be sorry. When you are ready, you will come see me. Yes?

Yes. I will come.

When?

I don't know, but I will come, Mother.

He felt a distant but strong wave of love. *I will wait an eternity if necessary, solnyshko moy.*

Solnyshko moy. After all the hurt and pain they had both endured, she still thought of him as her *solnyshko moy*, her *sun*.

I will come.

I await you, malchik moy, my little boy.

Chapter One

"I will wait an eternity if necessary, *solnyshko moy*."

"Palea? What's wrong?"

She didn't realize she'd spoken out loud. Palea Walker-Dumont opened her eyes and turned from the window. Across the darkened bedroom, lying naked on the bed they shared, was her bloodlust and the savior of her soul and her sanity, her husband of 108 years, Matt Dumont. She blinked, but could not prevent the tears filling her eyes from spilling over and rolling down her cheeks.

She wrapped her arms around herself, afraid she'd otherwise explode with happiness. "Matt! He called out to me, Matt! At last, he called out to me!"

He rose and crossed the room to her. He took her in his arms, holding her close. "Who?"

"Vladimir!"

He tensed, lifting her chin so he could stare down into her eyes. He had been ingesting her blood for a long time in human years. He had acquired many of the traits of a latent vampire. Still, she was surprised when his blue eyes glowed, because that only happened when he was angry. He was rarely angry in her presence. "Matt?"

"What did he want? I know how you feel about him, but I will not allow you to sacrifice yourself for him, Palea."

She sighed. Their first real argument in over twenty years had erupted when he had learned how close Vladimir had come to killing her months earlier. He had left the house in a rage, threatening to kill Vladimir before he killed her. It had taken much begging and tears on her part before he had begrudgingly returned home.

That night, for the first time since their marriage, they had slept in separate beds. She had spent the night sobbing, feeling torn between her boundless love for Matt and her eternal devotion to Vladimir. Just before dawn, as she was on the verge of sinking into despair, Matt had crawled into bed with her, taken her in his arms, and gently fucked her fears away.

She shook her head. "It's all right, Matt. He said he was sorry and—"

"And you believed him?"

"Yes! He says he's coming to see me. This is a good thing. Yes?"

He tensed again. "I don't know. When is he coming?"

"I don't know, but whenever he comes, he will be welcome. Yes? I will be waiting."

"And so will I."

She heard the steel in his voice; saw the resolve in his eyes. "There is no need for fear. He no longer wants to hurt me, Matt. This is a blessing from God. Yes?"

"Yes... if it is true."

She placed one hand on his arm, sliding the other down his body to cup his cock. She shivered with desire. Even flaccid, his cock was longer than most men's erect organ. "Matt?"

He pulled her hand away from his cock. "I have borne a lot since I fell in love with you and I know how much you love him, but I will not have him in this house disrespecting you or threatening Mik. Do I make myself clear, Palea?"

She blinked up at him, hurt by his harsh tone. He had never been weak or indecisive, but he had long ago recognized that she was far older and physically much stronger than he. As a consequence, for most of their marriage, he had been content to allow her to play the dominant partner. Gazing into his eyes, she saw that was no longer true.

"Do you think I would allow him to harm Mikhel?"

"No. Of course not, but you need to understand, Palea, that if it comes to a choice between him and Mik, I choose Mik."

She nodded. "As well you should. Mikhel is your son. But it will not come to that."

"If it does, I am fully prepared to do what I need to do to protect Mik."

This was the Matt Dumont she had fallen in love and in bloodlust with so many years earlier. While she feared for his response to Vladimir, she gloried in the return of the qualities which had first drawn her to Matt.

"Yes, my love, I would expect no less."

"As long as you understand where I stand, Palea."

"I do." She stroked a hand over his chest. "Now I have other needs."

They were both naked. Moisture pooled between her legs as she felt his cock lengthening against her. She had always found the greatest comfort while impaled on his rigid length. In the early days of their relationship he had often complained it was his cock rather than him she loved.

She reached down, closing her fingers over the thick, hard length. She pressed it against herself, shuddering as the big head slid between the wet folds of her sex. Leaping upwards, she linked one arm around his neck, while using the other hand to feed the rest of his length into her pussy. She kissed him, moaning with a combination of pain and pleasure as his cock drove into her body up to his large nuts.

Take me! Fuck me!

He cupped his big hands over her ass, drawing her closer. Thrusting his huge organ in and out of her, he carried her to their bed.

* * *

Feeling the distant connection with his mother broken, Vlad opened his eyes and looked at his son, Etienne. Vlad extended a hand. "I know I am not worthy. I have not been there for you when you needed me most. That's a pain I understand all too well. I am no Aleksei, who would know what to say to make the hurt in you vanish, but I am here now. I am your father. You are my son, and I am here now. My entire life has been one long failure after another. I don't know how to love or feel affection for any except my siblings. I don't know what to say to you to make up for all you have suffered, except to ask—to beg your forgiveness for failing you. If your forgiveness requires revenge…"

Vlad fell to his knees. Staring up into the angry, glowing eyes of his son, he spread his arms wide. "Take my life. I will not resist."

Etienne whipped out a short sword and pressed it against Vlad's neck. He felt it bite into his skin. He overcame a primordial urge to rip it away from his throat and attack—kill. He had accomplished nothing worthwhile in his entire life—except to help give life to this baby vamp. He would not undo that.

Vlad looked up into the gray eyes filled with fury. "Do it." He closed his eyes and prepared to die. "Dispatch me."

"You think I won't, but you are so wrong!"

Vlad opened his eyes but quickly closed them again as the sword was drawn back before swishing through the air toward his throat.

"No!"

"Etienne, no!"

Vlad snapped open his eyes. There was a blur of motion, then the sword was ripped from his throat, and his son was snatched away from him. He bounded to his feet, ready to defend the son who wanted to kill him with his life.

A male who was definitely Etienne's twin restrained Vlad's struggling son from behind, while Aleksei, Vlad's own twin, stood in front of him. Aleksei touched Vlad's throat, his blue eyes darkening with fury when he encountered blood. "Vladimir? You are all right?"

He drew away from Aleksei. "Don't interfere, Sei. I'm about to do the only worthwhile thing I've ever done in my life." He looked at his son's twin, a tall, dark, handsome male with long, dark hair. Strangely, he felt no particular connection with his son's twin. "Release him," he said. "This is between us."

The twin obeyed. Etienne immediately rushed at him. Vlad stood still, making no move to defend himself.

"No!" Aleksei flashed in front of him, knocking the sword out of Etienne's hand with one hand and backhanding him with the other.

Vlad felt the blow as if it had descended on his own face. "Do not strike my son again, Sei," he warned.

Aleksei swung around to stare at him. "If you think I'll stand by and watch him slaughter you, you are sadly mistaken!" Aleksei leveled a hand at Etienne. "No one threatens my twin. Stand down, pup!" Aleksei looked at the other male. "You are the elder twin. It is your place to control him. Tell him to stand down, Acier. I will not allow him to dispatch my brother."

The one called Acier knelt on the ground, cradling Etienne in his arms, his gray eyes glowing with anger. "You call yourself father and yet you dare strike my brother?"

Vlad watched the play of emotions across Aleksei's cinnamon colored face — pain, regret, and finally resolve.

"You call yourself humane and yet would stand by and watch another slain? I feel your devotion to your twin, Acier. I have a devotion to my twin that is even deeper, having been forged over three hundred years of being there for each other when we had no one else. Tell your brother to stand down... for all our sakes."

Acier took a deep breath and then rose, pulling Etienne gently to his feet. "You would kill us both?"

"I would willingly die for you both, but I will allow no one to kill my brother... not even one of you."

Vlad had not felt this close to Aleksei since his dispute with Mikhel. He knew the depth of feelings Aleksei felt for Acier. And yet Aleksei had aligned himself with his twin.

Etienne took a deep, shuddering breath before he buried his face against his brother's shoulder. Acier put his arms around Etienne and glared at Aleksei. Aleksei sighed and moved over to the two brothers. He put his arms around them both.

Aleksei spoke in a soft voice. "Trust us." He stroked his hands over both twins' shoulders. Neither twin protested. Aleksei lifted his head and looked at Vlad. *Come. They need us both, Vlad.*

He crossed the distance. Aleksei pulled Acier into his arms and stepped away, leaving Vlad and Etienne facing each other. After a moment of uncertainty, Vlad shuddered and opened his arms. *Forgive me, my son. Please?*

Etienne stood staring at him, his incisors still bared. "Forgive you? When I've needed you my entire life and you've never been there? How can I forgive you?"

Vlad felt as if his heart were being squeezed into stillness. "If you don't forgive me, you might as well kill me now!"

"Then die, bastard!"

Acier pulled away from Aleksei and turned his twin to face him. "Etienne! There may come a time when we will call them both to account for what we've suffered, but for now… for the good of the pack… we need them both alive."

Vlad watched, frowning. Why did he feel so close to Etienne, but not Acier?

Etienne jerked away from Acier. "Fine. They can both live… for now." Etienne turned to look at Vlad. "But you stay the hell away from me. You are not my father and I'll kill you the first chance I get!" Snarling the threat, Etienne shifted into a big gray wolf and ran into the surrounding trees.

After a startled moment, Vlad flashed through the night after his son.

Left alone in the woods with Aleksei, Acier hesitated, considering his options. Aleksei broke the silence. "Vlad will not hurt him."

Acier sighed, raking a hand through his long, dark hair. "I've never seen Tee so hurt. I have to go after him." He turned.

Aleksei caught his arm, swinging him around. "No. They need to be alone. Vladimir has a great capacity for love and affection. Up until now, I have been on the receiving end of most of it. Now he'll be able to share some of it with Etienne… his son."

Acier frowned. "I don't understand. I know he's Tee's father. I could feel how drawn Tee was to him. But you are our father… at least you're my father. How can that be?"

Aleksei shrugged. "I don't know... I just know that it is."

"But it doesn't make sense!"

"To mortals, our very existence might not make sense. Yet we not only exist, we thrive. You, Vladimir, Etienne, and I know which of you belongs to which of us. Does the how or why really matter?" Aleksei extended his arm. "Come, my son."

After a brief hesitation, Acier moved close to him and made no protest as Aleksei hugged him, pressing several kisses against his forehead. "You are my son and I will kill anyone who tries to separate us."

The softly spoken words infused Acier with a sense of belonging he had long abandoned any hope of feeling. This male was definitely his father.

Aleksei released him. "We will return to your RV and you will tell me about the danger facing you and your pack."

Acier glanced in the direction Etienne and Vladimir had taken. "You're sure he won't hurt Etienne?"

"I am positive."

Acier nodded slowly. In silence they raced back through the night to the RV. The barrier spirit dissolved to allow them through. As they entered, Aleksei turned to face the spirit. "Rest easy, Bentia. I will guard and protect those within for the remainder of the night."

Bentia disappeared. Acier closed the door and he and Aleksei sat facing each other in the dark room. Before they could speak, a tall, beautiful woman walked into the living room area. She wore one of Acier's sweatshirts over her lovely dark skin, leaving her long, shapely legs bare. She turned her green gaze on him. "Steele, is everything all right?"

Acier bolted to his feet. "Raven... this is—"

Aleksei rose.

"Your father? Yes." She nodded. "I know. Is everything all right?" The two small Keddi, Pen and Drei, hovered in the air near Raven's head, tense.

"Yes. He... he's come to help."

"Then I'll leave you alone." She smiled and walked back toward the bedroom at the back of the RV.

"Why does she call you Steele?"

Acier shrugged. "Her father is one of my dearest friends. When we met, she was young and couldn't pronounce Acier. When I told her it was French for steel, she started calling me Steele."

"I see."

Acier resumed his seat, motioning for Aleksei to do the same. When Aleksei had, Acier beckoned to Pen and Drei. They flew through the air. Pen landed on his shoulder. Drei hovered in front of Aleksei, his ears up, his tail down. *Friend?*

"What is your name, little Keddi?"

I am called Drei.

Acier arched a brow. As a rule, earthbound Keddi spoke in broken, ungrammatical sentences—except in the presence of the Supreme Alpha, Aime Gautier and his Keddi, Dominator. Yet Drei accorded Aleksei the same respect he would Aime.

"I have a younger brother named Andrei whom we call Drei." Aleksei smiled and extended his hand. Drei landed on his palm. "Who named you Drei?"

"Etienne named him."

Aleksei stroked a finger over Drei's back. Drei made a soft, growling noise of pleasure in the back of his throat. Aleksei turned his attention to Pen. "And you are called?"

Pen.

Acier sensed turmoil in Pen, who remained on his shoulder. He suspected Pen wanted a closer look at Aleksei, but wasn't sure if he was friend or foe. It was apparent Drei had already decided for himself.

"Well, Pen and Drei, I am Aleksei Madison." He locked his gaze with Acier's. "I am Acier's father."

Acier felt the now familiar ache. *His father.* After all the years of pain, heartache, and longing, his father sat across from him.

Will help? Pen inquired.

Aleksei nodded, his eyes glowing. "Yes. My son's enemies are my enemies."

Pen looked in his eyes. *Alpha?*

Acier inclined his head slightly.

Pen flew across the room and alighted on Aleksei's shoulder. *Help kill enemies?*

"Yes." Aleksei looked at him. "Now. Tell me who and what we will be facing."

Acier sighed. "The most pressing need is for a blood transfusion."

Aleksei shuddered. "Then it's true. You've been poisoned?"

Acier nodded. "How did you know?"

"Your Aunt Katie had a… vision. She saw you injured and poisoned. It was with her help we found you and Etienne." Aleksei rose and crossed the room to place a hand on his shoulder. "You are now a part of a large, powerful family. Call your physician and tell him to prepare for a transfusion. Then we will deal with those who dared injure you."

Acier shook his head. "I don't know how much you know about me, but I am Den Alpha as well as Alpha-in-waiting of the entire Pack Gautier. I have to fight my own battles… not turn them over to… to… my… my…"

Aleksei squeezed his shoulder. "The word you're having so much trouble with is *father*, Acier. Get used to saying it in reference to me. I am your father and you will not address me as anything else."

"Then I will just look at you and start speaking," Acier said coolly. He was not going to be pushed into addressing this vampire as father.

Aleksei laughed and slapped his cheek. "I will only allow that for a short time, my angry young pup. Now. Call your physician."

"I'm used to giving orders, not taking them."

Aleksei responded by slapping his cheek again, this time hard enough to make it sting. "Give all the orders you like to those of your pack… and to Etienne, but not to your father."

Acier took a deep breath. "Do not strike me again."

Aleksei curled his fingers in his hair. "I won't... unless you need it. I will gladly surrender my life to protect yours, but I will not be disrespected. Do not make the mistake of forgetting who I am." Aleksei released his hair and looked at Drei and Pen. "And that goes for you two as well."

Acier pressed his lips into a tight line. When the danger was passed, he was going to take great delight in giving the arrogant bastard in front of him a hefty backhand that would send him flying across the damn room and slamming into a far wall.

Aleksei arched a brow and laughed. "I wouldn't count on that, if I were you, Acier."

He stiffened. "Did you... read my mind?"

"So it would seem."

"Don't do it again! I have a right to my thoughts without you coming uninvited into my mind!"

Aleksei's smile vanished and he sighed. "You still hate me."

"Yes!" But even as he flung the word at the other male, he knew he lied. How the hell was he supposed to maintain his hate and anger for a male he knew would gladly die for him? Especially when he felt a wall of affection emanating from the other male threatening to overwhelm him?

"Would you like to off me as your brother was about to off Vlad?"

"Etienne wouldn't have killed him."

"Would you have killed me in his place?"

Acier looked away. After less than two hours of knowing the other male, he found he could not imagine a world that did not include this big, arrogant bastard. "No," he admitted.

Acier was rewarded by a warm smile and a hug. As he leaned against Aleksei, he closed his eyes. Just for now he would enjoy being close to him. When the danger to the pack was passed... well, there would be no reason not to kill Aleksei.

Chapter Two

Aware that he would not be able to outrun the vampire following him, Etienne stopped abruptly, and shifted back to his human form. Deep in the forest, he and the vampire faced each other. "Why are you pursuing me? What do you want of me, vampire?"

Vlad spread his hands wide, a helpless look on his bronzed face. "I don't want anything, but I need to be close to you. I know how you must feel about me… I know the hate and rage that no amount of words can assuage. But I did not desert you. I would never desert a son of mine."

Etienne clenched his hands into fists. He knew this vampire had sired him—he felt a connection with this vampire that he had not felt with the other one. This vampire was the bastard responsible for making his childhood so miserable. He had never realized how much he had missed having a father around—until he had heard him calling earlier that night and been drawn, almost against his will, to the RV park.

Rage ate at him. He felt feral. He longed to cut and tear into the other male's flesh until the forest ran red with blood. Yet another part of him longed to burrow against the other male and allow himself to be held.

Etienne shook his head. "I am an adult. The time when I needed you in my life is long passed."

"No! I am well over three hundred years old and I still have an abiding need for my mother who I thought had abandoned me. She hadn't. I did not abandon you. When you think yourself abandoned, you have a deep-seated need that eats at you and makes you bitter and dangerous—if you allow it. That's what happened to me. I will not allow the same thing to happen to you. You can run… you can deny who I am… you can try to kill me, but unless you succeed, I will be here for you. I will spend the rest of my life atoning for your pain, my son."

Etienne's chest tightened and he had to swallow hard to dislodge a lump in his throat. He wanted to hate and hate he did, but there was something else... something inside the other vampire that reached out and grabbed and twisted something in him—binding them together. "Did you leave us because you knew we would be hybrids?"

"No!"

"Then why? Why? Acier and I would have been the best sons any vampire could have wanted."

"I didn't know you *existed* until you started calling out to me and even then I didn't know who you were. Aleksei told me and we immediately took steps to find you and your brother." He extended a hand. "Come close... touch my mind and read the truth of what I've said. Touch my mind... my heart... the heart of one who will do whatever it takes to make things right with you... even if that means dying at your hands."

Even with the distance between them, Etienne could feel the other's pain as well as his sincerity. Whatever his reason for having deserted them, Vladimir now seemed prepared to die to ease his pain. That was far more than he had expected. The well of hate and fury burst inside him. Overcome, he dropped to his knees, gasping for breath.

When Vlad dropped beside him, Etienne turned and buried his head against his chest. Eager hands pulled him closer, cool lips touched his forehead, and Etienne allowed the tears in his eyes to spill down his cheeks.

Forgive me... my son. Forgive me.

The anguished plea released a wellspring of pain in him. Etienne collapsed against his father, releasing total control of his emotions. It wouldn't be easy, but granting his father forgiveness was what he'd always wanted to do. He'd never expected to have the opportunity.

Vlad rocked him in his arms, whispering softly to him in a language he suspected was Russian. *Malchik moy... solnyshko moy.*

The words meant nothing to him — and yet they meant everything. Hearing them chanted over and over, for the first time in his life, Etienne experienced the love of his father.

One silent word sprang from his heart. *Father.*

A great shudder passed through the other's body, then the two of them clung together, sobbing unashamedly in each other's arms.

* * *

Vampire fem Deoctra Diniti, naked and hungry to have her cunt filled with hard, hot cock, leaned over the end of the bed. She glanced over her shoulder. A tall, handsome blond stood behind her. Also naked, his erect cock sprang from a mass of dark blond pubic hair. His green eyes alight with lust, he closed the distance between them, cupping her ass in big palms.

"You are the loveliest female I have ever mated with." His low, warm voice sent a tingle through her.

"I require cock, not talk," she told him. "Fuck me now and romance me later!"

He parted her nether cheeks and pressed the head of his length against her puckered hole. "Get ready, my lovely."

"Bitch," she hissed, tensing. "Call me bitch and ram your entire hot cock in with one thrust." She braced her arms on the bed and looked forward, preparing herself for the coming onslaught.

"Get ready for the fucking of your life, pretty bitch!" He leaned over her and raked his teeth against the back of her neck. His hot breath there sent a jolt of anticipation through her.

She wiggled her behind against his groin. "Take me in your natural form."

He pressed closer. His skin slowly sprouted hair... fur. He pressed his hairy groin against her ass. Her small gasp turned into a scream of delight as his hot, silken dick forced its way between the cheeks of her nether regions and slammed deep into her cunt with a speed and power that nearly made her come.

She looked over her shoulder. Moisture and lust filled her pussy at the sight of her body impaled on the cock of a big, gray biped wolf with lusty green eyes. Without giving her time to adjust to the invasion, he wrapped his paws around her body, and shot his hot length in and out of her with a power and speed that left her gasping and shuddering with unmitigated lust.

She reached back to grab a handful of his hairy ass, grinding herself against him. Lord, who knew she'd love being fucked by a male in animal form. He leaned closer, grunting with pleasure, and thrusting wildly and viciously into her body, with no regard for whether his movements gave pleasure or pain. He didn't care. Neither did she. She loved sex that brought pain. One thrust shoved her onto the bed. As she sprawled on her stomach, he followed her down, driving his cock deep into her pussy and sinking his fangs into the back of her neck.

His large wolf body completely covered her small, slender form. Still biting her neck and tearing her flesh, he fucked her wildly, growling with his pleasure... wild and totally uninhibited, licking at her bloody neck. Waves of pleasure and pain dashed over her. She moaned and shuddered, her entire body teetering on the edge of an explosive climax. Only Acier and Etienne Gautier had given her a harder, more enjoyable fuck. But thoughts of the lust-filled night she had shared with them were washed away as Leon gave a particularly painful thrust, driving his cock deep within her wet cunt. Keeping his groin tight against her ass, he forced his knot into her.

She screamed and exploded. As the first wave of his climax crashed over her, she tightened herself so that his knot, hard and hot, was held inside her as he blasted her full of his seed. She lay under his heavy body, her hands curled into fists at her side, milking his plundering dick of the last few precious drops of his wonderful seed.

She turned her head, pressing her cheek against the bed. Hot breath fanned her face and a pair of wolf lips closed on her mouth. She parted her lips and welcomed the long, skillful tongue inside. They lay kissing and biting at each other while he continued to fuck her, gently now, his knot still inside her body.

She moaned, squeezing herself around his shaft. *You've made a mess of me. Now clean me up.* She whimpered with a combination of regret and pain as he withdrew his delicious knot out of her protesting cunt. Moaning and tingling, she turned onto her back, spreading her legs wide. Remaining in his natural form, he stood between her legs. Instead of eating her as she had ordered, he drew his hips back, and shot his still hard cock back into her pussy, knot included.

Lord! It hurt so good! She sobbed, blindly reaching up to draw him down to her. Wrapping her arms and legs around his big, hairy body, she fucked herself wildly on him, gasping and nearly coming each time he shot his knot deep inside her. Overcome with lust and need, she bared her incisors, and sank them into the side of his neck. As he shot jet after jet of seed into her receptive cunt, she fed on his blood, lost in an ecstasy of delight she had never expected to feel again.

She held him tightly, surrendering to the pleasure sweeping through her, setting her blood, her heart afire with need and more — for this male alone.

He collapsed on top of her. She continued to feed on him, drinking his warm, pure blood as she wallowed in the after bliss of the most incredible fuck she'd ever had.

They fucked over and over again until they were both so exhausted he couldn't muster the strength to pull his now limp cock out of her. It remained inside her because his knot was still erect. She licked her lips and growled softly.

They finally separated. He slept as she rose to wash. As she walked to the bedroom, she gloried in feel of his seed seeping from her body. There were few joys in the world as wonderful as being full of the seed of a lusty, handsome male.

She lay in the whirlpool bath for a long time, thinking of the future. Once Acier Gautier had been disposed of, she would send for her younger sisters, Tallia and Smovca. After Leon was installed as Alpha Supreme of Pack Gautier, Tally and Smo would be safe and welcome within the pack.

She smiled, thinking of the sensation her beautiful, sexy little sisters would create in the pack. Between the three of them, they would have their pick of the purebreds. She thought of Smo, so small and dark, lying on her back with her legs parted and Leon, with his cock and knot buried in her pussy, fucking her until she screamed with pleasure… while Tally, taller and lusty, sat on his face, with his wonderful tongue thrusting up into her cunt.

Thinking of the joys to which she would introduce her younger sisters got her so hot her juices flowed freely. She got out of the bath and hurried back to the bedroom. Leon lay on his back, still in his natural form. His cock, semi erect, lay along one hairy thigh.

She climbed onto the bed between his legs and popped his shaft into her mouth. Cupping his balls, she closed her eyes, sucking him slowly. He hardened in her mouth. Smiling, she rose, positioned herself above him, and quickly slammed down her hips.

His shaft pushed up into her anus. She sobbed with pain, but continued pressing down until her ass cheeks rested on his hairy groin. Delicious. So very delicious. Grunting with pain, she pulled up and pushed down rapidly, driving his entire length up into her bowels.

Groaning, he shifted his hands to his humanoid form, grabbed her hips, and pounded himself up into her with a ruthless lust in which she reveled. He thrust so hard and deep, she feared he would split her in two!

He released one of her hips and slammed a big palm down on one of her ass cheeks. Her flesh stung, intensifying her pleasure. She tossed back her head, bracing herself on her outstretched hands by his hips, riding his length with glee and delight. "Yes! Again!"

His palm rose and fell, stinging her flesh repeatedly, each slap harder than the last. The pleasure in her built, making her stomach muscles tighten and her pussy quiver. She fought for her release. It eluded her until he rubbed his thumb against her clit and thrust the fingers of his other hand into her pussy.

She exploded, falling forward onto his body, her breasts pressing against his chest fur, burying her lips in his hair. He cupped his hands on her butt, parted her cheeks, and fucked her with short, powerful thrusts until she felt his cum shooting into her ass.

So fucking good.

As she lay moaning, he lifted her lower body, withdrew from her ass, held her still, and shot his length into her cunt.

"Ooooh!" She shuddered and pressed closer to him, enjoying the feeling of his knot forcing itself into her body. It was times like these that she gloried in the fact that vampires, unlike unlucky humans, could not get STD's. They neither acquired nor passed them on.

You like that, bitch?

Like? She loved having his knot inside her well-satisfied cunt.

He licked the side of her neck, which had already healed. *You're my bitch!*

His bitch. Leon de la Rocque's bitch. It had a ring to it.

My sweet, sweet bitch. Together we will lead Pack Gautier to a new era of prominence.

He rolled her onto her back. As he poised above her, he shifted to his humanoid form. He slid his body on top of hers, sliding inside her. He made love to her gently, holding her tenderly and whispering words of love and lust that filled her eyes with tears and her heart with an ache she had thought herself incapable of feeling again.

After they came together, he shifted back to his natural form. She stroked her hands down his hairy back, turning her head to kiss his mouth. The fur on his face tickled. She smiled. For the first time since she had lost her erstwhile bloodlust, Mikhel Dumont, to a human whore, she could foresee a future which did not include only pain and revenge. Was it possible that she, a full-blood vampire, could be content, even happy, with a creature of another species? Some would call him a werewolf. Was it possible for them to be anything but temporary lovers? Was it possible or was she suffering from a case of moonlight madness?

She stroked her hands over his body. This body, this male, was hers. And damn anyone who dared come between them until she'd had her fill of him. As sleep overtook her, she tightened her arms around his big body, loving the feel and weight of him in his natural form, still impaling her. This might be as close to paradise as she could hope to come. Maybe... just maybe it was enough... not only for now but for the foreseeable future.

* * *

Acier... my son. Wake up.

Acier opened his eyes. Several people were crowded into his bedroom. Dr. Softee was the first person he saw. Raven stood beside him, a smile on her beautiful dusky face. Etienne stood to her right, with Vladimir on the other side of the bed, staring at Etienne. Next to Vlad stood a stranger Acier sensed was a vampire. To his right stood Xavier, with Aleksei at the foot of the bed, Pen and Drei on his shoulders.

Looking away from the intense affection he saw in Aleksei's blue eyes, Acier smiled up at Raven. She leaned down, pressing her lips against his. He reached up a hand to cup the back of her head and returned her kiss, feeling his cock stir at her touch. She drew back, a secret smile in her warm, dark eyes.

He smiled at Etienne, who sighed deeply and nodded. Xavier inclined his head and mouthed the words, *I live to serve, Alpha.*

Pen... Drei... it's good to see you, my friends.

Glad Alpha ok.

Knew Alpha make it.

"Okay. Everyone out," Dr. Softee ordered. Raven squeezed his hand and walked out the room, Vlad and Etienne following. The strange vampire remained, but Dr. Softee looked at Aleksei. "Everyone... please."

Aleksei shook his head. "The Keddi and I will stay."

Dr. Softee turned to look at Acier, a question in his eyes. Acier suspected nothing he or Dr. Softee could say would make Aleksei leave. He shrugged.

"Alpha, this is Dr. Grinkolo, who assisted me in your transfusion."

Acier inclined his head slightly. "Thank you, doctor."

The vampire smiled. "I have been the Dumont family physician for a number of years. When I heard that Palea's grandson was ill, I naturally came right away."

Acier blinked. Somehow he had never considered that Aleksei, who was well over three hundred years old, would have a living mother. He and Etienne had a *grandmother*. Oh, damn this was weird.

Dr. Softee took his pulse and checked his heartbeat and blood pressure before straightening. "Dr. Grinkolo and I agree that the transfusion was a success, Alpha. You're going to be fine."

"I'm *going* to be or I *am* fine?"

"I want you to take it easy for just a day or so. The transfusion has changed your blood chemistry. You now have more vampire blood in your veins than you've ever had. The change will take some getting used to."

"You will no doubt feel weak and maybe a little feverish for the next few days," Dr. Grinkolo explained. "But once that is passed, you will have a measure of power you have never felt. You will feel the call of your vampire blood stronger than ever."

What the hell? "Are you telling me that I am no longer a shifter?"

Dr. Softee sighed. "That is something only you can answer, Alpha."

If he were no longer a shifter, could he remain Alpha of even his den? He raked a hand through his hair, frightened at the thought of losing his personal den. That would be more devastating than surrendering his position as Alpha-in-waiting. He glared at Dr. Softee. "What did you allow them to do to me?"

"We did what was necessary to purge the poison from your body, Alpha. It was not easy and we nearly lost you."

"You nearly lost… how long have I been unconscious?"

"Two days. Take it easy for the next day or so and then resume your normal activities. I will remain at my hotel in Philadelphia should you need me, Alpha."

"As will I, Acier."

Acier glanced at the other doctor, pressing his lips into a tight line. The man had help save his life. So why did he feel as if the vampire doctor had gone out of his way to change his blood chemistry? What would be his motive for doing such a thing? There was only one person with reason to want him more vampire than shifter. He narrowed his gaze, centering it on Aleksei.

Aleksei stared back, his blue eyes concealing his thoughts.

He turned back to face the doctors, inclining his head. "Thank you, doctors."

Dr. Softee bowed briefly. "I live to serve, Alpha."

Dr. Grinkolo looked into his eyes. "I did no more than what was necessary to save your life. Whether you are shifter or vampire doesn't concern me. You are Palea's grandson and I did what I could to help."

Annoyed that the vampire doctor had invaded his thoughts, he spoke in a terse voice. "Thank you." Both doctors left the room, closing the door behind them.

Aleksei sat on the side of his bed and touched his cheek. "So, Acier Gautier… are you very attached to that name?"

"It is my name."

"I know. But would you consider changing it?"

"To what?"

"Madison." Aleksei stroked his cheek. "A son should have his father's last name."

He sucked in a breath and pushed his hand away. "I have the last name of Aime Gautier, the male who raised me to adulthood. I am and will remain Acier Gautier."

Aleksei sighed. "We'll see. In the meantime, tell me about this shifter. This Tucker Falcone and this Leon who attacked you."

He shook his head. "I'll take care of them myself. You've already provided all I needed from you. Now that the transfusion has been performed…"

"What? I can disappear into the woodwork? Fall off the face of the earth?"

"You can do whichever you prefer. But I will handle pack business. How serious would anyone take me if I showed up with my… daddy in tow?"

Aleksei leaned close to him, curling his fingers in his hair. "Since the moment I learned of your existence, I have been eaten up with the desire to find you. I've left my pregnant woman alone and neglected while I searched for you. You are a part of me I didn't even realize was missing. But now that I've found you, my life is almost complete. Understand this, Acier, you are too important to me for me to allow anyone to menace you! Whoever fucks with you, fucks with me! And I am not the damned vampire anyone with half a brain wants to fuck with!"

Drei nodded. *Not fuck with father!*

Be sorry if do! Pen added.

Aleksei had managed to win Pen and Drei's respect in a matter of a few days. The bastard had a way with him that made disliking him difficult.

Aleksei grinned. "I do have a way with me, don't I?"

He frowned. "I told you to stay out of my head."

"Told me? You don't tell me anything, Acier. I don't know who you're used to dealing with. If you ask kindly, I'll consider your request, but I am a full-blood vampire with special abilities not many vampires possess. You will learn to respect me or suffer the consequences."

"You are an arrogant bastard!"

He smiled again. "Yes, I am. Now about this Falcone and Leon."

"I can handle them."

"Yes. I believe you can, but I will not allow you to be double-teamed." He stroked his hair. "Now what can I do to help?"

Acier hesitated before speaking. He'd never needed to depend on anyone except Etienne. How could he expose his weaknesses to a stranger?

"I'm your father, Acier."

"But you are still a stranger. And stay out of my head!"

Aleksei curled his hand in his hair. "Then don't try to keep anything from me."

He pushed Aleksei's hand away from his hair. "We're not going to have much of a relationship if you can't respect my wishes! I am Alpha-in-waiting of my entire pack. I can't have you undermining me at every turn! Respect me or get the fuck out of my life and my face!"

The blue eyes cooled. Then Aleksei sighed. "I stand corrected. Your position demands a certain level of respect—as does mine as your father. Now, how can I help?"

"I don't require any additional help."

"So you expect what from me now?"

He wanted to tell him to go burn in hell. He looked into the hated blue eyes and found the words wouldn't come. "I don't need you."

"I can see that you're independent and proud. You don't need me? Fine. I need you."

"You've managed without me for the last forty years. I'm sure you'll do fine without me for the next forty."

He shook his head. "I can't. You are my son. Even if you don't need me any longer, I need you. No matter what you say, I am not going away, Acier. For me, there is nothing more important than family and you are a vital part of me that I can't be happy without."

Acier swallowed hard, trying to dislodge the lump in his throat. He hated how vulnerable and needy this useless vampire could make him feel.

Pen looked at him. *Let father help, Alpha.*

Drei pressed against Aleksei's neck. *Father strong. Can help, Alpha.*

He raked a hand through his hair. What was the use in denying he could use some assistance? "If you could manage to keep the rest of the Defense League of the Brotherhood off my back, I can handle Falcone and Leon."

Aleksei stiffened. "What interest would a group of rogue vampires have in shifter business?"

"A fem got them involved."

"What's this fem's name?"

"Deoctra Din—"

Aleksei bolted to his feet. His nostrils flared. His eyes glowed. "Deoctra!" He spat out the name. "She brought the Brotherhood down on your head?"

"Do you know her?"

"Yes. She thought Mikhel, one of my younger brothers, was her bloodlust. When he chose a human woman instead, she tried to kill the woman. I arrived just in time to stop her and her sisters. Vladimir went after her, but apparently spared her miserable life. The bitch has made her last mistake!"

"Etienne has a measure of affection for her."

"Etienne is a silly little pup who doesn't know what's good for him!"

"He wouldn't want her killed."

"What your brother wants is not my concern!"

Acier shook his head. "I don't understand this. Don't you have any feelings for him?"

Aleksei's eyes softened. "Of course I do! He's my nephew and I love and hold dear all my relatives. But his interest in some silly bitch who doesn't know when to call it quits can't supercede my concern for what's best for you. He is my nephew. You are my son. Your interests come first."

"He's my brother. His interests are mine as well. When our mother died, I vowed I would do everything in my power to keep him safe and happy." He shook his head. "I didn't realize until we met you and Vladimir what a lousy job I'd done."

"You didn't do a lousy job, Acier."

"Oh, yes I did. Out there in the woods, I could feel his need for a father's love. If I hadn't failed him, his need wouldn't have been so great."

"His need has nothing to do with failure on your part."

"Then why?"

"It's just that sometimes a boy needs his father... even when he's a man."

"If you're thinking I need you—"

"I have news for you, boy, not everything is about you. I was speaking from personal experience. I know because my father was killed when Vladimir and I were ten. That was well over three hundred years ago, but sometimes it feels like it just happened hours ago. I can still feel the pain of seeing him sprawled on that dirt road... and knowing he was dead. Dead! Gone forever.

"Part of me died with him. He had huge hands and a powerful build. I remember watching him when he would chop wood. He'd have his shirt off and I'd watch his muscles rolling under his skin and pray that one day I would grow up to be as big, strong, and powerful as he was.

"He was a big man, but he was gentle, kind, and loving. There were so many things he never got a chance to teach me. As I grew up, whenever I didn't know how to do something or couldn't understand something, I would wonder if this was one of those things he'd never had time to teach me."

Aleksei raked a hand through his dreads. "I have never... I will never forget him or stop missing him and longing for what we shared as well as what we never got to share. He would have made a great grandfather. You and Etienne would have loved him and been proud to have his blood running through your veins."

"What was his name?"

"Alexander. Alexander Walker."

"Walker? Not Madison?"

He grimaced. "Like you and Etienne, out of respect and love, we took the name of the family who saved us."

"From what? What happened to your father? How did he die?"

Aleksei shrugged, his eyes darkening. "He was a freed slave… freed by his father's family. When he and our mother fell in love, they went to Canada so they could be together. Our mother, Palea Walker-Dumont was a very young vampire then… younger than you and Etienne.

"Vampires, unlike humans and some other species, grow stronger as they age. Our mother was very young and she was denying her true nature to please our father. We were happy in Canada until we learned our grandmother, who was still a slave, was dying. Father had to see her one more time before she died. Mother convinced him to bring us along… me, Vladimir, Tatiana, and Andrei. We encountered some men not far from the plantation. They attacked us."

A wall of anguish from Aleksei assailed him. "What happened?"

"They shot our mother, disabling her."

"How is that possible? Didn't you say she was a vampire?"

"She was in fact a full-blood vampire, but she was weak because she was not living as a vampire. They were able to take her down in her weakened state by repeatedly shooting her."

"And your father?"

Aleksei raked a hand through his dreads. "He was killed… as were we."

He clenched a hand into a fist. "How?"

"They drowned us."

"What?"

"We didn't know what we were then. We thought we were normal… until we woke up from being dead. Even then we didn't fully realize what we were. That knowledge came later. As I was on the riverbank, holding a lifeless Vlad in my arms, he woke up… then Tat and Drei did as well.

"We were scared. This Quaker family came along and took us in. Even when it became clear we were not normal, they loved us and protected us to the best of their ability. To repay them, we took their last name."

Aleksei pressed a hand against his chest. "But inside, I am and always will be Alexander Walker's eldest son, and the one who misses him so much even after all this time I can taste my need for him."

Acier watched tears fill the blue eyes he had always hated. "There is... there will always be a little lost boy inside of me crying out for a father who will never answer! He's lost to me forever and I never got a chance to grieve for him because I am the eldest and I had three siblings for whom I had to be strong. The pain and anguish are as fresh and overwhelming now as they were the night it happened. It has not stopped hurting in over three hundred long, lonely years. As long as I breathe, it will never stop hurting! I will forever long for, need, and miss my father."

He felt Aleksei's ache as if it were his own. The pain stabbed through him, slicing his heart into small, battered pieces. His emotions laid bare, he tossed the light cover over his legs aside and rose. Without speaking, he put his arms around Aleksei. The confident, powerful vampire he had spent a lifetime waiting to meet turned in his arms, burying his face against his shoulder. He drew Aleksei down to the floor and held him, stroking his dreads, longing to comfort him. Aleksei shook. Acier tightened his arms and held Aleksei as he sobbed out a grief that had been held in check for centuries.

His own endless ache for a father's love filled his eyes with tears. He made no effort to control them. They spilled down his cheeks and mingled with his father's.

It's all right. It's all right. You don't have to bear your pain alone anymore. I am here and I will share it with you. I'm here to share your pain. Lean on me... father.

* * *

"Can I get you anything, Xavier?"

Xavier, who sat in the living room area of the RV with Raven and the others, shook his head. He rose. "Now that I know he's going to be okay, I must return to reassure the den and to make arrangements."

"What kind of arrangements?"

He hesitated, glancing toward the open door of the RV. "Unpleasant, but necessary ones. Acier is the most powerful shifter among us. If he could have so easily been taken to the brink of death during his battle with Leon de la Rocque and his enforcer, it will be necessary for some in the den to take steps to ensure the same fate does not befall those of us who will stand with him at the next battle."

"What kind of steps are you considering?"

"As unusual as it may be, there might be a need for some of us to… be vaccinated against the poison de la Rocque's enforcer can inflict."

"How do you plan to do that?"

"We'll do what is necessary, however unpleasant and dangerous." He inclined his head. "Please excuse me."

"Have you discussed these measures with Acier?"

"No, but then I don't need to. When he is away from the den, I have full authority to act in the den's best interests."

She shook her head, giving his arm a squeeze. "That's not what I meant. I only meant that Acier wouldn't want you to do anything that would be dangerous."

"We of Den Gautier will do whatever is necessary to protect his life. Now if you will excuse me, I must make those arrangements."

"Okay, but whatever you do, please be careful. He not only values your position in the den, but he values you personally."

He smiled, resisting the urge to kiss her hand.

He'd left his cell phone in his SUV when Etienne had summoned him to Acier's side. Back in the SUV, he picked up his cell phone, locating a familiar name, and hit send.

"What?"

He stifled a sigh. Vampires and their arrogant shit! "This is Xavier Depardieu. When can we meet to make the necessary arrangements?"

Chapter Three

Etienne stood in the doorway of an upscale vampire club in Society Hill Philadelphia. After his departure earlier from Vladimir, he felt in need of sexual comfort. The woman he hungered for with a passion that threatened to consume him belonged to Acier. So he had come to seek out the fem who had recently rocked his world and had almost succeeded in chasing away thoughts of Raven.

A beautiful, buxom brunette with dark eyes, seated on a barstool, turned to look at him. Her smile revealed her incisors. "Etienne, you handsome boy!" She rose and crossed the room.

"Kalista!" They met in the middle of the dance floor, her heavy breasts pressing against his chest as he hugged her. She slipped her hands down his back and cupped his ass, grinding her lower body against his. His cock sprang to rigid attention.

She moved her head until their mouths touched. Tightening his arms around her, he devoured her lips, sucking and pulling at her tongue. The extreme beauty of a vampire fem was her sensual nature, which gloried in her sexuality with no false pretenses of coyness. With her hands on his body, stroking his ass, and her lips and tongue inviting his to plunder, he released the tenuous control he had on himself.

All around them in the club, sounds of vampires fucking were interspersed with the pulse pounding music. He wanted her and he wanted her *now*. Swinging her up in his arms, he stalked across the big room, lit only by flashing strobe lights, to a spot against a far wall. He set her on her feet and pulled up her skirt, exposing her long, slender legs and the dark riot of curls surrounding her pretty pussy.

Locking her gaze with his, she slid down his zipper.

Her cool fingers closed around his fully erect shaft. He shuddered, urging her legs apart. She gave a tug and he moved closer, until the head of his shaft nestled against her pubic hair. A rage of lust washed over him. He growled and thrust forward, slamming deep within her tight, warm cunt.

She gasped. Grabbing his ass, she tugged, forcing the final inches of his cock into her. Her eyes blazed with lust. "Bang me, boy! Fuck me hard and fast! Ram your big hot dick deep and hard! Ruin me! Blast my cunt open! Blast me, boy!"

Her pussy felt hot and creamy. She was as wild for sex with him as he was with her. He fucked her hard and fast, slamming his cock into her with no fear of hurting her. It was difficult to hold on to his control long enough for her to come. He gritted his teeth, bit into one of her large breasts, right through her blouse, and stabbed his cock in and out of her in a frenzy of hunger.

She cried out, her cunt clasping and shuddering around him. Raising his head, he bared her neck, sank his teeth into her flesh, and fed on her as he blasted her full of his seed.

She held him in her arms, moaning softly as he pumped the last drop of his seed in her. "That's it, my lovely boy." She raked her incisors against his skin. "Give me every drop of your sweet seed."

He licked her neck, leisurely thrusting his cock in and out of her.

She lifted his head and kissed his lips. "You will spend the night with me and I will ride you hard and fast—all night long."

That's what he needed—to be fucked all night long. Maybe she could fuck thoughts of Raven out of his mind. With her still impaled on his cock, he looked into her eyes. "Yes."

She stroked his cheek. "Who is it that makes you so unhappy, my handsome boy? Tell me and I'll get her and together we will fuck her into submission."

He thought of Raven and shook his head. "I'm here because I need you."

A naked body pressed against his back. He stiffened.

"What about me?" a soft, sultry voice demanded. "Would you like to be fucked all night by two lusty fems, handsome?"

It had been a long time since he'd had two women outside of work. He'd never had two full-blood fems. His cock, still hard, pulsed in Kalista's cunt at the thought. "Hell, yeah."

The woman behind him licked the back of his neck, parted his cheeks, and touched his asshole. "You have a lovely ass. Can I fuck it?"

He pulled out of Kalista's pussy, placed his hands beside her body for leverage, and pushed back, shoving the woman behind him away. Swinging around, he found himself facing a tall fem with a luscious body. Her breasts were big and firm, her legs long and shapely legs. The sight of her dark, lovely body rekindled his ever-present hunger for Raven.

He bared his incisors. "No one fucks my ass!"

She cupped a hand over his cock and balls. "A pity." Keeping her fingers on him, she slipped the fingers of her other hand inside her pussy. She removed them, placing them against his lips.

The scent of her cunt sent him into a frenzy. He licked her fingers. The taste of her inflamed his senses. He grabbed her hips, swung her against the wall next to Kalista, and shot his cock into the liquid warmth of her tight cunt. She moaned and thrust back at him, stroking her hands over his back.

"Oh, damn, handsome, you feel so fucking good. Hmmm. Oh, yeah! Lord, I love a male with a big, hard dick and a yen for good, black pussy." She pressed her lips against his ear. "You do have a yen for black pussy, don't you, handsome?"

He thrust deep into her, shuddering with the pleasure as her inner muscles massaged and caressed his cock. "Yes," he whispered, his thoughts on Raven and her pretty, pink-lipped pussy.

"And I have a yen for big white cocks. So fuck away, handsome."

After a moment of watching them fuck, Kalista moved behind him. She was almost as tall as he. Pressing her body against his back, she leaned her face past his head. Moments later, she had locked her lips over those of the other fem. Kalista moved her hands until he was aware of her cupping her palms over the fem's ass. As he fucked into the fem's clinging pussy, Kalista jerked the other woman's hips forward, ensuring he got every inch of his cock deep into her with every downward lunge.

She has a sweet black cunt, doesn't she, boy? Fuck it hard and deep. Make the juices flow from her like nectar.

Trapped between the two kissing fems with Kalista projecting her wanton lusts directly into his head, the sensations assailing him were intense. He lost his ability to prolong and control his release. He shuddered and came, driving his shaft hard and fast in the lovely fem as he did.

Kalista pulled her mouth away from the other woman's and pressed her cheek against his. "Let's go to bed, handsome, and I'll fuck you and Adona all night."

Etienne reluctantly pulled out of Adona's slick, clinging pussy. He loved the way her swollen cunt lips clung to the head of his cock as he eased out of her. He cupped his hands over her hips. "I'd love to fuck your large, lovely ass."

"Got a thing for sweet black pussy and a large, luscious black ass, huh?" She smiled. "My mouth, my pussy, my ass, are all yours for the taking, handsome. What's your name?"

"Etienne."

She pressed her lips against his. "Let's go to bed and see if you can manage to get every inch of that hot dick of yours into my tight, eager ass."

The thought of sliding his cock between her dark cheeks, past her hole, and into her ass nearly made him come again.

Kalista cupped a hand between Adona's legs. "But first, I want to eat that sweet, black cunt of yours and taste your pussy juice." She looked at Etienne. "Lord, I love eating her fragrant black pussy. Would you like to watch me eat her?"

Normally the idea of two women eating each other left him lukewarm at best. And having fucked Adona, he was no longer interested in Kalista. Still, he decided that admission was best kept to himself. He smiled. "Lead the way, ladies."

As he followed them through the club, his gaze on Adona's lovely dark body with its long legs, and enticing big ass, for the first time in weeks, he didn't think of Raven.

* * *

Eight hours later, long after Kalista had left them alone together, Etienne eased his cock out of Adona's tight ass. He rolled onto his back and lifted her body on top of his. He stroked his hands over her warm ass.

"Someone needs another fuck, huh?"

He slapped one of her cheeks. "Yes!"

Smiling, she impaled herself on him. Her pussy, slick with their combined juices, closed tightly around his cock.

"Damn!" He shuddered.

She rubbed her breasts against his chest. "This is some fucking good black pussy, huh?"

"This is fucking good pussy of any color." He shoved his hips up, driving his entire length into her, groaning again. "Damn, I've never been inside a more addictive cunt."

She moaned softly, grinding her hips against his. "Like all fems, I love big cocks… the bigger and thicker the better, but I have a special hunger for watching a big white cock pushing between the dark lips of my pussy, and slowly sinking into me until it's difficult to see where the cock ends and my pussy begins. And baby, you have the best white meat this pussy's ever had. Fuck me, handsome!"

Even after hours of non-stop fucking, her pussy still felt almost unbearably delicious. He curled his fingers in her hair, bringing her warm lips over his, and they shared a tender, prolonged fuck. They both came multiple times. Finally, as he felt his cum and her juices oozing out of her pussy to settle on his pubic hair, he became aware of a familiar presence.

"I have to go," he told her. He kissed her slowly and reluctantly lifted her body off his, sliding out of bed.

"You sure you're ready to leave all this?" She lay on her back with her long legs spread wide. A stream of her natural juices, clouded with his cum, trickled out of her pussy to disappear down the crack of her big ass.

After all the hours of fucking, the lips of her pussy gaped open in a lascivious invitation he was hard pressed to deny. His cock stirred. Just looking at her well-fucked slit nearly drove him crazy with renewed lust. Left to himself, he could fuck her until his cock went limp and numb. But this was not the time to trade his hunger for Raven for a new one for this dark, luscious beauty.

"I have to go." He sat on the side of the bed, staring at her. "Are you bloodlusted?"

She sank two fingers between her legs and gently fucked herself. "I don't know if I believe in a vampire having only one perfect mate."

"So you're not bloodlusted?"

"If I were, I wouldn't have been able to spend the night with my pussy full of your thick meat." She pulled her fingers out of her body and popped them into her mouth. "Hmmm. Your cum, mixed with pussy juice, tastes delicious." She stroked a hand over his thigh to cup his cock. "Don't take my word for it, see for yourself." She plunged her fingers back inside her body, withdrew them, and pressed them against his lips. "Taste how good we are together, my handsome Etienne."

Unable to resist, he climbed onto the bed, settled between her legs, and buried his face against her pussy. His nostrils filled with the musky aroma of her aroused cunt, and the juices flowing freely into his eager mouth, he stabbed two fingers in her and finger fucked and ate her sweet pussy.

An hour later, he pulled his tongue out of her climaxing pussy, and rose to stand by the bed on unsteady legs. "I have to go."

She rolled onto her stomach, pressing her cheek against the bed. "Who's keeping you, handsome?"

He dressed quickly. Before he left the room, he pressed several greedy kisses against her ass cheeks and thighs.

"Hmmm." He hesitated, then eased her legs apart, and pressed a long, probing kiss against her cunt. He slid his tongue pass her swollen lips and into her pussy. He licked her warm flesh for several moments before he finally rose to his feet, breathing hard.

She turned to smile confidently at him. "It's difficult to leave pussy this good, isn't it?"

"Are you here often? If I want to see you again, can I find you here?"

"If I want to see you again, Etienne, I'll find you. Do not come looking for me."

"Why not?"

"Because I can only be found if and when I want to be found." She rolled onto her stomach and drifted to sleep.

He turned and left the room, closing the door behind him. He encountered Kalista in the deserted club. She gave him a long look. "She hooked you too, didn't she?"

"Too?"

She shrugged. "Like all fems, I love cock, but I swear whenever she shows up, I get this insatiable hunger to eat her pussy. Damn, it's good, isn't it?"

"What is she?"

"What do you mean what is she?"

"I sense she's not really a vampire."

"The hell she isn't."

"She projects all the signs and mannerisms, but she is not a vampire."

She grinned suddenly. "I really don't care what she is. All I know is she's now alone. And I am going to spend the next few hours eating the sweetest pussy on the planet."

"She's asleep."

"She won't be asleep long once I get my tongue inside that sweet hot box of hers."

He ignored the sudden, jealous rage that washed over him and headed for the door. He emerged from the club to find a tall vampire with dark auburn hair, green eyes, and chiseled features sitting in the driver's seat of his SUV. His shape shifting Keddi, in the form of a miniature wolf-shifter perched on the male's shoulder.

He walked around to the passenger side and got in. He closed his eyes and leaned his head against the headrest.

All right?

He nodded without opening his eyes. *Yes, Slayer. I'm all right*, he told his Keddi.

Sure?

Yes. I'm sure. "What are you doing here, Damon?"

"I'm your best friend. Where else would I be when you're troubled?"

"I'm fine."

"Then why did Acier call me?"

He sighed and opened his eyes, annoyed. "Because he worries too damned much. It's time he realized I'm not some damned silly teen who needs his guidance or interference."

Damon slid a palm against his neck. "He's your brother and I'm your friend. When you hurt, we hurt."

Slayer hurt too.

"I'm not hurt. I've just spent eight hours with two lovely, lusty fems."

"And?"

He shook his head. "And while I was with one of them, I stopped aching for Raven!"

"That's good. Right?"

"I don't know. I called her a fem, but I don't think she's really a vampire. She called herself Adona and—"

"Gorgeous, with yards of smooth, dark skin?"

"Yes. You know her?"

"I've seen her around, but I don't know anything about her."

He sighed. "Now that I'm away from her, my hunger for Raven has returned. What am I going to do?"

Damon's hand on the back of his neck tightened. "I told you what you need to do! You have to get with Raven, Etienne! This is not something you have much control over. You are more vampire than shifter, and damn if you're not a second away from entering a Feast of Indulgence."

He knew from previous talks with Damon, a vampire, that a latent or half-blood vampire moving to the status of a full-blood vampire entered a sex and blood orgy called the Feast of Indulgence. It was said to be a dangerous time for a vampire who bloodlusted with anyone who was not a vampire.

"I'm part shifter," he objected. "How can I possibly have a Feast of Indulgence? How can I become a full-blood vampire?"

Damon shook his head. "I don't know, Etienne, but I know the signs. Your feelings for Raven are making you more vampire than shifter. Okay. So maybe it's not a full-fledged Feast, but this incessant hunger for sex that no matter how good leaves you longing for Raven can't be denied."

"If that's true, shouldn't Acier be the one about to enter a Feast instead of me?"

Damon shrugged. "Hey, I don't pretend to understand how things work for vampire hybrids, but I think it's fair to say that's what you and Acier are. You're not shifter hybrids. Maybe things would be different for you two if you were shifter hybrids. But you're vampire hybrids. You know what's wrong, Etienne, and you know the remedy."

He shook his head. "I can't."

"I've talked to Acier, Etienne. He doesn't like it, but he understands what you need to do to retain your sanity."

"I can't touch Raven, Damon. He loves her too much. No matter what you say, he considers himself a shifter. We... they mate for life and do not share their mates. If I touch her, our relationship will never be the same again."

"If you don't... I fear for you, Etienne."

"I'll be fine."

Damon bared his incisors. "Damn it, Etienne, you will not be fine! You can't go on ignoring a large part of who and what you are. You are vampire, and we share our bloodlusts with our siblings. It's a part of our heritage. You have a right to fuck Raven. Acier has accepted that and Raven wants it. So go do her already, you stubborn bastard, so we can get on with dealing with the bastards threatening Den Gautier."

"We?"

Damon nodded. "You don't think I'm going to allow you to face danger alone, do you? Shaun and Brett stand ready to help too. Okay?"

He closed his eyes and leaned against the headrest again. From what he knew of Damon's older brothers, he didn't relish needing their help. Both were unpredictable with tempers shorter than a New York minute. "I appreciate their offer of help, Damon, but I feel like I'm going mad. I want sex all the time but no matter how great it is, it never satisfies me for long."

"I know." Damon squeezed his shoulder. "I know."

A picture of Raven danced behind his closed lids. He dismissed it only to have it replaced by one of Adona. Wonderful. Now he'd get to obsess over two different women. For all he knew Adona would prove just as difficult to possess as Raven had.

He swore softly. "Take me to the RV."

Slayer stirred on his shoulder. *Father at RV?*

"Father? Who are you calling—"

"He and I talked about Madison on the way here," Damon explained.

He looked at Damon. "And you called him father?"

"Not me. Slayer's been talking to Pen and Drei and that's what they call Aleksei Madison."

Father at RV? Slayer asked again.

No. Why?

Want meet father.

Why?

He's father. Pen and Drei met other father. Pen and Drei like... want meet yours. Want like yours.

You want to meet him? He shrugged. *Why not?* "Let's go find him, Damon."

Damon glanced at his watch. "Okay, but I can't stay long."

"Why not? Got something better to do?"

Damon grimaced. "I'd hardly call it better. Damn, the things I do for my friends. It's something I've agreed to do."

- 45 -

"For who?"

"Never mind who. I have a fucking unpleasant appointment with a number of supercilious bastards. That's all you need to know."

"Fuck you, Damon."

"Don't make me bitch slap you, Etienne."

He bared his incisors. "You and what army?"

Damon laughed and sent the SUV speeding forward.

* * *

Raven sprawled on her stomach, her cheek pressed against the mattress, her teeth gritted, her hands clenched into fists. Steele, naked and demanding, lay on top of her, his incisors buried in her neck, his big hands holding her hips still as he rutted his long, thick cock violently in and out of her pussy. He did it with little regard for her pleasure. In fact, he was hurting her… much as he'd done when he'd taken her virginity less than two weeks earlier. Although their sex play since that first time had alternated between tender lovemaking and raunchy fucking, he had always done his best not to hurt her.

She knew he made no such effort now. He seemed to delight in hurting her. Each time he slammed his huge length up into her, she gasped in pain and shuddered. As she did, he tightened his hands on her hips and thrust harder and deeper, bringing more pain. The moment he had tossed her onto the bed and fallen on her, knocking the breath from her, she had feared something was wrong. When he used his knee to force her legs apart and slammed his entire length into her with one painful, breath-stealing lunge, she had known that the man about to fuck her was not Steele.

She closed her eyes and tightened her hands until her nails dug into her palms. "Steele… please." She spoke in a low, pain-filled voice. "Not so hard or so deep. Please."

He lifted his head from her neck. His response, growled against her ear, shocked her. "I know you like it like this so shut the fuck up and enjoy it!"

She felt Bentia, the living barrier spirit who had granted Raven the right to command her, stir restlessly in her stomach. *I will make him stop. I will not let him hurt you.*

No. Angry tears tightened her throat, but she held them off. The man lying on her, rutting into her like some whore he'd picked up in some crack dive, was not the Steele with whom she had fallen so helplessly in love. And yet he was. *No. It's not his fault. His two natures are warring with each other like never before. Steele, my Steele would never hurt me.*

He is hurting you. He knows that and he's reveling in that knowledge.

She knew Bentia was right, but there was nothing to be done. She had willingly come to the bedroom, thinking they would make love. Instead, his vampire nature seemed to be conquering the sweet shifter for whom she had fallen. She knew it was the vampire who delighted in bringing her pain. Yet, somewhere inside him were the remnants of the shifter she loved, needed, and wanted to please and protect.

Let me handle this, Bentia.

The roiling in her stomach subsided and she lay in pain as Steele stabbed his cock into her with increasing violence until he shuddered, snarled, and blasted jet after jet of seed into her.

He collapsed on top of her, breathing deeply, almost suffocating her. Her pussy sore, her heart aching, she reached deep within herself and called on Bentia. *I've had enough. Get him off me!*

Feeling Bentia surging through her, she pressed her hands against the bed, and thrust her body up with a force powerful enough to force Steele's cock out of her and thrust him off of her. She rolled onto her side and exploded off the bed to stand staring down at him.

He lay on his back staring up at her with glowing eyes and bared incisors, his still erect shaft protruding up from his body. He fondled his cock. "I'm not finished with you," he said. "Get your sweet black ass back in bed and ride me."

Enraged and hurt, she reached down, curled her fingers in his long, dark hair, and glared down into his eyes. "I know this is a difficult time for you and you're struggling to retain the identity you feel you've lost or are losing, but if you ever try to abuse me like that again, Acier, you will be extremely sorry."

His gray eyes flickered with anger before slowly turning gold. He blinked up at her. "Abuse you? *Petite*, you know I would never hurt you." He pried her fingers loose from his hair and rose to face her.

"You practically raped me, Acier!" She leveled a finger at him. "Do it again and I will show you just who the fuck I am! I love you, but no one abuses me! No one ruts into me without my permission as you just did. Understand that or prepare to have your ass kicked by a Willoni who commands a living barrier spirit, you big bastard!"

His eyes flashing gray, he bolted to his feet, and bared his incisors. "You are my woman, Raven! Mine! I'll do whatever the hell I want to with you." He glared down into her eyes. "And don't think your living spirit will be able to stop me. No one comes between me and my woman."

Raven dropped her right hand down to her side, her fist clenched. She felt Bentia rushing up from her stomach to her chest. Like Steele and Etienne, she was not fully human. Her human father had married and mated with a Willoni Priestess. From her guide, Abby Valentine, she learned that Willoni, through mastery of a spiritual process called a *creed* or *soul song*, had the ability to see into and in some cases shape the future.

With power like that at her disposal, she was not about to allow any man to mistreat her. "Fuck you, Acier!" As a coil of energy shot down her arm, she thrust out her hand, opening her palm.

Swept off his feet by the force of Bentia, the living barrier spirit, being released from her fingertips, Steele slammed against the far wall. Snarling, he sprang to his feet. Raven thrust out her hand again and a shimmering wall, just barely perceptible to the eye, sprang between them. He rushed at it, but secure in the knowledge that he would not be able to get past Bentia, Raven turned and quickly pulled on her clothes.

"Where the fuck are you going?" He punched a clenched fist against Bentia.

"I'm going for a drive to give you time to come back to your senses. I know this is a difficult time for you, but I'll be damned if I'll be abused by you. You get your damn act together by the time I get back or I am out of here for good!"

"If you leave, Raven—"

"Fuck you!" She turned and stormed through the RV. Outside, with the afternoon sun warming her, she took a deep breath, allowing some of her rage to dissipate. She climbed into her car and pulled out of the RV court. As she did, she reached out to Bentia. *Hold him for ten more minutes, but do not injure him.*

I would not injure one who brings such pleasure.

A few days earlier, as she and Steele had made love, Bentia had exerted herself and caused Raven to react with an insatiable hunger, driving Steele to fuck her so violently Raven passed out. Bentia had promised not to allow her desire for Steele to emerge again. But now it seemed like a good idea to allow the two of them to go at each other without boundaries or restraints. She knew in future, she would be capable of satisfying all of Steele's hungers, but she wasn't there yet.

You can still say that after what he just did? she demanded of Bentia.

Yes. It is not his fault he brought pain.
Then whose fault was it? Mine?
It's the fault of the war within him. Forgive him.
I will — when I'm ready.
And now?
Now? You want him? Fine. Allow him to fuck you raw.
I... I have your permission to mate with him?

Raven sucked in a quick breath. She didn't like the idea of sharing Steele, but right now his passion and hunger for sex was more than she could handle alone. And if she had to share him, who better to share him with than Bentia, who had a thing for him?

I'm going to talk to Abby. As the Willoni guide charged with guiding her to her true destiny, Abby would be able to help. *Fuck him to your heart's content, but when I return, he is mine.*

He will always be yours... even as I mate with him. Would you like to retain our link so you may share the experience with us?

She shuddered at the thought of Steele with someone else. *No. It's one o'clock. I'll be back by six. Do not let me walk in on you pleasuring him when I return.*

Thank you.

Raven broke the connection. Pressing her foot on the accelerator, she sent her car speeding down the road. She cleared her head and concentrated not on what was happening between Steele and Bentia, but on the wonders and discoveries the future with him held. If they had a child, it would be part Willoni, part shifter, part human, and part vampire. Such a child would be a wonderful, miraculous gift to them both.

* * *

Aleksei sat in the driver's seat of his SUV, his gaze on the dark road just ahead of his vehicle's headlights. Vlad sat beside him. Pen had remained with Acier, but Drei, in his natural wolf form, perched on his shoulder, pressed close against his neck, projecting waves of warmth at him. The affection he and the small creature shared amazed and pleased Aleksei.

For the first time in a very long time, Aleksei felt at peace. He and Vlad had found their sons. He wasn't sure how they could both be so certain one twin belonged to either of them, but all four of them were sure. It wasn't logical but it made sense to them.

He noted a calmness and a sense of happiness in his twin he had despaired of ever witnessing. Meeting Etienne seemed to have had a profound effect on Vlad. Aleksei sensed a new purpose in him.

"When this is over, I'm going to see her."

"Her?" Aleksei cast a surprised look at Vlad. "Mother?"

"Yes."

He tensed. The last time the two of them met, Vlad had been determined to kill her. "Why?"

"I… need to see her, Sei. I want to talk to her. I told her I was coming."

"Why?"

"I think I know what she must have felt when I tried to… when I wanted to… no parent should feel as if they are hated by his or her child. It's not… natural. It's not something she… deserves."

Aleksei sighed, feeling as if a huge burden had been lifted off his shoulders. "She loves you more than ever."

"I know."

This was a new Vlad indeed. But before he and Vlad could settle down and become fathers, they had pressing business. "Tell me about the Brotherhood, Vlad."

"They are a powerful, dangerous group, Sei. Vitali Bourcaro is in charge. He's the one we'll need to convince to back off."

"Tell me about this Bourcaro."

"He's very powerful… anywhere from 700 to 900 years old, I think. He is devoted to ensuring vampires do not lose ground to humans or anyone else."

"Is he a reasonable vampire or will I have to kick his ass all over the countryside?"

"He will back Deoctra and Falcone."

"Do you know this Falcone?"

"We've met. He's a powerful shifter. He's Heoptin."

Aleksei frowned. His mentor Luc had spoken of an ancient god called Heoptin, who long ago commanded a breed of vampires who were healers rather than predators. Among those Heoptin commanded were a breed of warriors known as shifters who had been renowned for their skill in battle against superior foes. This Tucker Falcone, whose bite had nearly killed Acier, would present quite a challenge to Acier.

But he would only intervene if the tide turned against Acier. "His ass will be a dead Heoptin if he keeps fucking with my son."

"Sei, I don't know if Acier can take him. I know Acier is brave and strong, but perhaps it would be best if Etienne took him on."

Drei stiffened on Aleksei's shoulder. *Alpha stronger. Don't need help.*

Aleksei arched a brow. "Are you by any chance implying Etienne is more powerful than Acier?"

"I'm not implying it. I'm coming right out and saying it, Sei. I know he's your son, but facts are facts."

"Don't be ridiculous, Vladimir. Etienne is clearly a shifter to be reckoned with, but Acier—"

"Acier is a shifter. Etienne is a vampire."

The pride he heard in Vlad's voice both pleased and annoyed him. "Really? Let's not forget which of them shifted into a wolf. It wasn't Acier. He's vampire enough to take Falcone in a fair fight."

"I would hate to see you lose your son so soon after finding him, Sei."

"Don't you worry about Acier, Vladimir. He's the one who was chosen to be next Alpha Supreme."

"This Aime who chose him over Etienne must be a little... mentally deficient."

Aleksei laughed. Only days after finding them, he and Vlad were arguing over whose son was the strongest. "They're both worthy males, Vlad. Mother will be so pleased to learn she has two such fine grandsons." Remembering the promise he had made to Luc to bring Acier to meet him, Aleksei sighed. How the hell was he going to get the headstrong Acier to agree to meet Luc?

He'd worry about that later. For now, there was Vitali Bourcaro and the Brotherhood to deal with. A few miles from Vitali's suburban Philadelphia home, Aleksei felt a familiar tingling sensation.

"Stop, Sei."

He slowed the SUV and pulled it over to the side of the road. Moments later, another SUV stopped behind his. He and Vlad got out and waited. A tall male with heavily creamed skin with a hint of bronze and blue eyes alighted on the driver's side.

A tall, shapely female with skin the color of warm cocoa slid out on the passenger side, a welcoming smile on her pretty face.

Aleksei stepped aside. The two newcomers rushed at Vlad. Aleksei watched as his three siblings clung to each other, kissing and hugging.

Finally, Tatiana stood back, her head tilted to one side. "Vladimir, it's been a long time. It's so good to see you."

"Lord, Vlad, you get uglier every time I lay eyes on you," Andrei said.

Vlad laughed, his blue eyes alight with joy. "Drei, you ugly sucker!" His voice softened. "And Tat… you are more beautiful every time I see you."

She smiled and hugged him again. "It's been too long since we were all together."

Aleksei joined them, throwing an arm around Tat and Drei's shoulders.

Tat's gaze went to his right shoulder where Drei still perched. "And who is the handsome creature on your shoulder, Sei?"

"He's a Keddi, which is a living, sentient shifter." He smiled, looking at Andrei. "His name is Drei."

Andrei laughed. "No wonder the little sucker is so handsome."

"Drei, this is Tatiana and Andrei, our brother and sister," he told the Keddi.

Drei flew through the air to hover in front of Tat. *Pretty.*

She smiled, stroking a finger along his flank. "Hi, Drei."

Drei turned his attention to Andrei. *Drei let use name also.*

Andrei grinned. "That's mighty generous of you, Drei. I appreciate it."

Drei returned to Aleksei's shoulder. "So. What brings you two out tonight?"

"It's been a long time since we were together." Tat glanced at Vlad, who stood smiling at her. "We missed you both and decided it's time we reevaluated our situation. There's no purpose served in remaining separate from you two. If you can forgive us, we're back," she said.

"You're just in time," Vlad said. "We are going to talk to the Brotherhood."

"The Brotherhood?" Tat raked a hand through her short hair. "Why? What's wrong?"

"We... Vlad and I each have a son... they're twins and having problems with the Brotherhood."

Aleksei watched Tat and Drei exchange looks. "How can you each have a son who is a twin?"

"We don't understand it, but it's true."

Tat clasped her hands, her eyes shining. "Twins! I'm an aunt."

"Again," Aleksei reminded her. "Remember Mikhel's son, Dimitri."

Tat nodded. "Yes, I know, but I have not yet got to know him or Serge... or Katie. How old are your boys?"

"Forty."

"I can hardly wait to meet them. Are they vamps, human, or a combo?"

"They are part vampire, part shifter."

She sighed, then her eyes blazed. "But you said they had trouble with the Brotherhood."

"Yes."

She looked at her twin before speaking. "Drei and I will follow."

Aleksei shook his head. The last time he had faced a powerful foe and allowed his younger siblings to accompany him, one of his younger brothers, Mikhel, had nearly paid with his life. "You know we appreciate you and Andrei coming, but Vlad and I can handle this."

"Undoubtedly, but Drei and I will come as well."

Vlad shook his head. "No, Tat. Really. The Brotherhood is no place for vampires who are not... hardened."

She tossed her head. "Don't let the years Drei and I spent in the human world mislead you. We are still full-bloods able to do our part in protecting family interests. As Father used to say, we are family, no matter what. If someone threatens your sons, it's the same as threatening us personally. With or without your approval, Drei and I are coming."

Aleksei looked at Andrei. His younger brother shrugged and smiled. "Her mind is made up… and so is mine, Sei."

Tat looked at him. "We're wasting time, Sei."

He looked at Vlad. *We can't allow them to be hurt.*

We'll protect them, Sei… even if we have to die doing it.

He sighed. "Okay. So let's do this."

Drei pressed close to his neck. *Will help protect.*

Chapter Four

Forty-five minutes later, they stopped outside a large gated mainline Philadelphia estate. Vlad, now in the driver's seat, leaned out the open window and spoke into a microphone. "It's Vladimir. Open the gates."

"Who is that with you?" a cool voice demanded.

"My siblings. We're here to see Vitali."

The gates slid open and they drove down a long, winding drive. Five minutes later, Vlad stopped in front of a huge three-story mansion. As the four of them mounted the wide steps, a tall vampire with bronze skin, salt and pepper hair, and dark eyes appeared at the top of the steps. Flanking him were several large vampires.

"Vladimir, what brings you here?"

"We need to talk, Vitali."

Vitali eyed him in silence for several moments. "I see you've brought your big brother." He thrust his hand out to Aleksei. "For such a young vampire, you've managed to make quite a name for yourself, Madison. But then you have a powerful mentor."

Aleksei inclined his head slightly, but ignored Vitali's hand. "Bourcaro."

After a moment, Vitali allowed his hand to drop to his side. He arched a brow at Vladimir. "And your other companions?"

"This is Tatiana and Andrei Forester."

Vitali nodded briefly in Andrei's direction before turning to look at Tat. Their gazes locked, he smiled, and extended his hand.

After a brief hesitation, Aleksei watched Tat place her hand in his.

"Tatiana, a lovely name and a lovelier woman. You take my breath away." He lifted her hand to his mouth and kissed the back of it.

Aleksei heard her catch a quick breath before she tugged at her hand and stepped away from him, her dark lashes sweeping down to hide the expression in her blue eyes.

Andrei's gaze narrowed. Aleksei, watching his younger brother, gave a small shake of his head. Bourcaro was not the vampire for Andrei to piss off… at least not yet.

Vlad moved to stand in front of Tat. "This is my baby sister, Vitali. We came here to discuss Falcone and Diniti!"

Vitali shrugged, his gaze still on Tat's face, over Vlad's shoulder. "You know that I don't discuss Brotherhood business with outsiders, Vladimir."

Aleksei's patience evaporated. "Then let's speak frankly. Call Falcone off my son's back or you can pick up his remains in the nearest dump!"

Vitali turned to look at him, his eyes narrowing. "Don't allow your rep to go to your head, Madison. No one comes into my home and threatens members of the Brotherhood. If you have a death wish, I will be more than happy to help you fulfill it."

Drei stiffened on his shoulder.

It's all right, Drei. Do not interfere.

Won't let hurt. Will protect father.

Father can protect himself. Do not interfere. Understood?

Yes… but if father hurt… will tear to pieces.

Vlad flashed forward, staring into Vitali's eyes. "Do not threaten him, Vitali. Call off Falcone and tell Diniti to stay the fuck away from my son and nephew or you'll get more than you and the Brotherhood bargain for!"

Vitali's eyes glowed and he bared his incisors. "You want your ass whipped, you've come to the right place!"

"Vitali! Vladimir has been our companion for some twenty years. Why not hear them out?"

The speaker, a tall vampire with short, dark brown hair, dark eyes, and rather pale skin appeared at their side. He nodded at Aleksei. "I am Jacoby."

Aleksei sensed a well of immense power in the newcomer. He suspected he looked upon a vampire powerful enough to do what rogue vampire Wilfredo Miguel Santiago had not been able to do... kill him. And yet he didn't fear death. He didn't embrace it, but he couldn't imagine a more noble way to die than to do so protecting Acier's interests. He thought of Dani and closed his eyes briefly, praying that Luc would look after her for the sake of the child she carried, which Luc considered his grandchild.

Once again, he regretted allowing his siblings to accompany him into a situation from which none of them might emerge alive. As far as he knew, neither Tat nor Drei had ever bloodlusted. They were too young and too precious to die. For their sake, he decided now was not the time for this confrontation. If the situation allowed, he would walk away. If not... no one could expect to live forever — not even a vampire.

"I am Aleksei Madison," he said coolly.

Jacoby nodded. "You're Luc's boy."

"You know him?"

Jacoby frowned. "We've never met... at least I don't think we have and yet..." He broke off and turned to look at Vitali. "Diniti has been with us for a short time while Vladimir has been among us for some twenty years."

"But Vlad has never joined us, and Diniti has. And Falcone is one of us and has been far longer than Vlad has been amongst us." Vitali's nostrils flared. "And the last time I checked, Jacoby, I ran the Brotherhood. Don't you have some pressing business with Sean and Lover you need to attend to?"

Aleksei and his siblings remained silent, aware that they were watching a power play. Everyone who knew of the Brotherhood knew Vitali Bourcaro was in charge, while Jacoby was but one member. And yet...

Jacoby looked at Vitali, his lips tightening. "I do have pressing business elsewhere, Vitali, but do not make the mistake of underestimating me. I am far older and far more powerful than you can imagine. It would be unfortunate for you if I had to prove the point. Rein in Diniti and call off Falcone."

"Or?"

"Or I will."

"You think you're strong enough to wrest control of the Brotherhood from me, Jacoby?"

"I have no desire to lead the Brotherhood, but do not make the mistake of thinking I will allow you to lead us into an unnecessary and bloody conflict."

"Bloody conflict? You begin to sound like a squeamish old maid with no stomach for doing what is necessary, Jacoby!"

Jacoby leveled a finger at him. "Hear me and hear me well, Vitali. We have no quarrel with Aime Gautier's Pack."

Vitali peeled his lips back over his teeth. "I run the Brotherhood, Jacoby. I decide who we have a quarrel with."

Jacoby shook his head, baring his incisors. "I warn you, Vitali, tread lightly and carefully. You fuck with Madison and you risk bringing the wrath of Luc down on our heads."

"You can cower at his name in fear if you like, but I'm not afraid of any living creature… no matter what they are!"

"You're a fool if you don't fear Luc, but I don't have time for this shit right now. I have to find Sean and Lover." He swirled around and disappeared into the night.

Vitali watched him go before turning to face Aleksei. "Get out now while I'm inclined to allow you to leave with your dignity intact."

Aleksei thrust out his clenched right fist. When he opened his palm and exhaled, he pushed outward with his hand and his mind. He grinned at the startled look on Vitali's face as he quickly picked himself up off his ass, several feet away. "You were saying?"

The other vampires converged on them. Vlad, Drei, and Tat flashed forward to meet them and exchange blows. One vampire grabbed Tat and prepared to backhand her. Drei snarled with fury, tossed the vampire he held aside like a rag doll and charged to Tat's rescue.

Before he could reach her, she swung up her left forearm to block the fist of the attacking vampire and delivered a rapid series of vicious right jabs to what appeared to be a glass jaw. She stepped back as he dropped to his knees before slamming onto his face.

Another vampire rushed at her.

"Touch her and you die, Siti!" Vitali thundered.

The vampire rushing at Tat as well as the ones engaging Vlad and Drei stopped and looked at Vitali. "What the fuck? We're supposed to let her kick our asses?"

Vitali looked at Aleksei, his eyes still glowing. "For the sake of your lovely sister, go now, Madison, but know that you have made a powerful enemy here today. We will meet again."

Tat tossed her head angrily. "Do not make any concession on my behalf, Bourcaro. I am Tatiana Madison-Forester, full-blood vampire. Anyone who would threaten my brothers is my enemy. Come after my brothers and you come after me."

Vitali looked at her, breathing deeply. "We will meet again, Tatiana… under more pleasant circumstances."

"As long as you threaten my brothers, consider me your number one enemy." She stalked over to him and stared up into his eyes. "And trust me, Bourcaro, I may not be as old as you and I have not always embraced my vampire heritage, but I have learned the ways of dark magic. I am one sister you do not want to fuck with!"

Vitali's teeth flashed in a smile, his eyes softening. "You are one of the loveliest women I've ever seen. There is a magical quality about you I find… breathtaking. I definitely want to fuck with you. We will meet again." He cast a cool look at Aleksei. "You and I will also meet again, Madison."

Aleksei shrugged. "Anytime you want to be knocked on your ass, Bourcaro, you come see me. Bring your shifter with you and I'll—"

"We'll kill you both," Vlad stated in a cool, emotionless voice.

"Fuck you and your arrogant brothers, Vladimir." With a last look of longing at Tat, Bourcaro flashed away into the night. The other vampires, keeping their gazes locked on Vlad, quickly melted away, until Aleksei and his siblings stood alone on the steps.

Aleksei sighed. "Well, that didn't accomplish much." He turned and flashed into the night with the others beside him. At their SUV's, he paused. He looked at Vlad. "It's time I had a talk with Mother. She is powerful and will be able to help us protect the boys."

Vlad shuddered and shook his head. "I'm dealing with too much now, Sei. I can't face her yet."

Tat sucked in a breath. "Neither can I."

Andrei shrugged. "Hey, the time when I needed or wanted her in my life is long past."

Aleksei shook his head. "I know you all have issues with her. Hell, I still have issues with her, but she is not what we thought she was. And she wants and needs to reconcile with all of you. If you just give her a chance… get to know her…"

Tat shook her head. "In our own time, Sei."

"None of you have to meet her until you're ready. I'll talk to her and the others. I think it's time Katie and Etienne met. Together, they may be able to tell us what lies ahead."

Vlad shook his head. "I don't want to meet her yet, Sei."

"You don't have to… at least not yet. I don't like the idea of bringing Katie, Mik, or Serge into danger, but they are our siblings. If the Brotherhood doesn't back down, we're going to need all the help we can get."

* * *

"We need to move quickly and finish what we started." Deoctra paced the length of the luxurious living room of the house in suburban Bucks County Leon had rented for the short time it would take to get rid of Acier Gautier. Two males sprawled on the sofas—Leon, and a tall, heavily built shifter with long, wavy hair, chiseled features, and green eyes.

Although handsome, virile, and powerful, the shifter, Tucker Falcone, left her sexually cold. She turned her gaze to Leon, who had been lighting up her nights with an exquisite delight that still amazed her.

Tucker spoke. "Next time I'll kill him, his brother, and his infernal Keddi!"

Deoctra compressed her lips into a tight line. The hatred in Tucker's voice annoyed her. "This is business, Falcone. Not personal. Etienne Gautier has nothing to do with this."

Tucker touched his neck. Although there were no visible remaining wounds or scars, she had seen him after both Acier and his Keddi had torn into his neck. "It's very personal for me! His brother and his blasted Keddi forced me to do something I've never had to do in a fight—retreat. For that I will not only kill him and his Keddi, but his brother as well."

She turned away, lest he or Leon note her alarm at the thought of Etienne Gautier being dispatched. During the few hours they had spent together, he had been passionate, yet tender, showing her a consideration she had rarely received from a lover. He'd made her feel almost cherished.

Despite her increasingly powerful feelings for Leon, there was a small, annoying part of her that did not want Etienne Gautier hurt in any way. It was for his sake that she'd insisted Leon warn Acier that he'd enlisted the aid of a powerful Heoptin shifter in his conquest to remove Acier as Alpha-in-waiting of Pack Gautier.

She turned to face Tucker, aware that Leon's eyes were on her as well. Did he suspect her lingering feelings for Etienne? "Etienne is embraced by the vampire community. If you attack him, you risk running afoul of his friends and their friends."

Tucker rose and stalked across the room to stare down at her. "And you think I, a Heoptin shifter, fear him or his vampire friends?"

She didn't like the tone of his voice. Hell, she didn't like him or his superior attitude. She lifted her chin, her eyes glowing. "Heoptin you may be, but that means nothing to a full-blood vampire."

"That's only because some creatures are too dense to know the power vested in a Heoptin shifter. We are not like the shifters in Packs Gautier or LeMay. As descendants of those who served the original vampire father, Heoptin, we have power far beyond what you may imagine, fem."

Smug bastard. She smiled up at him, then moving with her full speed, she flashed up her clenched right hand and swung it at his jaw. She made no effort to pull the blow. Knocked off his feet, he landed in a heap against a far wall.

For a moment, he stared at her, a look of dismay on his face. Then rage took over. Eyes glowing, he bared his fangs and sprang to his feet. She stood still, hands clenched at her sides, waiting for his attack. She'd show the supercilious bastard why full-blood vampires were the kings and queens of the universe.

As he charged across the room toward her, Leon exploded off the sofa, shifted to his natural form, and raced to intercept Falcone. Although Falcone was bigger and heavier, baring his lovely fangs, Leon plowed into Falcone, stopping his charge.

Growling and tearing at each other, the two shifters fought. Fearful that Leon would be poisoned as Acier had been, Deoctra flashed forward, grabbed Falcone by the fur on the back of his neck, and lifted him away from Leon, tossing him across the room.

Leon, bleeding from several wounds, jumped to his feet and raced toward Falcone.

She flashed between them. "No, Leon!" She glanced over her shoulder at Falcone, who had shifted back to his humanoid form and now regarded her with a look of respect. "This meeting is not to fight amongst ourselves. It's to decide how to finish off Acier Gautier."

Leon shifted back to his humanoid form. She winced at the wounds on his body. "Go bathe and wash your wounds, Leon. Quickly."

Growling in Falcone's direction, Leon left the room.

Falcone rose to stand in front of her, staring down into her eyes. "I don't allow females to hit me with impunity, Deoctra."

She tossed her head, sending her long dark hair cascading around her shoulders. "I am not just a female. I am a full-blood vampire fem and we take shit from no one. I possess a physical strength comparable to yours and your poison can't harm me. Don't challenge me, Falcone. I want Etienne Gautier left alone."

"Why? You gonna fuck him when Leon's back is turned?" he demanded.

She stared into his eyes, a slight smile pulling at her lips. She knew that look. She could hear Leon moving up the stairs toward the bathroom with the whirlpool.

Soak, my handsome one, she told him. *I will deal with Falcone.*

You're sure? If he hurts you, I'll —

Soak and be well and strong, Leon.

She moved across the room to stand against the far wall. Keeping her gaze on Falcone, she undid tiny buttons in the one-piece cat suit she wore, sliding the sleeves down her shoulders. The lower section of the suit fell to the floor, revealing her bare groin. She pressed back against the wall, parting her legs. Keeping her gaze locked with his, she dipped a finger inside herself.

"Hmmm. Nice and moist and ready for action," she told him.

His eyes blazed with lust. He rushed across the room to her, unzipping his trousers as he came. When he stopped in front of her, his fully erect shaft protruded in front of his body.

She curled her fingers around him and urged him closer. Bending his knees, he thrust his hips forward, sending his length into her body. He was larger and thicker than Leon and he felt good going inside her. He did it slowly, clearly savoring the experience.

He cupped his hands over her face, found her lips, and kissed her hungrily, biting at her lips and sucking at her tongue. She immediately knew he was a skillful lover. Still, she did not feel the thrill she had expected when he began to fuck her with long, slow, measured strokes. Even when he sped up the pace and pounded her as she liked it, his cock felt no more than good.

As he pumped his way to his climax, she closed her eyes, held him close, and thought of Leon and his wonderful, hard knot! Now there was a lover to get hot and bothered over.

Although tingling, she had given up the idea of experiencing a climax of her own until Falcone forced two fingers up her ass. Then they exploded together, gasping and clinging to each other.

The moment she came off her high, she pushed him away from her. He stood in front of her, still hard, staring at her. "Damn, that was good. I want more."

She did too, but not with him. "You've had all you're getting for the moment. Behave yourself and we'll do this again sometime."

She smiled, watching his cock twitch at the thought of being back inside her. At least the arrogant bastard had enough sense to appreciate good pussy when he had it. "I want some more now!"

She moved close to him, palming his warm cock. "Another time."

"Don't make me take you by force."

The thought of his holding her down, forcing her legs apart, and thrusting his hard length deep into her cunt without her permission, made her heart race with excitement. She laughed and released his shaft. "I believe I'd like that, but some other time." She turned away. "Right now I need a fuck from my man."

He clasped a hand on her arm and swung her around to face him. "What's the fucker have that I don't?"

"A knot to die for."

"I have a knot too and I know how to use it!"

"I'm sure you do." She touched herself. "But there's only one knot going into this cunt and it belongs to Leon." She leaned into him, stretched up, and kissed his warm lips. "Have no fear, you can take me by force—rape me—one of these days when you're feeling brave, but right now, I want my lover."

He curled his fingers in her hair and stared into her eyes. "I always get what I want, bitch, and I want you!"

She laughed, squeezing his cock. "Hold that thought, Falcone. The next time Leon's not around and you're feeling brave, come rape me with your big, hot cock."

She slapped his ass and flashed out of the room and up the stairs to the master bathroom. Leon was just getting out of the whirlpool bath. The moment he saw her with the bottom of her cat suit open, his cock jumped to attention. His eyes, however, narrowed. "What have you been doing?"

She crossed the room to him. She linked her arms around his neck. "I've been fucking Falcone."

He stiffened. "What? You let him touch you? I'll kill him!"

She tightened her arms around his neck. "Stop and think, Leon. It's the only way to control him." She gazed up into his eyes. "Fucking him meant less than nothing to me. He wanted more and so did I, but from you, not him." She stroked her fingers through his hair. "*You* are my lover, Leon… my passion… my man and I am…"

"You are my what?"

The word bloodlust trembled on her tongue, but she swallowed it. If he had been her bloodlust, would she have allowed Falcone to fuck her? "Your woman, Leon."

His lips moved over hers. She reached between their bodies and brought his shaft to her cunt. He pushed forward and she closed her eyes, sighing with pleasure and delight as he slid forward, slowly filling her with his warmth.

"Oh, yes! Yes, my Leon! Your cock brings pleasure I never expected to feel again. Take me to heaven! Fuck me long and hard! Make me your bitch! Bang my ass and make me scream for your lovely knot, my Leon! I am yours to do with as you please! Make me beg for your love!"

"Before you two get too kinky, we need to talk, Deoctra!"

She gasped and jerked away from Leon. Vitali Bourcaro stood in the bathroom doorway. "Vitali! What brings you here?"

His dark eyes flickered over her and narrowed. She flushed and quickly buttoned her cat suit.

"We need to talk. Come walk with me."

"Now?"

"Now, Deoctra."

She glanced at Leon. "I'll be back." She shook her head quickly when he would have objected.

In the living room, Falcone stood with his jaw tight, his eyes narrowed, his lips pressed together. Their gazes met briefly. He gave an almost infinitesimal shake of his head.

Bad news then.

Vitali looked at Falcone. "I gave you your instructions. Why are you still here?"

Falcone bared his incisors and raced out of the open patio doors, disappearing into the surrounding woods in a blur.

Vitali motioned toward the patio doors. "Come. Walk with me."

They moved outside and into the woods. Several moments passed in silence before Vitali spoke. "This business with Acier Gautier is over."

She stopped and turned to face him. "It is? You took care of him? Oh, but I wanted to..." She looked at his face and trailed off. "That's not what you mean, is it?"

He shook his head. "The Brotherhood as an organization has no interest in what goes on within shifter packs."

"Falcone and I are members of the Brotherhood and we both have vested interests in Pack Gautier."

Vitali narrowed his gaze. "You and Falcone have no interests in anything that I do not approve and I do not approve of your interference in Pack Gautier's internal affairs."

Her plans for the future were in danger. "I have chosen Leon as my mate and he has aspirations to be Alpha Supreme of the Pack. He is a purebred while Gautier is not."

"If Leon aspires to lead this Pack Gautier, let him do it the normal way... challenge Gautier to a battle. Falcone's interest in this, as well as yours, is over as of now."

"Why? When we first told you of our intentions, you expressed no objections."

"Did you know that Gautier was Aleksei Madison's son?"

"His... No. How did you learn of this?"

Vitali's nostrils flared. "Madison, accompanied by Vladimir and two of his other siblings, came to see me, demanding I call off you and Falcone."

She stared at him in surprise. The Brotherhood had never been known to back down from a fight. "And you allowed him to back you down?"

Vitali bared his incisors. She tensed, preparing to dance out of his way if he attempted to backhand her. "No one backs me down!"

"Then why?"

His mouth softened. "Aleksei Madison has a sister."

"Katie Dumont?"

"No. Tatiana Forester."

"She's his sister? But what has she got to do with this? She and her twin don't even live as full-bloods."

"She interests me and she would not take kindly to you or Falcone injuring her nephew."

"You're asking us to back down for your own personal reason? That's not in the spirit of the Brotherhood. I—"

"I'm not asking you. I'm telling you. You put distance between yourself and de la Rocque."

"I can't!"

"You'd better or do not expect the Brotherhood to intervene if the Dumonts and Madisons and Foresters come after you… or your sisters."

The thought of Vladimir or Aleksei going after her remaining sisters sent a chill of fear through her. She wanted Leon, but she could not endanger Tally and Smo for anyone.

"Do I make myself clear, Diniti?"

She nodded, a knot of rage tightening her stomach. When would it end? When would the Dumonts and their siblings stop causing her grief? "I will not interfere with pack business, but I have some unresolved business with the Dumonts. Will you back me in that?"

He shrugged. "I personally will not stop you. If you can enlist the aid of other members, I will not interfere."

She lifted her head, her eyes glowing, her incisors bared. The time of accounting for the Dumonts would come.

Chapter Five

Etienne, with Slayer perched on his shoulder and Damon at his side, stood on the doorstep of an elegant single home in an exclusive subdivision in the Philadelphia suburbs.

Damon stretched out a hand toward the bell.

Etienne pushed his hand away. "Don't ring. I'm going in."

"Without letting him know you're coming? You know what they say about him."

"They lie," he snapped.

Damon shrugged. "I think I'll wait in the SUV."

"Suit yourself."

Using the key Vladimir had given him, Etienne opened the door and slid silently into the house. He paused in the foyer. The smell of sex filled the air. He tilted his head, his ears picking up the unmistakable sounds of sex coming from the upper floor.

Slayer stirred on his shoulder. *Father fucking. Go fuck with him.*

He hesitated before he flashed silently up the stairs. The door of the master bedroom was open. He stood staring at the scene unfolding on the bed before him.

A naked Vladimir lay on top of a pale, nude blond, thrusting a huge golden cock deep into the other male's ass. Each time Vladimir's cock slid home, the male moaned in ecstasy. Their faces, with the eyes closed, faced Etienne. He saw their tongues tangling together as they kissed and fucked, lost in a world of their own.

Having starred in numerous X-rated adventure movies, Etienne had seen his share of gay fuck scenes. But this wasn't a fuck scene. The tender passion between the two males was apparent. Vladimir wasn't fucking the man, he was making love to him.

Vladimir's hands stroked down the sides of the pale thighs as he eased his dick in and out of the other male's ass. The blond suddenly gasped and shook under Vladimir, clearly coming. Moments later, Vladimir groaned, thrust his cock deep into the man's ass, shuddered, and came.

Etienne watched as Vladimir and his lover exchanged kisses. "Is this someone I should know?"

Vladimir pulled out of the man and they both nearly fell as they jumped out of the bed and turned to face him.

Ignoring Vladimir, Etienne turned his attention to the other male. The man was tall and blond. Pressing a hand in front of his cock, he stared at Etienne with cool blue eyes.

Vladimir, his lips pressed tight, stared at Etienne. "I didn't hear the bell."

Etienne shrugged. "I didn't ring it."

"Why not?"

He nodded at the other male. "Who is he?"

"This is Adam Cady." Vladimir glanced at the blond. "Adam, this is Etienne Gautier… my son and his Keddi, Slayer."

Before Etienne or Adam could speak, Slayer streaked across the room from his shoulder to Vladimir's. *Father!* He flew in front of Adam Cady's face. *And father's lover. Lover like black cock? Slayer has big black one too.*

Etienne smirked as Slayer shifted until he became a miniature version of Vladimir, complete with a huge, golden cock protruding from a hairy groin. *Fuck lover hard and long just like father!*

Adam flushed. Feeling mean spirited, and unashamed of it, Etienne laughed. "You want Slayer to fuck you?"

"You want Slayer to get his little Keddi ass kicked?" Vladimir demanded, moving to stand in front of Adam.

Etienne narrowed his gaze. "Striking him would be the same as striking me."

"If you push me hard enough, that can be arranged too." Vladimir stared at him, his incisors bared. "Adam is my… bloodlust."

"So it's true. You're gay."

Vladimir's eyes glowed. "I'm me. Do you have a problem with that?"

"And if I do?"

"Then it will be your problem, Etienne. Not mine and not Adam's. Yours. You deal with it. Now what are you doing here?"

"Slayer wanted to meet you. So we came to find you."

Vladimir sighed and turned to look at his lover. "He and I need to talk. Do you mind?"

Adam shook his head. He looked at Etienne. "I know this must be a shock, but—"

"Why should I be shocked to walk in on my father fucking another man? It's just what every son wants to see."

Adam's nostrils flared and his eyes narrowed. "He's talked of little but you since he met you, Etienne. Please don't do or say anything to hurt him."

Etienne resisted the urge to backhand the man and bared his incisors instead.

Adam narrowed his lips. "Things will be easier for all of us if you at least try to be pleasant. But either way, I think you should know that I am here to stay, Etienne." He reached out and closed his fingers around Vladimir's cock. "This is mine and no one is taking it away from me... not even you. You're a big boy, learn to deal with the facts of life."

"I'm no damned boy. I—"

"Then don't act like one, Etienne! I fully intend to bend over backwards to like you. Meet me halfway." He turned and pressed his mouth against Vladimir's, who immediately returned his kiss. He pulled back to look at Etienne. "I'm going to shower and dress."

Slayer come with.

Etienne watched the other male. Would he allow Slayer to fuck him?

Adam left the room.

Slayer looked at him. *Going to fuck!* He shot out the room after Adam.

Vladimir dressed in a flash and stood facing him. "Is Adam going to be a problem for you?"

"You're gay?"

"No."

"Then how can you have a male bloodlust?"

"I don't know, but I still enjoy sex with women… particularly Aleksei's bloodlust, Dani."

"He doesn't mind your fucking her?"

"Of course he minds, but it's my right. It's our way."

"And does he fuck Adam?"

"No. Sei doesn't do men under any circumstances."

"How did you get Aleksei to allow you to fuck his bloodlust without getting your ass kicked?"

Vladimir gave him a long look. "Acier refusing to allow you to fuck his bloodlust?"

"He gave it his tacit approval, but I know if I do, our special relationship will change for the worst."

"Then so be it. You have a right to fuck his bloodlust. He'll just have to learn to deal with the facts of vampire life."

"What would you do if you were in my position?"

"I'd go fuck his bloodlust and to hell with the consequences."

Etienne felt an answering wildness in him responding warmly to Vladimir's words. He had a right to Raven. Damn if he wasn't going to have her. And after he'd satisfied his hunger for her, he would go looking for Adona.

He glanced toward the bathroom where he could hear the shower.

Vladimir shook his head. "You can safely leave Slayer here."

"He's very special to me."

"I know that."

"You won't hurt him?"

"No."

"If you don't watch him, he will fuck your lover."

To his surprise Vladimir arched a brow. "We'll see." Vladimir cupped a palm against his face. "Do what you need to do to keep your sanity intact. Go get your fuck, boy."

Etienne hesitated then flashed out of the house.

* * *

"Other grandchildren?"

Standing in the middle of the living room of the Dumont family home, the Dodge House in the Boston suburbs, Aleksei watched his mother's dark eyes widen. She bolted from her chair and rushed across the room to him. Her small, soft hands gripped his arms. She stared up into his eyes. "Tell me about them!"

He told her of Acier and Etienne.

She pressed a hand against her breasts, her eyes filling with tears. "What are they like? Tell me everything."

He described them.

She stroked a hand down his cheek. "Oh, Alexander! My first-born and Vladimir, my second born, both have sons! This is too much joy for this vampire."

"You're not going to ask how it's possible for each of us to have fathered only one of them?"

"No. I have heard many things that some would consider strange. What did Grinkolo say?"

"He had no explanation."

"It does not matter. When can I meet them?"

He sighed, took her arm, and led her over to her favorite chair. She sat down and he sank to the floor beside the chair. There was something about his tiny mother that always made him feel like a little boy who wanted to sit at her feet and have his hair stroked.

Her soft hand moved over his hair. "What troubles you, my Alexander?"

"They're having some problems, Mother. I need your help and the help of the others."

She tensed. "What kind of trouble?"

He told her of the Brotherhood.

She bolted to her feet, her incisors bared. "Let the Brotherhood attack at their peril. I will call the others and as a family, we will stand with them and protect them."

He sighed and rose. "Thank you, Mother."

"You will not thank me." She took his hand in hers. "We are family and as your father used to say, that is all that matters. Yes?"

"Yes, Mother. Family is all that matters."

"When can I meet them?"

"This is a really difficult time for them and us—"

"You want me to wait?"

He heard the pain in her voice. "I know that's a lot to ask, but they are both so fragile and… They both know about you and I know Acier would eventually be interested in meeting you. Right now he's undergoing so many changes. Do what you think is best, Mother."

She placed her other hand on his arm. "I will be mindful of their fragile state, Alexander. Now." She closed her fingers over his arm and they walked back toward the chair, resuming their former positions. "I believe that I have waited long enough to meet Dani. We must begin preparations for the birth celebration. When will she travel here?"

"I'll discuss it with her when I return home and call you, Mother."

She stroked his hair. "This is a troubling time for you, my little Alexander. One of joy for your new arrival and one of pain for Acier's pain."

"Yes." He leaned his cheek against her leg.

She sighed. "Fear not, my little one. All will be well or there will be hell to pay!"

His cell phone rang. He rose and removed it from his belt. He looked at the number and narrowed his gaze, telling himself not to panic. "Hello."

"Aleksei! Where the hell are you?" a gruff voice he immediately recognized demanded. "Never mind. Get your ass home now!"

His heart raced. "What's wrong? Where's Dani?"

"Come home immediately!"

He placed his phone back on his belt and turned to look at his mother. "That was Dr. Grinkolo. He was scheduled to do a checkup with Dani today. I have to go."

"Fear not, my little one. I will come with you."

She was so small and fragile looking, but just knowing she would accompany him somehow decreased his fear.

* * *

Aleksei paced the length of the large master bedroom of his Main Line suburban Philadelphia home. His bloodlust, Dani Tyler, lay on the big bed they shared. His mother stood by the window, her eyes dark with worry. Dr. Grinkolo bent over Dani, listening to her heart. He took her blood pressure next. Aleksei bit back the urge to ask him how she was. Dr. Grinkolo did not take kindly to being rushed.

After an eternity, Dr. Grinkolo straightened, patted Dani's shoulder, and looked at him. "A word with you."

He looked in the other vampire's eyes and could tell… nothing. He crossed the room to the bed. Leaning over Dani, he brushed the dark hair back from her damp forehead. She grabbed his hand, a frightened look in her lovely dark eyes. "I'm afraid, Sei. I can't lose our baby. I can't!"

"Don't worry, my love." He kissed her cheek. "I'll talk to the doctor and then I'll be back."

His mother crossed the room, sat on the bed, and placed an arm around Dani, who immediately clung to her.

He followed Dr. Grinkolo out of the bedroom. They walked down the hall to the head of the stairs. "She is stressed, Aleksei — dangerously so. If she is not unburdened soon, she will lose the child."

He felt as if a large hand had been thrust into his chest to rip out his heart. His legs buckled. He struggled to get sufficient breath into his lungs. "What — what can I do? How can I help?"

"You can keep your ass at home with her."

"I know I've been away a lot, but that was only because Acier—"

"I understand that Acier needs you and you have fences to mend with him."

"Yes, I do. He's in pain and—"

"He's also a healthy, able-bodied adult. Your woman and your unborn child need you with them. When you are gone, she suffers all kinds of agony, imagining you are engaged in some activity that will result in your death. For a human, she is having this baby very late in life. She needs you here with her until the baby is born. If you want your child to survive, you will need to remain at home and provide an environment where she feels safe and loved."

"She knows I love her," he protested.

"Does she? She knows you say you love her and yet you've spent very little time with her since she's been living here with you."

"She... said that?"

"She did not need to. I know what you've been up to."

"I had to find my son. I—"

"I will listen to no excuses, Aleksei! She gave up a lot to be with you and she's forty-three, old for a human woman having a baby. She needs you with her.

"In addition, she must spend the remaining weeks of her pregnancy in bed... no sex, Aleksei. Just cuddling, comfort, and reassurance. Do I make myself clear?"

"Very." He sighed. "I will remain here with her."

Dr. Grinkolo nodded. "Good. I thought you would agree. When it is time for the birthing, the family will gather here."

"Here? Mother is expecting us to travel—"

"She will be traveling nowhere. The birth will take place here."

On the rare occasions when there was a birth in the family, the entire clan gathered at the Dodge House. There was a special birthing room there where the extended family watched Dr.

Grinkolo deliver the baby. They had last gathered there for the birth of Mikhel's son, Dimitri.

Dr. Grinkolo spoke again. "I have sent for Margolis Cheyenne."

"Who is she?"

"She is a healer in her own right. A healer of the spirit."

"The spirit? Are you saying Dani's spirit is injured?"

"She has many insecurities which she has not shared with you, but which will impact negatively on your baby should she succumb to depression. Margolis's skills are still being refined, but those from the Cheyenne line will go to any length to ensure the spiritual health of those entrusted to their care."

Aleksei thought briefly of the silver-eyed, mysterious healer he had heard so many rumors about. "Then why not the best? Why not call upon Enola Cheyenne?"

"He is not currently available. Margolis will suffice. She will arrive sometime tomorrow and remain in the guesthouse until the delivery. I will, of course, be on call if I am needed." He stared at Aleksei. "You know what you need to do to ensure your baby survives. Let nothing and no one interfere."

He nodded. "I understand."

After he saw Dr. Grinkolo out, he stood by the door with his eyes closed. Damn! Why the hell did this have to happen now? He balled a hand into a fist and hit it against the wall. He stared at the resulting hole for a long time before returning upstairs. He paused in the hallway outside the bedroom. *Mother?*

Moments later, Palea appeared beside him in the hallway. She touched his arm. *Alexander?*

He told her what Dr. Grinkolo had said. *I'm torn, Mother.*

I can feel your pain, my Alexander. You want to be with them both. Yes? She pressed her cheek against his chest, slipping her arms around him. *It is a difficult thing, but we are a large, loving family. You remain with your woman. We will ensure Acier and Etienne are looked after. Yes?*

But you don't understand, Mother. We are just beginning to build a fragile understanding. If I'm not there for him now when he needs me—

She stepped away from him and studied his face. *I do understand. Do you not know how my emotions were nearly torn from my body when Vladimir threatened Mikhel? Do not misunderstand, my Alexander, but you know how I have always had a special love for Vladimir. I did not choose it to be so, but he has always been in need of a little more affection than the rest of you. You understand?*

Yes, Mother. We all understood.

Know this as well, Alexander. If it had come to a choice between Vladimir and Mikhel, I would have killed Vladimir to preserve Mikhel's life. Is this understandable?

Yes. I feared I would have to kill him for the same reason.

You would have done it, not because you love Mikhel more, but because he is the weaker of the two and must be protected. Yes?

Yes.

I would not have been able to live with myself afterwards. It would have been a hard decision, but I would have done it. In this family, we protect our young and innocent at all cost. I would have protected Mikhel... you protect your unborn child's life and leave Acier to the rest of us. We will ensure all is well with him and Etienne.

Mother—

All will be well, my little Alexander. Say goodbye to your Dani for me. She squeezed his arm, hugged him, and ran down the hall toward the stairs.

Dani looked up, smiling, as he entered the bedroom. He sat on the bed beside her and took her hand in his. "You will need to remain in bed until the baby is born."

"I was afraid of that."

"But everything will be all right."

"I know."

She nodded, but he saw the fear in her eyes. He sighed. "Tomorrow, Margolis Cheyenne, a sort of spiritual and physical nurse practitioner, will arrive to oversee your care."

"And then you will leave?"

Hearing the loneliness in her voice, he squeezed her hand. "No. I will not leave. I will be here with you and our child." He touched her cheek. "I'm sorry I've left you alone so much."

She smiled. "I'll admit I have missed you, but I have done this twice before, you know, Aleksei."

"I know, but you didn't expect to do it again."

"No, I didn't, and I was afraid at first." She touched her stomach, her smile widening. "But not anymore. I am so looking forward to having your baby."

"I shouldn't have left you alone so much."

"Aleksei, I'm a big girl. And you had to find your son."

"I did not realize that in devoting so much time to finding him, I was endangering our child."

"You didn't!"

"Dr. Grinkolo said—"

"I don't care what he said! This is not your fault. My last pregnancy was difficult even though my husband was there with me and I had no stress."

He caressed her cheek. "You are amazing. Still, I know part of this is my fault. It won't happen again."

She rolled her eyes. "You're a stubborn vamp, but I love you."

"I love you."

"What's he like?"

"Acier?"

She nodded.

He sighed. "He is everything a father could want in a son… proud, strong, a little stubborn, and very loyal to his brother and his pack."

"What does he look like?"

"He looks like a man."

She laughed. "Meaning what? Is he as handsome as you?"

"We don't look anything alike. He has long dark hair and gray eyes. I'm sure women would find him very attractive."

"I know they do if he's one tenth as handsome as you are."

"He's much better looking. He resembles his mother. He has her coloring… white skin… and handsome where she was pretty."

"Did you love her?"

"No." He knew she wanted to know something of his relationship with Acier's mother, but he didn't really want to discuss her.

"What was her name?"

"Chantel."

"Tell me about her."

"I'd rather not. If you need to know about our relationship, so be it, but—"

She squeezed his hand. "Never mind. You can tell me when you're ready. So will this handsome son of yours be here for the baby's birth?"

"Who told you about that?"

"Your mother."

"And you're okay with that?"

"Honestly? I don't know, but she tells me it's a family tradition."

"It is."

"So… okay then. I get to lay around with my legs open in front of a roomful of people… okay. I can handle it."

"You're taking this better than I'd hoped."

She stroked a finger down his arm. "If it's your custom, I'll deal with it because I can't imagine living without you."

He leaned over and kissed her cheek. He straightened before speaking again, choosing his words carefully. "There's someone who is very special to me who I would like to invite to the birthing."

"A friend?"

"He's more than a friend."

"A vampire?"

"He's… he's not human."

"What is he?"

"It's difficult to say."

"Don't you know?"

"For sure? No, but I do know that he's been like a third father to me and he's very important to me. His name is Luc and I really want to invite him. Before you say no—"

"Why should I say no? If your brothers, stepfather, sisters, and God only knows who else will be there, what's one more person?"

"He can come?"

"Yes. Now about Acier. Is he all right?"

He sighed. "He's entering a difficult and dangerous period of his life."

She bit her lip. "If you need to leave—"

"No! If he has problems he can't deal with, Mother or one of my siblings will stand in for me."

"Sei, if you need to go, go! I'll be all right. If I need you, I'll call you and you can—"

He shook his head. "I will be where I belong now—with you and our unborn child."

He saw the relief in her gaze. She smiled, squeezed his hand, and closed her eyes. He waited several moments before he left the room. In the hall, he took out his cell phone. After ending the conversation he closed his eyes and reached out with his thoughts. *Acier.*

A rush of anger assailed his senses. *Where are you?*

I had to return home.

When are you coming back?

I need to stay here for now.

Why?

"Sei? Where are you?"

He glanced down the hall toward the master bedroom. "I'll be there in a moment, Dani." *I have to go, Acier.*

Then go. It's what you do best, abandon me when I need you most... Father!

Acier—

I don't need you!

He closed his eyes, sighing, and made his way down the hall to the bedroom. Dani sat up, staring at the door, an anxious look in her eyes. She needed him. So did Acier, but even a vampire could only be in one place at a time.

Drei, now a miniature version of Aleksei, perched on his shoulder, wrapped his tiny arms as far around his neck as he could manage. *Father? Alpha be all right?*

Aleksei stroked a finger down the Keddi's long silky dreads. *This is a difficult time, but he will be all right.* He had to be.

Father sure?

Sensing Drei's fear for Acier, Aleksei did something he rarely did. He lied. *Yes.*

Chapter Six

The RV was empty when Raven returned from her visit with Abby. She closed her eyes. *Bentia?*

She felt a coil of energy fill her stomach. *I am here.*

Where is Steele?

He went off to write.

She wet her lips. *Is he all right? Did you and he...*

He is not all right, but he and I did nothing more than talk, Ravanni. He is going through a difficult time. You will need to call his father.

She sighed. "He'd hate that. He's proud and stubborn and it killed him to have to ask him for a blood transfusion."

I do not understand this... Feast of Indulgence. It is a vampire phenomenon his father would be best suited to see him through.

She hated thinking Steele needed help she could not provide, but she was still struggling to learn how to deal with the fact that she herself was not fully human.

Abby had warned her that as the daughter of a High Priestess of the Goddess Modidsha, of planet Aeolia, she would one day be called to temple service. That would entail leaving her family and Steele. The prospect of being torn away from those she loved to live on another planet sent a chill of fear and foreboding through her.

But she couldn't deal with her own demons and Steele's at the same time... especially when she did not understand either of them.

"I know Drei is with Aleksei. What about Pen? Where is he?"

Acier summoned Xavier to take him back to the pack. He was afraid he would hurt him.

She walked over to the phone and dialed the number Aleksei had left with her. As she hung up from their brief conversation, she heard a vehicle stopping next to the RV. She moved to the front of the RV in time to see Etienne alight from the passenger side of his SUV.

Usually delighted to see Etienne, this time she felt a prick of discomfort. She closed her eyes briefly, rocking from side to side. A series of unpleasant waves washed over her. When he knocked, she hesitated before opening the RV door.

She forced a smile. "Tee! Steele isn't here."

His cool gray gaze locked with hers. "I came to see you."

She stood in the doorway, blocking his entrance to the RV. "Why?"

"Since when have I needed a reason to see you?" He put his hands on her arms and urged her back into the RV, stepping inside. After locking the door, he leaned against it. His gaze moved over her, his nostrils flaring.

Realizing that she had not showered, she flushed. Tee's superior sense of smell would tell him she and Steele had had sex earlier.

"I can smell your pussy. It's full of Acier's seed. It smells delicious." He pushed away from the door and put his arm around her shoulders. As soon as he touched her, the bad vibes intensified. She pulled away from him and walked into the living room area of the RV.

"I want some of it."

She backed through the living room, coming up short against the kitchen cabinet. "No."

He closed the distance between them, trapping her body against his and the cabinet. His cock, hard and long, pressed against her. "I wasn't asking. I was telling you what's going to happen."

She stiffened and stared up at him. First Steele treated her like a tramp and now Tee, who'd always been sweet and considerate, was hinting at taking her by force? She couldn't quite bring herself to think of what Tee was threatening as rape. "You're not touching me, Etienne."

He curled his fingers in the long, thick hair hanging around her shoulders. "I'm going to do more than touch you. I'm going to fuck you until you can't walk!"

She sensed a turmoil in him... as if he were fighting an internal battle with himself. "No one takes me without my permission and you do not have my permission." She shoved at his shoulders. "Get away from me!"

He pressed closer. "I am going to fuck you whether you like it or not."

She stared up into his eyes. "That's usually called rape, Etienne."

"Call it whatever the hell you like! It's what's about to happen between us."

Her heart raced. "Oh, Tee!" She touched his cheek. None of the tenderness he usually possessed was apparent. Lord, she hated what the vampire blood had done and was doing to him and Steele.

His fingers closed over her wrists and he pushed her against the cabinets.

"Etienne! What the fuck do you think you're doing?"

Steele stood against the closed door of the RV, his eyes glowing, his incisors bared. Raven sucked in a breath. She had never seen him looking so feral or so out of control. Great. Now she would have to fight off both of them. She put her right hand down, fist clenched, channeling Bentia.

Etienne released her and swung around. "What the fuck does it look like? I've had it with your shifter shit! We are vampires. She is your bloodlust and as such, I have a right to fuck her—with or without her or your permission!"

"The hell you will. Get the fuck away from her or get your ass kicked from here to New Jersey, pup!"

Tee tossed back his head and laughed. "I've been itching to kick your ass for years now! You want a piece of me? Bring it on, big brother!"

Snarling and growling, Steele and Tee sprang at each other.

Raven thrust out her right hand. Bentia shot from her open palm, erecting herself between the charging twins. Bentia quickly spread herself out until she surrounded both men with her living energy.

The front door of the RV opened. A tall man with auburn hair and green eyes appeared in the doorway. He stormed past Steele to look at her. "I'm Damon duPre, Etienne's friend."

She narrowed her gaze. "I know who you are." *The one who's been egging him on.*

I'm the one who's been urging him to be what he is — a vampire. Whether you or Acier like it or not, that entails Acier sharing your charms with Etienne. Denying him his due is only making him crazy. Is that what you want?

I want the two of them to be close as they've always been. That won't happen if he and I sleep together. And make no mistake, vampire, no one takes me without my permission.

You're not human.

If I were, it would make no difference.

He considered her in silence for several moments before she noted an acknowledgment that she could not easily be dismissed. *Release him and I'll take him away.*

She drew her hand back. Bentia dissolved from around Etienne.

DuPre grabbed Tee by his collar and dragged the struggling Etienne toward the door. There he paused. "He and Acier are undergoing the Feast of Indulgence. If I were you, I would not allow Acier to be free until there is someone else with you to help control him."

She lifted her chin. "I don't fear him."

"If you release him without help, there's no telling what he will do."

"Suppose you leave that to me?"

Raven and the three males looked toward the RV door. A tall, beautiful woman with dark skin and startling blue eyes stood inside the closed door. Raven pressed her lips together. "You know there's a bell on the other side of the door."

The woman smiled, inclining her head. "So there is. My apologies."

Raven sighed. "I suppose you're yet another vampire."

She smiled. "Had your fill of us?"

"Yes!"

"I am Tatiana Madison-Forester. Aleksei has to remain at home with his woman, who's in the last stages of a difficult pregnancy." She touched Tee's cheek. "Etienne, my cherished young pup, Vladimir is my brother. I am your aunt. I know what you are going through. Go with your friend and know that along with him, members of your extended family will watch over you and see you safely through your feast. You and Acier are no longer alone."

Etienne bared his incisors, growling softly.

Damon wrestled Etienne from the RV. Moments later, Raven heard his SUV leaving. The woman turned her gaze to Steele, still imprisoned by Bentia. "Release him. I will ensure he does no harm."

Raven sank back against the kitchen cabinet, recalling Bentia. Steele sprang toward her, a look of lust and anger in his gray eyes. "I told you never to allow her to come between us again!"

Moving with unbelievable speed, Tatiana flashed between them, gripping Steele's wrists in her hands. "Acier, my handsome pup. I am here to help you through your feast."

"Then you can start by taking your hands off me and leaving me alone with my woman."

"If I did that, you would no doubt rape her."

"She's my woman! It wouldn't be rape!"

She laughed. "What a male response. You think because she's given herself to you willingly that you have a license to take her without her full permission? Oh no, Acier. No. Some things we can be forgiven for doing during our feast, some we cannot."

"Release me!"

"I am not here to deny you during your feast, but to ensure you do not tear down bridges you cannot rebuild."

As Raven watched, her heart aching for the pain and anguish she felt in Steele, the woman sank to the floor, forcing Steele down with her. Leaning against the refrigerator, she drew Steele into her arms and rocked him. "This is a difficult time, but you are among those who love and cherish you. Lean on me, Acier, as you would Aleksei. I am here in physical fact, but he is here in spirit and love."

"Where the hell is he?"

"With his woman. She is in danger of losing their child. He will need to remain with her."

"What about me?"

She curled her fingers in his hair, staring into his eyes. "You know in your vampire soul that he would die for you. But would you have your unborn sibling die so that he could be here with you?"

"Isn't that what he does best? Leave when he's needed most?"

The fem's eyes glowed. '"No! He has never done that. Never. He has spent his entire life putting the interests of his siblings and those he loves before his own. If you have touched his mind, you know that to be true."

Steele shuddered, burying his face against her shoulder. "I feel like I'm going crazy. I... need him."

"He knows that. He is torn between his children, but surely you see that the baby's need supercedes yours." Tatiana hugged him, kissing his hair. "Reach out to him, Acier. He will answer and help you all he can." She looked up, waving Raven over. "You are surrounded by those who love and cherish you. We are not Aleksei, but we will do our best."

Raven went to them, sinking down on her knees. She pressed her cheek against Steele's back, stroking his hair. "It's all right, Steele. It's all right. I'm here to help in any way I can. If you need rough sex, so be it. Whatever you need that I can give you, I will."

He turned and buried his face against her shoulder, clinging to her. "I'm sorry, *petite*... so sorry. I've never felt so out of control.

I can't stop myself from doing and saying things that I don't mean."

She kissed his hair. "It's all right, Steele. Nothing you say or do will be held against you. We will get through this together."

Moonlight Madness Part 2
Marilyn Lee

Prologue

Dressed in a dark, form-fitting cat suit, Deoctra turned to face the male staring at her from the large unmade bed where they'd spent so many nights fucking. She closed her eyes briefly. It had been a long, bittersweet night, made all the more so because Leon didn't know it would probably be their last. Though she had few illusions about a long-term relationship with him, she'd found their time together more than pleasant.

She sighed. Perhaps she *had* allowed herself to imagine a longer-term relationship with Leon. He was a handsome, purebred shifter, a den Alpha, and with Falcone's help, in a good position to wrestle control of Pack Gautier from Acier Gautier when the current Supreme Alpha stepped down.

Perhaps she'd envisioned herself in the role of Alpha Female Supreme, along with Leon, creating a new breed of hybrid vampire-shifters who would not only one day rule Pack Gautier, but all the shifter packs on Earth.

Vitali Bourcaro's visit had shattered those half-formed dreams.

"How long will you be gone?"

She sighed, surprised at how difficult this was. "That depends on you."

"Why on me?"

"I have been ordered to butt out of pack business."

"Why are you leaving? I need you."

"I have also been ordered to stay away from you. If you want me back, you have to take Gautier down without any help from me."

"There's Falc—"

"He has been ordered to stay out of this as well."

Leon raked a hand through his hair. "Fine! If I have to take Acier down to get you back, so be it! I'll take him down!"

She took a deep breath. "We can't help you, but you can use every dirty trick at your disposal. The sooner you take him down, Leon, the sooner I can return."

"You want to come back?"

She grabbed his hand and held it against her breasts. "You have no idea how much I hate leaving. If I didn't need the protection of the Brotherhood for my sisters' sakes, I would have told Bourcaro where to go. But without the Brotherhood, they are as much at risk as I am. I would risk my life to remain with you, but not theirs. I've already lost two sisters. I will not lose my remaining two."

He pulled her into his arms. "To get you back, I'll kill everything that moves."

She looked up at him. "When you do, I'll be waiting for you, Leon." She kissed his lips, then flashed from the room before the tears forming in her eyes could fall.

Chapter One

Acier woke feeling almost normal, his hunger for sex and blood temporarily appeased. Raven slept beside him, her long dark hair covering her face, a light sheet thrown over her body.

He leaned over, brushing her hair aside so he could kiss her soft cheek. The scent of their lovemaking lingered in the room. His nostrils flared as he savored the erotic scent of her sweet, delicious pussy, filled with his seed. He possessed no clear memory of the previous night, but judging by how satisfied he felt, they must have had a great time.

He wanted more. She lay on her side, her knees bent, clutching a pillow in her arms against her body. Tugging at the sheet, he eased her onto her back and lifted the pillow. Bruises covered her soft, dark flesh. He could actually see palm prints on both mounds of her breasts.

A flash of memory from the night before invaded his mind. He saw himself in his natural form, laying on her, rutting into her with little regard for her pleasure. Then another, more disturbing memory of him, in humanoid form this time, rutting into her tender, virginal ass. As she lay gasping and writhing with pain, he gloried in knowing he was taking his satisfaction at her expense.

Oh, God! He'd hurt her—and loved every minute of it! In his haste to get out of the bed and away from the evidence of what he had done, his feet tangled in the covers and he tumbled onto the floor beside the bed. He kicked the covers away and bolted to his feet, backing quickly away from the bed.

The closed doors stopped his backward flight. He swung around and pulled them open.

"Acier? Are you feeling better this morning?"

He closed his eyes briefly before turning to face her. In an effort to avoid the censure her eyes would shoot at him, he dropped his gaze... and saw the bruises on her stomach and thighs. Bile rose in his throat. Oh God, he'd brutalized her.

She pushed her long dark hair away from her face. "Acier?"

He swallowed. "I... I'm sorry. I didn't mean to hurt you."

She pulled the sheet up her body to cover her breasts. "The thing is, Acier, I don't think you are sorry. Oh, you say you are now and you probably believe it, but the moment you want sex again, you'll turn into an inconsiderate, vicious brute who thrives on giving me pain and leaving me bruised."

He shook his head. "Raven... *Petite*... you know I would never hurt you."

"I thought I knew Steele would never hurt me. But you're not Steele anymore. You're Acier." She sighed. "What I know of him, I don't like."

He sucked in a breath. "*Petite*... I don't know what to say. I... I love you. You know I wouldn't hurt you."

She pushed the sheet away, exposing her body with the ugly bruises. "You did hurt me." She shook her head. "Your Aunt Tat says that it's a combination of a Feast of Indulgence and the chemical changes taking place in you as a result of the massive infusion of vampire blood you received during the transfusion. She says that I have to be understanding and allow you to work your feast out with me or risk your going to other women."

He shook his head. "Other women? No! As long as you want me, there will be no other women. I'm a shifter and we mate for life."

"But are you really still a shifter, Acier? Or are you now a vampire who only knows how to brutalize lovers during sex?"

"Is that what you think I am, Raven?"

Her eyes filled with tears. She shook her head and brushed them away. "Look at me! If I were a normal woman instead of who and what I am, you might have killed me. And you wouldn't have cared. You would have taken your pleasure and left me dead somewhere."

About to angrily deny it, he remembered rutting into her ass, slapping her thigh and raking his incisors against her neck and shoulders hard enough to force painful exhalations from her. And he had come before he had pleased her.

But damn, she had a tight, hot ass and a luscious pussy. So maybe he had been a little rough with her. What did it matter? She was his to do with as he wanted. And he wanted her again. Now. Fondling his cock, he pushed away from the doors and crossed the room to the bed.

"Oh no you don't!" She exploded to her feet.

They stared at each other, the space of the queen-size bed separating them. "You're my woman!"

"You do not own me, Acier."

"The hell I don't."

She clenched her right hand into a fist. "You stay the fuck away from me until you get control of yourself. I'll be damned if I'll be turned into your punching bag!"

He leveled a finger at her. "I never struck you!"

"Not yet! Well, you know what? I don't plan to stay around until you do." She shook her head. "This is my fault. I was a fool to stay with you. At the first signs of your vampire insanity, I should have packed my bags and hit the road." She compressed her lips. "But I love you! I've always loved you."

He smiled, extending a hand across the bed. "I love you too, baby. Now come give me some pussy and ass."

She tightened her lips. "I'm out of here!"

He sprang at her and came up against that damned Bentia. He watched in an angry fury as she dressed quickly. She threw her clothing in her suitcases and stalked toward the bedroom doors. He knew he couldn't stop her. And hell, suddenly, he didn't give a flying fuck! "Go! But when you want some real cock again, don't think I'll be waiting for you!"

"Fuck you, Acier!"

"Oh, don't you worry, little bitch, I'll be doing a lot of fucking once I don't have you tied around my damned neck!"

She stared at him, her eyes wide. Then she turned and left the room.

Deep inside, he felt as if his heart were breaking. But he shook off the feeling. "Good riddance, bitch!"

* * *

In a fury of pain and anger, Raven roared out of the RV park. Several miles down the highway, she felt a churning in her stomach. Bentia had returned. She bit back the urge to ask how Acier was. He was in a mental place where she could no longer reach him. The ache inside her grew out from her stomach, threatening to devour her.

Her cell phone rang. She pulled over to the shoulder of the highway before she answered it. "Hello?"

"Ravanni, what is it? I felt a wave of pain from you."

She closed her eyes over sudden tears, leaning her head against the headrest. "Abby! It's Steele… he's changed and I can't… I don't know what to do… I want to stay with him and help him, but he's so brutal and I don't think he loves me."

"You are Ravanni Monclaire, she who wields the might of Bentia and daughter of a High Priestess. You are worthy of mating with gods. He is but—"

"But it's not gods I want! It's him. I want him! I always have. I always will."

"Even if he is not worthy of you?"

"I love him and he is more than worthy!"

"Of how much?"

"Anything."

"Then so be it. Where are you? I will come to you and we will begin the Progression."

"What Progression?"

"If you want him, you will have him, but there is a cost involved."

"What cost?"

"Nothing is free, Ravanni, not even love. The Progression will be painful and dangerous, but at the end of it, you will be able to satisfy his every need without fear of harm to yourself."

"Then why is it dangerous?"

"You have not fully accepted your destiny… and it is no longer allowed. You could die during the Progression—the steps necessary to complete the Ritual of the Talisman. If you do, many will grieve and I will be required to forfeit my life as well for having led you astray."

Raven opened her eyes and shook her head. "I'm more than willing to risk my life, Abby, but I will not risk yours!"

"Your concern for me warms my heart, Ravanni. It also strengthens my determination to aid you in whatever way I can. If I cannot do that, I have not fulfilled my purpose in life and do not deserve to live. I will come to you and we will begin the Progression… if you're sure that's what you want."

Raven nodded. "Yes, it is."

* * *

After Bentia released him, Acier tossed himself on the bed and fell into a deep sleep. Hours later, he showered and dressed in a pair of tight, black leather pants that emphasized his thick cock lying along one side of his leg. With his hair hanging long and loose around his shoulders, he felt wilder and more in need than he'd ever felt—even while in the grip of the heat that overcame him with the full moon.

Something deep and primitive inside him longed to tear after Raven and force her… beg her to come back to him. Something else, more powerful and far older and in great hunger, insisted he was well rid of her. Now that she was gone he was free to fuck every woman who caught his eye.

He snatched up his leather jacket, his motorcycle key, and headed for the front door, ignoring the fem, his Aunt Tatiana, sitting in the living area watching him.

As he reached the door, he heard a knock.

The bitch had come to her senses and come back to beg for forgiveness. He would grant it too—after he'd fucked her until she couldn't walk and was ready to admit she was his to do with as he damn well pleased.

Smiling and feeling confident, he pulled open the door. His smile vanished. The woman who stood there was tall, beautiful, and curved in all the right places. She sent his lust meter through the roof. But then, the last time he'd seen her, some ten years earlier, he'd been hard pressed not to fuck her senseless.

"Treena! What are you doing here?"

She smiled, revealing the tip of her tongue between her even white teeth. "What do you think? I'm getting married very soon, but before I do, I'm going to get into those tight leather pants and…" She cupped a hand over his cock, making him catch his breath. "… feel this big, thick dick of yours plundering my pussy, my ass, and my throat!"

The last time Raven's older sister Treena had come on to him, he'd turned her away. But this time he was going to ravish the sweet, pretty pink pussy she was so eager to share with him.

He stepped away from the door, allowing her to enter, then locked it. She stood inside, breathing quickly, her eyes centered on his cock. He hesitated. He saw no evidence Tatiana was still in the RV, but he could feel her. She was just no longer visible. He looked back at Treena. "You want cock? I'll give you more than you can handle."

"Oh, I wouldn't count on that if I were you, Acier!" She tossed her head, sending her long dark hair cascading around her shoulders.

Although she and Raven were both beautiful women, they didn't really look anything alike. Yet with her standing there reeking of lust for him, she reminded him of Raven. But Raven had made her choice and so had Treena. And he was going to take her and to hell with what Raven thought when she found out.

With his lust out of control, he went completely feral. He snatched her into his arms and crushed her lips under his, thrusting his tongue between her lips. Moaning, she pressed close, one hand cupped against his cock. He slid his lips over her neck, licking the soft, warm skin, as he slid down his zipper. Opening her pants, he was delighted to discover that she wore no panties. He maneuvered her back against the wall and bent his knees, searching for her opening with his fully erect cock.

She reached down to help him. He pushed her hands away and glared down at her. "No! I am in complete control here. I will decide when you get cock and for how long."

She opened her eyes and stared up at him. "I'm your woman, Acier. Do with me as you want."

"Damn right, I will." He found her opening, and quickly, roughly, shoved his entire length balls deep in her with one powerful movement.

She gasped, shuddered, and dug her nails into his arms right through his shirt. Without giving her time to adjust to having him fully inside her, he withdrew, and then quickly plowed deeply back in.

"Oooh!" The soft word was a combination of wonder and pain. He delighted in knowing he gave her pain with the pleasure.

Her hands pressed against his shoulders. He withdrew again, only to thrust back with even more force—again and again, making each homeward thrust more powerful. Before long, she was sobbing as her tight, creamy pussy exploded around his conquering cock.

Still fucking her hard, he tilted her head and sank his incisors into her neck. As her warm, sweet blood flowed into his mouth, he shuddered and came, shooting streaming jets of seed deep inside her.

He looked down at her as he withdrew. She leaned against the wall, staring back at him, her eyes wide. He relished the hint of fear he saw in her gaze. He smiled, stroking her cheek. It was appropriate for a woman to have a healthy fear of her man. And by the time he was finished with her, she would definitely fear to deny him anything he demanded.

"And now, I think I'll have some of that ass you were bragging about." He ripped off both their clothes, flung her over his shoulder, and stalked into the bedroom.

Leaving the doors open, he tossed Treena onto the bed where he'd last fucked Raven. He turned her onto her stomach, spread her long, lovely legs wide, fingered her pussy, and poked at her tiny, puckered asshole. Damn, sliding into that tight opening was going to feel too good.

He climbed on the bed, kneeling between her legs. He glanced briefly at the bureau top where he'd left the lube he'd used with Raven the night before. He remembered how Raven had moaned in pain as he'd invaded her tight, hot ass—and he'd lubed her ass and his cock liberally before knocking at her luscious back door.

Her muffled screams of pain had heightened his pleasure. Thoughts of the pain he could inflict on Treena if he took her without lube sent him into a mindless frenzy. He spread his body on top of hers, buried his incisors deep in her neck, and, pushing relentlessly, brutally drove his cock deep into her protesting ass as she gasped in pain.

Backdoor sex with her felt just as good as it had with Raven. Raven. He closed his eyes and pretended the woman lying under him was the one woman who had ever captured his heart. But that bitch had dared to defy him and then walked out on him when he needed her most. Silly, fickle bitch. Thinking of the rage her desertion had caused, he drew his hips back and slammed them down, forcing his cock back into Treena's tight ass.

Her moans of pain sent shivers of lust all through him. Holding her hips still, he fucked his length in and out of her, his passions rising with each homeward thrust until he exploded inside her in just a matter of minutes. Overcome with absolute bliss, he lay atop her trembling body, keeping his still erect cock buried in her warm, creamy ass. Pure, unadulterated ecstasy. He drifted to sleep with her still impaled on his cock.

Several hours later, he woke to the sound of muffled sobs. He got out of bed and made his way through the dark RV to the bathroom. Opening the door, he found Treena, naked and sobbing. For a moment, her eyes looked green and he fought to suppress a guilty thought of Raven and how she'd feel when she learned he'd not only fucked Treena, but had done it so brutally.

He gave an angry shake of his head. The old days when he allowed Raven to dictate his actions were long gone. From here on out he was going to do what felt good.

"I'm going out and I need to shower first," he told her, hardening himself against her tears. As she pushed past him into the hall he slapped her hard on her ass. Closing the door, he laughed at her outraged cry, and stepped under the water.

When he returned to the bedroom ten minutes later, she sat on the one chair there, fully dressed, her legs bent and pressed against her chest. Ignoring his instinctive urge to take her in his arms, he donned a clean pair of leather pants and a white shirt. Tying his hair behind his head, he headed for the door.

"Acier?"

He turned to look at her. "What?"

"Where are you going?"

"To get some pussy."

She sucked in a breath. "If you want more, I'll give it to you."

He smiled and walked back to stroke her damp cheek. "That's a charming offer, but you give it up too easily, sweetheart. I need someone who presents more of a challenge."

"You ignorant bastard!" Eyes flashing with anger, she swung at his face.

He caught her hand well before it touched his cheek. He bared his incisors and glared down at her. "Try that again and I'll give you a fucking you won't ever forget!"

"Are you threatening me?"

"What do you think?" He tossed her hand away. "Stay the fuck out of my face and you might not get hurt. I'm leaving now. Do not be here when I return."

Her eyes shot angry sparks at him and again he thought of Raven. Swearing, he swung away from her, storming out of the RV. Before he went in search of more pussy, he had a score of sorts to settle.

Chapter Two

Aleksei stood looking at the sleeping Dani. She lay on her side with Drei, in his natural form, sleeping soundly against her breasts. She looked so peaceful that he was tempted to summon Tat to watch over her while he went in search of Acier. Although he knew Dani needed him, Acier also needed him. It hurt that he had to leave his son when he was in such pain.

Acier's pain had become his own. Never had he felt so anguished, not even when he'd had to choose between the two brothers he loved most, Vladimir and Mikhel. Choosing between the woman he loved who was also his bloodlust and the son he longed to protect was a choice no vampire should have to make.

But not even he could change the unchangeable. Feeling the need for warmth, he stripped down to his briefs and slid into bed. Dani immediately murmured softly in her sleep and pressed into his arms.

He pressed a kiss against her hair and settled down to sleep. Sometime later, he came abruptly awake, aware that he and Dani were no longer alone in the bedroom.

He leaned close to Dani and whispered softly against her ear. "Sleep... sleep." He repeated the soft command to Drei before he sat up and looked around the room.

Near the open door stood a dark figure with bared incisors and glowing eyes. The rage emanating from the intruder was palpable.

Aleksei eased out of bed and flashed across the room to the other male. "What are you doing here, Acier?"

"You've abandoned me once too often. I've come to kick your sorry ass all over this fancy estate of yours."

Before he could speak, he was aware of two other presences, both of them familiar and loved. Tat was near as was their mother. He sent a quick, silent warning to Tat. He felt a panicked acknowledgement. Then Tat was gone and their mother stood between him and Acier. Although fragile compared to the two of them, she nevertheless exuded a sense of power that was undeniable.

"Acier... eldest of my eldest, I am Palea Walker-Dumont, your grandmother."

Acier stared at her, then looked at him. "Aleksei? This is her?"

Although annoyed at Acier's use of his name, Aleksei nodded. He would deal with Acier's lack of respect later. "Yes."

Palea took Acier's hand and drew him into her arms. He tried to resist, but he was no match for her strength. She lifted him in her arms, looking at Aleksei over Acier's head. *Your place is here with your woman. I will guard Acier. Mikhel and Serge will shadow Etienne and Vlad to ensure Etienne comes to no harm. All will be well, my little Alexander.*

With an aching heart, he watched her flash out of the room with a protesting Acier still cradled in her arms.

Acier. I will come to you as soon as I can. Until then, know that I am with you in spirit and that I love you, my son.

In response, he felt a wave of fury and pain from Acier. He returned to bed, took Dani in his arms, and laid awake for the remainder of the night. Near dawn, he sensed yet another familiar presence in the house.

He leaned close to Dani and whispered into her mind. *Sleep, sleep.* Drei was awake. *Keddi, guard,* he ordered.

With life and last breath, Father, Drei promised.

Slipping out of bed, he flashed down the stairs to the foyer. Vladimir leaned against the closed door, a troubled look in his blue eyes.

"Vlad? What's wrong?"

"I'm torn, Sei. I don't know what to do. Who needs me more?"

"You mean Adam or Etienne?"

Vlad shook his head, casting his gaze upward. "Sei? Is she… is she going to be all right? I feel drawn here with her, but… shouldn't I be watching over Etienne?"

Privately, Aleksei doubted that Vlad was in a state of mind to be of much use in ensuring Etienne did nothing to bring the authorities down on him and their community during his Feast of Indulgence. And there was no way he would allow Vlad too close to Dani. While he knew Vlad would never deliberately hurt her, he wasn't sure Vlad would be able to resist trying to satisfy his physical hunger for her.

"Mother was here earlier, Vlad."

Vlad stiffened, glancing around quickly. "Is she… still here?"

"No. She came to take Acier away. He came here to kick my ass."

"I thought you and he were working on your relationship."

Aleksei sighed. "That was before his vampire blood kicked in. He's almost feral now."

"How could you not go with him, Sei?"

The question annoyed him. "Don't you think I wanted to?"

"Then why didn't you?"

"I can't leave Dani, and even I can't be in two places at one time!"

Vlad squeezed his shoulder. "Yes, you can."

"What?"

Vlad grinned. "We are identical twins, remember. You can go watch over Acier and I will stay here and pretend to be you."

"She'd know the difference."

Vlad shook his head. "Not if I don't want her to. I'll cloud her mind."

His instinctive desire to do as Vlad offered shamed him. He shook his head. "No. It's my responsibility to be here with her. Not yours. Mother will see Acier safely through his feast."

Vlad's shoulders sagged. "I should be with Etienne, but he's so… wild. The rage and fury I feel in him… frightens me, Sei. Yet it excites me too. I'm afraid he'll go too far and I won't stop him."

"I know, Vlad. That's how I've felt with you for so long. I nearly despaired of ever seeing you happy and content."

Vlad's eyes filled with tears. "Oh, Sei, I'm so sorry I've caused you so much anguish and grief for so long. I didn't mean to—"

Aleksei pulled Vlad into his arms and sank down to the floor with him. "No. Don't apologize. Anything I have done or borne on your behalf, I would gladly do again. I regret nothing I've done for you."

The tears spilled down Vlad's cheeks. "I've never been worthy of your devotion or many sacrifices, Sei, and I never will be."

He brushed Vlad's tears away and cupped his palms over his face. "Don't you say that. Without you… without your unquestioning faith and absolute belief that I would do the right thing, I would not be who I am. You, with your belief in me, have helped sustain me when I feared I could not go on. I owe you as much or more than you owe me, Vlad. You are a vital part of my life that I could never bear to lose."

Vlad buried his head against his shoulder and they clung to each other in silence, each allowing their tears to flow freely for several long healing moments. Finally, they drew apart and rose.

Vlad glanced up the stairs. "Are you sure Dani will be all right?"

"Of course. In a few hours, Margolis Cheyenne will arrive to oversee her care."

Vlad leaned against the wall, his eyes wide. "Isn't she some kind of spiritual healer?"

"She's also a nurse practitioner and a forensic psychologist. She's more than capable of taking care of Dani."

"I guess I'd better go find Etienne."

Aleksei frowned suddenly. "Where is Slayer?"

Vlad grinned. "The little sex demon is with Adam. He likes to delude himself into thinking he can win Adam away from me. The last time I saw him, he was bent over my desk, looking like a mini me, trying to write Adam a poem."

"And you don't mind?"

"Why should I?" Vlad laughed. "Adam is mine. No one can take him from me—not even a sex-crazy mini me."

"Adam is good for you."

Vlad nodded.

He sighed. "When the baby is born, I'm going to come see him. It's time I mended fences."

"He'd like that, Sei. So you'll kiss and make up?"

Aleksei arched a brow. "I am not kissing him, Vlad."

"What would it hurt, Sei? Just once? It would mean so much to him."

"No!"

"Will you at least slap his ass?"

He grinned. "No, but I'll be happy to kick it."

"You're a hard case."

"I don't do men, Vlad."

"I know, but I can't see how one little kiss or one slap on the ass would hurt."

"No. No kisses, no slaps on the ass, but I promise to treat him as he deserves to be treated."

"Okay. Now I'd better go find Etienne. I only hope I can do right by him, Sei. I know I'm supposed to make sure he doesn't do anything to bring attention to us, but he's my son. I want to allow him to do whatever feels good."

"Which is understandable—and why Mikhel and Serge will be near. In case he does something you don't stop him from doing, they will." He palmed the back of Vlad's neck and stared into his eyes. "And I want your word you will respect their right to do that, Vlad."

"I have no problem with Serge being there, but—"

He tightened his hand around Vlad's nape. "Whatever you think of Mikhel, he is our little brother also. He has done nothing to deserve your scorn. And he is the elder of the two. You cannot disrespect him in front of Serge, who looks up to him, just as you do me. Would you allow Andrei to disrespect me?"

"No!"

"Then you must accord Mikhel the same respect. He and Serge will only show themselves if it becomes necessary. If they make their presence known to Etienne, do not challenge them, Vlad. They will only interfere if he gets too far out of control."

"Why should they be the ones to decide that?"

"Because you're too wrapped up in Etienne. They don't know him and will be more inclined to view his behavior with a clear head. Treat them with the same respect you would accord Andrei and Tat."

"Where are they?"

"Tat was with Acier. She left when Mother arrived. Andrei is keeping an eye on Falcone. Tat will hang around and run interference where needed, if necessary."

Vlad sighed. "Then everything is taken care of. I will go find Etienne… and for you, Sei, I will not break Mikhel's neck."

"I have your word?"

"I am never going to like him, Sei. Never. But out of respect for you, I will never threaten or lay a hand on him."

Knowing Vlad had never broken a promise made to him, Aleksei nodded. "Thanks, Vlad."

"Sei… will you tell Dani that I… I…"

He nodded. "She knows, Vlad, but I'll tell her anyway."

"Good… because the words don't come easy."

"I know."

"I'm going."

"Until we see each other again, know wherever you go, I go with you in spirit."

Vlad hugged him and then was gone in a blur.

About to return to Dani, Aleksei frowned, aware of another vampire approaching. He opened the front door and found himself facing a tall male with dark skin, a shaved head, dark brown eyes, a neat goatee, and a very muscular build.

He smiled. "Michelangelo!"

"Aleksei!"

"I thought you'd shaken the dust off your feet when you left for Europe… what was it… how long ago?"

"Sixty years, give or take a year."

"What brings you here?"

His smile vanished. "My last close living relative, my Great-uncle Charles, is dying. He knows what I am, but he's always been accepting. He won't allow me to do anything to help him, but I had to come be with him. I couldn't allow him to die alone."

"I'm sorry."

"When he's gone, I will be all alone, Aleksei."

Aleksei placed a hand on the other vampire's shoulder and shook his head. "Not as long as I breathe."

He nodded. "I hear life is good for you. I'm glad."

"Yes. I have a son and my woman is about to give me another. You are invited to the birthing."

Michelangelo inclined his head. "Call and I'll come… if circumstances permit."

"Understood."

"I should go. I just wanted to say hello."

Aleksei watched him disappear in a flash before he turned and went back into the house.

* * *

Several hours later, Acier woke in his bed. The small, dark woman who had called herself his grandmother was gone. But he wasn't alone. A naked, exquisite blonde with large breasts, long legs, and a bald pussy that made his cock jump, lay next to him.

He had no idea who she was or how she'd come to be in his bed. But he'd worry about that later. He rose above her, positioned himself between her parted legs, grasped his cock, and thrust his hips forward, sending his length burrowing deep into her tight, strangely familiar warmth.

She came awake with a gasp of pain. Her beautiful green eyes wide, her small hands pushed against his shoulders. Cupping his palms over her cheeks, he crashed his lips down onto her mouth, fucking her deep and hard. Jolts of lust cascaded through him as she contracted around him. Her warm, sweet lips parted under his and she clutched at his ass, welcoming him deep into her body. Being inside her felt so good… almost as good…

With his eyes closed and her hands raking down his back, he thought inexplicably of Raven as he came.

His climax thundered through him, leaving him feeling weak and replete. Burying his face against her neck, he sank his incisors into her skin and fed on her as she moaned and shuddered to her own orgasm.

When he'd had his fill of her luscious pussy and blood, he lifted his head and stared into her eyes. "Who are you?"

Still impaled on his cock, she smiled, stroking a finger down his cheek. "I am whoever you want me to be... ready to do anything you want me to."

Her voice, husky with passion, sent a tingle of desire through him. He stroked his hands over her thighs before sliding them under her body to cup her ass. He loved how warm and delicious her cheeks felt against his palms. His cock jerked inside her as he thought of how good it would feel sliding his aching length slowly between her nether cheeks, past her tight opening, and deep into her ass. "Anything?"

"Anything."

He smiled and kissed her lips softly, savoring the taste and texture of her mouth. "I'm going to fuck you until you can't walk."

"Walking is overrated." She locked her legs around him. "Now are you going to talk or fuck?"

He pulled away, withdrawing from her slowly. He turned her onto her stomach, spreading her legs. He bent, brushing his lips against her cheeks. Her skin felt soft and silken. His nostrils flared. The musky aroma of her well-fucked cunt excited his senses, much as the scent of Raven's did. Momentarily abandoning his desire to plunder her ass, he slid down her body, burying his face between her legs.

In an effort to chase away thoughts of Raven, he ate her slowly, delighting in her ecstatic cries of pleasure as he pushed her over the edge of passion again and again. As she lay moaning with her cheek pressed against the bed, he rose over her.

He parted her cheeks and ejaculated on the small, puckered hole. Keeping her cheeks separated, he shot a thick jet of cum into her. Overcome with lust, he plunged his shaft into her moist warmth.

"Oooh!" She balled her hands into fists and shoved her hips up at him. "I'm yours, Acier. Do with me whatever you want."

Sinking his incisors into her neck, he did just that. He fucked her tight ass several times before she lay limp under him. Still thoughts of Raven haunted him, infuriating him. He drifted to sleep with the memory of Raven's soft lips clinging to his and her soft hands holding him close as he exploded inside her plaguing him.

Damn the bitch! Why wouldn't she leave him in peace?

Chapter Three

"So. Where does Vitali's sacred pronouncement leave us?"

Deoctra stopped pacing the length of the bedroom of her cabin in the woods to face Tucker. Sprawled out on her bed, he looked cool and overly confident. Usually she admired arrogance in a male, but her unexpected concern for Leon left her in no mood for male bravado.

"We are forbidden from interfering with Pack Gautier business, but that does not mean we are left without options." She tossed her head angrily. "I will have my revenge."

"I thought you didn't want those two little Gautier boys hurt."

She sucked in an angry breath and leveled a finger at him. "Get this straight, Falcone. I have no feelings for them, but they are related to the Dumonts. They have wronged me for the last time. I will have my revenge."

He sat up, his eyes flickering with interest. "You have something in mind?"

"Yes."

"Need any help?"

"No!" She raked a hand through her hair. "However, I may have occasions to want help."

He smiled, running the tip of his tongue along his lips. "As you may know, as a Heoptin, my services don't come cheaply."

She stared at him. "What are you saying? You want to be paid?"

"Damn straight."

She considered him in silence for a long time. No one associated with the Brotherhood had any financial need. And he had not demanded money when she had first enlisted his aid. She knew what he wanted. "What is your fee?"

"Pussy... lots of it."

She shook her head. "No. But you can have as much ass as you like—after I've had my revenge."

He bolted to his feet, grabbed her arms, and tossed her onto her back on the bed. He stood over her, his eyes glowing. "I want pussy and I want a down payment now, or you can try your hand at taking revenge against the Dumonts solo while trying to protect your beloved sisters."

She tightened her lips, barely managing to hold her rage in check. If she were to protect her sisters and finally have her revenge, she would require help. His obvious lust for her made him the perfect patsy. She would need to play along with him until she could have everything she wanted—including Leon and the opportunity to sire a new breed of superior beings.

Lying on her back, she shimmied out of her one-piece cat suit, revealing her bare body. He ripped off his clothes and climbed onto the bed. Settling between her legs, he thrust his cock into her pussy. She closed her eyes, slipped her arms around him, and pretended the lips devouring hers belonged to another shifter.

Tucker was a more than competent lover. Since he was determined to please, she shuddered to her climax within a short time. As he filled her with his seed, she pressed her lips together to keep from crying out Leon's name.

She curled her fingers in Tucker's taut ass and reached out with her mind. *Leon... Leon... kill him quickly... take your pack and kill Gautier... and then return to me.*

* * *

"Not only would such a course not be honorable, Alpha, but any resulting victory would not be recognized by the other dens within the pack."

Leon considered the slender shifter with the short dark hair who stood in front of him in the living room of his temporary headquarters. Instead of standing with his head bowed in submission, he held Leon's gaze. "How long have you been my second-in-command, Marquee?"

"I have had that honor for five years, Alpha."

"What does your position as second entail, Beta?"

Marquee finally bowed his head, casting his gaze downward. "I live to serve, Alpha."

"And?"

"To obey."

"Obey how?"

"Without question, Alpha."

Leon nodded. "Damn straight. So don't dare challenge my decisions or orders again, Beta!"

Marquee lifted his head and his gaze. "I dare because I must, Alpha. If Den de la Rocque attacks Alpha-in-waiting as a group and defeats him, the other dens will be honor bound to call us to account. It is my job to protect the den in your absence. If we proceed against Alpha-in-waiting as a group, our entire den may be wiped out."

Leon exploded to his feet. "Once that half-breed pretender to power has been dispatched, none of the other Den Alphas will dare to move against us because we will have the backing of powerful allies. I have allies in the League of the Brotherhood, a vampire fem, and an Heoptin shifter."

"Those are powerful allies, indeed, Alpha, however there are rumors Alpha-in-waiting has powerful allies as well. He has been seen in the company of full-blood vampire Aleksei Madison. It is rumored Madison has been granted near immortality by a dark, powerful being capable of taking down not only our den, but our entire pack. If we proceed against Alpha-in-waiting in a dishonorable manner, we risk bringing condemnation on our entire pack, Alpha."

Leon's hand shot out. He closed his fingers around Marquee's neck. "You will obey me without question, Marquee. I have given you an order. Gather the adult males of the den together. We will move on Gautier as a group. Is that clear?"

Marquee's eyes glittered briefly with the first evidence of defiance he had ever displayed. Then he bowed his head. "It is clear. I live to serve, Alpha, as do all in Den de la Rocque."

Leon released his throat. "That's more like it. Contact me when the males are assembled and ready to take down Gautier."

"As you command, Alpha."

Marquee turned and left the house. Leon moved to the window, staring out into the night. He saw not the scene before him, but a vision of a small, exquisitely lovely fem he would gladly die for. *We will take down Gautier and then I will return to you.*

I await you, Leon.

He sucked in a deep breath, swallowing hard to contain his hunger for her. They could not be together again until Acier Gautier was out of the way. Gautier was going down—hard and fast. He would worry about the other Den Alphas later.

Several hours later, as he sat in his darkened living room, unable to sleep, Marquee returned. He saw the excitement in his second's face before he spoke, and knew he bore good news. "Alpha, it has come to my attention that Alpha Gautier may be a thorn in your side no longer."

Leon leaned forward in his chair. "Tell me. What has happened?"

"You were wise to assign shifters to shadow him. I've learned that after his confrontation with you and Falcone, he was so gravely injured he required a massive blood transfusion."

"So?"

Marquee smiled. "Gautier has been seen in and around the seediest sections of the city behaving for all the world like a vampire in the grip of bloodlust and a Feast of Indulgence! Those shadowing him say he's wild and almost bestial in his behavior. He's lost all restraint, ingesting blood in large quantities and whoring with anything with an open hole! He's even been with men pretending to be women!"

The thought of his erstwhile high-and-mighty friend so hungry for sex he'd stoop to doing men pleased him. "Gautier sticking that oversized cock of his into men. My, my."

Marquee shrugged. "Frankly, Alpha, it is a rumor that I personally do not believe, as many others are so willing to do."

Leon sighed. He knew Acier well enough to know the rumors were not true.

Watching his face, Marquee rushed on. "Still, since so many are so willing to believe it, when we move against him as a den, we can argue that we actually did the pack a favor by removing the threat of its being led by a shifter who is now, for all intents and purposes, a vampire!"

Leon hesitated, then shrugged. What difference did it make if he knew the rumor was not true if it helped him accomplish his goal?

Marquee smiled. "Den de la Rocque will retain its honor and you will rightly be perceived as the only choice to replace Alpha Supreme when he steps down."

Finally, fate was being kind. Leon sat back in his seat, a satisfied smile pulling at his lips. Now he and his pack could take down Acier without the worry of the other Den Alphas striking him down. "Have the news of Gautier's behavior spread to the other dens and to Alpha Supreme, but make no mention of our plans to take him down. When I am Alpha Supreme, Marquee, rest assured you will lead Den de la Rocque... no... Den Autena to prominence."

Marquee's smile widened. He bowed his head and dropped down to one knee, according Leon the respect reserved for the Alpha Supreme or his second-in-command, the Alpha-in-waiting. "I, and soon all in the entire pack, will live to serve you, Alpha."

Leon nodded. "So it will be."

"Then we will wait for the other Den Alphas to demand Gautier be ousted from his position as Alpha-in-waiting?"

The thought that Gautier would soon get what was coming to him buoyed his spirits, but he still had a desire for revenge. He shook his head. "Oh, no. In a fit of righteous, honorable rage, we will move on Gautier as a den and remove his scourge from the pack. We will exterminate him with extreme prejudice. And when we have dispatched Acier, we will go after Etienne. And then we will dispatch Depardieu and absorb Den Gautier into Den Autena."

Marquee inclined his head. "As you wish, Alpha."

"Yes. From now on, everything will be as I wish."

* * *

As he got out of his SUV and approached the door of the RV in the early morning, Xavier experienced a sense of unease. A small, dark woman seemed to appear out of nowhere to face him. He stopped, tensing, fully alert. She was not human or shifter. Her abrupt appearance indicated she was a vampire.

"I am Palea Walker-Dumont. What is your business here, shifter?"

"I am Xavier Depardieu."

A sudden smile lit her face. "You are Acier's second-in-command." Her smile vanished. "You bring bad news. Yes?"

He hesitated. "Who are you, ma'am?"

"I am she who bore Aleksei Madison."

That would make her Acier's grandmother. He relaxed. "Is Acier here? I must see him on a matter of pack business."

She took his arm and drew him several feet away from the RV. "He is here, but I fear he is in no position to discuss pack business."

Xavier felt as if the weight of the world had descended on his shoulders. He was glad he had not allowed Pen to accompany him. "Then the disturbing rumors I've heard are true? Is he out of control because of his... pardon my bluntness, ma'am... his vampire blood?"

She stiffened, releasing his arm, and stared up at him, her dark eyes shooting sparks of annoyance at him. "You speak of his vampire blood as if it is something undesirable, shifter."

"I have no wish to give insult, ma'am, but such an occurrence would not be desirable."

"And you are speaking for whom? Yourself? Your den? Your pack?"

"I am not authorized to speak for the pack. That is the privilege of Alpha Supreme Aime Gautier. In Acier's absence, I do speak for Den Gautier. To a cub, we are loyal to Acier and will remain so. My personal loyalty to Acier will never waver.

However, from a shifter viewpoint, having Acier out of control in the grip of a vampire… ritual… is not a good thing. There are those who will seize this opportunity to try to have him declared unfit to lead even Den Gautier, let alone the entire pack."

"Any foolhardy enough to challenge him when he is most vulnerable will find that they have made a grave error which they will not live long enough to regret."

He glanced toward the RV. "Where is Aleksei?"

"He is at home with his woman, who is in the last stages of a dangerous pregnancy."

Xavier swallowed. He had counted on Aleksei to help him gauge Acier's state of fitness. While he and Den Gautier would remain loyal to Acier, even in the face of a decree from Aime Gautier, he doubted the other dens would. "I must speak to him."

"He is not alone."

"I must speak to him to see if he is in a condition to direct me. If he is not, I will have to proceed on my own, as I think best."

She turned and walked with him to the RV. As soon as they stepped inside, his nostrils were assailed with the scent of sex. They got as far as the kitchen area before Acier appeared in front of him. The moment he saw Acier, his worst fears were confirmed.

Acier was naked and fully aroused. His eyes glowed and his incisors were bared. He emanated a sense of menace Xavier had never expected to find directed at him. He knew he stood in the presence of a vampire rather than a shifter/vampire hybrid. His hopes and fears for their den nearly overwhelmed him.

Schooling his features into what he hoped was a look of respect, he dropped to one knee, bowing his head. "Alpha, I fear I bring grave news."

Acier's hand descended on his shoulder. "How like a shifter, always bowing. Grow some backbone, boy. Look me in the eye like an adult male, not a sissy shifter."

Biting back the sudden urge to explode to his feet and backhand Acier for his disrespect to their species, he lifted his head. He found himself staring up into the eyes of a male he no longer knew and wasn't sure he could respect or like. "I have come to ask you to return to the den with me, Alpha. The rumors of your... the den needs to see you and be assured of your continued concern for our welfare."

"My continued concern is for my own pleasure. I have no interest in you or your den, Xavier. I am now a vampire. The den is yours to run as you see fit."

Stunned, he shook his head. "Alpha? You can't mean that. We live to serve you and we need assurance you are still one of us."

"There's the problem. I am no longer a shifter. I am now a vampire. I have no interest or concern for you or your den of misfits. Now leave me before I am tempted to show you why I glory in being vampire instead of shifter."

Xavier's nostrils flared. Rage ate at him. He sprang to his feet and bared his incisors. "Are you renouncing your leadership of Den Gautier?"

For the first time, he saw a flicker of concern in Acier's gaze. Or was that just wishful thinking on his part? He could not tell. Acier's lids swept down, concealing any hint of reluctance. "Yes. It is yours to do with as you will. Now get out and do not come back here again. If you do, I'll be tempted to kill you."

Xavier clenched his hands into fists, feeling as if the air had been sucked from his lungs. Even before he became Acier's second-in-command, he had always respected and longed to be like his older cousin, who had managed to put himself in position to be the first non-purebred to lead Pack Gautier.

He stared into Acier's hate-filled eyes. "I am a purebred shifter, Acier. You might not find me so easy to kill."

"Are you challenging me, boy?"

"I am demanding the respect I deserve as the de facto Alpha of Den Gautier."

Acier snarled and his right hand shot out. Xavier brought up his forearm and knocked Acier's hand away. Acier countered with a clenched right fist. Xavier danced backwards, quickly shifting to his natural form. Acier shifted as well and they stood staring at each other in silent aggression. Acier was bigger and heavier and Xavier knew he would give no quarter. But with the fate of the den riding on his shoulders, Xavier decided he could not afford to hold back. He would have to battle Acier as fiercely as he would anyone who threatened the den. If he fell, the den would be thrown into despair. In threatening him, Acier threatened the den.

Stand down, Alpha, or I will kill you.

You and what army? Acier leapt at him.

Heart filled with regret, he bared his incisors and sprang forward to engage Acier in a battle to the death.

Palea Walker-Dumont abruptly appeared, grabbed Acier by the scruff of his neck, and held him back. "I am sorry this happened. Go quickly, but please do not bear him ill will. He is in the grip of a Feast of Indulgence like none I have ever seen. Hurtful things said were not from the heart. He is not himself at the moment, but when his feast has burned itself out, he will bitterly regret giving you cause for pain. Go, Xavier, and know that if Den Gautier finds itself in need of allies, there is a family of full-blood vampires who will stand with you in the name of Acier Gautier."

Filled with rage and a hurt that made breathing difficult, Xavier shifted to his human form, and hurried from the RV. The sounds of Acier's snarls and curses rang in his ears.

In his SUV, he folded his arms over the steering wheel, fighting back tears. He knew in his heart that Acier was lost not only to him as a friend and mentor, but to the den as their beloved Alpha. He sat up and shook his head. Somehow he would have to find the strength to lead the den. In deference to the Alpha they had lost, he and the pack would do what they could to protect Acier.

Several hours later, he sat in the huge meeting room in Acier's house in the Arizona desert, facing as many of the den members as could fit into the room. He told them only that Acier would not be returning to the den for a while. Looking into the sea of concerned eyes, he had not had the heart to repeat the vitriol Acier had spewed at him.

"When is Alpha returning to us, Alpha Xavier?"

He turned his attention to a young female cub seated at the front of the room. The fingers of both her hands were curled in the long curtain of dark hair falling across her slender shoulders. Although sixteen, she had the look of a lost pre-teen cub. She was the cub who had run away in search of Acier weeks earlier.

She glanced at Pen, who sat on his shoulder. "When Alpha and the Keddi came to find me, he promised he would come home as soon as he could."

"Alpha is going through a difficult time, Cecily. It will not be possible for him to come just yet."

She stared at him then abruptly closed her eyes. Xavier felt a desperate probing of his mind and recoiled. He bared his incisors and sprang to his feet. "Cecily! Stop immediately. I command it."

Her eyes flew open and she stared at him, a look of horror in her gaze. He knew she had seen his confrontation with Acier in his thoughts. He stared at her, willing her to remain silent.

After a moment, she sank to her knees with her head bowed in submission. "As you wish, Alpha Xavier."

He resumed his seat and looked at the curious faces assembled before him. Sooner or later he would have to tell them the truth, but not yet. Not until he was sure Acier was completely lost to them. He looked at Pen. "I need to be alone with some of the shifters for a few moments."

Pen rose to hover in front of his face. *Alpha all right?*

He closed his eyes briefly. "I'm not sure, Pen."

Then Pen must return to be by his side!

"No, Pen. Please. He sent you back here for a reason. He's going through a difficult and dangerous time. And so I am. I need you here. Will you please stay?"

Pen shivered. *Should go with Alpha.*

"Please."

Pen bowed his head. *Will stay… for now.*

"Thank you."

He waited until Pen left the room before he turned to face those remaining. "Those who will accompany me to guard Alpha remain. The rest, leave us." He looked at Cecily. "Remain, cub."

"Yes, Alpha Xavier."

Ten minutes later he, Cecily, and six males remained in the room. The oldest of the males, slender with short blond hair and green eyes, approached him. "If Alpha will not be returning, then you must not go into battle with us, Alpha Xavier. I will lead the others and we will gladly surrender our lives in his defense, but with Alpha not among us, you are the hope and future of our den. Your life must become as precious to us as the Alpha's. We will battle to save him but if we cannot, we will battle to keep the fight away from the den and away from you. You must not fall, Alpha."

"Simeon—"

"No, Alpha. We will not allow you to fall in battle."

The remaining shifters all bowed their heads.

Simeon spoke. "We live to serve, Alpha."

"And willingly die to protect, Alpha," the other males intoned.

He sighed and fell back against his seat. They knew of his fear that Acier was lost to them. Cecily was not the only shifter among them with the ability to probe minds. Had they believed Acier to still be their leader, they would address him as Alpha Xavier instead of the more respectful Alpha.

"Have any of you felt any ill effects as a result of the experiment?"

Simeon shook his head. "And you, Alpha? Are you yourself?"

He nodded. "I am."

"Then why is Alpha so affected?"

He shook his head. "I don't know. I suppose because his natural blood chemistry made him predisposed to be more affected than a non-hybrid shifter."

Simeon nodded. "We will leave for Philadelphia immediately, Alpha."

The males bowed and moved toward the door.

"Simeon."

He turned. "Yes, Alpha?"

"Protect him. Please. Those of Den de la Rocque will seek to kill him."

Simeon nodded. "That will not happen while one of us lives. You have our word, Alpha."

He nodded. "Battle well and return safely to us."

"We will battle for the glory of our den and for you, Alpha."

Xavier shook his head. "For him."

"We will battle for you both with the hope of returning to serve you, Alpha."

He shook his head again. "I live to serve him."

"As do we all, but if it must be, we will follow you with as much devotion and zeal as we followed him."

Humbled by the words, Xavier inclined his head. "Battle well."

Simeon dropped to one knee. The others followed suit.

Xavier sucked in a breath. "No! Rise and do it quickly. That honor belongs to Alpha Supreme and his second. No other deserves to be so honored."

"You stand in the de facto position of his second, Alpha." Simeon turned and led the others up the staircase.

When they were alone, Cecily looked at him. "Is he really lost to us, Alpha Xavier?"

About to nod, he paused. Although Acier had declared himself a vampire, when he felt threatened, he had shifted into his natural form. Somewhere, buried deep under the layers of vampire shit, must remain the shifter Acier had once been. And he could think of only one way to bring Acier back to an awareness of what was really important.

He motioned Cecily closer. "You can help me determine that if you are as brave as I think you are."

She lifted her chin. "To save the Alpha, I will gladly surrender my life."

He smiled. "Spoken like a true cub of Den Gautier, but neither the Alpha nor I would have you die. Here's what we are going to do."

Chapter Four

The moment Palea released him, Acier shifted back to his human form and spun around to face her. He met the look of love in her dark eyes and swallowed the vile, hateful words trembling on his tongue. "Why didn't you allow me to kill him?"

"From what I understand from Alexander, he is the one who is charged with protecting and keeping the den together when you are away. He is also younger than you and your cousin. In this family, we guard and protect our young. We do not threaten to kill them."

"I don't give a fuck about that den anymore!"

She tilted her head. "So you now fully embrace your vampire heritage?"

"Yes! Won't dear Alexander be pleased?"

"Why should he be pleased? He loves and accepts you as you are. You understand this. Yes?"

"No! He's the one who allowed that vampire doctor to change my blood chemistry. What you see is what he made me!"

"You are mistaken, Acier. I know you are in a fever of rage and pain. I have undergone such a painful process twice in my life, but some things, even things done in the grip of the feast, are unforgivable. That is why I am here, to ensure you do not do any of them. Killing the cousin who loves you and who has taken care of your responsibilities would be such an unforgivable act. As it is, you will have much to atone to him for when you are yourself again."

Unbidden, he remembered a time when he was eighteen, coming upon the then eight-year-old Xay, bloody and bruised, heroically battling a much older and bigger shifter. When he had forced them apart, he had learned Xay had felt honor bound to attack the other shifter because he had made a disparaging remark about Acier's lack of purebred status.

Xavier had always had his back and had never let him down. And yet he had come within moments of killing him. He gave an angry shake of his head. "This is as good as it's going to get, baby."

Her eyes flashed and she backhanded him, knocking him to his knees. He stared up at her, wiping the blood from his mouth. "I am she who bore your father. No matter how deep in the grip of the feast you are, I will not tolerate disrespect from you." She curled her fingers in his hair and stared down into his eyes. "You will show respect or I will backhand the feast right out of you. Do we understand each other, Acier?"

He did the only thing he could in the face of her determination and power. He inclined his head and averted his gaze to hide the rage in his eyes.

She released his hair and put her arms around him. "I will willingly surrender my life to protect you. All I ask in return is your love and your respect. I can wait for your love. Your respect I demand now and always."

He burrowed against her, his fists clenched, the rage building in him. The day was coming when all the vampires who had hurt and humiliated him would pay dearly. But first there was the little matter of Leon. It was time he got his ass kicked. Even if he no longer wanted the position of Alpha-in-waiting, he was damned if he'd allow a little piss-ant like Leon to think he could take that prize from him.

He pulled away from her and stalked to the bathroom. After his shower, he looked at the buxom brunette lying on his bed, bruises all over her olive skin. "I'm going out. Don't be here when I return," he told her. He left without waiting for her response.

Roaring down the highway on his motorcycle with hair flying around his shoulders, he thought briefly of Raven. Then Etienne. For the first time in his life, he had no idea where his twin was or any particular care if he were all right. He frowned. Was this what being a damned vampire was about? Not giving a flying fuck about those who had once been most important to him?

He cleared his head and called out. *Leon! You little piss-ant bastard! It's time to pay the goddamned piper!*

* * *

Aleksei looked into the bedroom. A tall woman with olive skin, dark eyes, and an infectious smile glanced up from the bed where the sleeping Dani lay with Drei cuddled against her neck. The woman inclined her head slightly.

He backed out of the room and walked down the hall to the stairs. Moments later, Margolis Cheyenne joined him. He turned to face her. "How is she?"

"She is fragile, but I have not lost a patient in a very long time. I do not intend to have your family be the first." She considered him in silence for several moments. "In fact, I am more concerned with you than I am with them."

He arched a brow. "Me?"

"You." She closed her eyes briefly. He rebuffed the gentle probing of his mind. "Your state of agitation is clearly discernable."

He shook his head. "I appreciate your coming, but I don't need anything from you personally. I will be fine. Now if you'll excuse me."

She nodded, a slight smile curving her lips. "Of course, but the burden of pain you bear for your son will overcome you if you are not careful. Even a full-blood has emotional limits and boundaries. I sense you are close to yours. I have not yet acquired the great skill of my clansman, Enola, but I am far from a novice. I can see your woman safely through the remainder of this pregnancy and assist you." She extended a hand, her dark eyes beckoning. "Throw your emotional burden on me and I will bear your pain and see you through this dark time."

The weight of Acier's rage and pain had haunted him for days. Combined with his fear for Dani and their child, he sometimes felt as if he were tumbling out of control in a world of darkness where there was no peace or joy… just endless fear and dread at his inability to be a savior to those he loved most. He was tempted to gather up his anguish and toss it onto her slender shoulders. But the weight was too great. And it was his alone to bear.

Or was it? There was one person who had shared his darkest moments with him and never thought any less of him for his foul deeds and thoughts.

He shook his head.

She allowed her hand to fall to her side. "Do not let my fragile appearance fool you. I am a healer of the spirit among other things. Not all of our kind are so inclined, but those who are have a calling… a need to bear the burdens of others. If you change your mind, I will be here and willing to assist you."

While he had heard tales of the Cheyenne Healers from Shadow Mountain, he would not risk diverting her attention from Dani and their child. Still, he did require a measure of relief from the weight of guilt and futility weighing him down. He would not seek it at Dani's expense.

He shook his head again and flashed down the stairs. In his study, on the far side of the house from the bedroom, he sat in his favorite chair, picked up the guitar lying across the desk, and strummed slowly.

Sometimes music had the power to soothe him, but his agitation was too great for that. After several moments, he laid the guitar across his desk, closed his eyes, and reached out.

Luc… Luc… Father.

Although he felt no acknowledgement, moments later, he opened his eyes and found a tall, strikingly handsome male with shoulder-length blond hair and clear blue eyes standing in front of him. As always, the sight of the other male generated a sense of well-being in him.

Luc smiled. "You called me. You have not done that in a very long time."

"Calling you to ask for help smacks of a little boy calling for his father."

Luc's eyes searched his. "Would that be so wrong, Aleksei? Have I not done my best to be a father to you when you needed it? Have I not shared things with you… given you skills and abilities few other vampires possess? Would I not willingly surrender my eternal soul and life to keep you safe?"

He nodded. "Yes. You have always been good to me, Luc. But it's unbecoming of a vampire my age to always seek help from…"

"From who, Aleksei? What am I to you?"

"A father."

He sensed a quiet satisfaction in Luc at his answer.

In his lifetime he had been fortunate to know three men as fathers. His natural father, Alexander, who he would always love and miss, Mattias Madison, the man who had rescued him and his siblings hundreds of years earlier and had then lovingly provided shelter and seen them into adulthood. Then there was Luc, who had sheltered and taught him many things at one of the darkest times in his life. The others were long gone, but Luc had been a constant in his life from the moment they met.

"You know there are… others for whom I have affection and for whom I feel a sense of obligation and duty, but none are dearer to me than you, Aleksei."

He nodded. "I know." He motioned to the well-cushioned leather chair on the other side of his desk.

Luc sat and they considered each other in silence for several moments. "It grieves me to see you in such turmoil, Aleksei."

He rose and kneeled in front of Luc. "Help me… please… Father."

Luc averted his gaze, but not before Aleksei had seen a hint of moisture in his eyes. "What troubles you, Aleksei?"

"Acier. He's not going to be able to recover from his present despair. I can't leave Dani, but I can't lose him either. What am I going to do?"

Luc stroked a hand over his hair. "You need have no fear, Aleksei. There are many in his den who stand ready and willing to die to bring him back from the depths of despair."

He clutched Luc's hand. "But will they be successful? If he doesn't make it… how will I live with myself knowing I failed him when he needed me most? He's spent nearly all his life looking for me… needing me. I cannot lose him."

Luc remained silent for several long moments before he spoke. "He will survive and thrive. I give you my word that I will not allow him to be lost."

Aleksei suspected interference of that magnitude would constitute a big no-no for Luc. He wasn't sure who or what had the power or authority to hold Luc in check, but he knew such an authority did exist. He looked at Luc. "If you have to step in, will you be all right?"

Luc glanced away again. "Do not concern yourself with my welfare, Aleksei. I am far older than you can imagine. I will survive."

He suspected Luc could not die, but having lived in despair for a large part of his life, he knew there were worse things than dying. "But will you be all right?"

"That need not concern you. Return to your woman and trust me to ensure the well-being of your son, if necessary." Luc rose and turned away.

Aleksei rose and caught Luc's arm, swinging him around.

Luc stared into his eyes. "Do you doubt my word or my ability to keep it?"

"No! You know I don't."

"Then what is your concern now?"

"What is my concern now? Do you really think I don't care what happens to you?"

Luc smiled and touched his face. "Your capacity for love and concern for those you love is just one of the things which makes you so special. I consider it an honor and blessing to have had the privilege of knowing you… if only for a short time."

He swallowed several times. "Why are you speaking in the past tense?"

"If we do not meet again, know that wherever you are, a part of me will be there as well."

His heart raced. "Luc—"

"May Heoptin himself watch over you. Live long and be well and safe, Aleksei."

With those words ringing in his ears, Aleksei found himself alone in the room. Fear stabbed through him as he realized he had asked Luc to do something for which he might have to pay a great price. He fell on his knees. "Luc! Come back! I've changed my mind. I'm sorry! I'll find another way to ensure Acier's safety. Luc! Don't interfere! Please!"

Luc did not return or respond audibly. But a wellspring of warmth filled the room. Aleksei, still on his knees, shivered with a sense of dread, feeling chilled. To save Acier's soul, had he condemned Luc to God only knew what fate?

Chapter Five

Tatiana climbed out of the deep end of the pool. She pulled the swimming cap off her head, allowing her dark hair, which she had finally allowed to grow from a mass of short, dark curls to long, flowing locks, to cascade around her shoulders. Standing on the rooftop of the building where she maintained her penthouse apartment and private pool, she shivered. It was a warm night and the water temperature was fine, but even after all these years of forcing herself to swim, she still struggled to overcome her aversion to water.

Drowning at five had left an indelible scar on her psyche. The only time she had found water anything but a cause for alarm was when she and her former lover, Mike Timbersmith, had cuddled together on a float. For a time she had allowed herself to hope that after three hundred years she had found her bloodlust. But after three years as her lover, when she had felt confident enough in their relationship to confide in him that she was a vampire, he had rejected her.

Shaking her head to chase away thoughts of him, she patted a towel over her nude body, and stretched out on one of the plush, padded loungers around the in-roof pool. Closing her eyes, she let her thoughts turn to another male. Eric Jason... the vampire hunter with whom she had recently shared a brief but bittersweet encounter.

She trembled, recalling the feel of his cock pounding inside her as he bit and sucked at her lips and tongue with a hunger that had kept thoughts of him and their encounter uppermost in her mind. It had been a constant struggle over the last weeks not to seek him out and pursue a strictly physical, secret sexual relationship with him.

While with him, thoughts of her former lover had not tortured her. How ironic it had taken a hereditary enemy of her kind to momentarily free her of her hunger for Tim. Now instead of one man she couldn't have or forget, she was plagued by a thirst for two of them.

With so much going on in the family, this was not the time to lie around feeling sorry for herself. But even a fem required some downtime. Especially one who had only recently decided to return to her true heritage. Sighing softly, she emptied her mind of thoughts of the two males she longed for and tried to doze.

Her body's hunger for physical fulfillment kept her tense and held sleep at bay. As much as she would have once hated to admit it, as a fem, her need for carnal pleasure could not be denied. She needed to be fucked... and soon. Angry at being held hostage to her sexual needs, she willed herself to fall asleep.

Some time later, she woke abruptly and bolted to her feet. A man stood by the open French doors which led from her living room to the rooftop terrace, clad in black leather pants and an unzipped matching biker jacket. A formfitting white undershirt clearly emphasized the washboard abs and muscular chest she had spent countless happy hours licking and kissing when they made love. The strong sexual aura which had quickly drawn her into his arms against her better judgment sent a rush of moisture between her legs.

The first time they met he had been dressed in an expensive, but conservative, dark business suit. On the surface, he seemed a somewhat staid businessman. Only when she looked into his eyes had she seen the wealth of untapped passion. In that instant, her heart raced, her passion soared, and she knew she wanted that sexy young man as her lover.

His honey-blond hair, worn short in the front and sides and long in the back, fell down his back, past his broad shoulders. She curled her fingers, which longed to run through his soft hair, into fists at her side. She looked into the beautiful sea-green eyes which had made broken promises of love and devotion. How they had haunted her waking moments and dreams since their break-up. The diamond stud she had given him for their third anniversary sparkled in his right earlobe.

A large bouquet of roses and a huge box of her favorite chocolates rested in the crook of one arm. Recalling how they had both enjoyed what she'd come to think of as their chocolate ritual, a blast of sensual heat shot through her.

She blinked, shaking her head to chase away yet another dream that would end in frustration when she woke and found herself alone. Then he spoke.

"Remember me?"

His deep, warm voice raced along her heart, stirring up memories of long nights of love and near bloodlust spent lying under his big body as he sweetly fucked her until her entire world centered around her pussy and the long, thick cock plundering it… claiming her heart and branding her… making her his willing slave.

She lowered her gaze. Below his narrow, powerful hips, along the inside of one of his muscular thighs, lay the sizable bulge of his cock. Sexual desire and a gently remembered scent of leather filled her nostrils. She blinked again, her heart beating a tattoo against her chest. She was not asleep.

Why hadn't she heard him arrive on his motorcycle? She tossed her head. "Barely."

The crooked, Bruce Willis-like smile she'd always loved curved his lips and revealed a set of perfect, white teeth. "Timbersmith." His gaze rested on the dark hair falling over her shoulders and partially covering her breasts. She noted a spark of interest in his eyes, but he made no comment about her hair length.

But then he didn't need to.

While they had been lovers, she'd kept nothing from him… except her true nature. Her refusal to allow her hair to grow because he preferred women with long hair had been her one attempt not to lose herself completely in him.

She glanced at the open French doors. "How did you get up here?"

He held up a master key card.

She tightened her lips. "What are you doing with that?"

"You never asked for it back."

"Well, I'm asking for it now!"

With a flick of his wrist, he sent it whizzing toward her. She caught it while it still spun in the air and tossed it across the roof into her living room. "Now what makes you think you can just waltz in here uninvited?"

"If I'd called and asked to see you?"

"I would have told you to get lost!"

He sighed and placed the flowers and candy on the nearest table. "Leaving you was the worst mistake I've ever made." He extended a hand. "I need to be forgiven, honey."

"And just like that I'm supposed to forget all the heartache you put me through?"

"No. I don't expect that. I know I've hurt you and knowing that has been eating me up inside… that and coming to grips with how much you mean to me. I don't expect immediate forgiveness, Tat. I know that would be asking too much."

"Damn right it would!"

"All I'm asking is for a chance to make amends. You want me to beg? To crawl?" He dropped to his knees. When he spoke again, there was a noticeable tremor in his voice. "I'll do that and whatever else is necessary to win you back."

Although not unmoved by the sincerity and regret she heard in his voice, saw in his eyes, and read in a brief, cursory probe of his mind, she shook her head. "It's too late for that."

"Don't say that! It can't be too late!" He shot to his feet, the veneer of humility vanishing under a wave of passion she felt from several feet away. "If you tell me it's too late, all I've done and suffered to make myself worthy of you will have been in vain!"

She again probed his mind. This time he rebuffed her. "What have you done, Tim?"

"What I had to do to win you back!" He ripped off his jacket and tossed it on the ground. As he moved toward her, his tee shirt followed.

Her eyes roamed over the familiar contours of his bare upper body. The smattering of dark blond hair on his chest trailed down his tight abs to disappear into the top of his pants.

He stopped in front of her, his gaze drinking in the lines of her naked body. "I'm sorry! What more can I say when you know I mean it?"

She frowned, noting a difference in his aura. "What have you... done to yourself?"

"Does anything matter except I'm sorry and I know we both need comfort—even if it's only sexual and temporary?"

She told herself later that had her hunger been less intense, she would have tossed him out on his tight ass. She remained silent.

He unzipped his pants, and drew out his cock.

Her gaze was drawn to the long, thick beauty with the big, pink helmeted head that had given her three short years of near bliss. She swallowed hard. No matter what had brought him there, or how he had changed, she was going to have to feel that cock sliding between the lips of her vagina and deep into her pussy at least once more before she turned her attention back to pressing family business.

He stroked her hot cheek. "I have a surprise for you, love."

"What kind?"

He stepped back and quickly removed his pants, briefs, socks, and shoes.

When he stood before her completely nude, she caught her breath.

She'd always loved the beautiful symmetry of his naked body. His shaved pubes bore a full color tattoo of her face. A definite hint of lust sparkled in her tattooed blue eyes. The tattoo was centered low on his groin, covering the first few inches of his shaft as well so that it appeared as if her open mouth was in the process of swallowing his fully erect cock.

"Do you like it?"

She felt a brush against her mind, so familiar it might almost have come from her own mind. She tensed. *Stay away, Andrei*, she warned.

Who the fuck does he think he is getting your face tattooed sucking his tiny dick?

Tim's shaft, while smaller than Andrei's monster cock, was still a thick, pussy-pleasing nine inches, far more cock than the average woman wanted pounding her pussy.

I like the tattoo.

It's insulting!

As she'd sucked Tim's cock nearly every time they had sex and had loved every second, she shot back, *It's sexy as hell. Now stay away!*

She felt an angry acknowledgement. *I won't appear, but if he hurts you again, I'll –*

I can take care of myself, Andrei. I need and want this fuck.

I'll watch. If he doesn't satisfy you, I'll cut off his tiny little tattooed toy cock!

She cast a wave of anger his way. He would watch. It was their way. She had no objections to his watching as long as he didn't interfere.

"Do you like it?" Although Tim flashed a smile at her, she heard a hint of uncertainty in his voice.

She blinked at him, pulling her thoughts back toward him. "What?"

Tim tilted his head, his gaze narrowing. For a moment, she wondered if he were somehow aware of Drei's presence. "Where is he?"

"Where is who?"

"Your brother."

"Which one? I have several."

He glanced around the rooftop, frowning. "I didn't come here for trouble."

Andrei suddenly appeared in front of him, incisors bared, eyes glowing. "Then you should have kept your scared little ass out of my sight!"

Tat stepped between the two men, facing Drei. *I said I'd handle this, Andrei.*

No matter what you say, I'm going to kick his ass again, Tat!

She placed both hands on his chest and stared up into his eyes. *No you are not! I have needs right now and I can handle this.* She smiled and touched his cheek. *Trust me?*

The muscles in his face worked furiously for several moments before he stepped around her to stare at Tim. "Treat her gently this time or by God, I'll snap your neck like a twig and toss your useless body off the roof!"

Before Tat could object, Andrei growled and disappeared as quickly as he'd appeared.

She turned to face Tim, aware that Andrei was still around. But to hell with that. She had needs. "Does your equipment still work?"

"Judge for yourself." He hooked an arm around her waist and drew her body against his. She felt a leashed power in him where previously had only existed the humanity and sensuality for which she had so adored him.

She stroked a hand down the lines of his strong, handsome face. "What's happened to you, Tim?"

"When I realized what a fool I'd been to reject you, I took steps to make myself worthy of a beautiful fem like you."

She shook her head. "No, Tim. Please don't tell me you…"

He pressed his fingers against her lips and she was hard-pressed not to kiss them. "I did what I needed to do to atone for the biggest mistake of my life—leaving you. And now I want to be rewarded. I need to hold you and to make love to you."

Her thoughts turned to Eric Jason. Her encounter with him had been as bittersweet as her love affair with Tim. "There's been another since you walked out on me."

He sighed, but quickly shook his head. "I don't care about anything except the here and now. And right now I have you back, my lovely brown vixen. And I am going to keep you this time."

"You think I can so easily forget how you hurt me, Tim?"

"I know it won't be easy."

Recalling her anguish, she narrowed her gaze. "I'm not sure it's possible or desirable."

"Then I'll just have to change your mind."

"That's not so easily done either."

A smile curved his wine red lips. "I've done it before," he reminded her.

As she formulated an angry response, he bent his head and settled his warm lips against her right breast, taking the wide, stiff nipple into his mouth.

A jolt of lust sizzled through her body. The why and how of what he'd done and the question of whether she should forgive him or trust her heart to him again would have to wait. Right now, she had her lover back, if only for a short time.

She stroked her fingers through his hair while maneuvering her hips until she felt his length surging against her pussy with a furor and power that was shockingly exhilarating. It felt almost as if his cock had a mind of its own. Slipping his other arm around her waist, he drew back, then thrust his hips forward. She parted her legs, tilting her lower body. The big head of his cock probed her opening and then, sweet, blessed heaven, it slipped between the wet folds of her sex and surged deep into her aching pussy—oh, Lord, yes!

"Oooh!" She arched her back, lost in the harmonious joy of being fully impaled on the thick, hot cock which had enchanted and beguiled her after their first fuck.

For several timeless minutes, he kept his cock motionless in her while he took turns nipping, biting, and sucking at each of her breasts. The passion that she had been repressing since her encounter with Eric sprang forth, overwhelming her senses.

She shuddered, drew her hips back, and then sent them surging forward until his entire length was again buried inside her. She squeezed her inner muscles several times in quick succession, with a speed no human woman could hope to match.

As she had known it would, it triggered a helpless response in him. Dragging his lips from her breast, he slid his big hands down her back to cup her ass, slammed his mouth down on hers, and fucked his cock in and out of her with all the hunger of a man denied the pleasure for far too long.

Devouring each other's lips, they fucked with wild abandon. She gloried in the wonderful sensations assailing her senses. Like most fems, she had always enjoyed sex for the sheer, unmitigated pleasure it offered. But sex with a man she had been a breath away from bloodlusting with touched her on an entirely new level.

With all her senses engaged, she became his wanton slave, willing and eager to do anything to please him. But as always, he centered his energies around pleasing her. His hands stroked and slapped at her ass as they fucked. He raked his lips back and forth against her ear, whispering that he loved her… he needed her… she was his lovely fem… he was ready to accept her just as she was… he was sorry he hurt her… he couldn't live without her.

Lost in a world of sensual lust where she had no need to be anyone other than herself, her breasts crushed against the hard muscles of his chest, she fought against the primordial urge that had sent him fleeing from her in fear.

Overwhelmed with the climax crashing over her, her incisors descended, her lips drew back from her teeth. Her body shook with the effort not to bury her incisors in the strong column of his neck and feed on him.

Almost as if he knew of her struggle, he lifted his head. Cupping his hands over her cheeks, he looked into her eyes, which she knew to be glowing. She made no effort to hide her incisors. If he were really ready to accept her as she was, now was the time to prove it.

"Oh, Tat, my lovely, you are so beautiful… more beautiful than I could have ever imagined." He tilted his head, exposing his neck. "Be yourself with me, my lovely one. Take me."

Recalling his earlier horror, she hesitated. If he rejected her again, she knew no power on Earth would be strong enough to keep Andrei from killing him.

With his hands still on her face, he guided her lips toward his neck. "Feed on the man who loves you more than life itself! Take me! Make me yours!"

Unable to deny her hunger any longer, she licked his neck before sinking her incisors into his skin. His warm, delicious blood flowed into her mouth, heightening and prolonging her orgasm. Her pussy shook and convulsed around his cock as she shuddered in an agony of ecstatic delight.

Slipping his hands back down to cup her ass, he groaned, stabbed his hard dick in and out of her with a fury and rapidity he'd never been capable of before. Each time he surged back inside her, she felt tendrils of desire shooting through her, as his cock seemed to expand and cling to her pussy… kissing and caressing it.

She shuddered and came again. Only then did he cry out her name, and explode, shooting jet after jet of seed inside her.

Still feeding on him, she held him tight, keeping his cock buried in her, lost in the wonder of ingesting his blood while his seed fired into her. As the last shudder shook his body, she lowered them to the tiles. Lying on him, still full of cock, she continued to feed. He stroked his big hands over her ass and whispered how much he loved her.

Finally, reining in her hunger for his blood, she withdrew her incisors and looked down at him, his blood coating her lips and her chin.

Smiling, he cupped her face in his palms and brought her lips down to his. She felt his lips and tongue licking his blood from her tongue and lips as they kissed. It was an incredible, liberating moment for her… sexy as hell.

She lifted her head from his to gaze down into his eyes. "What have you done to yourself?"

He stroked his hand over her hair. "What does it matter? Don't you like the new, improved me?"

She climbed off his body and rose. She stared down at him, frowning, as her gaze slid down to his cock—still fully erect. He was definitely not the man she'd fallen in love with. In the past he'd always needed time to recuperate after their lovemaking and his cock had an annoying habit of deflating moments after he came. She well remembered having to kiss, massage, and caress him for what felt like forever before he was ready to love her again.

"I don't know, but now is not the time for this conversation. I'm in the middle of a family emergency. I want you to leave. Now."

His cock, coated with both their fluids, bobbed up and down as he rose. The tattoo appeared to move. Her heart raced as she realized it actually was moving! She could see her tattooed lips compressing on his thick length. The muscles in her stomach tightened. Fearful of surrendering to the desire to drop to her knees and suck the slick, delicious length between her lips, into her mouth, and deep into her throat, she stiffened.

Another fear assailed her. "Who did that tattoo, Tim? It's a Vamptu, isn't it?"

"I prefer the term blood tattoo, but yes, it's a living, evolving tattoo. She's a beauty, isn't she? Almost as beautiful as you. Watch this." He rotated his hips and massaged himself. He lifted his cock, pointing it toward his body. The tattoo's lips parted wider and he popped the head and several inches inside.

"Oh, yeah, that feels almost as good as your mouth does." He met her gaze. "While we were separated, she kept me from being too lonely."

So he had been getting his jollies by having her tattoo likeness suck him off. "The tattoo was done by a member of the Vamptues, wasn't it?"

He shrugged.

Combined with the change in his aura, the Vamptu, which required a skilled vampire tattoo artist, all of whom belonged to various vampire tattoo biker communities, was not a good sign. She liked bad boys as much as the next fem, but… "Please do not tell me you've joined the Vamptues."

He slipped his cock out of the sucking mouth. "It's done, Tat. I did it for you."

She shook her head. "No! I never wanted that! I want you to leave."

His gaze narrowed. "I'll leave… after I get another fuck." He hooked his arm around her waist, kneed her thighs apart, and thrust his cock balls deep into her.

"Oh, God!" Moaning with lust and love, she welcomed him back inside her. Clinging to each other, they tumbled to the ground. He pulled out of her, shifted his body behind hers, lifted her top leg, and shot his hard length back inside her.

She tossed her head back against his shoulder, parting her lips. Resting her top leg over his muscular thigh, he pressed his groin tight against her ass, forcing the last few inches of his sweet dick into her. He slid one arm around her body to cup her right breast while he cupped his other hand over her stuffed pussy. His mouth slammed down onto hers.

Clinging to the arm crushed around her body, she closed her eyes and wiggled her lower body. He responded by drawing his hips back, pulling half his length out of her. He quickly slammed back into her and they began a wild raunchy fuck that shook her to her core.

Chapter Six

Acier stood in the dark clearing, deep in the New Jersey Pine Barrens, aware that he was not alone. He could sense others slowly converging on him. Leon and his den of piss-ants were about to get their asses kicked and their throats ripped open.

He knew *she* was near. *Do not interfere*, he warned. *This is my fight.*

There was no response, but he knew she was still there.

He gave an angry shake of his head. Leaving his motorcycle, he stalked into the surrounding woods. Before long, at least twenty male shifters in their natural form surrounded him. Leon, still in his humanoid form, emerged from the forest to stand in their center. "Acier Gautier, hybrid, I hereby challenge your standing as Alpha-in-waiting to Pack Gautier. Will you voluntarily stand down or must we force the issue?"

"We?" He sucked in a deep breath, enjoying the adrenaline rush as he considered how satisfying killing Leon and his betas would be. He leveled a finger at Leon. "Afraid to take me on alone?"

A hint of red touched Leon's cheeks. "You, with that vampire blood running through your veins, have no right to lead the pack. The position belongs to a purebred shifter. Out of respect for our boyhood friendship, I will give you one last chance to stand down gracefully."

He laughed. "Don't you mean out of fear of having your heart ripped out of your cowardly chest?" He stared at the circle of shifters surrounding him. "Do not make the mistake of thinking these piss-ants will keep me from you! Nothing will keep me from you. I no longer desire to be Alpha-in-waiting or even Alpha of Den Gautier. I am now proudly vampire, but I will be damned if you will take the position from me. I will relinquish it in my own time and way. You have made your last mistake, de la Rocque!"

Leon's teeth gleamed in the moonlight. "Getting a little too much moon lately, Gautier? Suffering from a little moonlight madness maybe? You think you can take all of us alone?"

"Think? No. I know I can!"

Maybe so, but it ain't happening tonight!

He swung around. Etienne, in his natural form, padded silently toward him. At the sight of his twin, Acier felt a rush of affection. He swallowed it. "I don't need any help taking on these cowardly bastards!"

"Of that we are certain, Alpha."

Six shifters moved into the clearing. Leading them was Simeon, Xavier's second-in-command. Acier frowned. They were his shifters and yet he sensed a difference in them.

The six approached. Stopping several feet from him, each dropped to one knee. Simeon spoke. "Alpha, we live to serve."

The other shifters murmured softly, "And stand willing to die in your service, Alpha."

Acier fought back a wave of warmth. He was no longer the shifter they had come to protect. He didn't require or need their protection. And yet he could not force the harsh words in his heart out of his mouth. "Rise."

They did. Simeon moved forward, his head inclined slightly. "Those who live to serve you in Den Gautier will not stand by while cowardly shifters attempt to steal what is rightly yours by dishonorable means. If de la Rocque wants to challenge your standing as Alpha-in-waiting, we are here to assure he does it one-on-one."

"You can say that after he's just declared he has no interest in the position or your den?" Leon demanded of Simeon.

Simeon inclined his head. "We are shifters. Our loyalty, once won and given, is not easily swayed. We are here to defend our Alpha's life."

Leon's nostrils flared. "He just declared he is no longer your Alpha! Are you fools really prepared to die for a vampire?"

"You need not concern yourself with internal Den Gautier affairs, de la Rocque. You need only know we stand ready to fight to the death to ensure the challenge to our Alpha is a fair one."

"He's goddamned vampire now!" Leon pointed at him. "He said as much himself. You must have heard him."

"We heard what was said. It changes nothing. We stand with our Alpha. Attack him *en force* at your peril."

Although annoyed his plan to single-handedly decimate Den de la Rocque was in danger, his shifters' presence struck a chord in him. He turned to Simeon. "Does Xavier know you're here?"

"He sent us to defend you with our lives, Alpha."

So Xavier bore him no ill will… stupid bastard.

Leon curled his lip. "Xavier is a sentimental fool!" He glared at Simeon. "Look at your so-called Alpha. Does he look like a shifter worthy of your life or is he a vampire who cares nothing for you or our ways?"

"We're here to defend him against all unfair challenges. Nothing you or…" Simeon turned and looked directly into Acier's eyes. "Anyone else here can say will change that."

Acier felt an ache begin somewhere deep inside. He snarled and tore his gaze away from Simeon's.

Leon growled low in his throat. "Before you fools die trying to protect a damned vampire, look around you. We are twenty-one strong against the eight of you. It will be a slaughter."

"Oh, I wouldn't go counting my goddamned victories before they were won, if I were you, shifter."

What the fuck now? Acier swung around. Shaun, Brett, and Damon duPre appeared. The oldest of the brothers, Shaun, a tall vampire with green eyes and red-gold hair, stepped forward, eyes glowing, incisors bared. "And I sure as hell wouldn't continue your insolent whine about our kind, shifter."

Their appearance annoyed Acier. What business did their kind have meddling in shifter business? "I do not require your help!"

Shaun grinned. "Still as arrogant as ever, I see, Acier. Perhaps when this is over, I may give myself the pleasure of kicking your supercilious ass."

Acier bared his incisors. "Anytime you feel like getting stomped into the ground, bring it on, vampire!"

Shaun laughed. "Don't tempt me."

Leon stared at Shaun. "This is none of your affair, vampire!"

Shaun shrugged and inclined his head toward Damon. "No, it isn't, but Junior here is blood brothers with Etienne. If you threaten Etienne, you might as well threaten Damon. And no one threatens Damon while one of us lives. If having the odds evened out a little scares you as shitless as you look, stand down, shifter."

Leon growled. "Never! I will be the next Alpha Supreme of Pack Gautier!"

You talk too damned much! Etienne sprang toward Leon.

Acier flashed in front of him. "No! His ass is mine."

One of the largest shifters with Leon padded forward. *We have come prepared to fight to the death to ensure the leadership of Pack Gautier remains pure and untainted by vile outside influences.*

"And we are here to ensure the challenge is fairly met," Simeon told him. "We are Den Gautier and we follow Acier Gautier to death and beyond. Attack him and die!"

In the presence of shifters pledged to die protecting him, despite his having abandoned them, feelings of loyalty and kinship warred with Acier's vampire nature.

He bared his incisors, turning his gaze on Leon. "I accept your challenge, de la Rocque. Make your move."

"But only you, de la Rocque," Shaun warned. "At the first sign of movement from your den, they will be slaughtered with extreme prejudice." He looked around the circle of Den de la Rocque shifters. "If any of you want a demonstration of the devastation three vampires are capable of creating, interfere and be the first to suffer a very painful death!"

Silence settled over the clearing. Etienne moved closer. Acier turned to him. What he saw in Etienne's eyes chilled him. Although he was there at his side, he sensed none of the brotherly love the two had always shared. Etienne was not there to defend him because they were brothers, but for some other less noble reason.

He gently probed Etienne's mind and was roughly rebuffed. He turned his attention back to Leon, a new feeling of rage welling up in him.

"I grow tired of this incessant shit, de la Rocque. It's time for you to die!" He shifted to his natural form and charged forward.

Several of the de la Rocque shifters growled and rushed at him, while the others formed a circle around Leon, who had also shifted. Etienne streaked past him, engaging the largest of the oncoming shifters. Aware that Simeon and those with him were at his back, Acier leapt over the circling shifters, landing only feet from the surprised Leon. Before those closest to Leon could attack, Simeon and those with him were also in the inner circle, growling out an angry challenge.

Determined to kill Leon himself, Acier leapt forward. Leon spun around in a quick circle. Unable to retreat, he lowered his head and rushed at Acier, mouth open. His teeth grazed Acier's right shoulder. Acier roared. Rising on his hind legs, he lifted his left paw. Keeping his claws sheathed, he delivered a powerful blow to the side of Leon's head. Leon's legs buckled, but he shook his head and rushed at Acier again.

Acier dropped to all fours and charged Leon. Bigger and heavier, he easily knocked the already stunned Leon off his feet. He sprang forward. Using his head and front paws, he forced the struggling, growling Leon onto his back. He placed his front paws on Leon's chest to pin him to the ground.

Ignoring the sounds and smells of the battle raging around them, he looked down into Leon's frightened gaze. *Now, de le Rocque, you die like the dog you are!*

Let me up, Acier, and I will relinquish all challenges. I swear! Let me up! Have mercy for the sake of our childhood friendship. I beg of you!

I will show you as much mercy as you would show me were our positions reversed, de la Rocque.

He saw a glint of relief in Leon's gaze. *Do you recognize my authority as Alpha-in-waiting of Pack Gautier?* he demanded.

Yes! Yes! Just let me up and we will leave.

Declare your submission.

I do. I swear it. I... I live to serve, Alpha.

Keeping his paws on Leon's body, Acier lifted his head. He saw Etienne to his right, tearing at the throat of a shifter. Etienne tossed the dying shifter aside and rose, looking around for another shifter to attack. Several shifters lay on their sides, their lifeblood slowly seeping out of their still bodies. Four were his, most Leon's.

Etienne padded toward a shifter standing over one of the Den Gautier shifters' still bodies. *Etienne. Enough. de le Rocque formally withdraws his challenge. Is that not so, de la Rocque?*

It... it is so. Den de la Rocque... withdraw, Leon told his shifters.

The shifters from Den de la Rocque withdrew to one side, keeping their gazes locked on the vampires and the shifters with Acier.

Acier looked at those of his lying wounded and dying on the ground. His rage intensified. He looked at Simeon. *You fought bravely and well.*

Simeon inclined his head.

His gaze again shifted to his kin dying on the ground. A lump formed in his throat.

Simeon offered a soft assurance. *It was their privilege to surrender their lives in your service, Alpha.*

Leon struggled beneath him, his breathing labored. *With your permission, Alpha, allow me to rise. Breathing while bearing your weight is difficult.*

He looked down at Leon. In the moonlight, he saw not his hated enemy, but a slender, blond boy who had been his friend for a number of years. Memories of running free across the night desert with Leon and Etienne at his side assailed his senses. Those times had been carefree and relatively happy ones. Leon had been his friend. For those times he could spare him.

A gasp of pain shattered the silence. Simeon rushed toward one of the shifters lying on his side. Acier tensed then hardened his heart. He turned his attention back to Leon.

Because of your cowardly challenge, four of my kin lie dying. If you think I will allow you to live so you can plot against me again in the future, think again, de la Rocque. It's time to pay for your cowardice.

Acier. For the love of God have mercy! I have submitted. I –

Time to die! He bent his head, bared his incisors, and sank his teeth into Leon's throat. Allowing the rage in him free rein, he began tearing at the flesh in a frenzy until Leon lay still, his life force flooding out of his body from the tangled mess that had been his throat.

Acier rose, lifted his head to the moon, and howled in rage and pain for the loss of his kin. Then he turned and looked at the four shifters remaining from Den de la Rocque. *Let any of you remaining cowards who would dare challenge me step forth and I'll send you to meet your maker like your leader!*

The remaining shifters from Den de la Rocque put their tails down and bowed their heads. *We live to serve, Alpha.*

Overcoming the urge to rush forward and slaughter them where they stood, Acier padded over to his dying kin, brushing his muzzle against each head. There was only life left in one. He lifted his tail weakly. *Alpha... you live?*

He lay beside the dying shifter. *Thanks to you. You fought well and bravely, Arcane.*

Then I die with no regrets. Live long... Alpha...

Acier remained beside him until he took his last tortured breath. Then he rose, roared out his rage, and charged toward the remaining Den de la Rocque shifters. *You cowards will pay for his life with your own!*

"No!"

He broke off his charge as Palea appeared in his path. *Stay out of this!*

"They have submitted to your authority. To kill them now would make you as much a coward as they are. Grant them mercy and show them that Acier Gautier, Alpha-in-waiting of Pack

Gautier, is fierce and ruthless in battle, but capable of great compassion and mercy when the occasion calls for it."

I have no compassion for them! Had they presented their challenge honorably, none need have died except de la Rocque.

"As their Alpha, it will be your responsibility to teach them honor. Show mercy, my little angry one."

He stared at her and knew she would not allow him to give them what they deserved—death! But there would be another time when she would not be around. He treated each shifter who had stood against him with a long stare. *The time will come,* he promised. *Go, but know your time of accounting will come.*

Palea tilted her head and stared at him. He knew she had read his thoughts. Too damn bad. She wasn't his mother.

One of Leon's shifters padded forward, his head bowed, his tail down. *May we take the remains with us, Alpha?*

He nodded curtly. Although he had taken his revenge, he was still filled with rage. He looked at Simeon. *Will you see to our dead?*

It will be an honor to accompany the remains of those who fought so bravely back to Den Gautier for the Rite of Passage. Will you come to preside over the Rite, Alpha?

It was no more than they deserved, but how could he preside over a ritual so sacred to his people when he was no longer the Alpha they died to protect? He averted his gaze. *Xavier is best suited for that honor. He has guided them while I've been away.*

He ignored the disappointment he sensed in Simeon. *As you wish, Alpha.*

Simeon's disappointment settling on his shoulders like a giant weight, he turned and fled through the woods to where he had left his motorcycle.

Etienne followed him. He turned and faced him. He shifted to his humanoid form. "I need to be alone. Leave me."

Etienne shifted and moved to stand within a foot, his gray eyes alight with rage. "Shaun was right. You are a supercilious bastard. What makes you think I have any desire for your company?"

"Then what the fuck do you want, pup?"

"Who was that fem back there?"

His lip curled. "Palea Walker-Dumont… our Nana… or so I'm told."

Etienne gave him a startled look, glanced back over his shoulder. "She might be your Nana, but she's not mine. I'm done with family and you! To show you just how finished I am with you, I'm going to find your woman and fuck her until she can't walk!"

He tossed back his head and laughed. "Be my guest. I have no further interest in that fickle little bitch."

Lights of lust sprang into Etienne's eyes. He disappeared in a silent flash.

Acier got on his motorcycle and roared away into the night. There was an endless ache inside of him. He wanted to go to Aleksei, but feared being rebuffed. He would go fuck and blood-drink his way out of the pit into which he'd fallen. Acier, the shifter, was dead. He would begin his life anew—as a full-blood vampire. He wanted nothing from his old life—except his Keddi. When he'd had his fill of sex and blood, he would visit Aleksei to pick up Drei. God help Xavier if he did not return Pen.

Chapter Seven

Two hours later, Acier lay in the arms of a luscious vixen with smooth skin the color of black coffee. Her large, firm breasts cushioned his chest, her arms held him close, her lips clung to his, as he repeatedly plunged his hungry cock balls deep in her sweet, tight pussy.

Her soft cries as he ravished her roused thoughts of Raven... Raven... the love of his life. Raven... lost to him like everything that had once been important. He shook off the feeling of melancholy. He was a vampire now. He had no further need of Raven. She and Etienne were welcome to each other for all he cared. From here on out, any pussy he fancied would be his for the taking.

But right now, he fancied some tight, hot, black ass. He pulled out of the convulsing pussy of the woman, now full of his cum, turned her over, and without the benefit of any lube, rammed his fully erect cock into her protesting ass. It felt so good, he came as soon as he was fully seated in her.

Uncaring that she was gasping in pain under him, he buried his incisors in the soft skin of her neck and fed on her. Damn, her blood was as addictive as Raven's. Perhaps he would keep the sweet bitch around... at least until thoughts of Raven no longer haunted him.

Several days, and countless women later, Acier bolted up in bed, his heart racing with fear. He blinked, unable to remember when he had returned to the RV. In the early morning light, he saw a statuesque redhead lying beside him. Numerous bruises covered her pale skin. Palm prints on her round butt aroused faint memories of his slamming his raging cock up her tight ass late into the night.

She slept soundly. He looked around the room. What had awakened him?

Alpha. Alpha... help me... please.

His nostrils flared and he sensed the presence of a cub... one of his... lost and in need of his protection. He leapt out of bed, snatching his discarded clothes from the floor. He rammed his feet into his shoes and ran toward the bedroom door.

"Acier? What's wrong? Where are you going so early?"

He glanced over his shoulder at the redhead. "I'm going out. Don't be here when I get back!"

"Fuck you!"

He tightened his lips. If he had the time, he'd teach the bitch some manners. Outside the RV in the predawn light, he mounted his motorcycle and drove out of the park. He reached out with his mind. *Where are you?*

Help me, Alpha. Please. I'm so afraid.

There's no need to be afraid. I'm coming, my cub. I'm coming.

Alpha! Please come!

Ten minutes later, he left his motorcycle along a narrow dirt trail leading into the woods. He ran along the path, his heart racing with fear. If anyone hurt his cub, he would rip their heart out! He burst into a clearing. A crumpled body lay near a big tree. He immediately recognized her.

He raced forward. "Cecily!" Kneeling at her side, he reached out to lift her gently into his arms.

She looked up and collapsed against him in a storm of tears, her entire body shuddering.

He closed his arms protectively around her, keeping alert. "Cecily. What's happened? Are you hurt?"

She wrapped her arms around his neck and lifted her wet face to his. "Yes, I'm hurt! I feel as if my heart has been torn from my body!"

"Why?" He gently pushed her away. He could see no physical signs of injury, but sensed a level of pain and anguish in her that nearly left him breathless with fear for her. "What's wrong? Who has hurt you? Tell me and I swear I'll make them pay. Who hurt you?"

"You did, Alpha!"

He stiffened and stared at her. "I?"

"Yes! You!"

Acier released her and bolted to his feet, trying to hold back a sense of panic. He raked a hand through his hair. Faint memories of fucking a young female with dark hair and dark eyes assailed him. Oh, God! Had he taken her with a brutal disregard for her pleasure or any pain he might have caused her? He tried to recall the face of the elusive lover, but her features eluded him. But she had been dark and slender... like Cecily.

Had he, in his vampire rage of lust, taken one of his own precious cubs? Oh, God, no! No! He dropped to his knees and stared at her. "Oh, God, Cecily... I... I didn't mean to... I didn't know... I... I wasn't myself... I... oh, God, I'm so sorry!" He reached out a hand to touch her bare shoulder and then snatched it back, bolting to his feet again.

How could he have touched one of his own precious cubs?

She stared up at him, tears streaming down her cheeks, her dark eyes filled with pain.

How long had she been alone with him after he'd defiled her? He shuddered with revulsion, bile rising in his throat. "When... did this happen?"

"When Simeon came back and said you would not be coming to preside over the Rite of Passage, most in the den thought you were lost to us forever... they said you no longer cared about us. But I knew it wasn't true, Alpha. It couldn't be true... we are your responsibility. So I came to find you and..."

And had her belief in him shattered when he'd defiled her. He spread his hands. "God forgive me! I... didn't mean to hurt you, Cecily. I would die before I'd ever bring you grief or pain."

She sucked in a breath then threw herself onto the ground, sobbing.

Acier watched, feeling powerless. He had entrusted her to Xavier's care. Xavier would pay for his negligence. He would— but it wasn't Xavier who had defiled her. He had. And the ultimate responsibility for what happened to her was not Xavier's, but his. His. He had accepted not only the mantle of Alpha-in-waiting, but that of Alpha of Den Gautier. Tossing away his right to lead Pack Gautier was one thing. The responsibility inherent in leading a den of shifters ran much deeper and was not so easily tossed onto the shoulders of another—as he'd tried to do.

It was time he faced up to the mess he had made not only of his own life, but of the lives of those who had entrusted their hearts and well-beings to his care. Thoughts of the hurtful way he and Raven had parted, along with the rage he'd nearly turned on Etienne and Xavier, the disrespect he'd shown Aleksei and Palea, weighed him down. All those mistakes paled in comparison to letting the members of his den down. To have refused to preside over the Rite of Passage for those who had died in his service and having defiled Cecily were unforgivable. He was not worthy to be a shifter.

For the first time since the transfusion, his thoughts were clear and he felt in complete control of himself. He knelt beside Cecily. "I'm so sorry I hurt you, Cecily."

She lifted her head and looked at him. He felt a gentle probing of his mind. He made no effort to rebuff her. A sudden smile spread across her face, then she bolted to her feet, and burrowed against him. "Alpha! It's you! You're back! You've returned to us!"

Before he could tentatively put an arm around her, she broke away from him and turned to stare into the woods. "Alpha Xavier, Alpha Xavier, come quickly."

Xavier emerged from the woods.

She rushed at Xavier, who gathered her in his arms. She lifted her face to his. "It's him, Alpha Xavier! You were right. Alpha has returned to us—just as you said he would!"

Xavier kissed her cheek and released her. He walked to Acier, bowed his head, and dropped to one knee. "Alpha, I live to serve."

He stared down at Xavier before glancing at Cecily. "Did I... hurt... touch you?"

"Touch me?" She frowned, then he felt the gentle probing again. She shook her head, her cheeks red. "No! No, Alpha! You didn't touch me like that. Forgive me for causing you such pain, Alpha. When I said you hurt me… I meant when everyone thought… everyone but me and Alpha Xavier, that you were lost to us… it hurt. I know the den loves me… but you are Alpha… what would I have if my Alpha didn't love me as one of his cubs?"

"Then I didn't… defile you?"

"No!" She moved forward and clutched his hand. "I will help you recall the past weeks if you like, Alpha."

Did he want to fully remember the things he'd done while undergoing his Feast of Indulgence? He shuddered, but decided it was necessary. He could hardly atone for mistakes he couldn't fully remember. "Yes."

She kneeled, her head bowed. "When you are ready, I stand willing to serve, Alpha."

"Thank you, my brave little cub."

He placed a hand on Xavier's shoulder. "Both of you, rise."

Xavier rose, a hint of tears in his eyes. "Welcome back, Alpha."

He drew Xavier into his arms and they embraced. He cupped a hand on the back of Xavier's head. "I'm so sorry for the way I treated you, Xay. I—"

Xavier pulled away from him. "Nothing matters except that you have returned to us."

Acier raked a hand through his hair. "My return is a little late."

"How so?"

"I've come to my senses too late to preside over the Rite of Passage."

Xavier arched a brow. "No, you haven't. I was so sure that if one of your cubs called out to you in distress that you would return to us, I postponed the Rite."

Tears filled Acier's eyes and he dropped to his knees at Xavier's feet. "I don't deserve your faith in me, Xay."

Xavier placed his hands under his arms and pulled him to his feet. "While I appreciate your sentiments, it's unbecoming of you to kneel in front of anyone but Alpha Supreme. Will you return to Arizona with us for the Rite, Alpha?"

"Yes. Immediately."

Xavier smiled. "I have an SUV capable of carrying your bike waiting down the path to our right and Alpha Supreme's private jet and pilot is waiting to take us home for the ceremony and the celebration."

"Celebration?"

"I left instructions with Simeon to plan a party to welcome you back where you belong."

"Xay... I'm not sure I'm the person I used to be. I—"

"Whoever you are, you are our Alpha and we are far stronger and more content with you than we could ever be without you. Your return to us is a cause for great celebration. Can we leave now or are there affairs you need to tend to here first?"

"I have a lot of arrangements that require a great deal of tending here, but my first duty is to our den. We will return home for the Rite of Passage."

Cecily slipped her arm through his and smiled up at him. "And the celebration. Oh, Alpha, it's so good to have you back!"

He embraced her. "It's good to be among those I love and care for most." He looked at Xavier. "Something has been bothering me. When Simeon and the others came to meet the challenge, they seemed... different."

"They were. After you were nearly killed by Falcone's poisonous bite, I decided to take measures to ensure de la Rocque would no longer have that advantage when his challenge was answered."

"What did you do?"

"I contacted Etienne and he put me in contact with Damon duPre. Damon and his brothers agreed to provide transfusions for the warriors who would be going up against de la Rocque."

Acier nodded slowly. So Etienne's close friendship with Damon duPre had benefits after all. He could easily imagine Damon, who had the annoying habit of thinking of Etienne as his brother, convincing his real brothers to provide blood for the transfusions. duPre would not have wanted to risk losing Etienne in a battle with Falcone.

"And none of them have any ill effects?"

"No, Alpha, but they only had minimal vampire blood transfused."

"I see." It seemed he owed Damon and his brothers a debt. "Well thought out, Xavier."

An hour later, he sat in Aime's private jet with Pen pressed against his neck, staring out the window, his thoughts on Raven. Petite. *Oh,* petite. *Where are you?* As soon as he returned from Arizona, he would search for her and do whatever it took to win her back.

He closed his eyes and reached out. *Etienne?* He called out several times, but there was no response.

He reached out again. *Father?*

A wave of warmth washed over him. *Acier! Welcome back, my son.*

Nana?

Acier, my brave little one, you are yourself again. Yes?

Yes, Nana.

He smiled and settled back in his seat. He stroked Pen's head, content for the moment.

* * *

"Ravanni... Ravanni..."

Raven opened her eyes. She lay on her back on a soft bed. Abby, her eyes filled with worry, bent over her, stroking her cheek.

"Abby?" She swallowed and sat up, grimacing. She ached all over.

"How are you feeling?"

"Dizzy." She sat back against the headboard, looking around Abby's hotel room. "How long have I been here?"

"I brought you here two days ago."

She frowned, sliding back down in bed. The last thing she remembered was agreeing to undergo the Progression with

Abby... how long ago? It felt like far more than two days. "What happened to me, Abby?"

"You underwent the Ritual of the Talisman... and..." Abby closed her eyes and sank down on the side of the bed. "We nearly lost you. Forgive me."

She squeezed Abby's hand. "There's nothing to forgive. You did what I asked—insisted you do. And I'm not dead." She just felt like half of her was missing. "Abby... I'm feeling a little... strange and I can't remember much of what happened. Is that... normal?"

"It's a coping mechanism. If you want it, the memory is easily recalled."

"Do I want to remember?"

Abby sighed. "Only you can determine if the memories are welcome. However, you accomplished what you set out to do."

"Then I guess it was worth it." She frowned. "Except that I feel as if a part of me... a vital part of me is missing... and I don't just mean my memory. Something is wrong." She bolted up in bed suddenly, clutching her stomach. "Oh my God, Abby! She's gone! Bentia is gone."

Abby nodded. "I know. The Progression required your body be purged of everything that wasn't an integral part of you. I didn't realize until it was too late. I'm so sorry."

She pressed her clenched fist against her stomach. "Is she... all right? Where is she? She's not... dead. Is she?"

"She's a living barrier spirit. I don't think she can die, but I don't know where she is."

"Will she return to me?"

Abby's lips trembled. "I... I don't know. I'm so sorry."

Raven pulled her knees against her chest and wrapped her arms around them. "It's all right, Abby. Even if I had known the risk of losing her, I would have done it anyway. It's all right. I'll be all right. Being without her will just take a little getting used to." She released her legs and leaned over and hugged Abby. "It's all right," she whispered. "I'd risk anything for him. Bentia of all living creatures would understand that."

She closed her eyes and reached out with her mind. *Bentia... wherever you are... if you want to and you can forgive me, I'll be waiting for your return.*

Abby squeezed her hand. "Now, you must rest to regain your strength and reconnect with your creed song."

"I need to see Acier."

"No. You must rest first." Abby sighed. "We came too close to losing you. You are in no condition to do anything but undergo the Ritual of Creedal Reconnection."

"And just what the hell is that? God save me from all this Willoni shit!"

Abby's lips tightened. "You have been spending too much time around those not of our ilk. You must show proper respect for our rituals and traditions. They are in place for your protection and well-being."

"And just how long will this ritual take and are there any nasty side effects I need to know about?"

Abby sucked in a breath. "Ravanni—"

She shook her head. "Okay. I give up. I'll go through with your infernal ritual." Besides, as weak and empty as she felt she didn't really have much choice.

Abby nodded. "I must go see my sister. Rest now. We will begin when I return."

Sensing an abnormal fear in Abby, Raven frowned. "Something is wrong. What is it?"

Abby averted her gaze. "I am having... difficulties."

"What kind of difficulties? What's wrong?"

"I'm having blackouts. I fear what might be happening when I am not... myself. I am... I will visit briefly with my sister Belladonna, then I will return."

"Can I help?"

"I require the assistance of an experienced guide I can trust. Please remain here and rest and I will return as soon as I can."

She nodded, sliding down onto her back. "But if you need me..."

"I know. Thank you."

* * *

Aleksei looked up from strumming his guitar, which lay on his desk. Margolis stood in the doorway. "It will be time soon. I have called the doctor. Gather the family."

He exploded out of the chair. "It's time? She's having the baby? Is she all right?" He raced toward the door, knocking his prized guitar off the desk in the process.

Margolis reached out and caught his arm. "Calm down. I have spoken to your offspring and all will be well."

"What? You've spoken to... you have? Is he all right?"

She smiled. "Your offspring is well. Now contact your family. When they arrive, provided they don't take too long, the birthing will begin."

He nodded, took several deep breaths, and then began hyperventilating.

She closed her eyes and pressed her hand against his chest. "Breathe slowly and deeply. Breathe and relax."

Her voice was low and hypnotic. Within moments, his breathing slowed. He walked back to his desk and picked up his guitar. Clutching it against his body with one arm, he sank down into his chair, and reached for the phone.

He thought of the challenge of getting everyone together when Vlad, Tat, and Andrei were avoiding Palea. Then there was the worry over Luc, who had not answered any of his entreaties. While he knew Acier had been brought back from the brink of insanity and was duly thankful, he feared that Luc had paid a dear price for Acier's return.

After he'd summoned the family and the friends he could reach, he walked slowly through the dark house, feeling weighed down with grief. At the bottom of the stairs, he saw a shimmer of heat, as if reflected off a desert floor. Then Luc appeared in front of him. Staggering under a wall of relief, Aleksei's knees buckled and he sank onto the carpet.

"Then you are happy to see me, Aleksei?"

He stared up at him. "I called you, but you didn't answer."

Luc drew him up, keeping his hands on his arms. "I was in the middle of... a crisis of sorts."

"Why didn't you answer? I thought... I thought I'd seen you for the last time." He jerked away from Luc. "Do you know how that made me feel? You should have answered! I've been half out of my mind thinking I was responsible for—for I-don't-know-what—happening to you!"

"I am sorry, Aleksei. I did not mean to cause you pain, but even I have obligations I cannot ignore. You'll forgive me."

"Says who?" He turned and sprinted up the steps. At the top he turned and looked down into the hall where Luc remained staring up at him, an inscrutable look in his eyes. He sighed. What the hell. "I think it's time you met Dani."

The words were barely spoken before a grinning Luc stood in front of him with a huge bouquet in his hand. "Does she like flowers?"

Aleksei arched a brow. "You'll have to show me how you do that one day."

"Don't count on it. I have to keep some secrets from you."

"Some secrets? You're shrouded in mystery. Just who and what the hell are you anyway? I know who and what everyone thinks you are—even vampires, but really... who are you?"

Luc gave him a long, considering look before he spoke. "Does it matter? If I were who everyone thinks I was... Lucifer... the devil... would it matter to you?"

He answered from the heart. "No."

Luc closed his eyes briefly, almost as if in relief. He placed a hand on Aleksei's shoulder. "Soon. You will know who I am soon enough, Aleksei. But for now... for now know that like any mortal father, I am prepared to do whatever is necessary to keep you safe and happy. Is that enough for now?"

"Yes." He nodded. "So... let me introduce you to Dani."

"And Acier? When will I meet him?"

"Hopefully soon... Father."

Chapter Eight

Nineteen hours later, the extended family gathered in the master bedroom. Aleksei lay on the bed, holding Dani in his arms while she screamed, cursed, and panted out their child.

Drs. Grinkolo and Margolis stood at the end of the bed, urging Dani on. Aleksei had no voice, overcome at the magnitude of being there at the birth of his and Dani's child.

"You're doing great, my lovely. A couple more pushes. Push… push…"

Dani screamed and pushed and then Dr. Grinkolo bent. When he straightened, he held a crying baby.

He looked at Aleksei, who had stopped breathing. "Aleksei and Dani, you have a healthy baby girl."

Aleksei laughed, kissed Dani, and looked at Palea, who stood on the other side of the bed. "Mother… I have a daughter!"

She smiled, reaching out to clutch his and Dani's hands. "Alexander! She looks like your father!"

He arched a brow, uncertain how she could tell who the baby resembled already. But he could see the thought of his child resembling his father pleased her — as it did him. He smiled.

"And what shall we call her, Alexander?"

Grinkolo spoke before he could. "Before you decide that… we'd better deliver her sibling."

Aleksei swallowed. "Her… sibling?"

"Yes, Aleksei. Twins do, after all, run in your family." Dr. Grinkolo handed the baby to Margolis and bent over Dani's open legs. "Come, my lovely one… push. We have another baby to see safely into the world!"

Five minutes later, with a beautiful baby girl resting in each of his arms, and Dani leaning against him, Aleksei lifted his head and looked across the room toward the door. Luc and Acier stood there, both smiling. To his relief, Acier had taken one look at Luc when they met and dropped to one knee, murmuring, "My Lord." Luc, his eyes shining, had called Acier "son of my son" and immediately lifted him to his feet and embraced him. He had a feeling a firm bond had formed between the two.

Aleksei released an inner sigh. These first moments of his daughters' lives were bittersweet. Although those he loved most were present to share in the joy and wonder of the birth of his twin daughters, there was undeniable tension in the room.

Vlad, Tat, and Andrei stood to one side of the room, steadily avoiding looking at Palea, who could not keep her gaze from shifting between the three of them. While fully understanding his siblings' reluctance to acknowledge a mother they had all spent hundreds of years thinking had abandoned them, it pained Aleksei to see the hurt and yearning in his mother's dark, expressive eyes. Over the last half century, he had become reacquainted with her and had again come to appreciate the depth of her unselfish and endless love.

His siblings were not yet ready to forgive her for a sin she had not committed. True, they now knew she had not abandoned them, but the feelings of distrust and hate they'd harbored for so long were not easily overcome. Even Vlad, who had called out to her in his grief when meeting Etienne, had made no effort to approach her.

Then there was Acier's pain. Although his son was himself again, Aleksei knew he had yet to find Raven and make peace with her. He also had pressing den and pack issues to handle. Acier's concern for Etienne was palpable. Aleksei allowed his gaze to shift to yet another corner where Etienne stood, eyes stormy, incisors barely covered. Adam, apparently unafraid of Etienne's rage, stood near him, with a hand placed on his shoulder. While Acier's integral love for his den members had finally snatched him from the brink of insanity, it was clear to all that the danger of losing Etienne remained.

Drei, shifted into a miniature version of Aleksei, who had spent so much time with Dani during the last days of her pregnancy, flew around the room in a frenzy, informing everyone that he had two beautiful goddaughters. Pen and Slayer, both in their natural forms, sat on one of the dressers urging Drei to shut the fuck up or else.

Mikhel, with one arm around Erica and his son Dimitri asleep on his shoulder, grinned at Aleksei from across the room. *You're going to love fatherhood.*

Aleksei inclined his head. *I love it already.*

Katie and her bloodlust Mark stood behind Palea and Matt Dumont. Serge and his bloodlust Derri looked on with smiles, a hint of sadness in their eyes.

Aleksei caught his youngest brother's gaze and spoke softly to him. *Don't despair. Your time will come, pup.*

When?

Patience, Serge. We will gather like this to welcome your and Derri's child one day.

When?

Patience, he urged again. *Look how long it's taken me.*

Cal Harris, Mik's friend and employee, was there, as were Serge and Derri's best friends, a married couple, Chandler and Cassy Raven. Finally, Xavier Depardieu was trying unsuccessfully to keep his gaze from continually wandering to Margolis's face. Michelangelo, unable to leave his dying uncle, had sent his congratulations and best wishes.

Margolis's sultry voice interrupted his thoughts. "And what are we to call these lovely new latents, Aleksei?"

He hesitated. He and Dani had discussed names. To his surprise, she had left the choice up to him, with the proviso that he not come up with anything she considered too outlandish. Of course, he had assumed the child would be male. He pressed his lips against the warm, brown skin of the daughter resting in the crook of his left arm. "I think we'll call the oldest after the two women who made the deepest impression on me as I grew up. Palea..." He smiled at his mother who caught her breath and clutched at Matt Dumont's hand, her eyes filling with tears. "...Sarah, for Sarah Madison, who so unselfishly took on the task of raising four frightened, latent vampires into adulthood. Dani?"

Lying with her head resting against his thighs, she nodded. "Palea Sarah… maybe Pali for short?"

Aleksei hid a smile at the look of dismay on his mother's face at what he was sure she would consider the maiming of her name. "Pali it will be."

"And this little beauty, I think we'll call Alexandra Lucinda."

Dani stirred against him. "I like it, but… why Alexandra Lucinda?"

He smiled at Palea, who stood unashamedly sobbing with joy. "Alexandra, after a man I will always love and never forget no matter how long I live, my father."

"Your father would be so pleased, my Alexander."

"I know, Mother."

Dani nudged an elbow into his body. "And Lucinda because?"

"Lucinda…" Aleksei looked across the room and caught Luc's gaze. "After a man who stood in the place of a third father to me at a time when I was lost and felt alone… after a man whose unselfish nature continues to humble and inspire me."

He couldn't read the look in Luc's eyes, but he felt the surprised delight from him.

"We'll call her either Lexie or Cindi," Dani said.

Dr. Grinkolo spoke. "The naming is over, it's time for the healing to begin. While Mari and I are here we will check Dimitri as well." Dr. Grinkolo scooped the girls into his arms and bore them away. Margolis approached Mik, who rather reluctantly handed her Dimitri. With Dimitri cooing in her arms, she left the room.

Drei expanded his miniature chest. *Will go protect daughters.* Directing a superior look at Slayer and Pen, he flew out of the room. Growling softly, Pen and Slayer followed, their small bodies shaking with suppressed rage and jealousy.

Everyone crowded around the bed, and Dani, rediscovering her modesty, squeaked and turned her face against his shoulder. He laughed, slapped her on her ass, and lifted her so they were groin to groin. He wiggled his hips against her, allowing her to feel his cock stiffening.

"Aleksei! What are you doing?"

"What does it feel like?" Nibbling at her ear, he lifted her hips, centered her over his cock, and eased forward. Ejaculating, he slowly slid his length into her body. After being denied the pleasure for so long, he closed his eyes to savor the wonderful sensations thundering through him as he took full possession of her warm, addictive cunt. Pussy was always so much more enjoyable when it belonged to a beloved bloodlust. He shuddered and pulled her all the way down on his cock until he was balls deep in her. "Oh, shit, I love you!" he murmured, stroking his palms down her back and big ass.

"Oh… God! Everyone's looking!" Even as she protested, she burrowed closer to him and greedily tightened her pussy around his cock.

He felt the heat of her blush down the front of her body. "It's our way, love. And remember, my cum will speed the healing."

He closed his hands over her ass and gently eased his cock in and out of her pussy, ecstasy shooting through him. Damn, there was nothing like a BBW with a large, lovely ass and a sweet cunt. Allowing his eyes to drift shut, he continued the gentle, healing fuck.

He felt a soft hand touch his cheek. Burying his cock deep in Dani's pussy, he paused and opened his eyes. Palea leaned over him, a sad smile lighting her eyes. "We will leave you two alone for your private celebration now, my little one." She cast her gaze around the room, allowing her eyes to settle briefly on the faces of Vlad, Tat, and Andrei before speaking again. "The celebration to welcome our two new joys into the family will begin in two hours. Everyone out."

Holding his cock still inside Dani, Aleksei watched Palea hesitate before she moved across the room toward Tat and Andrei. Tat shook her head and averted her gaze. Andrei gave her an indifferent stare.

He reached out to them. *Tatiana… Andrei… please.*

Tat walked over to the bed, shaking her head. "Aleksei, I won't be staying."

He sensed a well of turmoil in her he suspected was not entirely centered around her desire not to be forced to welcome Palea back into her life. He searched her gaze. Was it that damned Timbersmith again? If it was, he had an ass whipping coming he would remember as long as he lived — however a short time that might be.

She shook her head again, her lips tightening. *Stay out of this, Sei. I can handle my own personal affairs without interference from my big brother.*

He'd stay out of it — when hell froze over! In the meantime, he was annoyed that his first fuck with Dani in weeks was put on hold. He reluctantly eased out of Dani, who immediately rolled to her side, trying to conceal as much of her naked body as possible. Shielding his thoughts, he smiled at Tat, inclining his head.

She sighed in relief.

He turned his attention to Andrei. "Will you stay?"

"I'd like to, Sei." Andrei glanced at Tat. "But I can't."

Aleksei looked at Tat. "When things aren't going well, you need to be with family. Tatiana… Andrei… please stay…"

She shook her head. "I know this is an important occasion… and I am so… thrilled for you and Dani, Sei, but I've had all I can deal with just now. Please understand and forgive me."

He glanced at Palea, who stood staring at Tatiana and Andrei with a look of longing in her dark eyes. His heart ached for them all. He smiled at Tat. "I understand and there's nothing to forgive. Call me if you need me, my lovely."

"I will, Sei."

She turned to face Palea. "Sei has told us we were wrong in thinking you'd deserted us. While we believe him… we… I… need time to adjust."

Palea's eyes filled with tears. "I understand and I will try to wait… but it has been so long, my lovely one. I have spent over three hundred years grieving your loss… never knowing you were all alive and needing... hating me." She pounded a clenched fist against her chest. "For the pain I feel now, it would have been better had I died that night than to be the cause of such grief and pain in your lives for so long."

Tat's lips trembled and her eyes filled with tears. "I... I'm sorry... I know this must be difficult for you... please... just give me a little more time."

Tears streamed down Palea's cheeks. "I will try, my lovely one, but if you knew how my heart aches to hold you both again, you would not ask this great impossibility of me." She gulped in a deep breath. "If I could just hold you both... for just a few moments... I would happily surrender my life for that privilege. The need eats at me... tearing my heart into pieces..."

Katie pulled away from Mark and approached Tat, tears in her eyes. "Please. I can sense your great capacity for love and forgiveness. If you can forgive him, why not her?"

Aleksei saw Tat stiffen. "Him? Who do you mean?"

"You know who I mean. I have seen you two together."

"I have not yet determined I will forgive him."

Katie stared at her. "I can see the future. You will face difficult choices... some of them dangerous. You will need us then as much as she now needs you. Make it easier on yourself by forgiving her now."

The two sisters, one under forty, the other over three hundred years old, faced each other. "My future and decisions are not guided by what you *think* you have seen, little one. Do not make the mistake of meddling in my affairs."

Katie's eyes sparkled with defiance. "You're hurting my mother!"

Tat's shoulders tensed. "Do not forget your place, Kattia. She was my mother first!"

"Then act like it!" Katie shouted. "Show her the respect and love she deserves!"

"I will! In my own time!" She stared into Katie's angry gaze. "You are very young yet, but you are a full-blood. You know the family hierarchy, which places you, as the youngest child, at the bottom. Do not challenge me again."

Katie lifted her chin. "To save her from a grief she does not deserve, I would challenge the devil himself!"

Aleksei tensed, certain Katie was about to be backhanded across the room—several times. Tat was not one to suffer insolence from a younger sibling, as Andrei had learned the hard way years earlier. Instead, Tat stroked Katie's cheek. "I can see that you would."

"Damn right I would!"

"It is going to be interesting to get to know you..." She glanced at Palea. "... and to get to know you again... Mother." With that, she turned and flashed out of the room.

Andrei sighed. *She's going through a very difficult time. She won't admit it, but she needs me. I'd like to stay and share in your joy, Sei, but I have to go after her.*

As I would go with Vlad. I know, Andrei. If either of you need me...

We know, Sei.

Andrei hesitated before he approached Palea. "She doesn't mean to hurt you..." He bent his head and brushed his lips against her cheek.

Palea sucked in a breath. "Andrei... my little lost Andrei." She clutched at his arm. "My little lost, handsome Andrei..."

"I have to go."

"Please... stay... for just a moment... just a moment... my Andrei... let me hold you... it's been so long... my heart and my arms have longed to embrace you... just for a few moments... my Andrei..."

He shook his head and gently peeled her fingers from his arm. "Tat needs me." With that, he turned and flashed out of the room.

Pressing a hand against the cheek Andrei had kissed, Palea dropped to her knees. Mikhel and Serge rushed across the room to kneel beside her, putting their arms around her. Katie and Matt

Dumont joined them and the five of them clung together, tears streaming down all their faces.

Dani sobbed softly and Aleksei knew she was thinking of her relationship with her two children. Feeling a lump of emotion lodge in his throat, he turned his gaze to Vlad.

Vlad, who now stood between Adam and Etienne, met his gaze. Aleksei saw his own pain and anguish reflected in his twin's gaze. *It's time to heal, Vlad... for you both... time to forgive and embrace what you lost so long ago through no fault of anyone still alive.*

He watched Vlad turn to look at Etienne, who gave his father a cold, hard stare. With Etienne still in the throes of bloodlust and filled with an almost murderous hostility, Aleksei suspected Vlad was going to need Palea's love and support more than ever.

Vlad touched Etienne's cheek and promptly had his hand slapped away. Aleksei resisted the urge to flash across the room and backhand Etienne. Instead, he turned his gaze to Acier. As he had done in the past with Vlad, Acier was now helplessly watching as his twin spiraled deeper into despair and near madness. Father and son shared a brief, pained glance before Aleksei looked at Vlad again.

It's time, Vladimir.

Vlad inclined his head slightly. Propelled by a hand in his back from Adam, he stumbled across the room to the spot where Matt Dumont and his children kneeled on the floor trying to comfort Palea.

Vlad paused by them, his shoulders slumped, his air of dejection plain. Aleksei sucked in a pained breath. Vlad looked much as he had so long ago — when a grief-stricken Aleksei had told him their father was dead — lost, alone, and afraid.

Reach out to her, Vladimir. Start the healing for you both, he urged softly.

Vlad's shoulders rose and fell. He extended a hand. "Mother?"

Palea, her small frame hidden by those of her husband and children, struggled free of the loving arms embracing her. At a quiet word from Matt, he and the others released Palea, rose, and stepped away from her, leaving her kneeling on the floor.

Mikhel, who Vlad had once threatened to kill, cast an anxious look at Aleksei. Of Palea's three youngest children, only Mikhel had witnessed the first reunion between Vlad and Palea just weeks earlier. Mikhel had seen firsthand Vlad's former hatred of their mother.

It's all right, Mikhel, Aleksei assured him. *He's hurting now and he just needs her.*

Mikhel inclined his head, looked at Palea still kneeling with tears in her eyes, and when Erica touched his back, turned, and buried his head against her, his shoulders shaking.

Derri urged Serge into her arms, stroking his hair. "It's all right, gray eyes. It's all right."

Matt put an arm around Katie and walked her across the room to Mark, who embraced her as she sobbed.

That left Vlad and Palea alone. She looked so small and helpless as she looked up at him, her dark eyes begging for forgiveness.

Vlad extended a hand to her. "Mother…"

Sobbing, she bolted to her feet and threw her small body against his. "*Malchik moy!* My *malchik moy!* God has forgiven me for my many sins and given me back my *malchik moy*… the child of my heart!"

Her knees buckled and she started to fall. His lips moving silently, Vlad swept her up into his arms.

No longer able to control his emotions, Aleksei allowed his tears to fall as he watched Palea wrap her arms around Vlad's neck, while pressing desperate kisses against his face. With his head bent and tears streaming down his cheeks, Vlad walked out of the room with her cradled in his arms.

The others slowly drifted out of the room until only Acier remained.

Dani lifted her head from his shoulder. "Sei? Are you all right?"

I am now. Wiping his cheeks, he beckoned to Acier, his joy tempered by the lingering pain he sensed in his son.

Acier crossed the room to them. "I won't be staying either. I need to find Raven and... I don't know what I'm going to do about Etienne... or Den de la Rocque leadership."

Aleksei recalled what Margolis had said about her kinsman. "Go and find your woman, Acier, and deal with pack business, but do not worry overmuch about Etienne. Margolis has a kinsman far more skilled than herself. He can guide Etienne back when the time is right."

"Are you sure?"

"Positive."

"I couldn't bear to lose him."

"I know. None of us could. While you tend to your dens, Mikhel and Serge will continue to watch over Etienne... as will Luc."

Acier frowned. "Who — what — is he?"

"Luc? Your guess is as good as mine. Now. About Xavier."

"What about him?"

"Can he remain?"

"Yes, but why?"

"Why?" Aleksei smiled. "Can you say Margolis?"

"Mar... really?"

"Didn't you see how he looked at her or how hard he tried not to look at her? He's been through a lot and deserves a little reward."

He nodded. "Simeon is capable of caring for the pack until one of us returns." He frowned. "Do you think she's interested in him? You know he's more than competent, but he's very young."

"I've heard some women like young men they can teach and mold. And if a third of what I've heard about the sexual prowess of the healers is true, Xavier is in for quite an experience."

"He deserves it. I put him through so much while—"

"I'm sure he doesn't hold that against you."

"I know, but that's what makes my actions so much worse. He idolized me and I came within a breath of killing him."

Aleksei shook his head. "In this family, we protect and cherish our young. You would not have killed him, Acier."

"I'd like to believe that, but I'm just not certain."

"I am."

He sighed. "Can I leave the Keddi here for a little while longer?"

"Of course. I think you'd have a problem getting Drei to leave right now anyway."

A brief smile touched Acier's lips before he glanced away, then quickly bent and kissed the top of Dani's head. "Congratulations. I will look forward to getting to know my beautiful little sisters."

Dani smiled and squeezed his hand. "And when you have time, I look forward to getting to know you, Acier."

Sensing Acier's lack of enthusiasm for getting to know Dani, Aleksei suppressed a sigh. God, would the problems never end?

To his delight, Acier pressed a quick kiss against his cheek. *Father, we need to talk about you and Mother. I know this isn't the time, but we need to do it... soon.*

Aleksei briefly closed his fingers in Acier's hair. *I know. After Dani and I deal with telling her kids about the girls and who and what I am, I'll come to you. Can you give me time to help Dani deal with her issues?*

Yes.

Thank you, Acier. If you need me before then...

He nodded. *I know.*

Left alone with Dani in the room, Aleksei turned her body so she lay facing him. Holding his aching cock in one hand, he slid it slowly back inside her.

"Yes! Yes! Oh God, yes! Give me all that sweet, golden cock, baby! Every hard, thick, hot inch! It's mine and I want it buried deep in my cunt where it belongs!" she screamed, thrusting her hips down until their pubic hair met.

Aleksei smiled. Now that they were alone, he had his wild woman back. "Hmmm. Someone is behaving like a cock-hungry wanton."

She grabbed his hips and fucked herself on his cock. "Shut up and fuck me, you big, handsome vampire, or I'll tie you up and beat your tight ass until you beg for the privilege of getting a little pussy!"

Dani was fond of stretching his arms over his head and binding them and torturing him by withholding her pussy until he was nearly mad with lust. Although he did not enjoy bondage, even when the bonds were silk scarves, he occasionally swallowed his distaste and allowed her to dominate him during sex.

But he was not in the mood to be submissive. He lifted her head, pressed his lips to hers, and lost himself in a long, sweet, healing fuck, sliding his cock in and out of her slowly, savoring the exquisite delight found only within the arms of his beloved bloodlust.

Sweet lips parting under his, she rubbed her big breasts against his chest, and overwhelmed his senses with a passion that was even more invigorating and exciting than it had been during their first night together. This beautiful, giving woman had risked her relationship with her adult children to pursue him. And now she had given him the ultimate gift of love, two precious babies.

"I love you so much," he whispered, holding her tenderly as she cried out and came. He caressed and stroked her as she shuddered through her climax, only then coming himself.

Afterwards while they lay in a tangle of arms and legs, he sensed tension in her. "Dani?"

"This has been one of the happiest days in my life. The girls are gorgeous and I already love them so much I ache with it, but…" She sighed. "I was just thinking… wishing Janie and Frank could have been here to share in our joy."

"I know. I'm sorry they weren't. Are you ready to tell them about what I am?"

"I don't know. Frank is… supportive of our relationship and I know that given time Janie will be too… but I don't know how they'll react."

"I could help."

"No!" She drew away from him, pulled herself off his cock, and sat up. "I don't want you clouding their minds, Aleksei. They either have to accept you as you are… or not. But I don't want you invading their thoughts."

He drew her back into his arms. "I'll leave it up to you if and how we tell them, Dani."

"I think we'll have to tell them. The girls are latents… will there be any indications they're not fully human?"

"I don't know. Latent abilities vary. When my siblings and I were latents we appeared human… until we survived being drowned. Even then we weren't fully sure of what we were until we were adults and Vlad and I encountered a fem one night and got our first taste of pussy and blood."

She settled against him. "We'll tell them."

"When?"

"When everyone leaves in a day or two. You'll be kind to Janie, won't you, Sei?"

He stifled a sigh. He liked her son Frank but he and Janie had never gotten along. "I'll be on my best behavior."

"Thanks, Sei."

"I would do anything for you, my lovely Dani."

She smiled and brushed her lips against him. "Ditto, handsome. Now, how about doing me again?"

"Oh, baby, I love it when you get all wanton and horny," he whispered and slid his cock back inside her. Damn, but sex with her was beyond good. Sliding his hands over her ass and urging her lips apart, he stroked both his tongue and his cock into her delicious openings. Nothing short of paradise.

Chapter Nine

Deoctra stood over the body of Leon, laid out for viewing in the rec room of his home in Arizona. The members of his den had done their best to convince her not to open his coffin, but she had been insistent. She needed to see what Acier Gautier had done to him.

She had no tears left, but the ache inside her swallowed all emotions—except hate and her thirst for revenge. Her hopes for the future lay before her in the form of Leon's battered body with his throat torn out. Although the sight of him hurt, she forced herself not to look away. The sight would help fuel her thirst for retribution.

She stroked her hand down his flank. "I will avenge you, Leon. I swear it. Acier might not die, but someone close to him will either die or know the pain I feel now. I will avenge you!"

She curled her fingers in his fur, forced the lump forming in her throat down, and hurried from the room. When she emerged from the house, Falcone stood by his SUV. He approached her, placing a hand on her arm. "Damn, I'm sorry."

She shook off his hand. "You're not sorry! You wanted me for yourself and now you think you have no competition!"

He grabbed her arms and jerked her body against his. "Okay, I'm not sorry and you will be mine." His lips crashed down on hers.

With the memory of Leon's kiss and taste haunting her, she parted her lips and melted against Falcone's big, hard body, seeking warmth and some shelter in physical pleasure from her mental anguish. He pushed her into the back of his SUV. She lay silent as he opened her cat suit. Allowing his gaze to feast on her exposed nakedness, he growled deep in his throat, and slowly mounted her.

Holding her hips, he pressed forward, forcing his cock between the lips of her sex, and deep into her cunt. Resting his body on hers, he rotated his powerful hips, allowing her to feel the full length and weight of his hard flesh. Full of shifter dick, she sighed. When she closed her eyes, she saw Leon. She curled her fingers in Falcone's hair and allowed a single tear to slide down her cheek. *Oh, Leon!*

"To hell with him. He's gone. You're all mine now, bitch!" He crashed his lips down on hers and fucked her with a hard, relentless passion which sent her body shattering in minutes. Even as he clutched her tight and fucked her harder still as she gasped through one orgasm after another, her thoughts centered on what was lost to her. *Leon. Leon...*

* * *

Acier saw Raven's car when he pulled into the RV park. He stopped his bike and raced to the RV. The door opened and Raven stood there. He stopped abruptly, his heart racing, his ability to breath and think or talk severely hampered by the lump of emotion choking him.

She looked as breathtakingly beautiful as she had when she'd first shown up what felt like months instead of weeks earlier. Her lips curved in a smile, but he sensed a difference in her... a sadness and a loss of innocence he knew could be attributed directly to him. She had come to him a virgin. He had deflowered her, brutalized her, and then slept with her sister and more women than he could remember.

The hurtful words he'd hurled at her the last time they saw each other rang in his ears. How could he ask or even expect her to forgive him? The hand he reached out to her shook. She took it between both of hers and drew him inside and into her arms. He embraced her, pressing his cheek against hers. "I'm sorry, *petite*... so sorry... forgive me... forgive me..."

"There's nothing to forgive, Acier."

He drew back, lifting her chin so he could look into her eyes. "Then why are you calling me Acier?"

She pulled away from him. "Things have changed, as have we. The girl who fell in love with Steele is gone."

He raked a hand through his hair. "I know... I killed her."

She shrugged. "It was time she grew up anyway."

"I... I never meant to hurt you, *petite*."

"Oh, yes, you did."

Oh, shit! "Okay, I did, but—"

"But?" She cast a cool look in his direction and walked into the living area where she sat.

He followed her, sitting across from her. He longed to reach out and take her back in his arms, but there was a decided touch-me-not aura surrounding her. "Have you come to say goodbye, *petite*?"

"Is that what you want? When I left you said—"

"I know what I said, but I did *not* mean any of that!"

"Oh, Acier, I think you did." She tossed her head, sending her long, dark hair cascading around her face and shoulders. "As a matter of fact, I know you meant every word of the hurtful things you said to me. You wanted to be free to enjoy other women. Did you?"

He swallowed slowly. If he had any hope of rebuilding what he'd destroyed, he'd have to be truthful with her. Noting the pain in her gaze, he prayed her remaining feelings were strong enough for her to weather the coming revelations. "Yes. Yes, I did, but I swear... you were never far from my thoughts. Even when I was with..."

"When you were with who, Acier?"

Oh God, when he told her about Treena, she would never forgive him. When she'd first arrived, he had berated her for desiring Etienne. How could he expect her to forgive his betrayal with her sister? "I... after you left I... she just showed up out of nowhere and I... I couldn't help myself. I... I couldn't stop."

She clenched her hands together. "Who showed up?"

"Treena." He watched her face, waiting for the dismay, shock, anger, and disbelief.

"Did you really think of me while with her and the others?"

"Yes! I know you'll find this difficult to believe, but you are the only woman I've ever loved and even when I was in the grip of my feast, you were never far from my thoughts." He rose and kneeled in front of her. "Can you forgive me, *petite*?"

She stroked a hand down his cheek. "I suppose I'll have to… I love you. Besides… I have a confession of my own."

She'd slept with Etienne! He knew it. He bolted to his feet and turned away. He had no right to be jealous or angry, but the thought of her with another man was not something he would ever find easy to take. He felt her hand on his back and reluctantly turned to face her.

"I know what you're going to say and—"

She pressed her fingers against his lips. "No, you don't. I did not sleep with Tee or anyone else while we've been apart."

He trembled with relief. Having finally accepted who and what he was, he knew she would eventually sleep with Etienne, but to know it hadn't happened yet acted like a balm to his aching heart. "Then what do you want to tell me?"

"You know all those women you slept with during your feast?"

His cheeks burned and he sucked in a deep breath. "Raven… *petite*, I'm so sorry. I couldn't help myself."

"It's all right, Acier. You have no need to apologize. There's a very good reason why you thought of me when you were with those other women."

"There is? What?"

She moved closer and stared in his eyes. "Because I was those women… all of them. You didn't sleep with anyone else, Acier."

He frowned. "What?"

"There is a talisman that is very old with origins on the home world of my mother, who, as you know, is not human. By undergoing this ancient ceremony called the Progression of the Talisman, I was able to master skills usually only acquired after hundreds of years of temple service. This ritual allowed me to tap into your innermost desires and fantasies."

"How?"

"I probed your mind."

"What? You invaded my thoughts?" He shot to his feet and stared down at her. "You had no right to do that, Raven!"

She lifted her chin. "After loving you for so long, I was not about to sit back and risk losing you to your vampire lusts. And I sure as hell was not going to allow you to fuck a succession of women and then crawl back into my bed. I'm not some weak woman to take shit like that lying down and then forgive you. Do you—"

"And that made it okay?"

She tossed her head angrily, sending her long, dark hair flying around her shoulders again. Her green eyes sparked with defiance as she rose to face him. "You would have preferred to have fucked all those other women?"

"That's not the point!"

"It is from where I stand! I did what I had to do to protect my interests." She hit a balled fist against his shoulder. "Your aunt said I had to let you work through your feast without taking your lust for sex with other women personally. But there was no way in hell I was going to sit back and wait while you roamed all over the place fucking any and every woman in sight.

"I am Willoni and I am strong enough to protect and keep what belongs to me. I found a way for both of us to get what we needed. If you think I'm going to apologize for doing what was necessary to keep what's mine, think again, Acier! Especially when I lost something precious to me in the process."

"What?"

Her eyes filled with tears. "Bentia… when I underwent the Progression… she was cast out and she hasn't come back."

Although he didn't personally regret the loss of the barrier spirit who had come between him and Raven too often for his taste, he regretted the pain he saw in her eyes. He stroked her cheek. "Will she return to you?"

Her lips trembled. "I don't know."

He drew her into her arms and held her. "I'm sorry, *petite*."

"So am I." She lifted her head and looked at him. "But I don't regret what I did."

"Neither do I, *petite*."

"You're sure?"

"Yes, but that doesn't mean I want you invading my private thoughts, Raven. I'm not going to have that. Is that understood?"

She nodded. "Yes."

"Good." He tightened his arms around her. "Now let's go to bed. I am mentally and physically exhausted."

Minutes later, lying with her warm, naked body cradled against his, he found sleep elusive.

She stroked a hand down his thigh. "Don't worry, Acier, Etienne will be all right in the long run… I have… seen it by means of my soul song."

"In the short run?"

"He is still in the grip of his feast, but he will be all right."

"Thank God!"

"What about you, Acier?"

"I'm… okay. I've finally come to terms with who and what I am."

She brushed her lips against his shoulder. "And who is that? Are you a shifter hybrid or a vampire hybrid?"

"I think it's clear that at least physically, I am now a vampire hybrid… but in my heart, I will remain a shifter hybrid."

"Does that mean you can deal with everything bloodlust entails?"

He stiffened. "If you're asking if I can deal with your sleeping with Etienne… I will never welcome it… but I now accept that it's a big part of who Etienne and I are. And I know he needs to be with you as part of his healing process. Perhaps if I hadn't been so selfish, he—"

"No! It wasn't selfishness, Acier. You were raised a shifter. The idea of sharing your woman was an alien concept. Given that, your attitude was perfectly understandable. And it's not your fault Tee is still feasting."

"You're sure he'll be all right?"

"Yes. I can't see my own future with any degree of certainty, but I do know, in the long run, he will be fine."

He caressed her ass. "And you, *petite*?"

"Me? I am Willoni."

"And what exactly does that mean for you and for us?"

"In the short run, it doesn't change anything for us. I am as much in love with you as I've ever been. I'll always be in love with and love you, Acier."

"And in the long run?"

She stirred against him. "One day I will be called upon to fulfill my temple service. That will require leaving you and Earth."

He stiffened. "And will you?"

She lifted her head and looked down into his eyes. "I don't know. Can you live with that uncertainty, Acier?"

"Yes."

"No hesitation?"

"No."

She frowned down at him. "Why not? Because you don't love me as much as I love you?"

"No! Because, when that time comes, I'll find a way to stay with you... just as you stayed with me and saw me through the darkest time in my life. I'm still shifter enough to know we belong together forever—regardless of what I have to do to make that happen."

A smile curved her lips. "You'd do that for me?"

He closed his fingers in her hair. "Isn't that what love is all about?"

Her eyes welled with tears. "Yes."

"*Petite*, I think when we go to Treena's wedding, I'm going to have to have a talk with Mo."

"Dad? What about?"

"I love you and I think it's time I made an honest woman of you."

"Oh. So you want me to believe you want to marry me because you love me?"

"Yes."

"Fat chance! I happen to know you're scared shitless of what Dad will say if I show up at Treena's wedding pregnant and unengaged!"

He laughed. "Okay. That too. So? You interested?"

She traced the outline of his lips with the tip of her tongue, sending jolts of desire through him. "I'm not sure. Convince me."

He slapped her ass. "Don't make me get physical, *petite*."

Her eyes darkened. "Have you gotten all the… need to be so… physical during lovemaking out of your system?"

"Raven… that was driven by the vampire part of me. I will do my best to never lose control like that again… but I will always be part vampire."

"I know. I love you just as you are and I wouldn't change a thing about you."

"Not even that?"

"Not even that." She reached between their bodies, cupped his cock, bringing it to rest against her pussy. "It took some getting used to, but I discovered I kind of like you wild and out of control in bed. I discovered I liked how you hungered for sliding that big, sweet dick of yours into all my openings.

"You know, Acier, while you were undergoing your feast, I discovered something surprising about myself. I kind of like rough sex and I love having your hard, lusty cock slamming deep into my ass, making my pussy tingle and flood with lust."

He shuddered as she slid his cock between the lips of her pussy and into her slick warmth. "Fuck me, Acier. Make me scream and sob as you did during your feast and I'll marry you in a heartbeat."

He sucked in a breath, feeling his lust rise. "One raunchy fuck coming up, my sweet, adorable bitch!"

"I'm yours, Acier. No matter what challenges the future holds, I will always belong to you."

"Even when Etienne has his oversized cock in you fucking you senseless?"

"Especially then!" But he sensed her excitement at the thought of being fucked by Etienne. Although surprised Etienne hadn't already tracked her down and fucked her, he feared the time was fast approaching when he would. When that happened, he would grit his teeth and learn to accept it as Etienne's right.

He cupped his palms over her face and stared into her eyes. "But your ass is all mine. Right?"

She gave him a wicked smile. "For now."

He sucked in a breath. "Don't fuck with me, Raven," he warned.

Eyes sparkling with mischief, she licked her lips and settled against him, pressing her sweet, warm lips against his mouth. He slid his hands down her back to cup her ass in his palms. Life offered no guarantees, even that he wouldn't eventually have to share her beautiful ass with Etienne, but as long as he had his woman… his bloodlust, the future was something to be joyfully embraced.

Moonlight Healing
Marilyn Lee

Chapter One

Raven Monclaire stood near the doors of the large ballroom in the prestigious Four Seasons Hotel. Dancing couples, arrayed in dark suits and beautiful dresses, swayed in rhythm with the pulse pounding music. An hour earlier, the music had been soft, the dancing slow and the couples close together. Her mood had been much lighter—until she'd shared a last slow dance with her fiancé, Acier Gautier.

After that dance, Acier and his identical twin brother, Etienne, left the reception. Recalling the intimate way Etienne danced with the bride, Treena, grinding his groin against her while he palmed her ass, Raven closed her eyes briefly. She'd prevailed upon Acier to insist Etienne leave with him when Acier headed back to Arizona. If her father had seen that scandalous dance… or if Derek had…

In the past Raven had always been delighted to see Etienne, or Tee, as she'd always called him, but he'd changed over the course of the previous months. So had Acier. Part vampire and part wolf-shifter, Acier and Tee had recently undergone a vampire ritual called the Feast of Indulgence.

This Feast of Indulgence, during which a vampire went from a latent or half-blood status to full-blood status, could be a dangerous time for any human who loved such a person—as she loved Acier.

She frowned. Not that she was completely human. Although her father was human, her mother had been a Willoni Priestess. Like vampires and wolf-shifters, the Willoni were an ancient race from the Aeolian planetary system. Unlike the other two groups, skillful Willoni could see and sometimes even shape the future.

Raven had discovered that the ability to see the future could be as much a curse as it was a blessing. Her recent visions disturbed and frightened her. If they proved true, there were grim and painful times ahead for her and those she loved most.

At the moment she had more pressing matters to consider than worrying about a future she might or might not have seen or interpreted correctly. The Goddess willing, the weeks and months ahead would not be as frightening as those that had gone before. During Acier's feast, she'd done what was necessary for Acier to work out his sexual aggression and hunger without harming her or being unfaithful. Acier had recovered from the near madness into which the Feast of Indulgence inevitably plunged a vampire.

The feast still held Tee firmly in its grip. Prior to his unexpected appearance at the church that morning, neither she nor Acier had seen Tee in weeks. The brothers who had once been so close were now emotionally worlds apart. She knew Acier worried about Tee's mental state. After that indecent dance with the newly married Treena, she knew Acier's fears were well founded.

But Tee was gone, and she should enjoy the rest of the reception without worrying about what he might do with Treena. She glanced at the large diamond engagement ring on the third finger of her left hand. If things continued to go well for her and Acier, the next time her family gathered for a wedding reception, it would be to celebrate her marriage to the big, handsome Acier.

Then she would be the one looking as if she were floating on air as she danced with their father. She narrowed her gaze and blinked. That wasn't Treena dancing with their father. It was her other sister, Kiki. So where was Treena?

"Hey, hon, can you do me a favor?"

The man in front of her was tall, well built, and extremely handsome. Small wonder Treena had taken one look at this Boris Kodjoe look-alike and fallen into lust and then in love with Derek. Raven slipped her arm through his. "Of course. What do you need?"

"Treena went to change nearly an hour ago. She made me promise not to follow her. Will you go and tell her to get the lead out?" He glanced at his watch. "I'm going to change in my parents' room and I'd like to get away in another hour. Tell her if she's not here by then I'm coming to get her."

The night before, Treena had told Raven and Kiki that she'd stopped sleeping with Derek six weeks earlier so he'd be hungry for her on their wedding night. Raven arched a brow and looked up at him. "What's the rush?"

"I'm eager to start the honeymoon. If she doesn't hurry up, we'll be starting it right here instead of tonight. Get her for me?"

"Of course. You know I've always wanted a big brother."

"And I've always wanted a gorgeous younger sister."

She kissed his cheek and left the ballroom. As she waited at the elevator bank, she smiled, remembering Acier's goodbye kisses. They had been deep, sweet, and scorching hot. Feeling his long, thick cock pressed against her as he held her had really aroused her. By the Goddess, she loved him. If her father had seen the passion she and Acier shared, he'd have insisted they get married immediately.

Her smile vanished as she recalled the look in Tee's eyes when Acier finally released her. Tee's gray eyes had turned that distinct gold, as they did when he was in what Acier had called prowl heat. Casting a quick look downward, she'd noted the clear outline of Tee's hardened cock against his thigh.

Flushing, she looked away from the raw sexual hunger in Tee's eyes to find Acier's gaze on her. Part of Acier and Tee's vampire heritage made it acceptable for brothers or sisters to sleep with their siblings' bloodlusts, or perfect mates. Since Acier had finally accepted his vampiric blood, they both knew she and Tee would eventually make love.

Despite her deep feelings for Acier, Raven shivered with desire at the thought of sleeping with his identical twin. She and Tee had always been close. She thought of his big, warm hands caressing her bare body... a body Acier had only recently introduced to the absolute joys of sex with a well hung, skillful lover. What would sex with Tee be like? Aside from their hair, which Tee wore short and Acier wore in a long, dark curtain that fell past his broad shoulders, the two were physically identical.

However, they had very different personalities. What would Tee be like as a lover? What—

The elevator doors opened and she stepped inside, pushed the button for the twelfth floor, and tried to clear her head. She and Acier would be apart for at least four weeks while he prepared to move his shifter dens from Arizona to the Greater Philadelphia area.

Acier had told her Pen would be mating with Emmanuel, one of the few female warrior class Keddi on Earth. Acier's other Keddi, Drei, would be there as back up, in case Pen and Emmanuel didn't like each other. Her smile widened at the thought of Pen, a diminutive shifter whose natural form was that of a gray wolf, fathering the next generation of earthbound Keddi. Drei, the younger of the two, had been driving everyone insane lately with his incessant crowing that he was the step-father to Acier's young twin sisters.

Raven wanted to meet Emmanuel, but the decision to remain in the Greater Philadelphia area had been easy once she'd seen how old and fragile her father looked. While she would miss Acier and their daily lovemaking, she wanted to spend some time with her father.

Her spiritual guide, Abby Valentine, had warned her most Willoni could not accurately see their own future. Nevertheless, her recent visions involving herself, Acier, and Etienne, and her father's imminent death, disturbed and frightened her. At a time when she needed her most, Abby had disappeared. She would have to discover what, if anything, could be done to help her father before she went searching for Abby.

She left the elevator on the twelfth floor. Halfway down the corridor she stopped outside the door to the suite where she and her sisters had spent the previous night. It was the first time the three of them had been together for an overnighter in months. They'd stayed up until after two a.m. exchanging news and gossip. Treena and Kiki had exclaimed over the size of Raven's engagement ring, exhibited good-natured envy that she had done what neither of them had been able to do—reel in Acier. All three sisters had spent years scheming to spend at least one night with either of the Gautier brothers.

Smiling, she remembered how grumpy they'd been when the alarm clock, followed by the wake up call, roused them. Treena was probably taking a quick nap. Raven glanced at her watch. Derek was impatient, but another fifteen or twenty minutes wouldn't make much difference. She swiped her keycard. Easing the door open, she slipped inside, closing it quietly.

Her eyes widened as she stared across the room. A naked Treena's lean, dark body was held against the wall opposite the door by the weight of the equally naked Tee's tanned, muscular one. From the way Tee's tight buns were clenching and unclenching, Raven knew he was already inside Treena—fucking her on her wedding day.

Raven could see Treena's long nails digging into Tee's broad shoulders. Her eyes were closed, her lips parted with her tongue peeking out. Each time Tee rotated his hips and thrust his cock into her, Treena moaned, her body shuddering.

After one particularly deep thrust, Treena gasped, raking her nails down Tee's back to clutch his ass. "Oh, God, Etienne. Your cock is so huge and delicious. So hard. Give it to me! Give me every hot, wonderful inch! Fuck me!"

Tee responded by widening his stance, pulling his powerful hips back, and then shooting them forward.

"Oh! Oh, shit! Oh, shit, Etienne, your cock feels so good. Fuck me harder! Harder! Dear God, I want every inch pounding into me until I come again! I need every inch of cock slamming deep into me!"

Tee wrapped his arms around Treena and swung them around with his back against the wall. He stared straight into Raven's startled gaze. A smile spreading across his face, he cupped Treena's bare cheeks and fucked her hard and deep. Raven couldn't look away from his intense gaze. She pressed a hand against her racing heart.

Treena moaned, tossed her head back, and ground her hips against his, clearly loving the relentless pounding he was giving her. "Oh, God. Oh, God, this is the sweetest cock in the world. Fuck me until I'm raw and full of your lovely cum!"

Keeping his gaze locked with Raven's, Tee linked Treena's arms around his neck, and lifted her off her feet. She wrapped her legs around him, impaled on his cock. He turned sideways, so Raven could clearly see his cock moving in and out of Treena's pussy. Treena's juices covered his pubic hair and the base of his shaft.

Raven bit her lip, feeling her pussy flex in response to the sight of Tee's big, slick length tunneling in and out of Treena. Tee kept his movements slow and measured, his gaze locked on Raven.

"Oh, yes! So good!" Treena tightened her arms and began bouncing on his shaft. "Harder! Deeper! Please. Almost there! Harder!"

He gripped her thighs and sliced his shaft in and out, his thrusts short and rough. Within seconds, Treena cried out as her entire body shuddered.

Tee groaned and kept pounding her pussy, his lids fluttering. Raven knew he was coming too. Tearing her gaze away from his, she looked down. A steady stream of their combined fluids trickled down from Treena's pussy to his pubic hair.

Raven caught her breath. By the Goddess, he was fucking Treena on her wedding day without a condom? Oh, no! The lustful spell broken, the muscles of her throat unlocked. "Etienne! How dare you!"

Treena gave a startled cry and tried to scramble off the cock still impaling her. "Stop! Oh, my God, Etienne, you have to stop! We've been caught!"

Easily overcoming Treena's efforts to be free, Tee maintained his grip on her thighs and leisurely shot his dick in and out of her pussy several more times. Despite her efforts to dismount him, Treena gasped, and shuddered. Tee continued fucking her, groaning softly as he thrust up into her, digging his cock in hard and deep.

"Oh, God!" Treena moaned and came again. Only after he'd clearly ejaculated inside her again did Tee lower her to her feet. Even then, he remained inside her.

Raven, feeling a combination of anger and jealousy coursing through her, stalked across the room, grabbed Tee's left shoulder, and tugged at it. "Get the hell away from her!"

With a deep-chested growl Etienne finally withdrew his cock. He turned to face Raven. "Ah, there's my jealous little *petite*. What's the matter, honey, afraid there won't be any cock left for you?"

Heat flooded Raven's cheeks. Ignoring him, she looked at Treena. "Derek's a good man. How could you?"

Treena pressed a hand between her legs and over her breasts. Sobbing, she rushed into the bedroom, closing the door. Raven turned to glare at Tee. He stood in front of her, making no effort to cover himself. Despite her anger, her heartbeat raced as she looked at him. He had a beautiful, tanned body with wide shoulders, a nice chest covered with a sprinkling of dark hair, washboard abs, long, muscular legs, and a long, thick erection that was every bit as breathtaking as Acier's. By the Goddess, what a big, beautiful cock!

She shook her head and sucked in an angry breath. "How could you do this to her?"

He leaned back against the wall, locking his gaze with hers. "Did it look as if I was raping her to you? I just gave her what she's been wanting for years."

She tossed her head angrily, sending her hair cascading around her shoulders. "You bastard! Have you no shame or sense of decency? It's her wedding day."

He grinned. "Those fucks were my wedding present."

Fucks? They'd done it more than once? Oh, no! A sense of dread filled her. He'd done it more than once in her visions with disastrous results. "The least you could have done was use a condom!" She bit her lip. "What if she gets pregnant?"

His smile vanished. "That's not too damn likely."

"It's not?" The Goddess willing, maybe she had interpreted her visions incorrectly. "You mean because she's on birth control?"

"I mean because I'm a hybrid. Do you really think a half-vampire, half-shifter male can impregnate anyone?"

Her visions had included a few of herself pregnant and strangely unhappy. "Yes, I do."

"You do? Didn't you pay attention in biology, *petite*?"

"Do you mean Acier and I... what *do* you mean?"

"Hybrids are almost always sterile."

Dare she believe him? She wasn't certain. Before Acier had first made love to her, his fear of sending her home pregnant had been real. "But Acier and I... I thought... he never said he couldn't get me pregnant." She touched her stomach. "In fact, he was worried that he would and then have to face Dad."

Etienne touched her cheek. "Biology was never Sei's favorite subject, *petite*. You two clearly have that in common."

He sounded as if he liked the idea of her and Acier being unable to have a child. She slapped his hand away. "Don't touch me!"

He narrowed his gaze. "Don't touch you?" He curled the fingers of one hand in her hair and slid an arm around her waist. "I'm going to do more than touch you, *petite*. I'm going to fuck you until you're walking bowlegged." He pressed his lips against her neck and raked his incisors along her skin.

A rush of moisture pooled between her legs where his erection pressed against her. She swallowed hard, trying to keep her desire under control. The sexual tension between her and Tee had been high since her eighteenth birthday four years earlier. Although she'd once come close to allowing him to make love to her, her fear of Acier's reaction had stopped her.

She loved having Acier ingest her blood as they made love. His huge cock often brought tinges of pain with the waves of pleasure. Thinking of Tee pleasuring and hurting her as Acier did sent a jolt of desire through her. She curled her fingers in the soft hair on Tee's bare chest. It would be heaven to wind her arms around his neck, part her legs, and have him love her against the same wall where he'd just fucked Treena.

He reached between their bodies and rubbed his cock against her. She shuddered, feeling the heat and hardness of it through her clothing. By the Goddess she wanted him... needed him.

She gave herself a mental shake. Now was not the time to surrender to her hunger for Tee. She turned her head to avoid kissing the warm, caressing lips moving against her neck. "Get away from me and put on your clothes before Kiki or Derek walk in."

He gave her a cold look. "If Kiki comes in, I'll give her what she's been wanting for years."

She flushed and glared at him.

"If Derek walks in, his life expectancy will—"

She pressed her fingers against his lips. "No! Don't you dare threaten him. Right now, he's worth two of you."

He growled softly. "You little—"

"If you dare call me a name, I'll slap you so hard your ears will ring for weeks!"

"You do that and I'll fuck you so hard up that big, dark ass of yours you won't be able to sit down for weeks."

She narrowed her gaze. "Don't threaten me, you half-crazy bastard! You put your clothes on and you do it now, damn it, Etienne, or hell will freeze over before I allow you to touch me."

He curled his hands into fists. "I don't require your permission to take what is rightfully mine—you!"

During Acier's feast, she had used her command of Bentia, a living barrier spirit, to help keep Acier in check. Bentia had been driven from her during a dangerous ritual she'd had to undergo after Acier's feast. While she no longer commanded Bentia, she sensed it would be unwise to show fear with Tee.

She lifted her chin. "I didn't allow Acier to take me against my will and I sure as hell will not allow you to do so."

"You won't dictate to me as you do to him. I'm going to get what I want and need from you—with or without your permission!"

She sucked in an angry breath. "Don't forget who and what I am." She leaned close and glared up at him. "I am the daughter of a Willoni Priestess and no damn male, no matter how crazy he is, takes me against my will. I know you're not yourself, but if you ever threaten me again, you're going to be one very sorry shifter." She stepped away from him. "Now dress and get the hell out of here before Derek shows up!"

Staring into his angry gaze, she knew he was very close to committing rape. Why hadn't Acier taken Etienne with him? Where the hell were all the friends and relatives who were supposed to be watching him to make sure he didn't do anything he shouldn't? Thinking of his best friend, full-blood vampire Damon duPre, she curled her lip. So much for his help. She was on her own. If she didn't back Tee down, he would rape her.

Raven compressed her lips and held his gaze. He swore softly, snatched up his clothes, dressed quickly, and then he was gone in a blur of movement. Closing her eyes, Raven leaned against the wall. She toyed with the idea of calling Acier, but decided against it. It would be a cold day in hell when she couldn't handle one half-crazy male. Besides, if her visions were true, such a call to Acier would only increase the chances of one of the brothers killing the other.

"You're not going to tell Derek, are you?"

Raven opened her eyes and straightened. Treena, dressed in a silk trouser suit, stood in the doorway of the living room, looking chastened and remorseful. Even if she hadn't expressed regret, there was no way Raven would betray her. "Of course not!" She pushed herself away from the wall and crossed the room.

The sisters embraced briefly before Treena shook her head. "I don't know what came over me, Rae. I didn't mean to sleep… to cheat with him, but when we were dancing, he made sure I could feel his erection. Derek has a very nice, satisfying shaft, but hell, Rae, I've never felt such a big, thick, long cock. I just had to have him. When he said he had to have me... I couldn't say no." She bit her lip. "I love Derek so much... I can't believe what I just did with Etienne."

"Just consider it a last crazy fling." Raven caressed Treena's cheek. "There's no need for Derek to know what happened. Go to him and have a great honeymoon."

Treena bit her lip. "Are you sure no one noticed?"

She wasn't, but she nodded anyway. The only person Treena needed to be concerned about was Derek and he hadn't given any evidence he'd seen that almost obscene dance between Treena and Tee. "Yes."

Treena sighed. "That was such a stupid mistake. God, I hope it doesn't come back to haunt me."

Recalling one of her more disturbing visions, Raven suppressed a shudder. "Derek's waiting."

With a troubled look in her dark eyes, Treena nodded slowly. "I better get back downstairs." She picked up her suitcase, and headed for the door. "Are you coming?"

"In a minute. I just want to call Abby."

"I expected to see her at the wedding."

"I know, but she hasn't been herself lately."

"Why not? What's going on with her?"

There was only so much Raven could share with Treena, who had no idea that neither Raven nor Abby were fully human. Abby hadn't returned any of the numerous calls Raven had placed during the last week. "I think she's lonely."

"She doesn't need to be. She's a beautiful woman."

She was a beautiful woman whose faith prohibited her enjoying carnal pleasure while she acted as guide to a Willoni acolyte. "Hopefully I'll be able to contact her soon."

Treena nodded. "I'll see you downstairs before we leave?"

Raven smiled. "Of course."

Alone in the suite, Raven sat on the chair by the window and took her cell phone from her shoulder bag. She felt a tingling sensation along the back of her neck and bolted to her feet, staring toward the door.

A man stood inside the closed door.

She'd thought Acier and Tee and their cousin Xavier Depardieu were handsome, but this man left her breathless. He was tall and muscular with long dark hair that fell around very broad shoulders. His eyes were more silver than gray. His skin had a reddish bronze tint. His dark, clearly tailor-made suit clung to his big body like the proverbial second skin. He exuded an air of sensuality that was almost palpable.

She immediately knew two things. He wasn't human, and she didn't need to fear him. Meeting his amazing silver gaze, she experienced a shock of recognition. They had never met, yet she knew his identity. Inclining her head slightly, she rose. She hesitated, then, moved by an instinct she didn't quite understand, she bowed briefly. "You're the one Acier said would help Tee."

He nodded. "I am Enola Cheyenne."

He had the most incredible smile she'd ever seen. It was at once reassuring, sexy, confident, and majestic. She had been right to bow to this Enola Cheyenne, whom she suspected commanded his people's allegiance.

"And you are the Willoni who will help me rescue Etienne's sanity."

"You just missed him."

He shook his head. "I sent him away so we could talk."

That explained Tee's sudden exit.

He extended his hand. "Come, little Willoni. We'll discuss how to rescue Etienne."

She shook her head. "I don't know what to do to help him."

"I do. Come." She crossed the room and he took her hand in his. "How much do you want to help him?"

"More than I can say, but right now I'm also worried about my father. He's sick and I need to be here with him."

"I have seen your father."

"You're a healer. Will you help him?"

"Although I have some small ability to heal physical maladies, your father's condition is beyond my capability. I am primarily a healer of the spirit or soul."

Tears filled her eyes. "You mean he's going to die?"

"What do his doctors say?"

She blinked hard. "That it's just a matter of time."

He hesitated. "I know someone who is a healer of the body. His father is a renowned healer."

She squeezed his hand. "What's his name? What's his fee? If I can't raise it, I know Acier will help."

"He doesn't heal for monetary reward and you won't have heard of him. He's from the planet Telmira."

"Will he help my father? Can he help him?"

"I'm sure he'd be willing, but I cannot guarantee that he will actually be able to help. Your father's condition—"

"Will you ask him? Please. I know Dad is human and he's not going to live forever, but I'm not ready to lose him yet."

"The healer's name is Eros. I will ask him to come see your father. Please don't get too hopeful—unless Eros gives you reason."

She nodded. "I understand."

"Before I contact Eros, we need to discuss Etienne and how much you are willing to endure to help restore his sanity."

Chapter Two

Adona stood in the dark shadows across from the hotel watching Etienne leave. Her eyes narrowed and she clenched her hands into fists. He'd been with her—with Adona's rival for his affection.

If the skinny, scheming, vampire-stealing bitch thought for one moment that Adona would stand by and allow her to sleep with her male, she would soon see how mistaken she was! There was only one way to deal with a Willoni who didn't know her place. Adona was just the female to give Ravanni Monclaire what she deserved.

She frowned. Ravanni wasn't alone. Adona had seen the tall, handsome, silver-eyed male enter the hotel room. Although Adona feared no one, she sensed a level of power in the male with which she wasn't prepared to deal.

The time would come when she would give the Willoni an all or nothing alternative. Either she stopped using her wiles to bewitch Etienne or she would pay with her life.

Casting a last look at the hotel, Adona turned and walked into the shadows.

* * *

Etienne, with his Keddi, Karol, perched on his shoulder, paced the length of his hotel suite, trying to control the fury building in his gut. Two full-blood male vampires, both tall with dark hair, one with gray eyes, and one with brown, sat on the sofa, watching him.

He stopped pacing and turned to glare at them. The presence of his so-called uncles, Mikhel and Serge Dumont, annoyed the hell out of him. It was bad enough having Mikhel issuing orders. Mikhel was some twenty years his senior. He turned his attention to the younger vampire with the gray eyes. At forty-two, Serge was only a year or so older than Etienne. There was no way he would obey Serge. He'd had enough of that shit from Acier to last him a lifetime. "I don't want or need either of you here. Get out and stop following me!"

Serge laughed. "Why don't you try putting us out?"

Mikhel frowned. "Serge—"

"I'm sick and tired of his whining, Mikhel! Instead of being home with Derri, I'm stuck watching over his ungrateful ass. I've had about all his shit I intend to take!" Serge leveled a finger at Etienne. "It's time you remembered we're your uncles or risk getting your ass kicked all over this suite."

"You and what army?"

"The day I need help kicking your sorry ass will be the day I stop calling myself a full-blood. Don't let your two- or three-inch height advantage go to your head. I'll kick your ass all the way to Boston and back if that's what you want."

Karol, in his natural form of a miniature gray wolf, flew off Etienne's shoulder. In battle mode, he revealed his three-inch incisors and four-inch claws.

Mikhel's lips tightened. "Tell him to stand down, Etienne."

Etienne shook his head. "You're going to be surprised at how much damage a warrior class Keddi can inflict—even on a full-blood vampire."

Mikhel shook his head. "Call him off, Etienne, or I'll kill him."

The threat to Karol increased Etienne's rage. "Hurt him and I'll rip your throat out! On second thought, I'll rip it out anyway!" Etienne flashed across the room toward Mikhel.

With a growl of his own, Serge exploded off the sofa and charged to meet Etienne. Karol flew at Serge. To Etienne's surprise, Mikhel growled. Flashing across the room, he leapt into the air, catching Karol in his hand.

Etienne only had time to see Karol sink his incisors into the surprised Mikhel's hand before he felt a powerful blow against his face that sent him spinning across the room.

When Etienne's head cleared, Serge stood over him—his incisors bared, his right hand clenched into a fist. "Call off your Keddi or he'll be killed and then I'll finish kicking your ass."

"Not while I'm here you won't," another voice intruded.

Serge swung around, allowing Etienne to bolt to his feet. Mikhel, trying to pry Karol's incisors out of his hand, flashed forward to stand by Serge.

Etienne watched the tall full-blood with auburn hair and green eyes stroll across the room to stand by his side, his incisors bared. Mikhel had his fist clenched, about to smash into Karol's small body.

"Karol, stand down," Damon ordered. He looked at Mikhel. "Release him."

"Who the fuck are you?" Serge demanded. "Never mind. Let me guess. You're Damon duPre. Etienne's so-called friend."

Damon looked at Mikhel again. "Release the Keddi unharmed."

Mikhel stepped in front of Serge and stared at Damon. "We're his blood relatives. Don't stick your nose into the middle of a family dispute."

"Do you know who I am? Who my brothers are?"

"Ask me if I care." Mikhel grabbed Karol by the scruff of his neck and pried his incisors out of his hand. He flung Karol across the room.

Roaring, Etienne leapt into the air and caught Karol before he could hit the opposite wall. When he dropped to his feet, he bared his incisors at Mikhel. "If you've hurt him—"

Mikhel swore and stalked across the room toward Etienne. When Damon stepped in his path, Mikhel backhanded him out of the way. Damon flashed after Mikhel and found Serge standing in his path.

Damon shook his head. "Get out of my way, pup, or I'll go through you."

"Pup? Don't let my age fool you, duPre. While you were depending on your nutty brothers to back you up, I was out killing a full-blood while still a latent. Unlike you, I've never needed my big brothers in a fight. But like you, I have big brothers in addition to Mikhel here," Serge warned. "You might have heard of them. Aleksei and Vladimir Madison and Andrei Forester."

"What the fuck is going on here?"

An overwhelming sense of relief filled Etienne as a tall full-blood with bronze-colored skin, blue eyes, and long locks appeared in the room. Etienne's second Keddi, Slayer, perched on his shoulder. "Father."

Slayer flew across the room to hover in front of Karol. *Karol hurt?*

Etienne watched as his father, Vladimir Madison, stalked across the room to face Mikhel. "You hit him?"

Serge frowned. "Actually, I'm the one who—"

Mikhel cast Serge a quick warning look before turning his attention back to Vladimir. "What if I did?"

Mikhel's response surprised Etienne. Mikhel seemed prepared to take the blame and the consequences for something Serge had done, much as Acier would have done for him. Etienne frowned. Like Acier, Mikhel clearly suffered from the delusion that he needed to protect a younger brother who required no such protection. Older brothers were pains in the asses.

Vladimir's nostrils flared. He clenched his right hand. "Why?"

"He needed it. Now get the hell out of my face with your attitude."

"You hit my son and then tell me to get out of your face?"

"Yes!"

Vladimir's eyes glowed. "Who the hell do you think you're talking to, pup?"

"I'm talking to you, Vladimir!"

Etienne smiled. Both his "uncles" were about to get their uptight asses kicked.

"Not for long you're not. I'm going to—"

Serge pushed past Damon, grabbed Vlad's shoulder, and swung him around to face him. "Don't you start any shit with

Mikhel! That brat of yours had it coming. He has no right to disrespect us."

Etienne, half expecting Vladimir to backhand Serge across the room, watched in annoyance as Serge raged on. "We're his uncles here doing our best to keep his sorry ass out of trouble! Etienne didn't get anything Aleksei wouldn't have given him in our place and you know it. You get that brat of yours to toe the line and there won't be any more trouble. Let him think he can continue to disrespect his uncles and he'll just have to get his ass kicked until he learns his damned place in the family order."

Aware of the tension between his father and Mikhel, Etienne waited. After that rant, the ass kicking was about to begin big time. Once it was over, he wouldn't have to worry about his "uncles" dogging him.

After several long, tense moments, Vladimir jerked away from Serge. Instead of backhanding Mikhel, he reached past him and closed his hand on Etienne's shoulder. "Come with me."

Etienne stared at him. "What?"

Vladimir pushed him into the adjoining bedroom, slammed the door, and turned to face him. He spoke in a low, barely controlled voice. "What happened?"

"All you need to know is that they attacked me!"

He watched his father's Adam's apple bob up and down as he made a visible effort to control himself. "Answer my question."

"To hell with your question!"

"What?"

"I said to hell with your question!" Etienne bared his incisors. "I want them off my back—now! Get them off my back or else!"

"Or else what?"

Slayer and Karol hovered around Etienne, their small bodies tense.

Father angry.

Don't make Father angry, Karol pleaded.

Etienne turned to look at Karol. "Fuck Fa…"

That's as far as he got before he found himself lying against the far wall. He pressed a hand against his mouth. Blood. He stared at Vlad. "You struck me!"

Vladimir stared at him in silence, his incisors bared.

Enraged, Etienne rushed across the room with Slayer and Karol flashing around him.

No!

Don't make Father angry again!

He ignored them and stopped in front of Vladimir. "You sorry bastard! You've never been around when I needed you and now when I could use your help, you side with them and attack me?" He sucked in an angry, painful breath. "Don't you ever again dare to call yourself my father. I have no father!"

He had the satisfaction of seeing a look of devastation in Vladimir's eyes before he stormed from the room. Avoiding the gazes of Mikhel and Serge, he flashed through the adjoining room and out the door with Damon and his Keddi at his side.

In the hallway, he came to an abrupt halt. A small, slender woman with dark hair appeared in his path. Damn, this day kept getting worse. The last thing he needed was his father's mother getting in his way. He knew enough about her not to yield to the urge to order her out of his way.

Damon sent him a brief message. *Oh, shit. I'll catch you later.*

Great. Damon was scared of his grandmother.

Palea Dumont looked up into his eyes. *Not afraid. Respectful, as you should be, my angry little one.*

Call it what you want, Etienne, Damon replied. *I'm out of here.* He turned and fled in the opposite direction.

The suite door opened. Mikhel and Serge joined them in the corridor.

Etienne stood in silent resentment as his uncles greeted their mother. Serge then turned to give him a long stare. "The next time we meet, you'd better have learned your place or I'll kick your shifter ass from here to Arizona."

Etienne bared his incisors. "I'll ask you again. You and what army?"

To his annoyance, Serge laughed, slapped his cheek, and walked down the hall to the elevator. Etienne overcame the urge to rush after the arrogant vampire and rip his throat open. One down. Two to go.

Mikhel arched a brow before turning to his mother. "What brings you here, Mother?"

"I've come to see Vladimir, but it appears I need to see Etienne first."

Mikhel's nostrils flared. "This young ingrate has been very disrespectful. Vladimir needs to see you."

Etienne found two pairs of dark eyes focused on him. He didn't care what Mikhel thought, but the disappointed look in Palea's eyes unnerved him.

"What of this little one who doesn't know his place?"

Mikhel narrowed his gaze. "Go see Vladimir. I'll deal with Etienne."

Nodding, she took Etienne's hand and drew him close. *I know this is a difficult time for you, my angry little one. But you and Acier are now part of a large, extended family. No matter how dark things might seem, one or more of us will be with you... in spirit if not in the flesh. The blood of the Walker-Dumont line runs through your veins. Whether a Walker, a Dumont, a Madison, a Forester, or a Gautier, we are all one family. We will do our best to give you all the love and sense of family you lost with the death of your mother.*

She stroked his cheek with her free hand. *And when you are more yourself, you will tell me of your mother. Yes?*

He hadn't experienced maternal affection since his mother's death thirty-one years earlier. The feeling of warmth and belonging her words spread through him made holding tears at bay difficult. She tugged at his hand. Obedient to the silent command and an inner need he'd long denied, he bent his head. Her soft, cool lips brushed against his cheek. *You are deeply loved... son of my most cherished child. You are dearer to me than you can possibly know, my precious and beloved Etienne.*

Moved despite himself, he gulped in a deep, aching breath.

Smiling, she released him and entered his suite. The moment the door closed behind her, Mikhel grabbed him by his collar and slammed him against the wall. "Now, Etienne, let's understand something very clearly. We all know you're having a difficult feast, but that's no excuse for disrespecting your father. In this family, we accord our parents and elder relatives the respect their positions deserve."

"Vladimir deserves nothing!"

Mikhel tightened his fingers around his neck. "He's your father and in my presence, you will show him the respect he deserves or face the consequences."

He glared at Mikhel. "Take your hands off me or—"

Mikhel tightened his grip. "Shut your mouth, boy, or I'll shut it for you! Vladimir may be prepared to take your shit, but I assure you, none of the rest of us will."

Etienne shoved Mikhel away and swung a fist at him.

Mikhel blocked it and slammed Etienne against the wall again. "Unless you try harder to fit into your proper place in the family, you're going to find yourself slapped around a lot during the next few weeks. Do I make myself clear, Etienne?"

He fought hard to control the rage building in him. "I have a long memory, Dumont!"

In response to the thinly veiled threat, Mikhel drove a fist into his stomach. "You'll call me Uncle Mikhel. If you ever use that disrespectful tone with me again, I'll slap your ass up and down this hallway until you develop some manners. Is that clear?"

Etienne swallowed hard in an attempt to overcome the urge to shift to his natural form and rip Mikhel's throat out. The time would come when this arrogant vampire learned not to fuck with him. For now, wary of being slapped again, he inclined his head slightly.

To his amazement, Mikhel suddenly smiled and put an arm around his shoulders. "Good. Now, boy, let's go see what kind of shit we can get into."

He pulled away. "What? You're not going to try and stop me from having a good time?"

Mikhel shook his head. "If you're lucky, you'll only feast once. It can be a difficult time, but it can also be one of the most intensely pleasurable times in a vampire's life. So, unless you do something that's completely off the charts, I won't interfere."

Etienne stared at him in silence for several moments. Just minutes earlier, he and Serge had been all over him for doing what he wanted. "Are you serious?"

Mikhel nodded. "Though my feast started badly and was painful for my bloodlust to watch, I enjoyed it. I had my fill of women and blood. I plan to do my best to see that you enjoy what's left of yours."

"You're serious."

Mikhel palmed the back of his neck. "Of course I am."

Etienne sighed. "In that case, I need several drinks and some pussy."

"I know a place where you can get both without any worries."

"Where the hell is that?"

Mikhel grinned. "One of the perks of being part of such a large family is our extended reach. Andrei owns numerous nightclubs across the country. He has two clubs in the area that cater to humans and vampires alike—Midnight Shadows and Eternity." He glanced at the closed door of the suite.

Etienne tensed, certain Mikhel was about to insist he apologize to Vladimir before they left.

Mikhel arched a brow and shook his head. "Not this time, but if you remember what I said about giving him the respect he deserves, you and I won't have any issues with each other."

Etienne nodded.

* * *

Five hours later, Etienne sat on a chair in one of the back rooms of Andrei's club. A beautiful, naked fem with long, dark hair ground herself on his cock as he ingested her blood. She had already come twice. The clenching of her tight vaginal muscles combined with the sweetness of her blood finally drove him to his fifth climax. Grasping her ass, he held her body still while he quickly drove his exploding cock deep into her wet pussy.

Buried in her pussy with his eyes closed, her blood flowing over his tongue and into his throat, he could pretend he was with Raven. That made his release all the sweeter. It was only when he lifted his head from her neck and met her blue gaze that the power of the illusion vanished—leaving him longing for Raven.

Giving him a sensual smile, the woman rubbed her large, firm breasts against his chest. "Everything I've heard about that big cock of yours is true." She stroked her fingers through his hair. "I know you're not bloodlusted, but are you otherwise taken?"

"Yes."

"Pity." Kissing him, she rose and stood over him with her legs on either side of his. Cum trickled from her pussy onto his pubic hair. She laughed, squatted over him, and parted the folds of her cunt. A tiny flood of their fluids gushed from her pussy onto his cock and pubic hair. She kissed him again and, straightening, stepped away from him. "Whenever you want another quickie, just think of me and I'll find you."

He'd enjoyed the two hours he'd spent with her, but there was something about her that unnerved him. Even as he smiled and nodded, he suspected she, like Adona, was not really a true fem and it would be unwise to have anything else to do with her.

She blew him a kiss, and without bothering to dress, she opened the door, and left the room—stark naked.

Etienne showered and, forty minutes later, joined Mikhel at a corner table in Eternity. Although his sexual hunger had been somewhat assuaged, his inner hunger and rage continued to gnaw at him. In addition, he feared he would regret that last fuck.

Mikhel arched a brow. "Is something wrong?"

The time spent in Mikhel's company had provided a surprising measure of comfort. Perhaps uncles weren't totally useless after all. He shook his head. "No."

He watched a pretty blond fem sink onto Mikhel's lap and link her arms around his neck. "There's an empty bed in the back."

Mikhel shook his head and rose, dumping the fem unceremoniously onto her ass. "Thanks, but I'm very happily bloodlusted and married."

The fem shot to her feet and tossed her long hair around her shoulders. "Your loss."

Etienne tilted his head. "Aren't you going to indulge?"

"In wine?" Mikhel lifted his glass and nodded. "Absolutely." He glanced briefly around the dimly lit club, filled with beautiful females. "I don't cheat."

Etienne sipped his wine before replying. "What about Derri?"

Mikhel shrugged. "She's Serge's bloodlust."

"But everyone says you're in love with her."

Mikhel arched a brow. "Who is everyone?"

"Are you in love with her?"

"Why should my feelings for Derri concern you?"

Etienne raked a hand through his hair. "I have the same problem."

"Problem? Who says my relationship with Derri is a problem?"

"You're in love with Serge's bloodlust. That sounds like a problem to me."

"Neither Erica nor Serge has a problem with our relationship. Why should you?"

"Because I ache for her."

Mikhel tensed. "Acier's Raven?"

"Yes."

Mikhel sighed. "It's like that for you?"

"Just like that."

Mikhel shrugged. "Your feelings for her are perfectly acceptable in our culture."

"Is that what you do with Derri? Make love rather than fuck her?"

He watched Mikhel's jaw clench and unclench before he responded. "I make no apologies for how I feel about Derri.

There's an invisible line between loving her and feeling something more compelling for her."

"Have you ever crossed that line?"

Mikhel's lids swept down, concealing his expression before he met Etienne's gaze again. "Derri will always be Serge's bloodlust. Erica will always be mine. Bloodlust trumps love every time. Erica is the mother of my son and I love her now more than I did when we first met. What I feel for Derri is powerful, but if I had to choose between saving her or Erica, I'd save Erica."

"You'd allow Derri to die?"

He watched a pained expression flicker across Mikhel's face. "I wouldn't risk Erica's life or safety for anyone—not even Derri."

Etienne sighed. "Then I guess I'm in worse shape than you because I can't think of a single person whose safety I would put before Raven's."

"Not even Acier's?"

"Not even his, but then he'd want it that way as well."

"Have you made love to her yet?"

"No."

"Why not?"

Etienne curled his lip. "Acier hasn't wanted it."

"So? It's your right."

"That's what everyone keeps telling me, but no one understands how close we used to be." He raked his hands through his hair. "I want her so badly that lately I've found myself wishing…"

"Wishing what?"

Etienne hesitated. He hadn't even told Damon how deeply his feelings for Raven ran. "Have you ever wished Serge was out of the way?"

Mikhel shook his head. "No! Erica would still be my bloodlust, the first woman I ever loved, and the mother of my son. Even if Derri weren't Serge's, I'd still be with Erica."

"Then Derri doesn't mean nearly as much to you as Raven means to me. Lately, I've even considered killing him."

Mikhel swore softly and reached across the table to clamp a hand over his. "The hell you have!"

He jerked his hand away. "Why shouldn't I? His feelings for her pale in comparison to mine. He wants her. I love, need, ache, and hunger for her. He doesn't deserve her."

"That's your feast talking."

Etienne shook his head. "I could easily kill him and take Raven. He's unfairly reaped the benefits of the seeds I've sowed over the last ten years. He ignored her for years while I kept in touch. If he had half a heart, he wouldn't have touched her!" He balled a hand into a fist and shook it at Mikhel. "Why should I allow him to come between us?"

"It's time for you to sleep with her and dispel some of your aggression."

"That won't change anything. I nearly ripped his throat out at the reception."

Mikhel's gaze narrowed. "What stopped you?"

"Raven wouldn't have forgiven me."

"And that's the only reason you didn't go after him?"

Powerful memories assailed his senses. Acier had always had his back. In college, Acier had worked two jobs while he'd had none. Acier had always provided comfort when he needed it most, putting Etienne's needs ahead of his own. Acier had never done anything to hurt him—until he took Raven. He swallowed a knot of rage and pain. "She should be mine."

Mikhel shook his head. "If your feelings for her run as deeply as you say they do, you'll learn to accept the role in her life and affections fate has given you. You can make love to her... love her... lust for her, but you can never allow yourself to forget that she belongs to Acier. You can never let your emotional guard down long enough to wish Acier harm just so you can have what is rightfully his. Learn to deal with your feelings for her, Etienne."

"Is that what you do with yours for Derri?"

"I've already told you I love her, but I would never place her above Erica. Everyone—except Dimitri—comes after Erica.

Once Dimitri is an adult and able to protect himself, he too will come after Erica."

"What if Raven is my bloodlust as well as Acier's? Who says two vampires can't bloodlust with the same woman? Are you in bloodlust with Erica and Derri?"

"I'll readily admit that I care more for Derri than I should, but I am not in bloodlust with her. Would I be in bloodlust with her had I met her before I met Erica? I don't know. All I know is that aside from Dimitri, Erica is the most important person in my life."

"That's how I feel about Raven! Can you honestly tell me she's not my bloodlust?"

"Only you can decide that, but you're going to have to deal with her belonging to Acier."

"So I'm supposed to be satisfied with making love to her when Acier allows it?"

Mikhel's eyes blazed at him. "Yes, Etienne, you are."

"That's not good enough!"

"It'll have to be."

He slammed his fist down onto the table. "I'm going to have her!"

"Yes, but you are not allowed to forget she belongs to Acier and you sure as hell are not allowed to wish him dead so your selfish, egotistical ass can have his bloodlust."

Etienne swallowed hard. The need to leap over the table and strangle Mikhel was difficult to overcome. "I expose my deepest emotions to you and you call me selfish and egotistical?"

"Yes. You've admitted he's always put your wants and needs first—until he fell in bloodlust. Instead of rejoicing with him, you selfishly want him to continue to put you first." Mikhel leaned across the table and grabbed him by his collar. "Do you know what it is to ask a vampire to give up his or her bloodlust? You selfish bastard! When is it your turn to put him first? When do you start giving him an ounce of the consideration he's always given you? What makes you so damned special that he's supposed to devote his entire life and happiness to your well-being at the expense of his own? Who the fuck do you think you are, Etienne, that he should continue to put your silly ass first?"

The rage engulfed him. He clenched his hand into a fist and shot it out—straight toward Mikhel's hateful face. It connected with enough force to snap Mikhel's head back. Before he could follow through with a second blow, a tall biracial full-blood with medium dark skin, short dark hair, and blue eyes appeared at their table and casually put out a palm to intercept Etienne's fist. "Don't start any shit you can't finish, Etienne."

Andrei Forester. Great. Just what he needed—another damned interfering uncle! Etienne snatched his hand away and shot to his feet. Mikhel rose slowly, fingering his jaw, his gaze narrowed. Etienne tensed, expecting to be knocked on his ass.

Instead, Mikhel shook his head. "It's okay, Andrei. Etienne and I were just testing boundaries."

Andrei nodded. "Fine—but you've done all the testing in here of that kind you're going to do. Understood?"

Mikhel nodded.

Andrei considered Etienne in silence for several moments. He palmed the back of Etienne's neck. "I understand what you're going through, Etienne. I know how it feels to hunger for a woman who belongs to someone else. I know it makes you want to strike out in anger and rage at everyone—especially those closest to you. In this family, surrounded as you are by vampires far older and stronger than you, all that will get you is a perpetual ass kicking."

Andrei slapped his cheek. "At least the woman you want is available for you." He sighed. "Which is more than I can say."

Etienne curled his lip. "If you want her so much, why don't you take her?"

"She's pregnant by another male she's determined to marry."

"She can't marry him if you kill him, can she?"

"Etienne!"

He ignored Mikhel's warning voice. Sensing that Andrei walked close to the edge of a dangerous precipice, he decided to try and push him over it. "She can't marry a dead man."

Andrei inclined his head slowly. "No, she can't."

"Kill him and take her."

"Shut the fuck up, Etienne!" Mikhel backhanded him, knocking him on his ass before he spun around to face his brother. "Don't listen to him, Andrei. He's bitter and full of rage. You can't kill the man she loves."

Andrei stared at Mikhel. "Why can't I?"

Pleased, Etienne got to his feet. Mindful of a warning look from Mikhel, he remained silent. Mikhel sighed. "Andrei, she'd never forgive you. I know you could coerce her, but if you did that, she wouldn't be the woman you want."

"But you'd have her!" Etienne pointed out and quickly stepped backwards as Mikhel swung around to glare at him.

"So I would."

"Andrei—"

Andrei looked at Mikhel. "I'll make my own decisions, little brother."

"Fine, but don't make any based on suggestions from a young, nearly insane nephew."

"Why not? He has a valid point."

"Andrei, he doesn't!"

"Yes, Mikhel. He does." Andrei nodded curtly and walked away.

Mikhel swore and turned to face him. "I've taken all the shit I intend to take from you, Etienne. Any more talk of killing Acier or anyone else who doesn't need or deserve killing, and I'm going to beat you to within an inch of your miserable, selfish life!" Mikhel grabbed him by his jacket and jerked him close to stare in his eyes. "Do I make myself perfectly clear?"

Such talk from anyone else, including Acier and Vladimir, would have infuriated him. Strangely, despite having struck and threatened him, Etienne felt close to the arrogant, holier-than-thou vampire. "Crystal."

Mikhel sucked in an angry breath. "Good. Now let's go find Raven."

"She wasn't pleased to see me the last time we met."

Mikhel shrugged. "Then you'll just have to charm her into your arms."

Chapter Three

Within moments of waking in the darkened bedroom of Acier's custom built luxury RV, Raven knew she was no longer alone. She lay with her eyes closed, trying to determine what had roused her. Abruptly she smiled and sat up, her eyes flying open. "Acier!"

But the dark, unseen presence did not belong to Acier. She bolted out of bed. The bedroom was at the back of the RV. Without turning on the lights, she reached for the sweatshirt Acier had worn the night before and slipped it over her nude body.

She opened the bedroom doors and made her way through the RV. Etienne, naked and gloriously aroused, stood beyond the living room area, by the closed entrance door. Standing there staring at her with glowing, golden eyes, he reminded Raven of a large, beautiful, majestic gray wolf.

Sensing his barely leashed fury, she knew the coming hours would not be pleasant. The morning would find her sore and battered—much as she'd been when Acier made love to her during his feast. Made love? Acier had fucked her without any concern for her feelings or pleasure—just as Tee was about to do.

While part of her rebelled at the thought of submitting to such treatment from Etienne, another part of her recalled all the good times they'd shared. When Acier had forgotten she existed, Tee had continued to visit. He'd always remembered her birthdays—something Acier had not done. His presence at her sixteenth birthday party had gone a long way in mitigating the hurt of Acier's continued absence. Under all the rage was the Tee who'd always made her feel special.

Tee pushed himself away from the door and brought one hand from behind his back. "For you, *petite*."

The sight of the dozen red roses sent a wave of warmth through her. Even in the midst of his uncontrolled lust, he remembered how much she loved red roses. She accepted them. "They're beautiful, Etienne, but—"

He pressed a finger against her lips. "I can't wait any longer, *petite*."

She'd known for weeks this moment would come. Still, she was afraid. She shook her head. "Etienne, I don't think I'm ready—"

"It's going to happen tonight, *petite*."

"I'm not ready!"

"I've waited as long as I can." He caressed her cheek. "Please don't make me take you by force."

Even as his barely concealed hunger excited her, it also sent a measure of fear and anger through her. How dare he try to intimidate her into sleeping with him less than two days after she'd caught him with her sister! She lifted her chin. As the daughter of a Willoni Priestess, she had no need to subjugate herself to any male.

She balled her right hand into a fist and stepped back. While she no longer wielded the power of a living barrier spirit, she felt a sudden sense of empowerment. Calm reassurance replaced her remaining fear.

Enola.

Have no fear, little Willoni. The coming hours will not be as you might have wished, but I will ensure he retains a measure of self-control.

Wonderful. Tee would hurt her while Enola watched.

If you are not ready to help him start the healing process, I will force him to retreat. The choice is yours and yours alone, little Willoni.

He's going to hurt me.

Yes, he is. Decide how much you can bear and we will proceed accordingly.

Knowing the choice was hers made the decision to submit to Etienne easier. She opened her right hand and relaxed her shoulders. Seeming to sense her surrender, Etienne took the roses from her, tossed them aside, and slipped his arm around her waist. For several moments, he held her close. His lips moved against the side of her neck with a feverish desperation that provided an insight into the depth of his feelings for her.

He abruptly drew away from her, his golden gaze narrowing. "I can smell him on you."

Hearing the near hatred in his voice as he spoke of Acier distressed her. She shrugged. "It's his sweatshirt."

"Not anymore!" He grabbed the top of the shirt and ripped it off her. Then lifting her in his arms, he stalked through the RV. In the bedroom, he tossed her across the bed and stood staring down at her.

As her gaze moved down his big, sculpted body to his fully erect shaft, her heartbeat quickened. Once his long, thick cock was buried deep inside her, she would experience that sexy stuffed feeling she so loved with Acier.

There was nothing in the world as wonderful as being impaled on a cock big, thick, and hard enough to make her fear it would poke a hole in her. With a knot of desire tightening in her belly, she raised her gaze to his. "Let's go back into the living room."

"Why?"

She sat up. "I don't want to sleep with you in the bed Acier and I share."

"Too damned bad!" He pushed her onto her back. Before she could react, he lay between her thighs with his cock pressed against her belly. He rubbed his balls against her pussy.

She looked into his eyes. He wanted her to struggle. Determined not to give him that satisfaction, she relaxed, closing her eyes. Her seeming acquiescence appeared to infuriate him. She felt the fury building in him. Muttering in French, he rubbed his shaft roughly along her slit. She trembled. "You want it. Don't you? Tell me you want my cock."

She sucked in a breath. She wouldn't beg to be brutalized.

"Playing hard to get, Raven?"

She compressed her lips and kept her eyes closed.

"No matter. I'll soon have you begging for it and me."

She tensed as he positioned his cock at her entrance. He curled his fingers in her hair, jerked her head back, lifted his hips, and slammed them back onto hers. The movement sent his hard, thick erection plowing into her. She wasn't quite ready for him. A wave of pain sliced through her. She gasped, gritted her teeth, and curled her hands into fists as he forced himself deep inside her.

Without giving her time to acclimate herself to him, he locked his arms around her. Bringing his mouth down on hers, he kept his thrusts short and fierce. He rutted into her with a superhuman speed that kept her gasping for breath and sent waves of pain crashing over her.

When she and Acier had rough sex, there was always a sweet undercurrent of pleasure just below the surface of the pain. Even at his roughest, during his Feast of Indulgence, Acier had never been as brutal with her as Etienne was now.

He ravished her with no regard for her feelings or pleasure. Each whimper of pain resulted in an increase in brutality. Angry, she raked her nails down his back. He retaliated by stabbing his cock deep into her with a ruthlessness that made her entire body shudder.

He bit her lips, pawed at her breasts and thighs, and curled his fingers into her ass cheeks. Each time she attempted to draw away from him, he growled and raked his incisors along her throat.

Alarmed, she gasped, and opened her eyes. He bared his incisors and slowly began to shift. "No," she whispered. She didn't want to have sex with Etienne in his natural form.

Even as she protested, she felt his pelt on her belly and thighs.

"No!"

Gripping her hips in his hands, he pressed his knot against the lips of her pussy.

"Don't!"

She felt Enola's calming presence. *If you want me to stop him, Raven, I will, but he needs this.*

Enola would only let him go so far. She bit her lip and clenched her hands into fists. She could get through this to help him.

Holding her still, Etienne shoved his hips forward. Tears filled her eyes as he forced his knot between the lips of her slit and into her pussy—something Acier had never done, even when they made love in his shifted form.

Since surrendering her virginity to Acier two months earlier, she'd developed a taste for rough sex, but what Etienne was doing to her went beyond rough. She could feel him feeding on her discomfort.

His violent lovemaking overwhelmed her senses and injured the warm feeling she had always held for him. Sensing none of the tenderness he'd always displayed with her and fearful of the knot of anger and hate igniting in her belly, she released her grip on consciousness.

But even that provided little relief. As she fell through a dark void, she was aware of Etienne ejaculating into her sore pussy. He remained hard after coming and within seconds was rutting into her again.

She shuddered and sobbed. Suddenly, she was aware of a light in the dark void. Gentle hands lifted her… soft, reassuring words washed over her. *You've done all you can for now, little Willoni. Sleep. I will watch over you as you sleep and recuperate.*

* * *

The sound of soft, incessant sobbing roused Raven. After she woke, she lay on her side with her eyes closed, orienting herself. She ached all over and was aware that her vagina throbbed in an unpleasant way. She knew she was naked under the light sheet that covered her body.

It took a few moments before she realized where she was and what had happened to her—at Etienne's hands—in the bed she and Acier shared.

With consciousness came the return of her anger. She could feel him lying in the bed behind her. She'd swing around and rake her nails down his face. The satisfaction of making a temporary mess of his handsome face just might help ease some of the fury consuming her.

She opened her eyes and turned onto her side. Etienne lay on his back. Her rage dissipated as she noted the tears streaming down his cheeks from his closed lids. Recalling their shared good times, she reached down to touch his face.

His eyes fluttered and opened. They were gray again. "*Petite,*" he whispered in a low, broken voice. The timbre of his voice and the misery in his gaze spoke to her of his remorse.

His one act of brutality paled in comparison to his years of tender affection. She stretched out beside him and drew his body against hers. He trembled in her arms as he pressed his face against her neck. "Shhh." She kissed his hair while stroking his shaking shoulders. "It's all right."

He lifted his head and met her gaze. "Can you forgive me?"

Much of the uncontrolled rage he'd let loose on her the previous night seemed to have dissipated. He still wasn't the Tee she'd always known and loved, but, for the moment at least, she no longer feared him. She wanted to help this Tee. Nevertheless, she wanted to make it clear she wouldn't forgive such behavior again.

I know it's difficult, but he needs you more now than he's ever needed anyone, little Willoni.

Raven stiffened. *So you're still here, Enola? I thought you said you'd keep him from getting too out of control. Why did you allow him to brutalize me as he did last night?*

Had I not been here, it would have been worse. As unpleasant as it was for you, you are Willoni. You have the power to heal yourself. He needed that interlude with you — just as it was — to even begin the healing process. That fact notwithstanding, he still has a long way to go before he can resume a semblance of normalcy. That the process has started at all is a testament to you. Because of your generous spirit he has a measure of peace this morning. How much is that worth to you, little Willoni?

Put like that her lingering resentment seemed downright churlish. *I don't know how much more of this I can take.*

Take only as much as you can bear, Raven. If we are lucky, it will be enough.

I thought you were the one who was supposed to save him. Not me!

I am committed to helping him, but I can only do so much without harming him.

Harming him? I thought you could control him.

His level of rage would require I bend his will to mine. Because of the danger involved, I'll only do that as a last resort.

Why a last resort?

Because there's a danger that some of who he is would be forever lost.

"Petite?"

Etienne's tense voice interrupted her silent conversation with Enola. "I'll do my best."

He stroked her face, then trailed his fingers down her body to her breasts. They were sore and tender. She winced and he gentled his touch. "I didn't mean to hurt you."

"Oh, yes, you did and you enjoyed it."

She saw a flicker of excitement in his gaze. Not only had he enjoyed hurting her, but the assurance that he had increased his excitement level. Enola was right. The Tee she had known and loved would never have treated her as this familiar stranger had.

Her nickname for Etienne, Tee, was as dead as Steele—the nickname she'd used for Acier for years. Tee was dead. In his place was an Etienne she wasn't sure she liked.

He gently traced the outside of her lips with his tongue. As he explored the contours of her mouth, he cupped, stroked, and caressed her breasts.

She sucked in a quick breath as he rolled her nipples between his fingers. They quickly pebbled. Great. Her body was about to betray her.

Pulling his lips away from hers, he nibbled his way down from her neck to her breasts. "Hello," he said softly.

Raven smiled. He'd been known to call her breasts "bad girls" and "tasting tits." She usually objected to such nicknames, but she liked his obvious reverence for her body.

He dragged his tongue along the undersides of her breasts several times before he sucked her right nipple into his mouth. She shivered and cupped her hands over his head.

The movement of his warm, moist tongue against her nipples stirred her passions as only one other man had—Acier. She closed her eyes and enjoyed the delicious eddies forming in her belly. He skillfully made love to her breasts, tenderly tasting, nibbling, licking, and sucking them. Waves of delight buffeted her body, leaving her trembling with need.

He lifted his head. "*Petite?*"

She opened her eyes, meeting his lovely, sensual golden gaze. She stroked his cheek. He eased her onto her back and lay on top of her. The feel of his big cock pulsing against her belly sent a rush of moisture between her trembling thighs. Her body's reaction annoyed her. Numerous bruises covered her. She didn't want to respond so wantonly to him, which might give him the impression that she was a slave to her body's desires. Thank God she wouldn't see Acier until after her various hickies and telltale signs of rough sex had vanished.

Cupping her face between his palms, Etienne bent his head. His warm, persuasive lips moved slowly over hers, infusing his gentle kisses with all the tender affection she had longed for the previous night.

He rolled over onto his back, taking her with him, and continued kissing her, coercing her lips apart. She heard him whisper something soft and sweet against her mouth. It was in French, but she knew the words well. *I love you. I've always loved you. I always will love you, Petit Corbeau.*

Petit Corbeau. Little Raven. She had cherished the sweet nickname since Etienne and Acier had given it to her years earlier. Neither had used it recently. Hearing it on Etienne's lips coupled with a promise of eternal love touched her deepest, innermost feelings and desires. The eddies in her belly ignited. She had the Tee she had always known and loved back. Her eyes welled with tears. "I love you too," she whispered.

He rolled them over again so that she lay on her back with him sprawled between her thighs. "Do you? Do you really love me, *petite*?"

She heard the need for assurance in his voice. She caressed his cheek. "Yes. Oh, yes."

"Even after last night?"

Oh, boy, he was pushing it. She decided now was not the time to warn him against future displays of sexual aggression. "Yes. Even after last night."

He rolled off her and reached between her legs. His fingers parted her wet folds. She shivered and eased her legs apart, offering silent encouragement. He traced the entire outline of her slit before he slipped his fingers inside her. He stroked and probed gently, stirring her passions. She closed her eyes and moistened her lips. Nice. Very nice.

He gently finger fucked her for several moments, getting her wet and hot before withdrawing his fingers and pressing his thumb against her clit. She moaned softly and rotated her hips. More. She wanted so much more.

He removed his fingers. Leaning down, he pressed a moist kiss against her slit. The tip of his tongue slid against her clit. "Oh!" She shivered with need.

He laid his cheek against her lower belly, inhaling deeply. "I love the aroma of your pussy. You're wet."

And ready for him. She reached for him. He lay between her legs, supporting most of his weight with his arms. She trembled with need as his cock pulsed against her.

He brushed his lips against her neck. "I need you."

At the moment she needed him too. "I'm here for you. Take me."

He lifted his hips from hers. "Show me you forgive me for last night."

She frowned. "How?"

"You know what I want and need."

Yes. She did. His need matched hers. Reaching between their bodies, she closed her fingers around his cock. A tingle danced up her arm at the contact with his hard, warm flesh. Despite her love and desire for Acier, she'd always cherished a secret yen for Tee. Finally, he was going to make love to her. A surge of anticipation shook her body. Eager to have him love her, she brought his cock to rest against her entrance. Moistening her lips, she lifted her gaze to his.

He stared down at her in silence for several moments before he spoke. "I'm sorry about last night, *petite*. I know I hurt you, but I was out of my mind and I couldn't stop myself. A part of me wanted to stop and be gentle with you, but there was another part of me that wouldn't allow it."

She wasn't sure she believed that.

"I never envisioned our first time together being anything but loving and tender," he told her.

That she did believe. She smiled up at him and caressed his shoulders. "I know."

"I didn't want it to be like last night."

She slid her fingers down his back to his ass. "Make love to me and chase away the memories of last night."

"As you wish, *petite*." He gently lowered his hips. The big head of the shaft which had angrily sliced into her the night before gently parted her wet folds. He eased his hips forward. Several inches of hard shaft slid gently into her body.

She closed her eyes. "Oh... oh." *Yes. Yes!* This is how their first time together should have been. *Yes! At last!*

He stiffened on her. "Am I hurting you? Do you want me to stop?"

She'd burst with frustration if he stopped. "No! I don't want you to stop." She slipped her arms around him, lifting her hips off the bed. "I want you inside of me. Now."

He resumed his downward motion, driving her butt back onto the bed. Within moments she felt his pubic hair brushing against hers. *Yes. Oh, yes.*

He lay on top of her in silence for several moments, seemingly content to hold his cock still inside her.

She wanted and needed more. Slipping her hands up to his shoulders, she rotated her hips and quickly rocked them against his. "Love me."

He groaned against her ear. "I do. I do. I always have."

Just as she'd always loved him. She turned her head, touching the tip of her tongue against his lips. "Oh… Etienne…"

"Oh, God, Raven, I love you so much!"

"Show me," she encouraged, stroking her hands down his back to cup his tight buns. "Make love to me."

Brushing his warm lips against hers, he obeyed with a slow, sweet deliberation that threatened to make her melt into him until they were two parts of one, finally completed, whole. Each touch of his tongue and mouth against her lips, neck, and breasts felt like a tender promise of an eternal love as old as time. His big, caressing hands created tiny fires wherever they touched. Each stroke of his big, hard cock sent an electric shock of desire and pleasure surging all the way from her stuffed pussy down to her curled toes. Even more wonderful was the sensation of drowning in an emotional bliss. His tender lovemaking erased her anguish from the previous night and created a new, urgent need for him.

Every move, touch, and kiss filled her with delight. She felt worshipped, cherished, loved, and adored. She clung to him, lost in a world of bliss and mindless pleasure. Under the long, endless kisses was a voracious passion and hunger for her that she'd never experienced with anyone else. Not even Acier had wanted or needed her with the endless depth that she felt with Etienne.

The intensity of his desire for her shook her… encompassed her… bound her to him in a way she had never wanted or expected. She felt a need in him that, if encouraged or allowed to continue, would infringe on her relationship with Acier. That was the last thing she wanted. Nevertheless, his deeply held feelings heightened her pleasure even as they frightened and threatened to overwhelm her.

The ball of fire in her belly roared to life and raced down her body, setting her pussy ablaze. She sobbed, shuddered, raked her nails over his ass, and exploded into a thousand mindlessly happy pieces.

He held her close, whispering softly to her in French and gently fucking her, as she luxuriated in a long, very satisfying orgasm. As the last shiver of pleasure shook her, he cupped her ass in his palms and pushed his cock in and out of her with a deep, slow deliberation that brought her close to a second climax before he groaned, held her body still, and exploded deep inside her pussy.

His entire body shook with his orgasm. She ground her hips wildly against his in a fury until he rotated his hips in response. His pubic hair brushed roughly against her clit.

"Oh, yes! Yes!" she moaned through a second climax.

Clinging to each other, they collapsed together, rolled over onto their sides, and lay shaking for several long, sweet moments.

Then he pulled the sheet over their bodies and stroked her breasts. "*Petite?*"

Feeling sexually sated and happy, she kept her eyes closed. She rubbed her cheek against his shoulder. "Hmmm?"

He stroked her breasts again. "I love you."

She smiled. "I love you too."

"No." He lifted her left hand in his. "I mean I really love you."

"I know," she said sleepily. "And I really love you too."

"You mean that."

"Of course I do."

She felt his fingers moving against her left hand. Her smile vanished. She bolted up in bed and snatched her hand away—too late. He'd already removed her engagement ring and leapt out of bed with it.

She stretched out her hand. "Give it back."

He shook his head. "No."

She took a deep, calming breath before she spoke. "Why not?"

He raised his gaze to hers. "Because you have no business wearing his ring."

Seeing the rage in his gaze, she sighed. Admitting the depth of her feelings had probably been a mistake. This was going to get messy. "We're engaged, Etienne."

He bared his incisors and leaned down to glare at her. "Well, you shouldn't be."

"We're in love."

"I can see why he loves you." His gaze softened and he caressed her cheeks with his free hand. He straightened abruptly. "But give me one damn reason why you love him and not me?"

Oh, God. "I love you both."

"You shouldn't! What has he ever done to deserve your love? Name one damned thing he's done. Did he keep his word to stay in touch with you? Hell, no! But I did. I was the one who made an effort to be there for your important days. I was there for your sweet sixteen party. Not him. I was there for every birthday after that until…" He paused and swallowed slowly, closing his hand over her ring. "You had to chase him down! Is that what made him so irresistible to you when you should be mine?"

Raven sat on the side of the bed, her heart racing. "Yours?"

"Yes! Mine, damn it!" He reached down and closed his fingers in her long hair. "And you know what? Hell will freeze over in August before I allow him to have what's mine—you!"

A wall of hate for Acier emanated from him and slammed over her, nearly drowning her. Fear seized her… not for herself but for him and Acier. There was no way he could get better while harboring that vitriol. The thought of what it would do to Acier if he knew how Etienne really felt about him added to her fear and horror.

She knew Etienne would not return her ring, no matter how much she begged or pleaded. She'd need to have another one made before she saw Acier. The worry of where the money would come from would have to wait until after she'd found a way to calm Etienne down. She reached up to touch the wrist of the hand gripping her hair. "Come back to bed."

He released her hair, but instead of returning to bed, he flashed from the bedroom. Moments later he returned and opened his hand. A diamond solitaire, similar in size to the one Acier had given her, rested in his palm.

She looked up at Etienne. "What… what's that?"

"It's an engagement ring." He shrugged. "I've been carrying it around since your nineteenth birthday."

Oh, no.

"I've been waiting for the right moment to give it to you and ask you to marry me."

She gasped, feeling as if one of her lungs had collapsed. "Marry you?"

He dropped to one knee. "I've known since you were sixteen that I wanted to marry you. I stopped seeing you when you were nineteen because being around you was becoming too difficult. I was afraid I'd pressure you into sex before you were ready. I thought I'd wait until you were twenty-two or -three before I told you how I felt. And what the hell did I get for trying to do the right thing by you? Kicked in the ass by my own brother! You should be wearing my ring. Not his."

Enola! Aren't you supposed to be helping? Where the hell are you?

You're doing fine, little Willoni.

He was starting to piss her off. *Is that what you thought last night while you stood around and allowed him to brutalize me?*

He needed last night. You knew that or you would have called out to me and I would have intervened.

He had an answer for every damned thing.

If I had, I would be more popular at home, little Raven.

Whatever! She turned her attention back to Etienne. "Come back to bed."

"After you put on my ring."

How could she possibly put it on in place of Acier's ring?

"Put it on, Raven."

When she sat staring at it in silence, he took her left hand in his and slid the ring onto her third finger. Then he slipped into bed and drew her into his arms. After a moment of resistance, she relaxed in his embrace. She'd remove it the moment he fell asleep.

He kissed her forehead and drew her closer. "I love you so much it hurts."

For the first time she understood why his feast was so difficult. He'd considered her his and had been fighting against his natural inclination since he learned she was in love with Acier. When she'd been certain Acier was indifferent to her, instead of reinforcing her belief and trying to steer her away from Acier, Etienne had gone out of his way to portray Acier in the best light possible.

Etienne had been a loyal brother to Acier — at the cost of his own happiness, peace of mind, and sanity. Now he was going to need the understanding, love, and support of both her and Acier. "I know, Etienne. I know."

He lifted his head. "But I don't just love you. I have to have you. You know why. Don't you?"

Oh, no, Etienne. Not that. Please. Not that. That would make this whole situation untenable.

He tipped up her chin. "Look at me."

She sighed and opened her eyes.

"I love you."

"I… I love you too."

He caressed her breasts. "I've known since you were sixteen who and what you are."

She swallowed slowly. *Please, Tee. Don't. Anything but that.* "A Willoni?"

He bent his head and gently brushed his lips against hers. "My bloodlust… the one being who completes me like no other ever could… and for whom I have an overwhelming need for sex and blood." He licked her lips with a sensuality that made her toes curl. "Now I need to taste your blood."

Even as a little voice urged her to resist, she tilted her head. She made a small sound of pleasure as his incisors pierced her skin. *Yes. Yes.* She arched her back, cupped her hands over his head, and experienced one of the sweetest, most delicious climaxes of her life. It was all the sweeter for having been entirely blood induced.

Afterwards, they lay facing each other, exchanging long, lingering kisses. Finally, feeling content, Raven fell asleep with the sound of Tee's deep voice whispering how much he loved her… his bloodlust.

Chapter Four

When Raven woke, it was dark in the RV. She lay on her side with a warm, naked body curled spoon-fashion behind hers and a firm arm across her waist. Recalling remnants of a chilling dream-vision, she shivered. "Acier," she whispered.

He moved behind her.

She froze. She shared the bed with Etienne, not Acier. His admission that he considered her his bloodlust sent a chill of fear through her. She couldn't be his bloodlust. She was Acier's bloodlust. Her visions could not come true. She belonged to and with Acier.

Acier. Driven by the need to see Acier, she eased from under Tee's arm and slipped from the bed. She dressed quickly and left the bedroom. In the living room area, she was annoyed to find Mikhel and Enola sitting over a drink. Her world was falling apart and they sat around drinking?

Both males rose. Mikhel frowned. "Raven? Are you all right?"

She gulped in a breath. He opened his arms and she rushed into them. He held her as she sobbed. She tried to calm down, but she started to shake uncontrollably.

Enola approached and placed a hand on her back. *It's all right, Raven. You'll be all right. You're afraid. Go to the man you love for comfort.*

She lifted her head from Mikhel's shoulder and looked at Enola through a rush of tears. "But Acier's in Arizona and I need to stay here in the Philadelphia area to be near my father in case he needs me."

"Eros has your father in a deep, healing trance from which he won't emerge for at least a week. Eros will remain with your father and if anything changes, he'll be in touch. Go to Acier."

She glanced back toward the bedroom. "I… I don't think Etienne will allow me to leave."

Enola arched a brow. "He can't stop you if he's asleep."

"He's a light sleeper. I'm surprised he hasn't already awakened."

"I'll put him into a deep slumber."

"What?" Mikhel released her and swirled around to face Enola. "No, you won't."

Enola placed a hand on Mikhel's shoulder. "If your family trusts me with his mind, surely you can trust me with his body. I promise you I won't hurt him. I'll put him in a deep sleep for a few hours and then see Raven safely to Acier."

Mikhel stalked away and paced the length of the living room area twice before he turned to face Enola. "I have your word that he won't be harmed?"

"Of course you do. I have a number of… duties, but the one that is more a part of me than any other is that of healer. I attempt to live by the oldest healer creed — to do no harm."

Mikhel sighed. "Okay."

Enola turned her back into Mikhel's arms before he walked toward the bedroom. She stood with her hands balled into fists pressed against Mikhel's chest. It seemed to take an inordinately long time for Enola to return. When he did, he had her suitcase. "Are you ready?"

She nodded. "Yes… I think so."

Mikhel wiped her face with his handkerchief and kissed her cheek. "You'll be fine and so will Etienne."

She clutched Mikhel's jacket. "He's full of hate for Acier…"

"I know, but under it all, he loves Acier."

Remembering her visions, she shook her head. "I'm not so sure about that."

"I am. Go visit Acier."

* * *

After Raven and Enola left, Mikhel went into the bedroom. Etienne slept deeply. Mikhel returned to the living room area of the RV as his cell phone rang. He pulled it from his waist clip, and noted the incoming phone number. He lifted it to his ear. "Hi, sweetheart," he said, a smile spreading across his face.

"Mik, I didn't want to bother you, but Dimitri has been crying for you. I know Etienne needs watching, but Dimitri isn't eating and he's not sleeping. He just keeps crying and asking for his dada. I called Serge and he said he'd come take your place so you could come home and spend a few hours with Dimitri."

Serge and Etienne alone together? That was a sure formula for disaster. Both were hot headed, liked their own way and weren't particular about who they had to backhand aside to get it. On the other hand, Etienne was in a deep sleep. Maybe he could spend a few hours with Dimitri and be back before Etienne woke. "I'll be home in a few hours."

"Are you sure?"

"I'm positive."

"We'll see you then. We love you."

"And I love you both."

"See you soon, love."

"Soon," he echoed and ended the call.

He called Serge. Serge answered his cell phone almost immediately. "Mik? I'm on my way, but there's fog here in Boston so it's going to take me a few hours."

"Okay. I'll see you then." He paused. "How's Derri?"

"She's preparing for a big case so she's a little on edge."

"I'm sure she'll win."

"So am I. I'll be there soon."

Ten minutes later Damon duPre arrived. About to send him away, Mikhel changed his mind. Etienne would sleep for a number of hours, but it would be better if Damon was there along with Serge when Etienne woke.

Damon's nostrils flared when he realized he couldn't wake Etienne. "What did you allow that damned weirdo to do to him?"

Mikhel arched a brow. "If I had the time, I'd slap your happy ass all around this room, but my son is missing me. Etienne will be in a healing sleep for a number of hours. I'm leaving now. Take better care of him than you've been doing."

Damon bared his incisors.

Mikhel laughed and left the RV, eager to reassure Dimitri and to see Erica.

*　*　*

After several failed attempts to awaken Etienne, Damon sat in Acier's bedroom, watching him sleep. Although having Etienne in such a state unnerved him, he hoped the sleep would accomplish its purpose. Over the course of the last few months, he'd been forced to watch Etienne slowly spiral out of control into near insanity because of Etienne's misguided loyalty to his supercilious and self-righteous twin. As far as Damon was concerned, Acier was undeserving of all the anxiety Etienne had suffered on his behalf. He was delighted that Etienne had finally fucked Raven. Hopefully that, along with this healing sleep, would allow him to get through the rest of his feast without any more angst.

Two hours later, Damon's cell phone vibrated. He rose to his feet and left the bedroom. Closing the doors, he moved down the hall. "Shaun?"

"Where are you, Junior?"

"With Etienne."

"Who else is there?"

"Just the two of us."

"Damn! Where the hell are all his useless relatives? What the hell are they good for if none of them are available to watch over his useless ass?"

Damon frowned. "I'm just relieving Mikhel for a while. What's wrong? Do you need me?"

"It's Brett."

Damon tensed at the mention of his other brother's name. "What about him?"

"The Brotherhood has snatched him."

Damon clenched his hand into a fist. The brotherhood in question was the Defense League of the Brotherhood, a group of powerful vampires dedicated to seeing vampires retain their superiority and ability to prey on humans at will. "Why?"

"I don't know why. I just know we have to get him back. I need you with me, Damon."

Damon's heart raced. He'd never heard fear in either of his older brothers' voices. If Shaun was afraid, Brett must be in real danger. If he left, he'd be leaving the sleeping Etienne defenseless. If he didn't, he'd have to allow Shaun to face the Brotherhood alone. Brett might be killed, or worse, they might both be killed.

"Damon? Can we count on you?"

He glanced back at the bedroom where Etienne slept. Etienne had no real enemies. Serge Dumont was on his way. Etienne would be fine until then. "Yes. Tell me where you want to meet and I'll be there ASAP."

He ended his call with Shaun, checked on Etienne, and quickly left the RV.

* * *

As Damon duPre's SUV sped out of Acier Gautier's second parking space, several figures emerged from the surrounding darkness. The most striking of the four was a tall vampire with dark skin, short, straight salt and pepper hair, and light brown eyes. He carried himself with the air of one used to wielding authority.

The lone female, tall, with dark skin, smiled. "I told you my plan would work, Vitali."

He nodded. "So you did."

"And now I get to fuck him?"

The vampire shrugged. "Why not? You've earned it, Adona. But only once. We have plans for him and not much time to set them in motion."

"Then I'd better go fuck him!"

* * *

Acier sat at the head of the table in the conference room of his Arizona ranch house. On his left sat a tall woman with brown eyes and dark skin the color of cocoa. At forty-five, Anais Toussaint had the distinction of being the only female in pack history to lead a den that included adult males. Aime Gautier, the Alpha Supreme of their pack had stunned both the den members of his pack and those of rival Pack LeMay when he had allowed Anais to battle a male of her late brother's den for leadership.

To everyone's dismay, Anais had won the death battle and had followed her father and brother as the leader of Den Toussaint. Whereas a human woman would have either had plastic surgery or kept her damaged skin covered, Anais had been known to proudly display the scars of that historic battle on her shoulder and taut belly.

Next to Anais sat a tall shifter with short dark hair and gray eyes. Although most of the available females in Pack Gautier had made a play for the thirty-year-old ex-model, Antoine Chenault's gaze was so often turned in Anais's direction that Acier suspected Anais's second was in love with her.

On Acier's left sat two tall, surly shifters with silver hair, thin moustaches, and dark, scowling eyes. Arnaud LeMay and his second in command, Gabriel Neville, from Pack LeMay.

Looking at the two shifters who did their best to ensure Aime's last days as Supreme Alpha were unpleasant, Acier was hard pressed not to leap across the table and tear out both their throats.

Acier glanced at his watch. "Perhaps we could get to the point of this meeting some time tonight?"

Arnaud LeMay glanced around the room before looking at him with clear disrespect in his gaze. "Where is Gautier?"

Acier attempted to mask his annoyance at the lack of respect in LeMay's voice when he spoke. "Alpha Supreme has pressing business elsewhere."

"Then call him here now because I don't deal with underlings."

Acier watched both Anais and Antoine tense. He shook his head and turned his attention back to LeMay. "As the Alpha-in-waiting of the oldest and most revered Pack on this side of the Atlantic, I can hardly be called an underling. As you know, LeMay, Pack Gautier is several generations older than your little pack."

LeMay's second exploded to his feet and found himself facing Anais and Antoine. Neville bared his incisors. "Out of my way, female."

At roughly 5' 10" Anais had a few inches on Neville. Although he was far more muscular, the male shifter she had defeated and killed to win the chance to lead Den Toussaint had been of a similar build.

When Antoine would have objected to Neville's tone, Anais held up a hand to silence him. "Perhaps you'd care to try to remove me from your face."

Acier decided this was not the time for a showdown between Packs Gautier and LeMay. He met Anais's gaze. Without a word, she inclined her head and she and Antoine returned to their seats.

Neville remained standing until LeMay jerked his head.

"Now, as I said, LeMay, anything you have to say to the Supreme Alpha you can say to me."

"Fine, Gautier. It's time Pack Gautier was reined in with all its firsts before it weakens all other Packs—even those with much higher standards."

Acier arched a brow but remained silent.

LeMay went on. "This Gautier you speak so highly of has a lot to answer for. He's allowed too many firsts and the rest of the packs will not permit any more firsts."

"Too many firsts?" Acier shrugged. "I'm sure I'm on the negative side of your list."

"You're damned right you are! In fact, his allowing you, a non-purebred, to lead a den was bad enough. But to choose you to succeed him was an outrage over which the other packs are still disgusted." LeMay turned his cold gaze on Anais. "Then he compounded that gross error in judgment by allowing this female to lead a den which contains adult males." He cast a quick, dismissive glance at Antoine. "It's unthinkable that any shifter male worth the name would serve under such conditions!"

Acier narrowed his gaze. Normally, he would accord LeMay the respect Aime had taught his pack all Alpha Supremes deserved. However, Acier was not in the best of moods. Etienne was still close to insanity, Acier missed Raven, the den he had inherited when he'd dispatched his arch rival Leon de la Rocque was filled with a bunch of surly shifters he couldn't trust, and Aime was pressing him to finally assume the position of Supreme Alpha of Pack Gautier. In addition he was still struggling to deal with his lingering resentment for Aleksei Madison, the vampire father he'd only recently met. Their relationship was complicated by the fact that Aleksei's bloodlust had recently given birth to two twin girls on whom Aleksei doted. Aleksei and his new family had accompanied Acier to Arizona from Pennsylvania.

While Acier adored his delightful new sisters, he found it difficult to conceal his dislike of Aleksei's bloodlust, Dani. Aleksei showered her with all the love, care, and attention Acier's mother had never received. His mother had struggled to raise him and Etienne on her own.

He had to release his pent-up rage on someone. Who better than the despised LeMay? He stared at LeMay. "This female? Anais is a den alpha—just as you once were. And even you would have to admit that she earned the right to her present position. Nothing was given to her. She battled to the death and won. She's earned the right to be respected and while you're in my house you'll show her the respect she's earned or you'll regret it!"

LeMay laughed. "Do you know how many LeMay shifters I can summon to my defense, Gautier? Unlike you, with your divided pack, Pack LeMay is united. I doubt very much that you can count on those from Den de la Rocque whereas I command the respect and loyalty of each member of each den within my pack."

Acier bared his incisors. "Pack Gautier is ready and able to defeat all those foolish enough to challenge us. Do so at your own risk, LeMay. Now I think I've extended you as much courtesy as I can stomach." He rose. "Leave now while I'm still inclined to allow you and your second to depart in one piece."

LeMay shot to his feet. "This isn't the last you've heard from us, Gautier. You'll learn the hard way that I have a long memory and that I never leave my enemies behind. When you least expect it and are least able to defend against it, there'll be hell to pay."

Acier glanced at Anais. "Den Alpha Toussaint and her very able second will see you out."

"So be it, Gautier. The next time we meet, one of us will not be leaving alive."

"Then I'd advise you to say goodbye to your loved ones before we meet again, LeMay. Now get out of my sight!"

When Acier was alone in the room, he sighed and sank back against his seat. A tall vampire with bronze-colored skin, long locks, and blue eyes entered the room. The full-blood sat in the seat Anais had occupied. "Difficult meeting?"

Acier shrugged. "Nothing I couldn't handle."

Aleksei inclined his head. "Of that I'm sure. How are you?"

"I'm okay."

"Is there anything I can do to help?"

The sincerity behind the question, coupled with the look of love Acier saw in his father's eyes, dispersed some of his anger. It continued to annoy and amaze him how easily a vampire he'd spent the first forty years of his life hating could handle him. "Not at the moment, but… it helps to have you here."

Aleksei gave a deep sigh, as if a burden had been lifted off his shoulders. "I know that's not an admission you make easily. I can't tell you how much it means to me to hear you say that."

During the ensuing silence, Acier felt a level of affection and love he hadn't known since his mother's death. It was impossible to continue to hate or resent a male so capable of making him feel as if he were worth dying for—and all without speaking a single damned word. Even as he wanted to hate Aleksei, he loved him more with each passing moment—damn the over-confident bastard.

Aleksei arched a brow.

Acier frowned, certain that despite all his warnings, Aleksei had read his mind again.

Aleksei smiled suddenly. "You have a visitor."

Acier sighed. "I'm not in the mood."

"I think you'll want to see this visitor."

Acier tensed. "Why? Is it Etienne?"

"No. It's me."

At the sound of the soft, sultry voice, Acier shot to his feet. He raced to the door to enclose Raven in a bear hug. "*Petite*! I didn't expect to see you for several weeks! What a wonderful surprise." He tipped up her chin and hungrily devoured her sweet lips. It took him several moments to realize her trembling wasn't desire induced.

He lifted his mouth from hers. Her dark eyes glistened with tears. "You've been crying." He cupped her face. "Oh, honey, has Mo taken a turn for the worst?"

She shook her head, gulped in a breath, and burrowed into his arms.

He released a relieved breath. Raven's father, Maurice Williams, was a twenty-year friend and Acier's literary agent. It seemed an age since Acier had had the freedom or drive to work on his overdue next adventure serial.

"Mr. Williams is still in the healing trance into which Eros placed him. Raven needed to see you so I accompanied her here."

Acier glanced over Raven's shoulder at Enola Cheyenne. He frowned. "Thanks for accompanying her, but who's with Etienne?"

"He's in a brief healing trance with his uncle Mikhel watching over him. I didn't come here just to accompany Raven. You and I need to talk—after you and Raven have spent some time together." He turned to look at Aleksei. "A word with you?"

Aleksei nodded. He and Enola left Acier alone with Raven.

Acier lifted Raven in his arms and carried her down a long hallway with doors on both sides. At the end of the corridor, he opened the door that led to his personal suite. He closed the door and carried Raven over to a dark leather loveseat, where he sat down with her sprawled across his lap. He brushed the long, dark hair away from her beautiful face. "What's wrong?"

She pressed her cheek against his shoulder. "I needed to see you."

The more he embraced his vampire heritage, the more in tune he became with her. One of these days the ability to read thoughts wouldn't be all on her side. For now he sensed her fear. He lifted her chin. "I know something's wrong. Are your sisters okay?"

"Yes."

That left Etienne. He hesitated before he spoke again. "Have you seen Etienne?"

She nodded and lowered her eyelids.

"No, Raven. Look at me."

She sighed before she raised her lids to meet his gaze.

"Have you seen Etienne?"

A flash of guilt danced in her eyes. He swallowed slowly, in an attempt to control the feeling of rage knotting his gut. "I can see that you have." His nostrils flared. He could smell Etienne's scent on her. "You've been with him."

"I... I... yes."

He took a deep breath. "I see." Just days earlier, she'd insisted he force Etienne to leave the reception with him. Yet she'd now slept with Etienne while Acier had been celibate.

He'd always known she and Etienne were close—far closer than he and she had ever been. How close were the two of them now that they'd become lovers? He sat her on her feet and rose.

She touched his hand. "Acier?"

He shook his head but turned to face her. "Did you enjoy sleeping with him?"

She bit her lip. "Acier... please..."

"Please what?"

"Please understand that he needed me."

"Oh. I see. So you only slept with him because he needed you? Does that mean you didn't enjoy it? Is that what you want or expect me to believe?"

She closed her eyes briefly and sighed. "You gave us your permission."

He knew Etienne had needed her and God knew he wanted Etienne well again. Furthermore, her sleeping with Etienne was part of the vampire heritage he'd recently accepted. He had given them his permission to sleep together. Nevertheless, he felt betrayed by the two people closest to him. He glared at her, fighting hard to control his fury. "When did you two arrange this?"

She blinked at him. "Arrange what?"

"Sleeping together—or should I say fucking?"

"We didn't arrange it! It just happened."

"How the hell do you just happen to sleep with someone?"

Her gaze narrowed. "I was at the RV so I could be near Dad. When I woke in the middle of the night he was there."

"And so naturally you felt obliged to drop your thong and spread your legs wide for him!"

"Damn you, Acier!" Her eyes shot off sparks. She swung her right hand.

He caught her wrist before she could slap him. "Oh, no, you don't!"

"I'm not in the mood for any of your jealous shit, Acier! I'm going to sleep in the guestroom. When you're feeling more reasonable and can hear me out, let me know. If that doesn't happen before tomorrow, I'm going back to Philly." She jerked free of him. As she did, the evening sun reflected off her engagement ring.

He turned her to face him.

"Let me go!"

He jerked up her left hand. "What the hell is this?"

"What is what?"

He resisted the urge to shake her with difficulty. "Where the hell is the ring I gave you?"

"What do you mean…" She followed his gaze to her left hand. A look of horror flashed in her eyes. "Oh, my God!" She pressed her free hand against her chest. "Acier! I can explain."

Some of the rage he'd felt during his Feast of Indulgence returned. He released her wrist and stepped away from her. "You have about two seconds to explain why you're wearing that instead of my ring."

"Oh, Acier!"

"Answer me, Raven, or I promise you there's going to be a problem between us."

Her nostrils flared. "Fine. Tee gave it to me."

He blinked. "What the fuck? It's an engagement ring."

"I know."

"Are you telling me you're engaged to him instead of me?"

"No!" She moved forward.

He shook his head and held up a hand. "Stay away from me, Raven."

"I can explain, Acier!"

"Where is my ring?"

"I don't know."

He clenched his right hand into a fist. "What?"

"I… Tee took it."

Despite his efforts to retain a measure of control, Acier's incisors descended. "He took it? Took implies he used force." He stepped close so he could stare down into her eyes. "Did you give it to him?"

She took a deep breath. "No, but I need to explain—"

"There's nothing to explain! I'm going to kill him!"

"Wh-what?"

"I said I'm going to kill him!" He swung around and started toward the door.

"No! Acier!" She ran after him and wrapped her arms around his waist. "No! Acier, please don't hurt him!"

The panic in her voice on Etienne's behalf only increased his wrath. He pulled away so he could face her. "I'm not going to hurt him. I'm going to kill him and there's nothing you can say or do to stop me."

She lifted her chin and met his gaze. "I wouldn't be too sure about that, if I were you."

"Well, you're not me, sweetie, and I'm very sure about it."

"I'm not going to allow you to hurt him."

Her words hit him with the force of a stake driven into his heart. There was only one explanation for her desire to protect the man who'd forcefully taken her engagement ring. That reason did not bode well for his relationship with her. The one thing he'd feared most had obviously happened. He'd lost his bloodlust to Etienne.

Despite her earlier denial, she'd clearly come to Arizona to tell him she'd thrown him over for his own brother. Hell would freeze over before he allowed the ungrateful Etienne to be happy at his expense. "I'd like to see you or anyone else stop me!"

Her expression softened. "Acier… please. You've misunderstood everything. I love you, and—"

"Fuck off, Raven!"

"You jealous bastard!" She rushed past him and ran from his suite.

Chapter Five

Crossing the room to sit on the loveseat, Acier covered his face. Moments later he felt a calming presence. He knew without looking up Aleksei was there. He offered no resistance when Aleksei sat beside him and put an arm around his shoulders. Even as he told himself it was unbecoming of a male about to take command of an entire pack of powerful shifters to collapse in his father's arms, he clung to Aleksei.

Cool lips touched his forehead. Soft, reassuring words permeated his mind. *There's no need to grieve, Acier. You've misunderstood her. She doesn't want to leave you for Etienne.*

She's wearing his ring!

Not by choice, Acier.

But she wants to protect him by choice!

And well she should. He's not himself. If your heart weren't involved and you were comfortable with who you've become, you'd want to protect him too. When she needed reassurance, she came running to you.

Acier frowned. So she had. He lifted his head and met his father's blue gaze. "Women have always preferred him to me."

Aleksei shrugged. "There's no accounting for taste, but the only woman who matters ran away from him right to you."

Acier smiled. "So she did. You know, when I remember how much Etienne and I needed a father when we were growing up, I hate you so much I can't bear it."

"I know and I understand."

"On the other hand, I don't know what I'd do if you hadn't found us."

Aleksei sighed. "I feel as if I've waited a lifetime to hear you say that."

"Don't let it go to your head." Acier shrugged. "I'm just glad to have you here now and in my life."

Aleksei's eyes welled with tears. He clasped a hand over the back of Acier's neck. "I would gladly walk through the fires of hell a thousand times to hear you say that once. I'm so sorry I wasn't there for you when you needed me most."

"I know that now."

"Do you know why I feel that way, Acier?"

"Yes, I do, but…" He shrugged. "I'd like to hear you say it anyway."

"I love you."

Acier closed his eyes. He let the words flow over him like a healing balm. He blew out a breath before he met Aleksei's gaze. "The thing is… I…"

"I know, Acier, I know."

"Good. So I don't have to say it."

Aleksei slapped his cheek. "We need to discuss Etienne."

"I despise him!"

"Believe me, Acier, I know the feeling. I've long since lost track of the number of times I felt as if I hated Vladimir and yet had anyone dared to pluck a single dread from his head, I would have killed them without hesitation. There's a special bond between vampire identical twins that only another set of vampire identical twins can truly understand. Venting your feelings for him will come soon enough."

"You think I should go after him?"

"Things will soon work out for you and Etienne. Right now you should go comfort your woman."

"I don't think she wants to see me."

Aleksei shook his head. "You know, boy, there's only one thing more pitiful and fragile than a vampire in love and that's one in bloodlust. She's part of an ancient clan who have the ability to read minds. She'll forgive you."

"Are you sure?"

"Of course I'm sure. You love her. She's your bloodlust. She can read your mind so she knows how you feel. Nevertheless she's female and they can be unpredictable at the best of times. Go make things right with her."

He rose.

"Acier?"

He turned at the door. "Yes?"

"I know you love her very much, but you're going to have to learn to share her with Etienne—just as I've had to learn to share with Vladimir. I never had a problem doing that until I met Dani. If you need help with that, I'm here, but the master at sharing a beloved and cherished bloodlust is your uncle Serge. You should talk to him. Go make sweet music with your *petite*."

He nodded.

* * *

Raven sat at the vanity in one of the guestrooms in Acier's ranch house staring at her reflection. Her eyes had changed from brown to green. Abby had told her most Willoni had green eyes at some point in their long lives. The angry spark that had been in her eyes earlier had been replaced by pain and confusion. Why was Acier so unreasonable? Why was he so ready to assume she wanted Tee more than she did him?

If she had half a brain, she'd prove him right and go back to Tee. She'd do that in a second—if she didn't love Acier so much. The more irrationally he behaved, the more she loved him—fool that she was.

She looked down at the top of the vanity where she'd placed Etienne's ring. She'd been in such a fever to see Acier, she'd forgotten to remove it. Small wonder Acier had lost it. If she'd given him a ring and then found him wearing a ring given to him by another woman, she'd have lost it as well.

She had to find a way to dispel Acier's belief that she and Etienne were colluding against him. If she could forgive Etienne, she could be more understanding with Acier. Besides, she hadn't come all the way from the Philly suburbs to sleep alone in a guestroom.

She rose and moved across the room. She opened the door. Acier stood on the other side of the door. They stared at each other in silence. Then she smiled and took his hand. "Hi, sweetie."

"*Petite*, I—"

She pressed her fingers against his lips. "Me first." She urged him into the bedroom and shut the door. She held up her bare left hand. "Before you say another word I need to make something perfectly clear to you—once and for all."

He nodded but she noted the wary look in his eyes. Even now he wasn't sure of her or her feelings for him. She placed her hands on his chest and looked up at him. "I've adored you since the moment we met when I was a child. I can still remember how much I looked forward to your visits."

"Just mine?"

She shook her head. "No. I looked forward to seeing Tee, too, but I always felt cheated if he showed up without you." She smiled. "I've loved you since I was a teenager."

"That's a strong word to use for a teen's feelings."

"I don't mean a sexual love. That came later. I'm not exactly sure when, but by the time I was sixteen, I knew you were the man I was going to belong to one day. I knew I loved you with all my heart. That hasn't changed. That won't ever change." She slipped her right hand up his chest to his cheek. "It may sound like a cliché, but I love you more each day. I love you, Acier. I always will."

She stroked her fingers through the long, dark hair that fell just below his broad shoulders. "Sleeping with Etienne won't change how I feel about you." She leaned against him. "I do love Etienne. But you?" She looked into his eyes. "Etienne means a lot to me. He always will, but you mean the world to me. I'd be very unhappy if I never saw him again, but I'd be devastated and inconsolable if I had to try and live without you in my life."

"What are you saying, Raven?"

"That I love you more than I do my own life. I am not one of those women who prefer him over you." She watched his gray gaze turn that lovely golden shade she loved. "Now what did you want to say?"

He sighed. "I've been an idiot for jumping to conclusions and—"

"Oh, no. No one gets to call the man I love and adore an idiot. A hothead? Absolutely, but a very sexy hothead."

He rubbed his nose against hers. "I'm so sorry, *petite*."

"So am I. If our positions had been reversed, I'd have been angry too."

"Yes?"

She recalled her feelings of jealousy, anger, and pain when she'd discovered Tee with Treena. Those feelings would have been off the chart had she discovered Acier with her sister. "Yes."

He frowned.

She tilted her head. "What? What's that wary look in your eyes?"

"That's it? You're forgiving me that easily?"

Lord, what a hard male he was to convince. "Yes!"

"Why?"

She laughed. "Suspicious to the very end, huh? How very vampire of you."

His nostrils flared. "Does that bother you, Raven?"

"Does what bother me?"

"That I've decided to accept that I am part vampire?"

"No. It doesn't bother me."

"Why not? That's not what you expected when you came after me."

"Hey, sweetie, don't forget who you're talking to. I'm Willoni. I can see the future. What makes you think I didn't know you were part vampire?"

"So that's okay with you?"

"I love you, Acier, and I'll happily be your woman, your bloodlust—just as you are." She nibbled his lips. "Now tell me what would possibly make you think I'd choose any other man over you?"

She watched a flicker of fear in his gaze. "Most women who have expressed a preference between us have preferred him."

"Maybe so, but—"

"And when I wanted to go after him, you sounded so protective, I thought—"

"You were the one I chased down. You were the one I saved my virginity for. You're the one I have to have."

She saw the beginning of distrust in his gaze. "Just me?"

"Let's not have any more misunderstandings, Acier. I love Tee and I want him, but I don't have to have him." She rubbed her palms over his chest. "You I have to have—regardless of the cost. I've never left you to go to him, but I did leave him to come to you because I needed to be with you. I want, need, and love you more than I know how to explain. Is that clear enough?"

He nodded, a small smile curving his lips upward. "Yes."

She linked her arms around his neck. She tugged gently. "Now you get to show me how much you love me."

* * *

Etienne was lost in a world of sensual delight. Warm, lush lips caressed his. Soft, eager palms stroked over his shoulders and chest. A tight, slick pussy slid up and down his cock. Jolts of pleasure buffeted his body. His stomach muscles tightened. He was close to coming. He struggled to prolong one of the sweetest, most erotic fucks he'd ever had.

Don't struggle so, my handsome Etienne. Come. Come for me. Fill me with your seed, my love. Brand me. I'm already yours, but I want to be branded so everyone who looks at me will know I'm yours and will always, always be yours.

The tender, seductive words echoed deep in his mind. They seeped into his heart... softening his rage. They made him feel wanted, needed, and loved as no woman ever had before. There was no need to hurt or ache when he had the devotion and love of this giving woman.

She lifted her hips until only the head of his cock remained inside her. Just as he hungered to feel her hot tunnel encasing him again, she eased her hips down, slowly impaling herself on his full length. *Oh, yes! Yes!* She fit around him as if her pussy had been made for that one purpose. Sex didn't get any better than this.

He slid his hands around her body to cup her ass. It was big and round, like a woman's ass should be. He stroked her cheeks as she rode him. Soft, gasping sounds of pleasure escaped her lips.

He liked the sounds. He was so close to coming, but he wanted her to come before he did.

It's all right, my love. Come. Come for me, my handsome Etienne. She tightened herself around him. *Come for me.*

Unable to hold back the tide of the orgasm building in him, he exploded, shooting his seed inside her. He hadn't come so long or hard since he was a teenager. Finally, he slumped back against the bed. Oh, damn, what a climax.

She rode him hard, bracing her hands against his shoulders. Her nails dug into his flesh. He thrust his hips upward, sending his cock shooting into her. She moaned, and he reached around her body and eased a finger into her ass.

"Oh, yes! Yes, Etienne!" She shuddered, her pussy tightening around him as she came.

Etienne snapped awake. A pair of dark eyes stared down at him from a pale face. Large, naked breasts pressed against his bare chest. A tight, clingy cunt covered his erect cock with slick bodily fluids. Her climax was long and the contractions of her pussy so intense, his cock erupted again.

There was only one woman he'd tolerate fucking him without his permission—and it was not this woman. He growled, bared his incisors, and tossed the woman off. Before the startled woman landed in a heap on the other side of the small bedroom, Etienne jumped from the bed, landing in a crouch.

Sensing he and the woman were not alone in the RV, Etienne responded instinctively, shifting into a large gray wolf. He sniffed the air and padded slowly toward the open bedroom door.

Three males stood there, all vampires, crowded beyond the door. *What are you doing here and what do you want?*

A tall vampire with salt and pepper hair stepped forward. "I'm Vitali Bourcaro and I assure you that you have no need to be on the defensive with us. We, and Adona, who's lying unconscious on the other side of the room, are here to help you."

Adona? She was the only female who had been capable of helping him forget Raven for even a short period of time. The woman he'd tossed off him was not Adona. But at the moment he had more pressing concerns. He'd heard of the Defense League of the Brotherhood and Vitali Bourcaro. What he didn't know was where the hell Raven was and what the Brotherhood wanted with him.

Etienne shifted back to his human form and crossed the room to examine the crumpled form. The naked, pale body of a mildly attractive woman with short, dark curly hair did not belong to Adona.

"What the hell." When he kneeled to press two fingers against the side of the woman's neck, he received another surprise. She was unconscious, but alive. He caressed her cheek. *Forgive me.*

Sighing, he lifted her into his arms and carried her to the bed. He laid her on her back, covering her naked body before he faced Bourcaro. "What do you want?"

"To talk."

"Where is Raven?"

Bourcaro shrugged. "Probably with Acier."

That Raven had fled to Acier the moment he fell asleep annoyed the hell out of him. His nostrils flared. "That still doesn't explain what you're doing here and why you stood by while that... female used me like a damned sex toy."

"We have more important things to discuss than sex."

"Such as?"

"We've been watching you for some time. You're strong, intelligent, and fierce—all qualities I look for in those I invite to join the Brotherhood."

He knew both his father and his uncles had issues with the Brotherhood. Normally that would have been enough to ensure he kept his distance from the vampire group. But why should he dismiss the opportunities the Brotherhood could provide just because his father's family didn't like them? He cared nothing for his father and even less for his family. "Why would I want to join an organization that stands in opposition to my family?"

"Because you deserve more than your short-sighted family has given you. Why should a male with your abilities take a backseat to Acier? Why should he have the woman you deserve?"

Why indeed? He narrowed his gaze. "What do you suggest I do about Acier?"

Bourcaro shrugged. "What can you do—except kill him? Do that and she'll come running back to you for comfort."

"He's my brother."

"He's a brother who has no problem hogging the family spotlight and taking the love of a woman he doesn't deserve. What brother worth the name would expect you to stand idly by while he robs you of your bloodlust? You owe him nothing—except a quick, painless death!"

Etienne nodded slowly. With Acier gone Raven would have no reason not to rush back into his arms, his heart, and his bed.

Bourcaro placed a hand on his shoulder. "If I were you, I'd call Acier and tell him to prepare for a battle to the death for Raven."

The idea, which once would have been unthinkable for him, now held undeniable appeal. "He won't come alone." Etienne's lip curled. "He'll probably bring Aleksei."

"Afraid to face you alone?" Bourcaro shrugged. "You won't be alone either. We will accompany you to ensure it's a fair fight."

* * *

Acier swept Raven's long, dark curtain of hair aside. He cupped his hands over her cheeks. She was one of the sexiest, most seductive females he'd ever met. He knew she could have any man she wanted. Luckily she loved and wanted him. He saw that assurance in the vibrant green eyes gazing up at him... encouraging him to stake his ownership of her anew.

"I love you more than I love anything or anyone else, Acier."

He pressed her against the door and devoured her soft, sweet, willing lips. The feel of her large, firm breasts crushed against his chest sent his desire spiraling out of control. His need and hunger for her consumed him.

Sweeping his tongue into her mouth, he lifted his right knee and nudged her thighs. She parted her long, lovely legs for him. He shifted his body so that she could feel his cock. "Oh, yes, my Acier."

He loved how quickly she was ready for him. He kissed her, sucking her tongue into his mouth. She responded to his intimate kiss with a warmth that delighted and aroused him. His nostrils flared. The intoxicating aroma of her pussy signaled her readiness for him. He had to have her immediately.

Slipping her hands between their bodies, she quickly unzipped his pants and hers. Moaning against his lips, she drew his cock from his pants and briefs. His ability to control his desire vanished. He pulled her blouse open, sending the buttons scattering over the carpet. With her help, he pushed her panties and jeans over her hips and below her big, round ass. Then, groaning against her lips, he shot his hips forward and drove his cock into her tight, hot, luscious pussy. She gasped and arched her body into his, encouraging him.

Her pussy fit around him as if it had been custom-made to accommodate his cock. Buried deep inside her, he experienced an almost immediate climax. With her he enjoyed both a physical and an emotional satisfaction he had never known with anyone else. His need for her frightened him.

It doesn't need to be scary, Steele, because I have the same hunger for you.

Steele. She hadn't used the English word for his French name since his feast—when he had done his best to hurt and frighten her.

You'll always be my Steele.

Somehow her use of her nickname for him released a knot of tension in his gut. In turn some of the hate and anger he felt for Etienne evaporated. This was the time to satisfy his need for her while assuring himself of her love. He eased in and out of her slowly. He loved the way her vaginal muscles clung to his cock, trying to impede each withdrawal, but then opened to welcome him as he slid back inside her... deep inside her wet, tight channel. This is why he'd been born—to love and worship this sweet, beautiful, giving female. He'd had more explosive sex, but only with her did he feel as if he was where he belonged... where he'd always belong.

He slid his hands below her waist. Cupping her ass, he drilled her slowly... loving each second of each slow slide into her wonderful warmth.

Oh, Steele. That's very nice.

You like it?

Yes, I do, but what I'd like even more is to be fucked.

Pressing his face against her cleavage, he gripped her hips. *My pleasure,* petite. He thrust hard and deep in her warm, slick tunnel. Ripples of pleasure splashed over him in a series of endless waves. His ability to do anything but feel was compromised... impaired... immobilized. He shuddered and tried to hold back the explosion threatening to swallow him. She wasn't ready and he wasn't going to come before he'd pleased her.

But I want you to.

No. He eased his hips backwards until only the tip of his cock remained inside her.

She tightened herself around him. *Yes. Yes, Steele. Let go. Come. Come for me, sweetie.* She pushed her hips forward, impaling herself on his cock. He shuddered and gritted his teeth. Wrapping her legs around him, she humped herself on his cock, squeezing and massaging it until he thought he'd lose his mind. *Let yourself go, Steele. Fill me up with your seed!*

Oh, hell, petite! He released the slender thread of his control. Sinking his incisors into the side of her neck, he thrust his cock in and out of her tight, clinging pussy in rapid succession.

Oh, yes. Yes, Steele. Feed on me... consume me...

He groaned as she pressed a finger against his asshole. Moaning, she pushed her finger past his tight, protesting hole, and into his ass. He shuddered, slammed his cock into her, hurting her. He ejaculated into her, shooting jet after jet into her hot channel. Her finger inside his ass intensified and prolonged his climax.

Yes, my Steele... the love of my life... come for me... come in me... feed on me. She held him close while he continued to ingest her addictive blood long after she'd eased her finger out of him and he'd finally stopped coming. The taste, scent, and rush of her blood onto his tongue created a unique feeling of satisfaction in him.

After the last rush of pleasure had crashed over him, he drew her down to the carpet. Holding her in his arms, he continued to feed on her until the bliss was almost a pain. Only then did he lift his head and embrace her.

She clung to him. *You are the love of my life, Steele. You... only you.*

Only him. That's the way it should be with a vampire-shifter and his bloodlust. They lay in silence until she slipped her hands down his back to cup his ass. He wanted her again, but not against the wall and not on the floor. He rose and lifted her to her feet. "Let's go to bed."

She shook her head and fixed her clothes. "Let's do that later. I haven't seen the girls yet. How are they?"

She watched his face light up. "As gorgeous as ever."

"Your father is very lucky."

He drew his trousers over his hips and zipped them up. "He's very proud of them."

"He's proud of you too."

His immediate nod and slight smile pleased her. "I know."

She pushed her breasts into her bra cups and sighed at the state of her blouse. Only two buttons remained. Oh, well. She looked up at him. "What about you, Steele? Do you want kids?"

"Yes."

"Good, because I'd very much like to have your babies—as soon as possible."

"But?"

Flashes of her conversation with Etienne and of her visions sent a shiver through her. "Etienne said the chance of our being able to have a baby together is practically nonexistent. He said hybrids are usually sterile. Do you know any that aren't?"

He swore. "Etienne talks too damned much!"

"I'd really like to have your baby."

"Just maybe Etienne doesn't know everything he thinks he does." He hugged her. "Now let's go get you into another blouse and then we'll go see Pali and Lexie."

After spending an hour with the twins, she and Steele had dinner in the large dining room. The table had been custom made to seat forty-two people to allow as many shifters as possible to share meals with Acier when he was at the complex.

After a walk in the moonlight, she and Acier took a bottle of wine and went to his suite. In the living room, they listened to soft jazz and sipped wine while enjoying the moonlight shining in through the floor to ceiling glass wall.

Halfway through the second drink, Acier rose suddenly, urged her to her feet, and moving with supernatural speed, he stripped her. He stepped back to survey her. The smile on his face vanished.

"What?"

He swore at length in French.

She frowned. "Steele? What's wrong?"

"Lights!"

The lights in the room came on. She followed his gaze downward and saw the remnants of the many bruises covering her body. Oh, no! She reached down to pick up her blouse. As she struggled to put it on, he snatched it from her and tossed it aside.

"He brutalized you."

"He... he didn't mean to."

"I'm going to kill him!"

She closed her eyes briefly. How could she make him understand? "He's going through his feast, Steele. Please don't forget that. You can't expect him to be anything but centered on his own pleasure. I know it looks bad, but I'm not hurt." She stepped closer to him and put her arms around him.

He shuddered against her, his fingers digging into her flesh. They would create new bruises. The depth of his pent-up fury frightened her. The brothers who had once been so close would probably attack each other the moment they met again. "Let's go to bed, Steele. Please. I'm afraid and I need you to hold me."

"You have no need to fear him. If he dares lay another hand on you—"

She pressed her fingers against his lips. "I'm not afraid of him. I'm afraid of what's happening to the two of you. You used to be so close. Now you're both talking about hurting each other. I never wanted or expected to come between you two."

"You haven't."

"I have. It's because of me you're both filled with such anger."

"It's not because of you. There'd be no problem between us if he got off of his lazy ass and found his own bloodlust instead of expecting me to allow him to take mine."

Therein lay the problem. "What if he thinks he's found his bloodlust?"

"Then he should stay the fuck away from you! If..." He trailed off and stared at her. "Is he so delusional he thinks you're his bloodlust?"

"He's confused, Steele."

"If he doesn't get a grip, he'll be dead!"

"You don't mean that."

"The hell I don't!"

"Well, then you'd better rethink your position."

"What?"

"Get this straight, Acier. I will not stay with you if you hurt him."

"Well, I sure as hell have no plans to let him hurt me—even if that is your personal preference."

About to snap at him, she took several deep, calming breaths before she spoke. "If that were my preference, I'd be with him begging him not to hurt you."

"The day—"

"Enough of this shit, Acier! My father is in Philadelphia fighting for his life. My best friend has disappeared. I'm still trying to deal with who I am. I'm not in the mood for any more shit from you. Give me what I want or I'm leaving."

He curled his fingers in her hair and tugged her head back. "Who the fuck do you think you're talking to? It's time you realized the way this relationship is going to work. I love you and you're my bloodlust, but I don't take orders from you or anyone else. Get this straight, Raven. You are not leaving—unless I allow it. And I guarantee I am not allowing you to leave here just so you can run straight to him."

"I don't require your permission to leave." She peeled his fingers from her hair and stormed toward the door.

He pushed the door closed as she pulled it open. Using the weight of his body, he pressed her against the door. She felt his lips brushing against her left ear. "Don't..."

"Don't what, Acier?"

"Don't... go."

"I think I should."

He turned her around and tipped up her chin. "There's a lot going on in my life right now. Some of those things I'm not sure of, but I'm very sure that I need you."

"Oh, Steele." She linked her arms around his neck. "I need you too. Hold me."

He swept her off her feet. Moments later as she lay in his arms with him whispering to her in French, she shivered. She knew he was still determined to confront Tee. He tightened his embrace, drawing her closer.

She closed her eyes. If the tension between the brothers remained high, she'd need to do something drastic.

Chapter Six

As soon as Raven fell asleep, Acier left his suite. Walking through the dark, quiet, L-shaped house, he paused outside the guest suite. Before he could lift a hand to knock, the door opened. Aleksei, holding Pali, stepped into the hallway.

Acier sighed. "I need to talk."

"I need to listen."

He glanced at Pali, sleeping peacefully against Aleksei's shoulder. He stroked her cheek. "She's... they're both so beautiful."

To his surprise, Aleksei cupped a palm against his cheek. "So are you. Where would you like to talk?"

Acier glanced at Pali again. She wore a fuzzy pink outfit. A pair of pink socks covered her feet. "Can we sit in the moonlight? Would she be warm enough?"

"Yes."

They left the house and sat on the back terrace. Acier listened to Aleksei cooing softly to Pali. Each time he did, Pali made a soft, pleased sound in her sleep. Acier sighed. If Etienne was right, and he usually was, this was a pleasure Acier would never know. He glanced at Pali. "May I..."

Aleksei smiled. "Of course." He kissed Pali's cheek before he gently placed her in Acier's arms.

Pali opened her dark eyes, smiled up at Acier, and immediately wrapped her tiny fingers around the one he stroked against her cheek. "I think I'm going to have to kill Etienne."

"No, you won't. Enola tells me that both you and Etienne have deep-seated resentments of each other you need to work out physically. I have no doubt you'll kick his over-privileged ass, but we're not going to entertain any talk of killing him." Aleksei clamped a hand over the back of his neck. "That is out of the question."

Acier shook off the hand. "He took the engagement ring I gave Raven and made her wear one he'd bought her. He's not going to leave us in peace."

"I'll say this just once more, Acier. I don't care what he's done, you are not going to kill him. Is that clear?"

"He says she's his bloodlust!"

"Perhaps she is."

Acier blinked. "What? How can she be his when she's mine?"

Aleksei shrugged. "And who says a female can't be the bloodlust of more than one vampire at the same time?"

"You mean… it's possible?"

"I've heard of a few cases."

"How did the cases you've heard of turn out?"

Aleksei sighed. "Badly."

"What happened?"

"In each case, the older, stronger vampire killed the younger one. The women, feeling as if they were the cause of the death of their soulmates, killed themselves."

Acier sucked in a breath.

"But that won't happen with you, Etienne, and Raven."

"She's not his bloodlust."

"Enola believes she is."

Acier felt his incisors descending. "Maybe Enola doesn't know everything."

"I'm sure he doesn't, but I wouldn't bet on his being wrong about this, Acier. He's very old and very skilled at what he does. He's probed Etienne's mind on more than one occasion. If he says it's true, I think you're going to have to accept that it is."

"No! She's mine."

Aleksei sighed again, placing a hand on his arm. "There are difficult times ahead of us as a family, Acier, but we are strong and we will survive."

"But—" Acier's cell phone rang. Handing Pali to Aleksei, he lifted his cell phone from his waist. Noting the number on the

Caller ID he frowned and took the call. "You've got a lot to answer for, pup."

"Where is she, Acier?" Etienne demanded.

"Where is who?"

"Raven! She belongs to me."

"The hell she does."

"If she's with you, send her back."

"Why the hell would I do that?"

"Because I'll have to come get her if you don't."

A knot of rage formed in Acier's gut. "I wouldn't advise that, pup, unless you want your ass kicked all over the desert."

"Don't you call me pup in that condescending voice. You'd better send her back, Acier, or so help me, you'll be sorry."

Acier laughed. "The night I fear you is the night I'll be dead."

"Which is exactly what you'll be if you don't send her back where she belongs—to me."

"Why don't you come here and give taking her from me your best shot? But I warn you, pup, the fact that we're brothers won't stop me from ripping you a new one."

Aleksei shook his head. *It might not be wise to have a confrontation with him here in front of the pack. Go to him.*

He was loath to leave the den again, but decided Aleksei was right. "Better yet, I'll come to you."

"You do that, Acier. I'll be waiting for you in the Pine Barrens." Etienne abruptly ended the call.

Acier turned to look at Aleksei. "I'm going to ki—"

Aleksei stared into his eyes. "Not only are you not going to kill him, you're going to allow him to kick your ass."

Acier jerked away. "Why would I do that?"

"Because he's your younger brother. He's feeling sick, alone, and afraid. He's in bloodlust with a female he thinks he has to kill you to have. I know how you feel. Not only can I read your troubled thoughts, but I've been in similar positions with Vladimir more times than I care to remember. I know you've spent most of your life doing your best to protect and take care of him. I've done the same thing with his father."

Aleksei sighed. "Sometimes... often it seemed an endless proposition with Vladimir. Before I met Dani, there was a woman I loved and wanted to be with, but I had to allow her to leave because of family obligations. Subjugating your own needs and desires for the good of your younger siblings is a large part of being the eldest sibling."

"How many more times am I expected to do that for him? When we left the pack against Aime's wishes, I worked two jobs while going to school full time so he wouldn't have to work at all. While I spent four years getting barely four hours of sleep a night, he was out partying and whoring all over town! I paid back the majority of his student loans! I walked to classes while he drove around in the secondhand car I saved to buy! How much more am I supposed to do for him? When does he start doing something for me?"

Aleksei nodded. "I understand you feel you've done enough for him, but he's never needed you more than he does now. He needs you to do this one more thing for him. When you meet him, put up a good fight, but let him get the upper hand."

"If I do that, he'll kill me."

"Take that chance."

"Why should I risk allowing him to kill me?"

"Because I ask you to and because I'll be there. Do you really think I'd allow anyone to kill you while I'm alive?"

Acier shook his head. "No, but—"

"No buts, Acier. We have to rescue him now or risk losing him. Do you really want to spend any more time alienated from him?"

About to snap that he didn't care, Acier swallowed slowly. After their mother had died, knowing that Etienne always had his back had made their love-starved life much more bearable. He did miss the close relationship he and Etienne had once shared. "No."

"Then we'll do what's necessary to help rescue him." Aleksei smiled and held Pali out to him. "Now give your sister a good night kiss. I have to put her to bed and go call Vladimir."

Acier kissed Pali's cheek and smiled when she gave him a big, gummy smile. He stroked a finger down her cheek. "I love you," he said softly.

She rewarded him with another smile.

He looked up at Aleksei. "Why are you calling Vladimir?"

"He's Etienne's father. He'll be there."

Acier tensed. "He'll expect me to allow Etienne to beat me senseless or—"

Aleksei frowned. "He's my brother and I love him more than I love my own life, but you, Acier, are flesh of my flesh, my son. I will not allow him to slap you around. Understood?"

He nodded. "Yes... Father."

Aleksei smiled. "Yes. I am your father. Now, you'd better go prepare your dens for your departure. The sooner we get this over and done with, the sooner we can welcome Etienne back to sanity."

* * *

"Don't go, Steele. Please."

Standing in his bedroom watching a naked Raven slip out of bed, Acier longed to spend the rest of the week lying between her thighs. But that would have to wait. "If I don't go, he'll come here. I'm having enough problems with Leon's den without having them witness Etienne and I battling each other."

Crossing the room to gaze up at him, she placed her hands on his chest. "If you go, I'm afraid one of you will end up dead."

"Why?" He saw the fear in her green gaze. "What have you seen?"

"One of you dead—over me—and I can't allow that, Steele!"

He sucked in a breath. "Which one of us?"

"I don't know."

"Raven, his hair is a lot shorter than mine. Surely you can tell us apart."

She shook her head. "In the vision, both of you had short hair. I couldn't tell who was dead. All I know is that I don't want either of you killed!"

He caressed her cheek. "You told me yourself Willoni often can't foresee their own future."

"If you face him and one of you is killed—"

"It wouldn't be your fault."

"It would be because I came between you two!"

"Aleksei and Vladimir will be there, along with Enola to ensure neither of us gets seriously hurt."

She gripped his shirt. "Don't go, Steele. Please."

"I have to face him. Enola says it's something he and I both need." He gave her a small smile. "As you might have guessed by now, I too have some unresolved and until now unacknowledged issues with Etienne. Both he and I need this cleansing."

"Cleansing? How is beating each other physically going to cleanse either of you?"

He shrugged. "If it'll make you feel better about this, I promise I won't kill him."

She stepped away from him, compressing her lips. "And what if he kills you?"

"Despite what he thinks, I'm physically stronger and far more driven than he's ever been. He's not going to kill me."

"You wouldn't be so certain of that if you knew the level of his resentment. If you go to face him, don't expect me to be here waiting when you return."

His incisors descended. "I have too much going on now for you to start this shit with me, Raven! I'm going to face him because I have to."

"You're going because you *want* to!" She leveled a finger at him. "Well, I'm not some object you and he can beat each other senseless over. Go if you must, Acier, but just understand that the spoils don't always go to the victor."

He clenched his hands into fists. "Are you implying that when I give him the ass kicking he's needed for a long time now, you'll leave me for him?"

Her green eyes flashed at him. "Perhaps I'll decide I don't need or want either of you!"

"Really? And just maybe I'll decide I don't need or want a woman who sleeps with my brother the moment I turn my back, Raven!"

She sucked in a breath. "I won't be here when you return."

Even as he felt as if she were driving a sharp knife through his heart, he shrugged. "That's your choice, Raven."

"That's all you have to say to me?"

"No, it isn't. If you're not here when I return, I won't come looking for you. And should you change your mind and return, you just might find that I've changed mine about wanting you."

He watched a look of hurt dismay spread across her face before he turned and stalked out of the bedroom. It would be a cold damned day in hell when he allowed a twenty-two-year-old to jerk the chain to his heart again. If she was there when he returned, he'd mend fences with her. If she wasn't, even with his heart ripped out, he'd get on with his life. He would not chase her or beg her to return to him. If she wanted him, she'd have to prove it and understand he wasn't going to be held hostage by threats of her leaving whenever they had a disagreement.

* * *

Etienne's thoughts kept returning to Raven. He hungered for her with an intensity he feared would consume him. He had to have her—even if it meant killing Acier. For a brief moment the thought of Acier's death sent a streak of dread through him. He shook it off. He would lose his mind without Raven. Without her, he would have no reason to live.

He felt a warm, familiar presence and glanced up. Adona, naked, with her dark, beautiful skin glistening from a shower, walked into the living room. "Are you all right?"

She shook her head.

He saw tears in her dark eyes. Damn. This was a fine time for her to turn feminine on him. "I'm sorry," he told her. "I didn't mean to hurt you."

Her lips trembled. "I know you hunger for her, but she's not here. I am." She lifted her arms. "Love me, Wyatt."

Etienne frowned. He made a living acting in adult films under the name Wyatt Diamond. Clearly Adona, or whoever this woman was, had seen his movies. However, during their previous encounters she'd always called him Etienne. Within minutes of meeting her weeks earlier, he'd known she wasn't the vampire fem she purported to be. After her incredible change earlier in the bedroom, he had no idea who or what she was.

He was certain of one thing—her ability to ease his hunger for Raven deserved a measure of consideration. He stared down at her. "Who are you?"

She wrapped her arms around herself. "Someone who shouldn't, but can't help wanting and loving you."

"Why shouldn't you want me?"

She shook her head. "I don't know. I just know it's wrong for me to want you, but I do. Hold me, please? I need you."

The need he saw in her dark gaze mirrored what he felt for Raven. No one should suffer that level of deprivation when such a basic, overriding need went unmet. He picked her up.

She linked her arms around his neck, laying her cheek against his shoulder. "I need you."

"You're going to get me." He carried her through the RV to the bedroom.

He tore off his clothes while she played with her breasts and fingered herself. "I'm getting nice and wet for you, Etienne."

The aroma of her pussy intoxicated his senses. She was so sweet. He couldn't wait to slip back inside her.

"Then don't." She leaned against the wall and smiled at him over her shoulder. "You look hard. I'm wet and ready. What are we waiting for? Take me, my handsome Etienne. Put your mark on me. Brand me as yours." She reached back and parted her cheeks. "Take me."

She was so lovely with her dark flesh still glistening with moisture. He moved to brush his lips against her lovely neck. Her skin was soft and warm. She turned her head, and the look in her eyes shook him. No one had ever looked at him with such unconditional adoration. He kissed her, rubbing his groin against her round ass. *Damn, what a nice ass.*

Fuck it! she invited, sliding her tongue along his.

He pulled away from her lips and kissed his way down her body, over her lush, beautiful skin. Dropping to his knees, he nibbled at her ass cheeks, loving the feel of her warm flesh. Reaching around, he slipped two fingers inside her. She was wet. Withdrawing his fingers, he rose, and parted her cheeks. He slid his cock along her crack before he positioned it at her rear entrance.

Fuck my ass. Please.

The beauty of non-human women was their ability to take a hard shaft up their asses without lube. He eased his hips forward. The head of his dick pierced her tight hole.

"Oh! Yes!"

"Hell, yeah!" He thrust forward, sliding his entire length into her tight rear. "Oh, damn! You have a sweet ass."

She ground herself against his groin, tightening her muscles as she did. "It's sweet because it was made for your fucking pleasure alone, my handsome hunk. So fuck it—as hard as you like."

"Oh, baby, you know how to get me hot!" He gripped her waist. He fucked her with long, slow strokes. Pounding her would offer a quick, sweet release, but he didn't want to come before her. Within a few slow strokes his passion rose.

Don't worry about me. If you're satisfied, I'll be satisfied. I want you to come. Come! Come! Come!

He closed his eyes and struggled to hold back his impending climax. She made that harder by slamming her hips back at him, forcing his cock balls deep in her ass again and again until he trembled with the effort to keep from coming.

Come! Come! Come for me… come in me, Etienne. Please. Brand me with your seed!

He surrendered to her persuasive words. Wrapping his arms around her waist, he sank his incisors into the side of her neck. As he fed on her, he fucked her with a hard, furious motion. Within minutes, he groaned, rutted into her tight ass, and exploded, jetting his seed in her.

Oh, damn! That was incredible. With his cock still in her ass, he slipped the fingers of one hand into her pussy. He rubbed the thumb of his other hand along her clit. He sighed with relief when she gasped and came. *Oh, yeah.*

Cupping his hands over her breasts, he continued to feed on her until she stopped trembling. He removed his incisors from her neck and eased his cock out of her ass. Then he lifted her into his arms and carried her to the bed. They cuddled together in silence.

She lay with her cheek resting against his shoulder. The sex between them had been very satisfying. As before, while inside her, he had been able to forget Raven. He stroked her hair and tensed. Adona was gone—again. In her place was the pale woman. He lifted her off his body and rolled away from her.

She reached for him. "Wyatt? Please stay with me."

He shook off her hand and slipped out of bed. "The name's Etienne, not Wyatt. And I can't stay. I have a date with brother dearest shortly."

"To fight him over her? What does she have that I don't?"

Her tone when speaking of Raven annoyed him. "She's my bloodlust."

"What am I?"

He sat on the side of the bed, surprised by the urge to soften the coming blow. "It's been a long time since I've met a woman half as exciting as you are."

"But?"

Women. They were never satisfied until they'd wrung a confession from a man—and then they still weren't satisfied. He rose and moved away from the bed. "But you're not my bloodlust."

She slipped out of bed and pressed her breasts against his chest. "I could be."

Sometimes when he was with her he almost believed that. It was only when he was away from her that his hunger for Raven overshadowed his feelings for her. "You're very sexy, but I don't even know who or what you are." He stroked her cheek. "And frankly, honey, I prefer women with darker skin and a bigger butt."

Her cheeks reddened. Her eyes welled. He immediately regretted his hurtful, tacky outburst. There was no need to hurt her just because she wasn't Raven.

"I love you far more than she ever could. Give me a chance to help you forget her."

"If forgetting her was easy, she wouldn't be my bloodlust."

"I can help you forget."

"I don't want to forget her."

She clutched his hand. "I could make you far happier than she ever could."

He withdrew his hand from hers. "I'm going to shower, get dressed, and leave."

"I'll wait for you."

"Don't." He sighed. "If you feel half of what you say you do, you deserve far better than what I can give you."

"I don't want better. I want you. If she were gone, would that increase my chances with you?"

He bared his incisors. "She's not gone, so don't get any ideas. Is that clear?"

"Very."

He gave her a cool look. "It would be better if you're not here when I return."

She gasped. "Wyatt—"

"How the hell do you expect me to want a relationship with you when you don't even know who I am? My name's Etienne." He turned and left the room. He heard her sob and stopped. She was the only woman who had given him a measure of peace in months. What difference did it make what she was or what color her skin was? She was willing to accept him just as he was. Why couldn't he do the same with her?

He returned to the bedroom.

She had thrown herself across the bed where she lay sobbing. She was Adona again. He sat on the side of the bed and lifted her. When she turned into his arms, he felt a rush of emotion. He wrapped his arms around her and crushed his lips down on hers. He made love to her slowly, ensuring she came before he allowed himself to enjoy the sweet release of coming inside her.

Later, as she slept, he eased from the bed. He bent over and kissed her dark cheek. He was aware of a sudden desire to remain with her, but he ignored it. After dressing quickly and quietly, he left the room. He had a date with Acier.

As he unlocked the doors of his SUV, Vladimir slipped into the passenger's side. Etienne was surprisingly glad to see him. He started the engine before he turned to look over at him. "I didn't expect to see you again."

He watched Vladimir's jaw clench. "Didn't you? You're my son. Did you think I'd allow you to face Aleksei's brat alone?"

Etienne hesitated before he spoke again. "I'm going to kill him."

"As much as it pains me to say this, we don't kill our siblings, Etienne."

"It's the only way I can have Raven, and I have to have her. She should be mine, not his! And if I have to kill him to get her, so be it." He shifted the engine into gear and pulled out of the parking space.

"She's Willoni. It's up to her to choose who has mastered her soul song. If she's chosen him, you'll have to learn to deal with having her when you can."

He shook his head, tightening his hands on the steering wheel. "It's not enough."

"Even if we would allow it, killing him would not change how she felt. You'd just ensure she loved him all the more. Possession of her body alone would be small comfort if her heart continued to belong to him."

"I'll take my chances," he snapped. "If you're going to try and talk me out of what I'm determined to do, get out."

"And leave you to face him alone?"

"No. The Brotherhood will be there."

"The hell they will!" Without warning, Vladimir's hand shot out and grabbed the steering wheel. The SUV veered sharply to the shoulder.

Etienne slammed on the brakes. He cut the engine and turned to glare at Vladimir. "What the hell is your problem?"

The words had barely left his mouth before a backhand blow from Vladimir sent him sprawling against the driver's side door. Vladimir leaned close and stared into his eyes. "My problem is having a son who doesn't know his place! I've taken all the disrespect I intend to take from you, boy. I am your father and I expect you to act like it! I'm not taking any more shit or backtalk from you. Do I make myself clear?"

He bared his incisors. "Get away from me."

Vladimir grabbed his collar and jerked on it. "Do I make myself clear, Etienne?"

There was a resolve in Vladimir's voice he'd never heard. It matched the steel in his angry, blue gaze. The tone and the look said one thing clearly: *I am not the vampire to keep pissing off, boy*!

"Crystal."

"Good. And if I were you, I would not expect the Brotherhood to show up."

"Why not?"

"Because they have better sense than to show up any place where Aleksei and I will be together… especially after they've clearly been stirring up trouble between you and Acier." Vladimir released his shirt and returned to his seat.

Etienne sucked in a deep breath before he started the engine again. "Where are Slayer and Karol?"

"They're with Mother."

Great. Just great.

They made the rest of the drive in silence.

* * *

The ringing of her cell phone interrupted Raven's pacing. She glanced at the Caller ID and gasped in relief as she answered the call. "Abby! Abby, where have you been?"

"Ravanni, I've... I'm in trouble. I need help. Will you help me?"

"Of course I will! Just tell me where you are and I'll be there as soon as possible."

"I'm in Philadelphia. Can you meet me at my hotel? It's just outside the city limits."

"I'll get on a flight and be there as soon as I can."

"I'll be waiting for you, Ravanni."

Raven ended the call and went in search of Acier's cousin, Xavier Depardieu, who led the dens in Acier's absence. She found the tall, handsome, blue-eyed blond relaxing in an easy chair in the communal living room. He rose as she entered the room, a smile spreading across his face. "Raven, what can I do for you?"

"I need to get back to Philly. Can you help me?"

"How soon do you need to arrive?"

"As soon as possible."

"Perhaps Alpha Supreme will make his private jet available."

Raven shook her head. "Oh, no! I couldn't presume to even consider asking him that. He'll think I have awful nerve."

"You are the life mate of the Alpha-in-waiting. If Alpha Supreme has no pressing plans for his jet, I'm certain he'd be delighted to put it at your disposal."

"Are you sure?"

"I'm positive." He gestured toward the chair he'd vacated at her entrance. "Make yourself comfortable while I go see Alpha."

Two hours later, accompanied by two shifters from Den Gautier, Raven sat aboard Aime Gautier's private jet on her way back to Pennsylvania. Her thoughts were in turmoil. Fear overwhelmed her. Acier and Etienne would soon be trying to kill each other because they both wanted her.

Many hours later, Raven and the two shifters Xavier had insisted accompany her stood outside the airport. "I'll be fine making my way to the hotel." She extended her hand. "Thanks for accompanying me this far."

The taller of the two smiled and placed a hand under her elbow. "Alpha Xavier insisted we see you safely to your destination."

Certain that they would follow her regardless of her protests, she smiled. "Thank you."

At Abby's hotel room door, she thanked them again, and offered her hand.

The taller shifter took her hand in his and inclined his head. "No thanks are required. You are the life mate of our Alpha. It was an honor to accompany you, ma'am."

If only she felt certain she was still Acier's life mate. They hadn't parted on the best of terms. She smiled and turned to look at the second shifter. He inclined his head, but remained silent. "Thank you both very much."

She knocked on the door.

"It's open," Abby's voice called. "Come in."

Raven opened the door and stepped inside.

Candlelight lit the interior of the suite. Raven looked around the living room. "Abby?"

"In here."

Abby's voice came from the open door on the other side of the room. Raven walked across the living room and into the bedroom.

Even though Abby looked pale and shaken, it was a relief to see her unharmed. She smiled and crossed the room. "Oh, Abby! I'm so happy to see you. I've been so worried about you."

It was only as she embraced Abby that a chill of apprehension ran down her spine. She released Abby. "Abby? What's wrong?"

Abby's lids lowered, concealing her expression. "I sensed you needed me so I called you."

Raven frowned and stepped away from Abby. "Where have you been? Why haven't you answered any of my calls?"

Abby sighed. "I've been having a very difficult time. I know I haven't done my duty by you and I'm so sorry." She curtsied. "Forgive me."

Raven hesitated. Where was the warmth and eagerness to help Abby usually exuded? Why did she avoid eye contact?

"Forgive me, Ravanni." Abby curtsied again, deeper this time. When she lifted her head, there was a smile on her face. The warmth had returned to her gaze.

Raven relaxed and smiled. "There's nothing to forgive." She extended her hand. "I'm just glad you're okay."

Abby took Raven's hand in hers and squeezed it. "I can feel your agitation. Let me give you something to relax you and then we'll sing the Willoni creed song together."

She did need to relax, but she would not be singing the Willoni creed song which celebrated the Willoni's vow to forsake all physical pleasure in pursuit of higher goals. "I'm not ready to sing, Abby."

"But you are ready to relax?"

She nodded and sat on the side of the bed. "Yes. I have so much I need to discuss with you."

Abby smiled and nodded. She moved across the room to an open door which Raven guessed led to the bathroom. She returned moments later with two white pills and a glass of water. Raven took the pills and drank the water.

Abby's eyes gleamed with satisfaction as she took the glass from Raven. "Lie down on the bed and as soon as you're feeling relaxed, we'll begin."

Raven removed her shoes and lay on the bed. Instead of relaxation, she experienced a sense of agitation and fear. She closed her eyes and attempted to rock side to side to enhance her ability to focus her senses. She hummed softly. An abrupt sense of danger shot through her.

She attempted to bolt into a sitting position, but she couldn't move. Her eyes snapped open. A tall, dark woman with a malevolent smile on her face stood over her. "Yes, bitch, you're in trouble all right."

Raven attempted to speak, but her throat muscles were locked. She pushed back a wave of panic. *What are you doing, Abby? Why are you doing this?*

"Abby is gone. I'm Adona, and you have something I want."

What do I have that you want, Abby?

"I told you Abby is gone! My name is Adona, and Etienne is mine."

Raven struggled to regain control of her limbs. *I'm Acier's bloodlust, not Etienne's.*

"You think I don't know you've been with my man? I smelled your scent on him when we fucked!"

This was getting worse by the minute. Abby had clearly undergone the forbidden ceremony called the Progression of the Talisman that had enabled Raven to change her appearance so she'd had the ability to become any woman Acier desired during his Feast of Indulgence. That would account for her drastically changed appearance, but the woman calling herself Adona was definitely Abby.

That was necessary to begin his healing process.

"Lying bitch! Once you're dead he'll turn to me for comfort and pleasure." Abby grimaced and moved toward the bed.

Raven noted the large knife in her right hand. *Abby! I know you're in there somewhere. Listen to me. You can't do this. You are my spiritual guide. You can't do this!*

"Oh, but you are so very sadly mistaken, Raven. That speech might work on Abby. But that sorry Willoni who would stand by and allow you to take her man isn't here. You're dealing with Adona, and no one takes Adona's man."

Abby climbed onto the bed and straddled Raven's body. She smiled as she placed the sharp edge of the knife against Raven's throat. "I'm going to do this slowly and as painfully as possible. If you somehow survive, you'll know better than to try and steal any other man."

Looking up into the hate-filled eyes, Raven knew no amount of heartfelt appeal would help. In order to avoid death at the hands of the person chosen to guide her, she would have to help herself.

She closed her eyes and began a silent chant that her mother had taught her as a lullaby. *A Willoni is mistress of her own destiny. None can enslave a Willoni who accepts her destiny. None can enslave a Willoni who accepts her destiny.*

As the words flowed over and through her, she felt the telltale tingling sensation which signaled the return of blood circulating in her body. *None can enslave a Willoni who accepts her destiny. I accept my destiny and thus am mistress of my own fate.* The painful sensation of blood returning to her limbs spread from the fingers of her right hand up her arm. She needed more time before she had a hope of defending herself.

"Open your eyes, Raven!"

She kept her eyes closed and continued the silent chant. *None can enslave a Willoni who accepts her destiny. None can enslave a Willoni who accepts her destiny. I accept my destiny and thus am mistress of my own fate.* The fingers of her left hand tingled. *None can enslave a Willoni who accepts her destiny. I accept my destiny and thus am mistress of my own fate.* The muscles of her left arm burned with the return of circulating blood.

The knife was removed from her neck. "Open your eyes or die with them closed like the coward you are!"

Sensing Abby was about to stab her, she opened her eyes. A fine sheen covered Abby's face. The hand clutching the knife over Raven's body shook. What she was about to do went against everything she believed. If only Raven could reach her. *This is not the Willoni way, Abby. You can't do this. You've spent seventeen years watching over me. To do this would dishonor everything Willoni believe.*

"I am not Willoni and I'm not Abby! I'm Adona and you have something I want. If you have to die—so be it."

Raven tried again—appealing to Abby using her clan name. *Abigail Valanti, as the daughter of High Priestess Deliah, I demand you stop!*

Abby tensed on top of her, but only for a moment. She shook her head, as if shaking away momentary weakness. "Demand all you like, Willoni. I don't owe you or your mother any loyalty." Abby smiled as she drove the knife down toward Raven's chest.

Raven forced her hands up from her sides. Her fingers closed around Abby's wrist with the knife just inches from its target. She closed her eyes as they struggled, focused her energies on keeping the knife away from her body. Raven was slowly forcing the knife further away from her chest when Abby suddenly drove an elbow into her side.

Raven gasped in pain as she felt the blade pierce her chest.

Chapter Seven

"Are you sure?"

"Yes. I'm sure, but I can't afford to have this information traced back to me."

"Understood." Serge Dumont ended the call on his cell phone and started one of the SUVs the Dumonts kept at the airport. As he sped away from the airport, Serge made another call. Moments later he heard his older sister's voice. "Serge?"

"Tat, I just got a call from Deoctra. She's learned the Brotherhood has maneuvered everyone away from Etienne. Mik had to return to Boston and I'm on my way to Acier's RV. I have no idea where Aleksei or Vladimir are."

"Are you sure you can trust the information from Deoctra? I thought she'd made a break from the Brotherhood."

"She has, but her lover, Tucker Falcone, is still aligned with them. The information came from him."

"The last I heard Falcone had no love for our family."

"He doesn't, but he seems to have some for Deoctra and she and Mikhel have declared a truce."

"So you're certain the information is reliable?"

"Yes."

She swore softly. "Damn Bourcaro. I'll contact Andrei and we'll meet you at the RV with Jace."

Serge frowned at Tat's mention of her vampire-hunting lover, Jace Makefield. "Is it necessary to bring Makefield?"

She swore again. "Now is not the time to start any shit with me about Jace, Serge. He's my bloodlust and as you might know, he's made a habit of killing vampires and staying alive for the last fifty years. If we're going to face the Brotherhood, we'll need all the help we can get."

But the help of a vampire hunter who had once sought to kill Vladimir? Damn, he'd like to put his size twelve foot all the way up Makefield's ass. "Fine. I'll see you at the RV."

Forty-five minutes later he arrived at Acier's RV, located in an RV park outside of Philadelphia. Tat, her twin Andrei, and a tall, dark man with dark hair arrived moments later. Serge gave Makefield a cool look before turning to face Tat. "Etienne's not here."

She frowned. "Damn! How did this happen?" She shook her head. "Never mind. We'll figure that out after we find Etienne."

Serge took out his cell phone and tried Vladimir's number. This time Vladimir answered. "This had better be important, pup."

"I'm at Acier's RV with Tatiana, Andrei, and Makefield. Etienne, who was supposed to be here, isn't."

"He's with me."

Serge sighed in relief. "Then he's okay?"

"As okay as he can be under the circumstances."

"What circumstances are those?"

"We're on our way to a beat down with Acier."

Serge frowned. "They're going to fight each other? Let me guess. Over Raven?"

"Yes. Imagine two brothers wanting to kill each other over a woman."

Serge arched a brow. Having experienced similar emotions, he understood the fury between Acier and Etienne. "A few women are worth it."

"Not in this life they aren't."

Serge smiled. He'd expect such a sentiment from a vampire with a male bloodlust. "Do you want us to come?"

"No. Aleksei will be there with Acier and we don't really need an audience for this nonsense. When things have been settled, we'll call."

"Okay."

"Aren't you going to wish Etienne luck?"

When hell froze over. Instead of being satisfied with the mores of their culture which allowed him to sleep with Raven on certain occasions, the ungrateful bastard wanted Acier's bloodlust for his own. Imagining his own rage if Mikhel tried to take Derri from him, Serge knew Etienne was going to need all the luck he could get. Besides, as far as Serge was concerned, Etienne needed a good ass kicking. "They're both my nephews," he said and ended the call.

Tat swore when Serge repeated the conversation he'd had with Vladimir. "Will this family's problems ever end?"

Andrei grinned. "I don't think this is such a bad thing. Acier looks as if he's needed his uptight ass kicked for a long time."

Serge laughed. "It'll be a cold day in hell when Etienne can take Acier."

Andrei arched a brow. "Oh, come on, Serge. Surely you don't think Acier can take Etienne?"

"Any day of the week."

"Really? Are you interested in backing that opinion up with a small, brotherly wager?"

Serge shrugged. "Sure. What did you have in mind?"

Tat glared at them. "Are you two out of your minds? You are *not* going to bet on which of our nephews is going to win a fight that should never happen in the first place." She paced the living room. "I can't imagine what Aleksei is thinking."

Serge grinned. "He's probably thinking it's time that Etienne got the ass whipping he's needed for years."

Tat snarled at him.

Serge shrugged, his lips twitching. When he looked at Andrei, he saw clear amusement in his older brother's blue gaze. He turned his attention to Makefield, who'd been silent since his arrival. The hunter glanced quickly away, but not before Serge noted the gleam in his eyes. Moments later, the sound of the three males' uncontrollable laughter filled the RV.

"All three of your asses are mine!" Tat's angry promise only increased their mirth.

* * *

Acier stood in the Pine Barrens staring up into the night sky. The full moon had once sent him into prowl heat. In that state, he'd been incapable of thinking of anything beyond shifting and spending the night having sex with a series of women who meant nothing to him.

Since his transfusion of vampire blood, which had saved his life, and his Feast of Indulgence, the moon no longer held the unique majesty and beauty for him it once had. While he was not indifferent to the full moon, he felt no pressing need to shift into what he'd always considered his natural form—that of a big gray wolf.

The last time he'd been in these woods, it had been to face his ex-friend, Leon de la Rocque. That confrontation had ended in Leon's death. Little had Acier known he'd be back within weeks facing Etienne in what the other thought would be a fight to the death.

He looked to the shadows of the tall pines where Aleksei and Enola Cheyenne stood. On the flight from Arizona, he'd been eager to arrive and accept Etienne's challenge. Now memories of all he and Etienne had been through together assailed him. How could he fight the brother whose welfare and safety he had spent most of his life protecting? He raked a hand through his hair. "I don't think I can do this."

"I understand this is going to be difficult for you. It's not something I would ordinarily recommend or suggest. In this case, it's necessary for the completion of your own healing and for the start of Etienne's," Enola told him.

"I'm fine," he objected, turning his gaze to Aleksei's.

Aleksei shook his head. "Our conversation at your complex says differently, Acier."

"I was upset. I didn't mean those things."

"Yes, Acier, you did mean them. It's time to get everything out in the open. We'll deal with the situation between you and Etienne now and be done with it. When we leave here, we'll leave all angers and resentments behind and start fresh."

"I can't hurt him."

"He'll do his best to hurt you, Acier," Aleksei pointed out. "While I insist you don't get carried away, I don't expect you to allow him to use you as a punching bag. I expect you to defend yourself."

He swung away from the two males who seemed determined to force him to fight Etienne. "Fine, but let's do it some other time."

"The healing process will be most beneficial for you both under the auspices of the full moon."

Acier glanced up at the moon again. "It doesn't mean as much to me as it used to."

"I'm aware of that, Acier, but there is a part of you that will always respond to the call of the moon."

In the distance Acier heard the approach of a vehicle. He tensed. "It's Etienne."

Aleksei nodded. "And Vladimir. Like you, I can always sense when my twin is near."

Minutes later Etienne and Vladimir appeared at the edge of the trees, stopping next to Aleksei and Enola. At the sight of Etienne, a sudden, powerful rage filled Acier. His incisors descended. His eyes glowed. This ungrateful bastard dared to think he could take Raven? She was his! He barely overcame the urge to flash across the clearing to attack Etienne.

Rocking back and forth on the balls of his feet, Acier watched Vladimir speak to Aleksei. "Are you sure this is a good idea, Aleksei? I'd hate to have any bad feelings between us when Acier gets his ass kicked."

Although infuriated by the comment, Acier remained silent.

Aleksei arched a brow and smiled. "Vladimir, as much as it's going to pain me to watch, I'm afraid your pampered, selfish, over-privileged boy is in for the ass whipping of his life. Acier has promised not to kill him, but I'll be damned if he won't defend himself."

Vladimir bared his incisors. "Pampered, selfish, and over-privileged? What the hell are you talking about, Sei? Have you forgotten how he struggled growing up?"

Acier watched his father cast a quick look at Etienne. "Vladimir, I know he's your son and you feel compelled to defend his sorry ass, but Acier is the one who did all the struggling. It was Acier who worked two jobs so his lazy ass brother could spend all his time whoring with anything with a pussy! Hell, Acier probably did his damned homework for him as well! Everything he has he owes to Acier's struggles. He wouldn't know how to struggle or share if his miserable life depended on it!"

Listening to Aleksei, Acier's rage increased.

"Watch what you're saying, Aleksei," Vladimir warned.

"What's the matter, Vladimir? Can't stand the damned truth? Acier has done everything possible, but is that selfish brat of yours ever satisfied? Hell, no! Now the ungrateful pup has the nerve to think Acier should relinquish his bloodlust to him." With his eyes glowing, Aleksei bared his incisors. He moved around Vladimir to face Etienne. "Just when are you going to do something for Acier? Like find your own god-damned bloodlust and leave him and Raven in peace?"

Faced with the unexpected anger of the powerful, centuries-old vampire, Etienne stepped backward. Vladimir pulled Etienne behind him and faced Aleksei. "Stay out of his face, Sei! If you have issues with me, don't think for one goddamned minute I'll allow you to take them out on my son. Nor will I allow you to place that supercilious brat of yours on a pedestal at Etienne's expense."

Aleksei snarled and Acier could feel his father's rage across the distance separating them. "Are you challenging me, Vladimir?"

Before Vladimir could respond, Enola pulled Aleksei back and stepped between the two brothers. "Clearly, you two have some issues that need to be settled as well, but this is neither the time nor the place for that. This is about Etienne." He placed a hand on each brother's shoulder. "Calm down, both of you. Please."

Vladimir shook Enola's hand off his shoulder. He leveled a finger at Aleksei. "There was no need for you to disrespect Etienne or to get in his face as you've done. Acier has a face as well."

"Yes he does, and you'd do well to stay out of it, Vladimir. He has enough on his shoulders without any shit from you."

"I won't forgive this, Sei."

"Ask me if I care!"

"Enough!" Enola snapped. He swung around to face Aleksei. "You are the elder twin, Aleksei. It's your place to set the proper example. Do you really think this display of temper and emotion between you two is good for either of your sons? Do you want them trying to kill each other to please you two?"

Aleksei sucked in a deep breath before he shook his head. He turned to look at Acier. *Don't kill him, but kick his ass.*

Instead of fueling his anger, this time Aleksei's command diminished it. He and Etienne had always been close. No one had ever come between them before. They both wanted Raven, but she didn't want them at each other's throats on her behalf. He would not fight Etienne.

He half turned away.

"Acier!"

At the warning from Aleksei, Acier glanced over his shoulder. Etienne, shifted into his natural form, charged him. He barely had time to step back before Etienne slammed into him, knocking him on his back. Etienne lunged at his throat. Acier wrapped his hands around Etienne's neck and held him off.

Steele. Steele, I love you. I always have and I always will.

The desperate words projected directly into his mind startled Acier. He froze. *Raven? Raven?*

Etienne took advantage of his distraction, and Acier found himself pinned to the ground with Etienne's paws on his shoulders. Etienne's gaping jaws were inches from his exposed throat. His brother's rage-filled golden eyes stared down at him.

* * *

Raven overcame a wave of panic. She redoubled her efforts to force Abby's hand away, but couldn't stop the blade from sinking further into her chest. Feeling blood on her blouse, Raven feared she was about to die. She reached out to the most important person in her life. *Steele. Steele. I love you. I always have and always will.*

Raven felt a strange sensation in the room and then heard a commanding female voice call out. "Willoni! Stop!"

"Abigail! No!"

Raven opened her eyes. Two females stepped from a widening circle of light in the middle of the room. She recognized the bronze-skinned woman in the cream-colored dancer's tunic as Abby's sister, Belladonna. The woman next to her was beautiful—tall, with smooth, dark skin and eyes, and a regal bearing that led Raven to believe she was at the very least a Willoni High Priestess.

While Belladonna rushed across the room to the bed, the other woman lifted her right hand. Abby froze and the downward movement of the knife stopped. Belladonna pulled Abby off Raven.

Raven grabbed the knife, which was still embedded in her chest. The other woman quickly crossed the room and eased the blade from Raven's chest. Raven gasped and then sobbed as she felt her blood quickly soaking her blouse.

"It's all right, Raven." Speaking in a soft, consoling voice, the woman grasped Raven's hand in hers and placed her other palm over the wound. "Close your eyes and together, we will heal you."

Raven squeezed her hand. "I... I can't... breathe... I can't breathe."

"The worst is over. Close your eyes, Willoni." *Feel the wound... feel it closing... feel it. Feel it.*

She closed her eyes. *Feel it closing. Feel our combined strength willing it to close, Willoni.* Raven felt the blood stop flowing and the wound slowly closing. She lay still for several minutes, clutching the woman's hand. Finally she became aware of Abby, sobbing hysterically, and Belladonna's soft, insistent chanting.

"Are you feeling better, Raven?"

Raven opened her eyes and looked up at the woman. She nodded. "Yes. Thank you. I owe you so much and I don't even know who you are."

"I am Venus Amisha."

Raven sat up slowly, her lips parted in surprise. "Venus Amisha of the Golden Hills Clan?"

"Yes, Willoni."

"Goddess Ascendant of Bliss?"

Venus smiled. "I see you know something of our history, Raven."

Memories of tales her mother told her years earlier surfaced. Hadn't her mother talked of Venus in the past tense as if she no longer existed? Perhaps the memory was faulty. She would probe her memories later. There was something more pressing she needed to do. She struggled to get off the bed and knelt in front of Venus. "Goddess."

Venus reached down and lifted her to her feet. "Those days are long gone, Willoni. These days I am simply Venus Ryan. You're still weak. Lie on the bed while I help Bella attend to Abby."

Raven sat on the side of the bed while Belladonna clutched the sobbing Abby in her arms. She still had dark skin, but Raven sensed this really was Abby rather than Adona. Venus knelt next to them and placed her palm on Abby's cheek. "Be at peace, Willoni." She looked over her shoulder and met Raven's gaze.

Raven nodded. "Yes, Goddess."

Venus smiled and turned back to Abby. "Ravanni Monclaire, born of Deliah, High Priestess of Modidsha, is as gracious as her mother. She freely absolves you of all blame."

Abby shook her head and pulled out of Belladonna's arms. She sat against the wall and hugged herself, her dark gaze trained on Raven's face. "I… she… I tried to kill the Willoni I was charged with guiding. There can be no forgiveness for that, Goddess."

Venus turned to look at Raven again.

Raven slipped off the bed and knelt in front of Abby. "It was Adona who attacked me, Abby, not you. I don't hold you responsible for what she did."

Abby touched the large bloodstain on her blouse. "She… I would have killed you."

"But you didn't." Ignoring the dull ache in her chest, Raven smiled. "And I know you would never have hurt me."

"But she only exists because of my many mistakes."

Raven pressed a finger against her trembling lips. "I freely forgive you, Abby. I just want you well again."

Abby drew back, closing her eyes and rocking from side to side. As they watched, her skin tone grew lighter until it was pale. Several long minutes later her Adona persona had vanished and Abby was herself again.

"Abby! You're back!" Raven stretched out a hand.

Abby shook her head and drew away again. "Raven…" she whispered, and collapsed.

Belladonna dropped to her knees beside her sister and felt for a pulse. Raven shivered with fear. Belladonna gazed up at them with a stricken look in her eyes. "She has no pulse. Goddess, she's gone! She's gone!"

* * *

Etienne lowered his head, sinking his teeth into Acier's throat. Acier grabbed Etienne's ears and forced his jaws away. Etienne responded by dropping his weight onto Acier's chest, impeding his ability to breathe. Then he sank his teeth into Acier's throat again.

Before that call from Raven, Acier had intended to follow Aleksei's earlier advice and allow Etienne to have the upper hand—at least as long as his life was in no danger. He could no longer afford to do that. He needed to end this quickly so he could make sure Raven was all right.

Acier jammed his open hand up against Etienne's nose. Etienne roared in pain and jerked his head back. Acier wrestled Etienne onto his back, exposed his throat, and sank his incisors into Etienne's neck.

Steele. Steele. I love you. The desperation he'd felt in her earlier declaration of love had disappeared. He closed his eyes and sighed in relief. Thank God she was all right.

He couldn't afford to lose his concentration. Etienne raked his teeth against Acier's cheek before sinking them deep into his shoulder, ripping and tearing in a near-mad frenzy. Roaring in pain, Acier curled his hands into fists and slammed them against Etienne's ears.

Etienne shuddered and tore into his shoulder again.

Acier hammered his fists against Etienne's ears with increasing fury until Etienne released his grip on his shoulder and bounded away. With blood pouring from his damaged shoulder, Acier staggered to his feet.

Without warning, Etienne growled and sprang at him again, knocking him onto his back. Within seconds Acier felt Etienne's incisors sinking into his throat. Oh, shit. How the hell was it going to look if Aleksei had to pull Etienne off him? He'd let that happen when hell froze over. He'd had enough. He grabbed Etienne's ears and pressed his knee against Tee's ball sac. *Don't make me neuter you, pup!*

* * *

With Acier lying helpless under him, Etienne experienced a surge of triumph. Even if Acier kneed him in the balls, he could still rip Acier's jugular open. There would be nothing the prowling Aleksei could do to stop him. Within seconds, he could put Acier out of the running for Raven's heart. With Acier dead, there would be no one standing between him and Raven.

On the other hand, with Acier dead, he'd lose what he'd always considered the best part of himself. Acier had always gone out of his way to ensure life ran as easily and as smoothly as possible for him — until they both fell for Raven. He could kill Acier. But what would that accomplish?

Raven had left him and fled to Acier. As painful as the revelation was, it was time he accepted that simple fact. She had run to Acier. She'd made her choice. Killing Acier wouldn't change her preference. It would just ensure she despised him.

If, by some miracle, she was able to forgive him, the last thing he wanted was to kill Acier. That would be like committing suicide. It would also make him as ungrateful and selfish as both Mikhel and Aleksei had accused him of being. Acier had never denied him anything he wanted—except Raven. How could he rightly expect Acier to give up his bloodlust?

Yet, if he gave up his fight for Raven, he'd have no reason to live.

He looked down at Acier. *Forgive me, Sei. I surrender. She's yours.*

Withdrawing his incisors from Acier's neck, he rose, turning in time to see both Vladimir and Aleksei racing toward them. Shifting, he extended a hand to Vladimir. As Aleksei flashed past him to kneel beside Acier, Etienne's knees shook. Vladimir placed a hand on his shoulder, a concerned look in his eyes. "Etienne?"

"Fa... Fa..." His knees buckled and he collapsed, falling to the ground. His body rolled and rolled—toward a cliff. He could hear voices, Vladimir, Acier, Aleksei, calling to him. He fell off the cliff. Encouraged by the voice ringing in his head, he reached out to catch the edge of the cliff—breaking his fall.

He looked down into the dark pit over which he dangled.

Etienne! Pup. Hold on.

Give me your hand, son.

He looked up toward the edge of the cliff. Both Vladimir and Acier knelt there, each imploring him to give them his hand so they could pull him to safety.

Give me your hand, pup. It'll be all right. We'll work things out with Raven. We'll share her. It won't be a problem because she loves us both. You know she loves you too. Give me your hand.

I can't live without her, Sei.

You won't have to. I promise. We'll work things out. Just give me your hand.

Lifting his head, he saw desperation in Vladimir's and Acier's gazes. Aleksei extended his hand. *Forgive me, Etienne.*

Etienne, my love, I need you.

At the sound of the soft, sultry voice, Etienne glanced down into the pit. Raven stood at the bottom, naked and smiling. *Come to me, Etienne. I made a mistake in leaving you for Acier. I've come to my senses and come back to you, my love. Release your grip and come to me.*

No, pup, no! Give me your hand.

Your hand, Etienne. Now. Give it to me.

Despite Acier and Vladimir's pleas, the lure of what Raven promised was more than he could resist. He released one hand.

Etienne, no!

No, pup, no! Please.

Come to me, my Tee. Come to me. Release your grip and we can be together forever.

"Raven. *Petite.* I'm coming. I'm coming." He released his grip on the cliff. He tumbled through the cold, black depths. It was only as he hit the bottom of the dark pit that he realized Raven wouldn't have asked this of him.

Lying crumpled at the bottom of the void, he heard cold, triumphant laughter that did not belong to Raven. He'd made a huge mistake and was now going to pay with his life. He could hear Acier, Vladimir, and Aleksei calling out to him, begging him to hold on. But he couldn't—not when the darkness was so close and offered an end to his physical and mental anguish.

A small circle appeared, quickly widening. A large male with long dark hair and silver eyes stepped from the circle. The man easily moved through the darkness, bringing the light with him. With his hand extended, he knelt beside Etienne. "Etienne Gautier, I am Enola Cheyenne."

"Go away."

Enola's silver eyes stared down into his. He felt his mind being probed. Ashamed of the secrets he'd allowed to consume him, Etienne tried to erect a mental barrier.

"No, Etienne. Don't struggle. The burden you carry is too heavy. Release it and I will bear it for you."

"Get out of my head and let me die in peace!"

"Die?" He felt a warm sensation brushing against his mind. "No, Etienne. There are too many who love and need you alive and well to allow that. The burden you carry is too cumbersome for one of your tender years. Release it to me."

"I don't deserve to live. I've betrayed the one person who has been in my corner for my entire life. I tried to kill him! All he's ever done is sacrifice so I could have things he didn't get to enjoy himself, and I repaid him by trying to kill him. I don't deserve to live."

"And yet he's here, pleading for you to hang on. He forgives you."

"I don't deserve his forgiveness. He's always been worth ten of me and I've never done anything but use him. Let me die so he can be happy with his bloodlust."

"Without you, a large part of who he is would no longer exist. Take my hand and let me bear your burden."

"I don't want to live without Raven. She's my bloodlust too."

Enola reached out and grabbed his hand. "I know she is. Acier realizes that now too. He will make allowances, but you need to hold on."

Etienne jerked his hand away. "No. I've tried to kill him. I've created problems between my father and his twin where none existed. I've done nothing but bring the family grief. Everyone will be better off without me."

No, Etienne!

No, pup! Don't you leave me, Etienne!

He felt two anguished cries echo in his mind. Acier and Vladimir.

Please! Come back to us, Etienne. If you do, I promise things will be better between us. I won't begrudge you time with Raven. I swear it. I know she's your bloodlust too. I know you need her as much as I do. Don't leave me, Etienne. If you do, part of me will die with you. Part of her will die as well. You know she loves you.

Etienne, please, give Enola your hand. Let him guide you back to us. I've just found you. I couldn't bear to lose you now. Live, solnyshko moy. *Live.*

Solnyshko moy. *My sun.* Moved by the pleas of the two males who meant so much to him, Etienne extended his hand. Both of Enola's hands closed over his.

"Let go of your pain, Etienne. Release it to me. I will bear it for you."

Etienne gasped, shuddered, and surrendered. He felt a warm, healing touch spreading out from the hand Enola held. It slowly moved along his body, with the power of healing moonlight. It consumed the pain, guilt, and darkness that had overwhelmed him for weeks. Light and hope surfaced in its wake.

Hope. Light. No more darkness. No more shame and guilt for his unjust feelings toward Acier. No more pain.

No more pain, pup. You are a vital part of who I am. Come back to us. Come back to me.

He felt moisture on his face and opened his eyes. Enola cradled him in his arms. Vladimir and Acier knelt beside him, each holding one of his hands, each crying. Behind them Aleksei knelt with a hand on his brother's and nephew's shoulders.

With Enola's help, Etienne sat up and turned to Acier. Seeing the blood and wounds he'd inflicted, he sobbed. "Oh, Sei, forgive me! Please!"

"For anything, Etienne. For anything."

Acier reached out for him. They embraced, hugging one another with a feverish intensity. As they clung together, Etienne felt the special bond they'd always shared returning. "I'm so sorry I hurt you, Sei. I wasn't myself."

Acier drew away from him and cupped his face between his palms. "I know that. What happened here is over. You're back and that's all that matters. You're back." He kissed Etienne's cheek and released him.

Vladimir took Acier's place and drew him into his arms. Etienne clung to him, pressing his cheek against his shoulder. He whispered one word — "Father."

Vladimir froze, then his body shook. He sobbed. Within moments Aleksei and Acier were kneeling next to them and the four of them clung together, whispering words of love and forgiveness. They huddled close, reinforcing the special bond that only identical vampire twins could fully understand or appreciate.

Three pairs of arms touched him. Three hearts beat in relief at his redemption and return from near insanity. He was where he wanted to be... where he belonged—surrounded by those who loved him most... those he loved most.

His thoughts turned to Adona. His desire for her and hers for him would help alleviate his need for Raven. Her affection would lessen his hunger. Hopefully, that would be enough for her—at least until he could feel more for her.

He closed his eyes and reached out to her. *Adona. I'm coming for you. Wait for me, Adona.*

Chapter Eight

Venus leaned over Abby. Placing both hands on either side of Abby's head, she closed her eyes and chanted softly in what should have been a strange language. Raven was surprised to find that she understood the words.

Abigail Valanti. Hear me and let the healing begin. All is forgiven. All is forgiven. Come back to the clan that waits to welcome you. Return to guide Ravanni Monclaire, who still needs your instruction. All is forgiven. Return to us. Return to us, Willoni.

Unbidden, Raven joined the chant. *Abby. It's Rae. I've been so lost without your guidance these last weeks. There's so much I don't know about our people. I need you to instruct and guide me. Please come back.*

Venus and Raven fell silent. The only sound in the room was that of Belladonna's sobs. Venus waited a few moments and began the chant again. *Abigail Valanti. She of the Golden Hills Clan...*

Abby stirred and slowly opened her eyes.

Belladonna gasped and wrapped her arms around Abby. Abby shook in her embrace, pressing her face against Belladonna's breasts. Raven stroked her hand over Abby's hair. "Welcome back, Abby."

Abby reached out and clutched her hand. "Forgive me, Rae?"

She squeezed Abby's hand. "Of course I forgive you."

Venus rose. "Let's get her on the bed to rest. Then we will begin the ritual to reverse the progression."

Belladonna sucked in a breath. "She's so weak, Venus."

"I know. We'll take all the precautions necessary, but we must begin soon or lose the small window of opportunity we have to perform the ritual successfully."

They helped Abby onto the bed. As she rested, Raven went into the living room and called Acier's cell phone. Acier answered on the second ring. "Raven! *Petite*. Are you all right?"

"Yes."

"Are you sure? I felt you call out to me. You seemed to be in danger."

"I was, but I'm fine now."

"Where are you? I'll come and get you."

"I'm with friends and I'm safe." She bit her lip. "Steele... are you all right?"

"I have a few more battle scars, but yes. I'm all right."

She took a deep breath. "And... Etienne? Is he all right?"

"Yes. You'll be very pleased to hear he's hardly scratched at all."

A long silence ensued.

"Steele? What's wrong?"

"You're his bloodlust too, Raven."

"I know. That's why I was so afraid for you both."

He sighed. "We're going to need to work things out between us... that is, if you're still interested."

"Still interested? I love you both. You know that, but you're the love of my life."

"We're going to need to share you. Can you handle that, *petite*?"

She knew how difficult accepting the knowledge that she was both of their bloodlust had been for him. "I love you both," she said. "It might not be easy, but we'll work things out, Steele."

"Where are you? I need to see you." He paused before he sighed. "We both need to see you."

"And I want to see you both, but right now I'm with Abby. She's sick. I want to make sure she's all right and then I'll come to you. Will you be returning to Arizona?"

"I'll be staying at the RV for a few days. Can you meet us there when you can? I don't want to return to Arizona until after the three of us have... seen each other."

"Okay. I need to get back to Abby. Steele, I love you."

"I love you too."

"Tell Tee that I... love him too."

"I already have."

"I'll see you as soon as I can."

"We'll be waiting for you, *petite*."

Raven ended the call and returned to the bedroom where Venus and Belladonna sat on either side of the bed, chanting over Abby. Raven moved to the window and watched in silence. One day, she would need to know all things Willoni, to prepare for the time when she would serve at temple.

She wrapped her arms around her body. That would require leaving Acier, Etienne, her family, and the child she carried.

* * *

Two days later, after ending a call to Steele, Raven looked up to find Abby emerging from the bedroom. Venus and Belladonna followed. Raven saw no trace of Adona in Abby's gaze.

Raven rose, a smile spreading across her face. "Abby! Welcome back!" She crossed the room and clasped Abby's hand. "How are you feeling?"

Abby sighed. "Ashamed that I allowed my obsession with Etienne to drive me insane. I'm so sorry for hurting you."

She shook her head. "It's forgiven, Abby. We don't need to talk about it again." She released Abby's hand and led her over to the sofa where they sat. Venus and Belladonna shared the loveseat.

"You're very gracious, Ravanni—"

"Please. We've been through so much together. Call me Raven."

Abby nodded. "Raven. As the final step in the healing process I need to explain why this all happened... why Adona was... created."

"Okay."

"Willoni guides have one purpose—to successfully guide and instruct earthbound Willoni in the ways of our people. While we are acting as guides, we have to follow the Willoni creed that requires us to forsake all carnal pleasure and devote ourselves exclusively to the instruction of the acolyte. This is particularly true in the case of a future High Priestess—such as your mother, Deliah, whom I successfully instructed in our ways. After she entered temple service, I was free to pursue personal pleasure. When she was granted leave to have a child, I was put on notice that I would have five years of carnal freedom after you were born. On your fifth birthday, I would have to return to the creed code and watch over you until such time as I deemed you were ready to learn who you were.

"While I watched over you, I was supposed to refrain from all carnal pleasure." She glanced at the loveseat. "Such as my sister did as she watched over the Goddess." Abby pulsed, balling a hand into a fist. "I did that… until I got lonely one night and went into an adult movie. I saw Etienne in a movie. At the time I just thought he was Wyatt Diamond. I tried to forget him, but I couldn't.

"I told myself there was no harm in watching his movies. I bought them all and then I got sex toys to pleasure myself as I watched his movies and pretended I was with him. At first that worked. Then I wanted more. I had to have more. I knew I couldn't and yet I had to. So I secretly underwent the Ritual of the Talisman that allowed me to change my appearance—and Adona was created.

"Willoni are sexual creatures with healthy sex drives. Once I had created Adona, I lost my ability to control mine. The more I became her, the more I wanted sex. The more I had sex, the sicker I became until she started to dominate me. Then… one night at a bar, I finally met Etienne—the man of my dreams. I'm very old and I've had countless lovers, but I've never needed one as I did him.

"When I—Adona realized he was in love with you, she decided you had to die. You know the rest of the story."

Venus rose. "What you do not know, Raven, is that Caldera, the enchantress who took my rightful place as Goddess of the Willoni through treachery, perverted the Willoni creed. It was never intended to drive a faithful guide such as Abigail to despair because she was forbidden to seek the love of the man who had mastered her soul song. Much of what has happened to Abby can be laid at the feet of Caldera."

Abby shook her head. "You are ever gracious, Goddess, but I was weak."

Venus's eyes flashed. "You were driven to despair by a vengeful enchantress intent on ensuring all Willoni were as miserable as she was!" Venus took a deep breath. "If you're all right, I have a personal matter I need to attend to."

Abby rose and bowed. "Thank you for your graciousness, Goddess."

"Rise, Abigail. As I've said, those days are past." She turned to smile at Raven. "When you've seen those you love, go see Belladonna. She'll guide you to a portal that will allow you to visit someone who's very interested in seeing you again."

"Who?"

"Your mother."

Raven caught her breath. "My... is that possible?"

"Yes. Tend to your loved ones here first and then Belladonna will arrange a meeting."

Abby blanched. "I can do that, Goddess."

"Call me Venus. I want you to concentrate on getting well. That means spending time pursuing your handsome Etienne."

Abby blushed. "He's in bloodlust with Raven."

"True enough, but I have it on good authority that he cares deeply for you as well." Venus smiled. "Who is to say that he will always be in bloodlust with our lovely Raven alone? Or that he may not have dual bloodlusts, one of them being you? Or that you may not meet someone else who has an even greater mastery of your soul song?"

"Goddess!" Abby caught her breath. "You've foreseen..."

"I've foreseen a great many things. Your faithful service will not go unrewarded." She turned her attention to Raven. "The road ahead might not be as smooth as you would have liked it to be,

Ravanni, but things will be well…" Her gaze drifted down toward Raven's stomach. "Fear not."

Raven bit her lip. "But I'm afraid of who's—"

"I know of your fear."

"Is it well founded?"

"Who is to say for sure? Now, I must go."

They all rose and then bowed as Venus left the room.

Raven turned to Abby. "If you're feeling better, I need to see Acier."

Abby nodded. "Bella will be with me for a few days. Go."

They embraced before Raven left the suite. Forty-minutes later she was at the RV being kissed breathless by Acier.

* * *

Etienne watched Acier ravish Raven for several minutes before he cleared his throat. "I should go and leave you two to say hello without an audience."

Raven pulled away from Acier and turned to look at him. "How are you?"

"Better." He raked a hand through his hair. "I'm sorry, *petite*… for everything."

She hesitated, glanced at Acier, who inclined his head slightly, and then crossed the living room area of the RV to smile at Etienne. "I'm so happy that you're well and you and Acier are close again."

He stared down at her and felt his cock hardening. God, he wanted her as much as he ever had. "I don't deserve it, but Sei's forgiven me."

"So have I." She linked her arms around his neck and lifted her chin.

He tensed and glanced at Acier. *Sei?*

Acier nodded. "Give me the keys to your SUV so I can take a ride in the country while you and Raven get reacquainted."

He took his keys from his jacket pocket. "Are you sure, Sei? I know this is difficult for you."

"It will be an adjustment for us all." Acier walked over to him and took the keys from his hand. He bent and kissed Raven's cheek. "I'll see you tomorrow."

She nodded and kissed Acier's lips. "I love you."

"I love you too, *petite*." Acier left the RV, closing the door behind him.

When they were alone, Raven slipped her arms around his neck. "I love you too, Tee."

He wrapped his arms around her waist. "I love you too, *petite*."

She stroked her fingers through the hair at his nape. "Show me how much."

He lifted her into his arms. She rubbed her cheek against his shoulder as he carried her through the RV to the bedroom. He took his time undressing her, delighting in slowly exposing her dark, beautiful body.

She lay naked on her side, watching as he pulled off his clothes. When he was nude, she rolled onto her stomach, parting her long, lovely legs for him. Damn, she was beautiful with a nice ass. It was almost as nice as Adona's large, brown bottom.

Eager to love her, he lay on top of her, holding her hips as he slid his cock balls deep in her hot, tight ass.

"Oh... Tee..." She ground her ass against his groin.

He shuddered. When she did that he could feel every inch of her tight anal tunnel along his hard cock.

He slipped his hands under her body to cup her large, lovely breasts. "You are so beautiful."

"Love me," she whispered.

"This will be our last time together for a while. I want to go slow and make it last."

"I'm on fire, Tee. I don't want sweet and gentle. I want to be fucked."

The tightening of her muscles around his cock made retaining his control difficult. Nevertheless, this time he would not come before his partner. He slapped the side of her thigh. "Stop trying to make me come now!"

She laughed, but relaxed her ass muscles. He made slow love to her luscious ass, enjoying the leisurely build up of both their passions. When the tension in her body signaled her coming orgasm, he rolled them onto their sides and found her clit. He scraped his thumbnail over the hard bud until she let out a low, gasping moan, and came. Only then did he ejaculate inside her warm ass.

He eased out of her ass and she turned into his arms and kissed him. He held her until he drifted to sleep. A few hours later, he slipped out of bed and picked up his pants.

"Tee? Come back to bed."

He retrieved a box from his pants pocket before he slipped into bed beside her. He turned on the light. "I have something for you."

She sat up. "What?"

He opened his hand and revealed a small jeweler's box. Noting the wary look in her eyes, he shook his head. "Take it."

She shook her head, pulling the blanket up to cover her breasts. "I thought you understood that I'm going to marry Acier, Tee."

"Open it."

She bit her lip.

"Please."

She took a deep breath before she took the box. She moistened her lips before she opened it. When she had, she gave a happy scream. "It's my ring! It's the ring Acier gave me!" She slipped it on her finger and threw her arms around his neck. "Oh, Tee, thank you so much! I thought you'd thrown it away."

He hugged her. "I couldn't. A part of me knew it meant too much to both of you."

She drew back and caressed his cheek. "Thank you."

He shook his head. "Don't thank me. I should never have taken it from you."

"You've returned it and that's all that matters now." She lay on the bed and parted her legs. "Come love me again."

He stroked her pussy. "That's a tempting invitation, *petite*, but there's someone I need to find."

She sat up. "Abby?"

"No. Adona. Does that bother you?"

"Bother me?" She shook her head. "No! I'm delighted. She loves you so much."

"I know."

"How do you feel about her?"

"She's the only woman who has been able to help me assuage my hunger for you and her feelings for me are so real and so deep… it's difficult not to want to reciprocate."

"Oh, Tee, if you could love her half as much as she loves you, you'll be a very happy vampire."

"Actually, you know, these days I'm feeling more like a shifter than I have in years."

"Vampire or shifter or delicious hybrid, she'll make you very happy."

"I'll do my best to make her happy too."

"I know you will. Do you know where to find her?"

"No."

She gave him Abby's cell number and told him where he could find her.

"Thanks, *petite*." He slipped out of bed and dressed quickly, eager to see Adona again.

"Before you go, there's something I need to tell you about her. If it matters, don't go. If it doesn't, please go reassure her."

He listened in silence as she told him about Adona and Abby. He frowned, his jaw clenching. "She tried to kill you?"

"She couldn't help herself. Don't hold that against her."

"How can I when Sei has forgiven my own murderous behavior?" He stroked her cheek. "And when you've forgiven me for raping you?"

She shook her head and pressed her fingers against his lips. "Oh, no, Tee! It was rough and not very nice, but it wasn't rape. I didn't have the physical strength to stop you, but Enola was there willing to intercede the moment I wanted him to. I didn't ask him to stop you because I knew you needed it. Please don't ever think of it as rape."

"You said no, Raven."

She nodded. "I know, but Enola was there to enforce that no had I really wanted you to stop. So don't ever think of it as rape again."

"You're as forgiving as you are beautiful. You are a worthy bloodlust for Sei who is equally as forgiving."

"And we both love you."

"And I love you both."

"And Abby?"

He shrugged. "Adona was very exciting, but I wasn't in love with her."

"So it…"

He recalled the incredible climax and sense of joy and wonder he'd felt when he awakened from Enola's healing sleep to find Abby making love to him. "It doesn't matter."

"Thank the Goddess!"

He smiled and kissed her lips before he left the RV. His SUV was parked several spaces away. Acier sat inside with his eyes closed.

Etienne tapped on the driver's side window. "Sei?"

Acier sat up. "Why are you dressed? The moon won't rise for another few hours."

"I'm eager to see Abby."

"You are?"

He nodded, smiling. "I can see you're surprised, and to be honest, so am I."

"I'd like to meet her."

Etienne nodded. "You will. Now if I could get started."

Acier got out of the SUV. Etienne got in and started the engine.

"Oh, there's something you should know, pup."

"What?"

Acier grinned. "I'm looking forward to getting to know your Abby — in the biblical sense."

Etienne stared at him. "What?"

"You heard me, pup."

"But what about Raven?"

"What about her? She knows I'm far more vampire than shifter these days. She'll expect me to sleep with your Abby."

"Maybe she will, but I'm feeling more like a shifter these days and I won't!"

He drove off with the sound of Acier's amused laughter annoying the hell out of him. This vampire shit was overrated. He drove home and took a quick nap before he showered and dressed. As he headed back to the SUV his phone rang again. Noting the number on his Caller ID, he lifted the phone to his ear.

"Etienne! Are you all right?"

"I'm fine, Damon. Where the hell have you been?" Listening to Damon's tale of how the Brotherhood had tricked him into thinking they'd kidnapped Brett, Etienne realized he'd had a lucky escape from Vitali Bourcaro's clutches. "And it wasn't Shaun who called you?"

"No, but damned if it didn't sound like him. Brett and Shaun had gone to Vegas for the weekend. Somehow the Brotherhood got a hold of Shaun's cell, but he was never actually in any danger from them."

"I'm glad to hear that."

"So things are okay with you and Raven?"

"Yes. I'm on my way to see Abby."

"And who the hell is Abby?"

"Someone very special. I'll tell you about her when we see each other again."

"And when will that be?"

"I want to spend some time with her. I'll call you."

"I'm delighted to hear you're all right."

"I know. I'll talk to you in a few days."

While he was driving the SUV to Abby's hotel, Mikhel called. "I'm fine, Uncle Mikhel. I'm on my way to see someone very special. If it's all right with you, I'd like to fly out to Boston in a week or so. I have to pick up Slayer and Karol from Nana and I thought you and I might be able to spend some time together while I'm there."

"I'll look forward to that, pup."

Pup. He supposed he was going to have to get used to being called pup by everyone.

* * *

Etienne stood watching the tall, pale woman cross the hotel lobby toward him. His cock tingled with each step she took. Not only was he happy to see her, but he was also eager to fuck her.

She paused a foot from him, an uncertain smile playing over her lips. He took her hand and drew her close. She turned a dark, troubled gaze up to his. "I'm so happy to see you, Etienne. Once you found out about... I didn't think I'd ever see you again."

"We need to talk. Let's go up to your suite."

She nodded.

He held her hand on the short walk to the elevator. In her suite, when he would have taken her into his arms, she shook her head and stepped away from him. "We need to talk. You need to know..." She compressed her lips. "I know you were attracted to Adona."

He caressed her cheek. "What's your point?"

Her eyes welled with tears. "I... I can't change into her anymore. If you're interested in me... it has to be me as I am now."

The desperation in her voice matched his when he'd awakened to find Raven had fled from him straight to Acier's arms. He cupped his hands over her cheeks. "I knew you couldn't change anymore before I came."

"You did?"

"Yes. Raven told me."

"And you came anyway."

"What does that tell you, Abby?"

"That you... that there might be a chance for us? I know how you feel about Raven."

"Is that going to be a problem for you?"

The tears spilled down her cheeks. "I wish you didn't love her, but I know you do and I'll work hard not to be a pain when you need her."

He wiped away her tears. "I'll do my best to make those times as painless for you as possible. Having said that you should know that one of the most incredible, sensual feelings I've ever experienced was with you, just as you are now, in Acier's RV before I went to face him."

"But... you were furious when you woke. You tossed me across the room and I lost consciousness."

He sighed. "I'm so sorry about that. I was confused and half-mad. But even in that condition, while you made love to me, I didn't think of Raven once. I thought only of you and how natural being with you felt."

She sucked in a breath. "You're serious."

He nodded. "Yes. I am." He bent his head and kissed her lips before lifting her off her feet. "Now let's go to bed and you can tell me what you like."

She linked her arms around his neck. "You. I like... I love you so much I ache with it, Etienne."

The emotion in her voice, the love in her gaze overwhelmed his senses. As he sank into her arms while slowly sliding his cock into her sweet, addictive pussy, he suspected his hunger for Raven would not be nearly as debilitating as he'd feared. The lovely woman under him, surrounding him with a longing and love he could almost taste, would see to that. In turn, he would do his best to keep her happy and content—just as he knew she'd do for him.

Marilyn Lee

Marilyn Lee lives, works, and writes on the East Coast. In addition to thoroughly enjoying writing erotic romances, she enjoys roller-skating, spending time with her large, extended family, and rooting for all her hometown sports teams. Her other interests include collecting Doc Savage pulp novels from the thirties and forties and collecting Marvel comics from the seventies and eighties (particularly *Thor and The Avengers*).

Her favorite TV shows are forensic shows, westerns (*Gunsmoke* and *Have Gun, Will Travel* are particular favorites), mysteries (She loves the old Charlie Chan mysteries. Her all time favorite mystery movie is probably *Dead, Again*.), and nearly every vampire movie or television show ever made (*Forever Knight* and *Count Yorga, Vampire* are favorites).

She loves to hear from readers who can email her at MLee2057@aol.com or visit her website—www.marilynlee.org. Join Marilyn's Yahoo! Group—Love Bytes—by sending an email to: marilynlee-subscribe@yahoogroups.com. Marilyn occasionally blogs at Ladies of the Club, http://ladiesoftheclub.blogspot.com.

The Dumont Family Tree

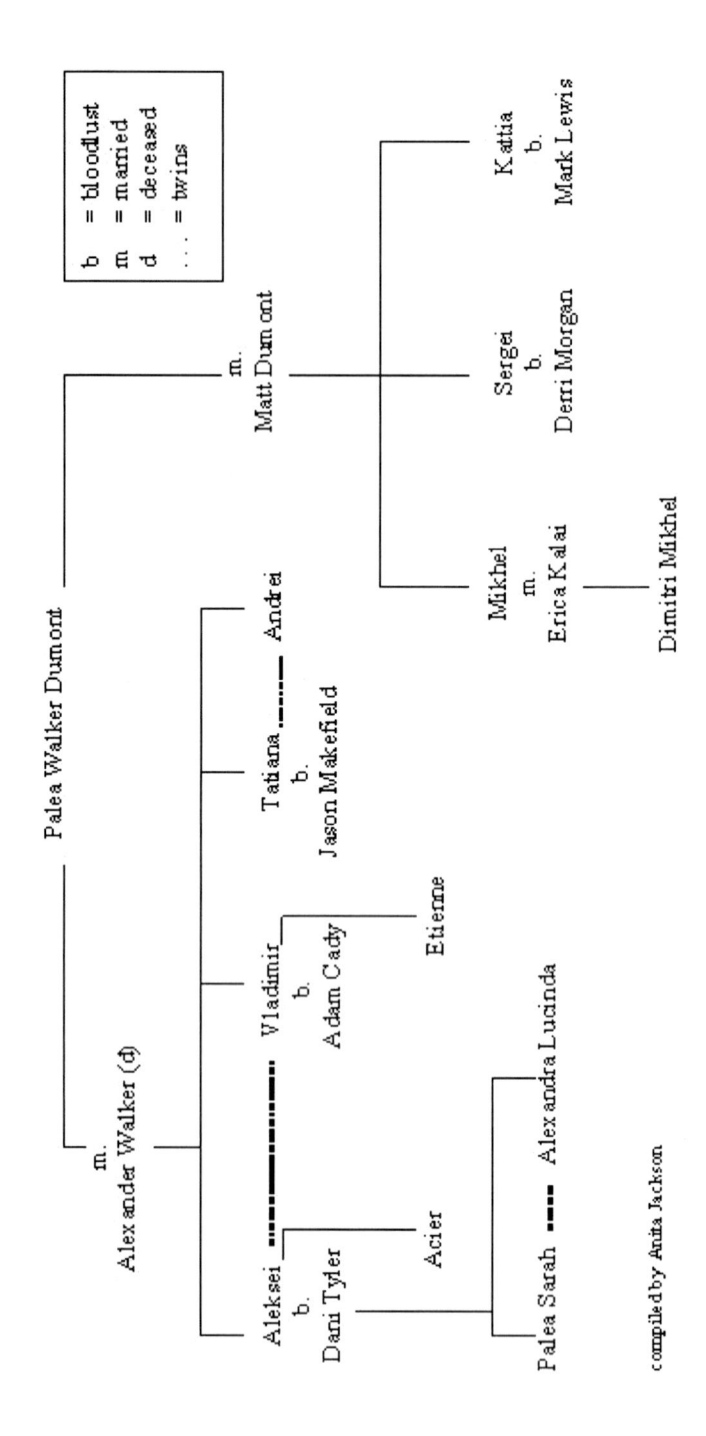

Legend:
- b = bloodlust
- m = married
- d = deceased
- ... = twins

Alexander Walker (d) m. Palea Walker Dumont

Children of Alexander Walker & Palea Walker Dumont:
- Aleksei — b. Dani Tyler
- Vladimir — b. Adam Cady
- Tatiana — b. Jason Makefield ———— Andrei
- Matt Dumont

Aleksei's children:
- Acier
- Palea Sarah ···· Alexandra Lucinda (twins)

Vladimir's child:
- Etienne

Matt Dumont's children:
- Mikhel m. Erica Kalai
- Sergei b. Derri Morgan
- Kattia b. Mark Lewis

Mikhel & Erica Kalai's child:
- Dimitri Mikhel

compiled by Anita Jackson

Changeling Press E-Books
Quality Erotic Adventures Designed For Today's Media

More Sci-Fi, Fantasy, Paranormal, and BDSM adventures available in E-Book format for immediate download at www.ChangelingPress.com — Werewolves, Vampires, Dragons, Shapeshifters and more — Erotic Tales from the edge of your imagination.

What are E-Books?

E-Books, or Electronic Books, are books designed to be read in digital format — on your computer or PDA device.

What do I need to read an E-Book?

If you've got a computer and Internet access, you've got it already!

Your web browser, such as Internet Explorer or Netscape, will read any HTML E-Book. You can also read E-Books in Adobe Acrobat format and Microsoft Reader, either on your computer or on most PDAs. Visit our Web site to learn about other options.

What reviewers are saying about Changeling Press E-Books

Elisa Adams — Sleepless

"5 Angels! The build up in the bar was fantastic and the first sex scene absolutely rocked my world. The chemistry between these two was amazing."
— Missy, Fallen Angel Romance Reviews

B.J. McCall — Lycaon Moon

"The story is very well written and the love scenes are very erotic… A very enjoyable werewolf romance."
— Maura Frankman, The Romance Studio

"5 Angels! Lycaon Moon was a delicious snack by B. J. McCall."
— Dana P., Fallen Angel Romance Reviews

Emma Ray Garrett — AWU: Torqued

Two Lips Recommended Read: "The action-packed, non-stop thrills start from the first page and continue to the last…. In addition to the heat there is a deep and detailed story encompassing centuries of pain and betrayal, making the plot morph into something different entirely. Curious? You'll have to pick up a copy to find out what I'm talking about."
— Kerin, TwoLips Reviews

Kira Stone — Bayou Shifters: Chase

"Danger filled action and the budding relationship between two sexy male werewolves define Ms. Stone's intriguing new tale. A fascinating read with characters I hope to read more about in the future."
— Water Nymph, Literary Nymphs

www.ChangelingPress.com